Dear Reader,

This month we have four wonderful new *Scarlet* romances for you which we hope will help chase away those winter blues.

Share *That Cinderella Feeling* with Anne Styles's heroine and find out if 'Cinderella' Casey really does live happily ever after . . . When the lawyer meets the dancer, sparks are bound to fly – and they do in *The Marriage Dance*, as author Jillian James brings us a new slant on the old problem of reluctance to commit. We are delighted, too, to bring you *A Darker Shadow*, the latest long novel by Patricia Wilson, in which Luc Martell is forced to remain in England with computer buff Amy Scott – the bane of his life. And finally, *Slow Dancing* by Elizabeth Smith shows us that life in Hollywood isn't always the stuff of dreams.

As always it has been a pleasure *and* a challenge for me to select these latest *Scarlet* titles for you and I hope that you enjoy reading these books as much as I did.

Keep those letters and questionnaires flooding in, won't you? We are always happy to hear from you. And don't forget, if you want to write to a favourite *Scarlet* author, I'll be glad to pass on your letter.

Till next month,
Best wishes,

Sally Cooper

SALLY COOPER,
Editor-in-Chief – *Scarlet*

ELIZABETH SMITH

SLOW DANCING

SCARLET

Enquiries to:
Robinson Publishing Ltd
7 Kensington Church Court
London W8 4SP

First published in the UK by Scarlet, 1998

A copy of the British Library Cataloguing in
Publication data is available from the British Library

ISBN 1-85487-950-2

Printed and bound in the EC

10 9 8 7 6 5 4 3 2 1

In memory of my father,
Bill Ferriter
And for my mother,
Virginia Ferriter,
with love

CHAPTER 1

Love is a lot like slow dancing:
Sometimes the best part is what happens
when the music stops.

March 1997, Memphis, Tennessee

The idea first came to her that dismal day at Casey's funeral while she stood shoulder-to-shoulder with the other mourners in her somber, perfect black suit, her head bowed. The cold, bone-chilling rain seemed to elude the numerous umbrellas held overhead and settled instead upon the dark garments of the silent group that had gathered to pay their last respects.

At first, she dismissed the thought as irreverent and outrageous, sinful even, but it wouldn't go away. Instead it danced on the fringes of her sorrow, taunting her with the promise of long-denied pleasure, and promising as well to fulfill her shameful desire for revenge.

There should have been tears, but they wouldn't come. Instead there was a heavy ache that gathered around Hallie Prescott's heart. With each beat she was reminded that she was only here for appearances' sake.

1

The family needed the young widow at their side.

The day had been as gray and bleak as her mood, and while the voice of the minister droned on and on, extolling the virtues of her husband, the now-deceased Casey William Prescott, Hallie Prescott wondered if he was indeed speaking of the same man with whom she had lived for most of the past four years.

There had been many nights, especially during recent months, when she had wondered exactly what it was that she could do to even the score with Casey. But he was dead now. And what kind of woman would seek revenge against her dead husband?

By the time Hallie returned to Los Angeles the following day, she knew.

It was a dangerous game in which she was about to participate. For some women it was the excitement, the lure of the unknown, the thrill of the chase. Unspoken was their secret hope of finding someone and falling in love. But that had been the farthest thing from Hallie's mind tonight.

Nervously she straightened the thin shoulder straps of her dress and smoothed her hands down the sides of the black silk that skimmed her slender body.

Only yesterday she had returned from Casey's funeral, and she should have felt a certain shame for what she was about to do, but she didn't. Not now. Tomorrow morning she might feel differently.

From her small beaded purse she removed the gold and white package of cigarettes she had purchased earlier. Trying to appear at ease to anyone who might be watching, Hallie took a cigarette from the package and let it dangle for a moment from her slender fingers. When it was lit she propped her elbow on the shiny gold railing that stood slightly higher than her waist.

Once more her dark blue eyes searched the crowded nightclub, expecting only to see the faces she had found there minutes ago, faces that mingled with the glittering reflections of the glass and gold and black accents of the room. Instead she was stopped in her search by a pair of riveting gray eyes. They held hers and connected.

Quickly she lowered her lashes. The brief visual contact had left her strangely shaken. With her head bent, she fumbled ineptly with her cigarette, feeling as if she had more hands and fingers than she needed. Her shoulder-length hair fell forward, forming a full wavy cloud of copper that nearly obscured her delicate profile.

The beat of the music began to pulsate, sending invisible waves of heat through the dancers on the floor. For Hallie it warmed her blood and sent it rushing through the maze of veins inside her. Shadow and light acted as a kaleidoscope, forming ever-changing patterns and designs that obliterated the shapes of the dancers but accentuated their frenzied movements.

She raised her cigarette to her lips; as the smoke curled and wound its way upward, she only hoped that she didn't look as rattled as she felt. From not more than a dozen feet away she could feel his eyes on her, and she knew she could not continue to ignore the tall, sexy stranger whose attention she had attracted.

Nor did she want to. He, or someone like him, was the reason she was here tonight, alone and available.

When she ventured another look in his direction their eyes locked and held.

'You look like you could use some company.'

Hallie jumped at the sound of the smooth voice that was much too close behind her. She turned quickly, catching a flash of gold at his throat, then took a step back. The strong, spicy scent of his cologne drifted in the air.

'I see you're alone. Can I buy you a drink?' he asked as he moved closer, confident that she would welcome his company.

Damn. This was not going at all like she planned.

'Uh, no, thank you.' Hallie replied, instinctively bringing her hand to the neckline of her dress and pressing it tight against her. His nearness and his unmistakable interest in staring down the front of her dress sent her backing up another step.

He advanced. 'Hey, you're alone, I'm alone. Why not?'

Hallie took another step backward along with a deep breath and announced with a self-conscious laugh, 'Oh, sorry. I'm . . . I'm not alone. I'm meeting someone. Ahh . . . there he is now,' she said, wagging her finger emphatically toward the bar. 'Over there. But thanks, anyway.' With a quick nod she manuevered around him and threaded her way through the crowd toward the gray-eyed stranger who waited at the bar.

Silently, and so slightly that she might have almost imagined it, he raised his glass in toast before downing the remainder of its amber contents. It was a salute, almost as if he knew exactly what she had done and what she was about to do. He stood then, turning his broad

4

shoulders away from her, and reached into the back pocket of his gray slacks for his wallet. When he had extracted some bills he laid them on the bar, then turned back to watch her approach, his eyes traveling over her slowly and deliberately. When she had covered half the distance, he left the bar, intent on meeting her halfway.

The tempo of the music had changed and now the beat matched his slow, sensual gait. Hallie swallowed as he came closer, until finally he stood before her. She held her hand out in invitation. 'Will you dance with me?' she asked. Nervously she looked over her shoulder. The man she had thought she had left behind only seconds ago was rapidly closing in on her. 'Now?' she pleaded. Without waiting for an answer, she grabbed the stranger's hand and led him through the crowd.

'Do you want to lead too?' he asked with a grin, holding his hands up in surrender when they were out on the dance floor.

Hallie blushed. 'Sorry,' she mumbled. 'I don't usually . . .'

'Grab strange men and insist that they dance with you?' Grant Keeler smiled at her discomfort.

'Something like that.' She returned his smile.

'If you're going to hang out in places like this, you're fair game for any man here,' he warned. 'Don't you know that?'

'I do now.'

'Are you with someone?' he asked after a moment.

'No,' she replied. 'What about you?'

'Alone, also. I'm here in Los Angeles on business.'

He was silent for a moment. 'You don't look like you belong here,' he observed with narrowed eyes, as they moved slowly on the dance floor, their bodies brushing against one another.

Hallie looked up at him, and felt compelled to respond to his observation. 'I'm not sure I do,' she replied candidly, 'but I have this overwhelming desire to live dangerously for one night.'

Grant seemed to consider this, and the thought brought a devilish gleam to his silver gray eyes. Then he lowered his head and inhaled the sweet fresh scent of her hair as he pulled her closer. After a while he pulled back to study her face, the flawless ivory complexion, the perfectly proportioned nose, the eyes, rimmed in dark lashes, that were deep blue.

'And does living dangerously appeal to you?'

She smiled and, rising on her toes, leaned against him to whisper in his ear, 'Tonight it does.'

Grant raised his brows in a small show of surprise. There was no mistaking her message.

As they swayed in rhythm to the music, Hallie felt the heat from him. It seemed to burn everywhere his body touched hers, even through the barrier of clothing that separated them. She closed her eyes and gave herself up to the sensations that flowed over her. Neither of them knew when one song ended, and the next one began. They were only aware of each other.

Hallie had forgotten how good it felt to be held by powerful arms, to inhale the clean scent of a man, to move against him and know without a doubt that his body craved hers. This time when the music ended,

Hallie and Grant stood without moving, each reluctant to break the spell between them.

Finally, he stepped away, his hand still holding hers, then led her back through the maze of tables past the bar to a dim corner. Without letting go of her hand, he turned and pulled her closer, then let his eyes travel over her head to survey their surroundings. He took a deep breath, feeling suddenly uncomfortable, and wondered if she was looking for the same thing he was: a night that would ease the pain of loneliness. So far, all the signals had been right.

'Look,' he said in a husky voice, 'I don't know what you had in mind for tonight . . .'

Hallie looked up at him, sensing his uncertainty, and silencing her nagging doubts. 'This . . . this is exactly what I had in mind,' she said in a whisper, knowing even as she spoke that she could not back down now. With a small silent prayer that she would be forgiven for what she was about to do, she placed her hands against his chest. Tremors of anticipation and fear raced through her side by side.

Only yesterday, with apparent ease, she had relinquished her place as a member of the grieving Prescott family, then boarded the flight from Memphis to Los Angeles. Tonight, just as easily, she had shed the somber black funeral suit that threatened to smother her, and replaced it with the black silk dress she now wore that bared so much of her ivory skin and outlined her slender curves.

Tonight she was going to put her grievances with Casey to rest. The score would be even. After this evening she would rid herself of the scars she had been bequeathed. She would know beyond a doubt whether another man would find her desirable.

It had taken a long time, but now she was ready to take this final step. It was time to put an end to the mourning that had begun so many months ago, long before the actual demise of the relationship, long before the death of one of the partners.

'Do you want to go?' he asked, his voice husky with meaning.

Hallie nodded. 'Yes,' she replied, breathlessly. 'Yes, I do.' Deep in the pit of her stomach excitement had begun to build and was now spreading in a rush.

It was only a short drive from the nightclub to Grant's hotel, but to Hallie it seemed as if it took forever. To reassure herself that this was real, she kept looking over toward him. His profile was rugged, his features not quite handsome, but compelling. Somehow the silver gray eyes, the nose that looked like its shape had been altered on more than one occasion, and the well-defined lips joined together to compose a face that was infinitely more interesting than a perfect version would have been. The lights of a passing car outlined the thick dark hair that fell over his forehead.

With one arm Grant reached out to pull Hallie closer to him. 'Nervous?' he asked.

She shook her head in denial. What a lie. Now that she had come this far, she was terrified.

'Are you sure? You don't look like someone who does this all the time.'

'How am I supposed to look?' asked Hallie in a small voice.

'Not like this,' he laughed. 'You look . . . like you want to change your mind.'

'Then, by all means, take me back. I'm sure that club is full of women who –' she said, her tone bordering on the defensive.

'Hey, I didn't mean to hurt your feelings. I just meant that you seemed apprehensive.'

Apprehensive. She was that, all right, and a whole lot more. Hallie looked toward him and spoke more sharply than she had intended. 'If you're trying to make small talk, don't bother.'

'A woman who knows exactly what she wants,' he mused, keeping his eyes forward.

By now Hallie was having serious second thoughts about what she was about to do. She had never before entertained anything as bold or foolish as this. 'Are we almost there?' she asked. To her own ears, her voice sounded tinny, as if it was coming from far away.

'Why? Are you ready to run?'

As far as I can. 'I wouldn't even consider it,' she said. 'Now that I've come this far, I just want to get on with it.'

Grant flashed her a quick glance. The darkness hid his wry smile. 'Sure,' he answered. 'We can get right down to business, if you prefer. Most women like conversation, a little flirtation, maybe a drink, something that would make this seem more acceptable. But it seems you're just here for the sex. No frills, no attempts at polite conversation necessary.'

Grant turned left sharply into the hotel parking garage and, without meaning to, Hallie slid even closer to him. He pulled into a parking spot and shifted in the

9

seat, turning toward her. He took his time, looking Hallie over slowly. His gray eyes reminded her of the color of the sky on an icy winter day. 'Well, honey,' he drawled, 'we'll just do it your way.'

'You've obviously had a lot of experience at this,' she mumbled defensively.

The darkness hid Grant's sudden smile. *Way more than you, babe.*

The glittering lights from the crystal chandeliers in the opulent and ornate lobby cast a harsh glare. Hallie squinted at the brightness as she hurried alongside him toward the marble-fronted elevators. He turned toward her as he pushed the button, once more studying her. Her behavior in the car a few minutes ago was at odds with his original impression of her. Perhaps she was trying to forget something, or someone, just as he was.

A few minutes later they reached his room. He inserted the plastic card in the slot and turned the handle. The door silently swung wide. Hallie waited as he entered the room and switched on a lamp that cast a dim glow that didn't quite reach to the dark corners of the room.

Grant stood where he was, his stance relaxed as he leaned against the dresser. Hallie watched his gray eyes as they ran the length of her. She shivered at his perusal, not knowing if what she felt was apprehensiveness or anticipation. Satisfied with what he saw, he motioned for her to come to him.

Slowly, she crossed the room as though she had all the time in the world. Inside, her heart was beating fiercely. Then she was standing before him with her hands at her sides. Grant spread his powerful legs and reached to pull her into the space he had created there for her. His hands moved slowly, delicately over each side of her face. Then he let them slide through the mass of copper hair as he pulled her closer and leaned down to kiss her. His lips moved boldly across hers, seeking a response. Voluntarily, she answered him by parting her lips in invitation.

He felt a jolting surge of excitement. The lady wasn't as business-like as she pretended to be. How easily she fit his contours, he thought, as he locked her into place with his muscular thighs. He hadn't gone out that night looking for anyone to share his bed, he had gone out of loneliness and a need to be with other people. Normal people. There was a scarcity of them in his line of work.

Then he had found Hallie standing alone across the crowded club. There had been no doubt as to the message she was sending, but he had been surprised at how strongly he had responded to her.

'Why are you here?' he whispered as he reached to gently push the thick waves of hair away from her small face. He studied her intently as he waited for her answer. Hallie raised her face and he was able to see the fleeting look of uncertainty in her eyes. Purposely, Grant kept his expression unreadable.

'Because I want to be,' she answered, her voice soft as she breathed deeply and added silently, *because I have to be.*

When he moved both hands in unison to her shoulders her skin was as smooth and satiny as he had known it would be. Gently he pushed the thin black straps of her dress down until the straps pinned her arms at her sides. Slowly he moved to caress her

11

breast with one hand while he deftly reached around her with the other to unzip her dress.

The dark silk slid to her waist, and Hallie felt herself growing warm and flushed all over. Grant leaned back slightly, appraising what he had just uncovered. She fought for a moment against the panic she felt at being observed like this. Like someone's prize, someone's possession.

This is what I came here for, she reminded herself. This is what I was hoping for, she thought, forcing herself look up at him. What she saw in his eyes made her breath catch in her throat and suddenly she felt a renewed confidence. He was looking at her as if she were some rare work of art, worthy to be on display, to be loved, then to be revered.

In that moment, this stranger, this man she had never seen before tonight, had reaffirmed that she was beautiful, that she was desirable. It was something she hadn't seen in Casey's eyes for a long time.

Grant lowered his mouth to her breast and Hallie arched her back, unable to ignore the slow, liquid heat that wound its way downward to a place deep inside. In return she reached for the buttons on his shirt and began to work them. Impatiently, Grant set her hands aside and moved her away to finish undressing. The pace between them had accelerated and now it was more frantic than before, but still he managed to keep from rushing her.

The rustling of silk was the only sound in the room as he slid her dress and panties over her hips. Grant drew his breath in sharply as she stood before him. For a moment he was unable to move. It was as though the sight of her had hypnotized him.

12

Then he leaned down to swing her into his arms, carrying her the few steps across the room to the bed. As he laid her down, he followed with his body half covering hers. They both lay still for a moment, then she moved restlessly against him. It was the signal he had been waiting for.

For every place his mouth touched her skin, Hallie burned. For every place he left untouched, she ached. With him, she felt as if something wild and primitive had been unleashed; some part of her she had never known existed had come to life and had taken complete control. Tonight with this man she would discover a passion she would never again be able to hide.

With his eyes and his hands and his mouth, Grant awakened every part of her body, forcing her to acknowledge her own sexuality, demanding that she take pleasure from it. Then he moved his legs between hers, urging hers to part. Momentarily, he hovered above her as he struggled to regain control before his invasion. Hallie gasped as he pushed into her.

Grant stilled and reached up with one hand to gently push a few strands of hair off her forehead. 'Are you all right?' he whispered.

She nodded, and began moving against him, creating a rhythm that caused a deep pressure along with intense pleasure to build within her. Grant never took his eyes from her as she met each of his thrusts with a passion that matched his own. A series of expressions played across her features. It was almost as if she was surprised by what was happening to her.

By now Grant was sure she was operating on pure

13

instinct, not artifice, and for him it was unbearably exciting. He watched her eyes in the dim light as they widened and felt her tighten her grip on his shoulders, then he thrust into her harder and faster, the rhythm now accelerated. And for Hallie it provided a shattering, crashing release that sent waves of pleasure radiating through her. Grant climaxed only moments later, then lay heavily on top of her.

Time was suspended as they were caught together on another plateau where the only experience allowed was pleasure. Rolling to his side, he wrapped his arms around her, pulling her with him. Hallie couldn't get enough of his warmth. This stranger had made her feel all the things she needed to feel.

Almost as if by prearrangement, there were no more questions about one another and no shared confidences.

'I should go,' Hallie said quietly after a while.

'Stay,' he whispered, kissing her shoulder lightly. And for the rest of the night, Grant reaffirmed his desire for her.

They made love again and again and never once was it the same as the time before. He was a skilled, practiced lover and Hallie, surprised by her own boldness and passion, was a challenging partner.

Toward dawn Grant gathered Hallie in his arms once more and slept soundly. When she was sure he was asleep, she moved quietly from his arms, gathered her clothes from the floor and went into the bathroom to dress. In the dim light she looked into the mirror and marveled at the magical hours she had just spent with

14

this stranger. Almost simultaneously, she was appalled and ashamed at what she had done.

When she was dressed she turned out the light, shut the door quietly and made her way across the room. At the door, she paused and turned to look at the man with whom she had shared such intimacy. Silently, she wished this night could go on forever. Knowing it couldn't, she fervently hoped she would never meet him again. Her shame and embarrassment at what she had done tonight would be too great.

Then she stepped out into the silent corridor and pulled the door closed behind her. Hurriedly, she walked to the elevator and pushed the button. The doors parted and she stepped in. When they closed, she leaned her head against the cold stainless steel of the control panel and squeezed her eyes tight in a futile effort to control her tears. She cried for the way things should have been. Most of all she cried for Casey. 'Damn you,' she whispered. 'Damn you and every-thing you did to us.'

Several hours later sunlight pierced the narrow crack between the drapes, causing Grant to stir. With his eyes still shut he reached across the tangled sheets, expecting to touch her soft skin, warm and tinged with the lingering scent of sex. When he failed to find her, he opened his eyes and pushed himself up in bed with his elbows. It was the first morning in three years that his first thought hadn't been of Libby and how much he missed her.

He sank back against the pillows. Without looking further, he knew she was gone. All at once he felt a curious loneliness and a sense of loss.

15

It was ironic, he thought, remembering the beautiful copper-haired woman and the night they had spent together – he knew every inch of her body intimately, but he didn't know her name.

CHAPTER 2

July 1996, Los Angeles, California

The Spanish-style house with the pale beige stucco and the terracotta tile roof had been built in the thirties, and it reminded Hallie of an aging actress – well-groomed but slightly out of style. Inside, the house was white and cool and altogether pleasing. It was the place they would call home for the next six months, and she loved it.

Casey had always heard that it cost a small fortune to live in Los Angeles and after leasing this place he believed it. But things had changed for the better and the Brentwood address was worth it. Their days of stretching Hallie's paycheck from week to week – while resisting the impulse to spend the ready cash she brought home from tips she earned each day from her job as a waitress until all their bills were paid – and living in cramped quarters in the tiny carriage house in mid-town Memphis were over.

When Hallie had voiced her concerns about a house this expensive, Casey confidently reassured her. 'Don't worry, honey. I intend to make my next

17

fortune here.'

'I think you've already made a fortune,' she giggled, still amazed at the turn their lives had taken with the sale of his book, *Journey to Fear*, and its appearance on everyone's best-seller list. Now it was going to be made into a movie, and soon Casey would begin work on the screenplay.

When Hallie recalled how she had begrudged him the past two years that he had spent writing while she labored waiting tables, she felt petty and childish. Those traits were not a part of her character, and she knew that much of the resentment she had felt had been prompted by her intense disappointment at having to put her plans aside. But now Casey had made all her sacrifices worthwhile. And here, in Los Angeles, she felt like she was living a fairy tale.

The next morning Hallie stretched and blinked her eyes as the bright sunlight flooded the bedroom. It took her a minute to remember where they were. Then she rolled across the bed and snuggled up against her handsome husband, fitting herself easily to his body. When she felt him responding to her, she playfully scooted away. He groaned as he reached out an arm and encircled her slim waist.

'Not so fast,' he commanded, 'I've got plans for you.' Casey nuzzled the back of her neck with his mouth, then covered her lips with his.

'But I don't want to waste the morning,' protested Hallie when his lips began a slow descent toward the swell of her breasts.

Casey pushed aside the nightshirt she wore, and

taking her breast in his mouth flicked his tongue teasingly over her nipple. 'To hell with the morning,' he muttered.

Hallie couldn't have agreed more.

An hour later she stepped out of the shower and dressed in a pair of shorts and a T-shirt. She found Casey outside near the pool. 'I want to go see the movie stars' houses,' she informed him, 'after we get something to eat. I'm starved.'

Casey wrapped his arms around her, turning her so that he stood behind her. Together their eyes traveled over the sparkling pool that was rimmed with cobalt blue tile, the lush green lawn and the flowering geraniums and impatiens that formed brilliant borders of red and pink. 'Food and movie stars. Is that all you can think of?'

'Uh huh. What about you?' she asked, rubbing her cheek against his freshly shaven face.

Casey took a deep breath and waved his hand at their surroundings. 'I think about this. I am so lucky, Hallie. Some people wait all their lives for an opportunity like this and they never get it. Well, I've got mine and I'm going to make the most of it. Nothing is going to get in my way.'

She tilted her head to one side, laying her cheek against the rough hair on his arms, and thought about the way things had been between them. If she were completely honest, she would admit that her love for him had tarnished during their three years of marriage, and together they had failed to bring back its original luster.

It had been so different in the beginning, but maybe

all relationships diminished in intensity after a few years. She closed her eyes, feeling the sun's warmth steal over her and let her thoughts drift back to when she and Casey first met.

It had been a sticky, humid Memphis night, the kind that follows on the heels of the first few warm days of spring. Almost everyone at the fraternity party had sported some evidence that they had spent time outside in the hopes of acquiring an early tan. Inside the red-brick fraternity house with the big wraparound porch couples were packed shoulder to shoulder, hip to hip. Hallie was there with Skip Beckwith. Both were seniors at the University of Memphis. They were also friends, having grown up together in Mimosa, a small town in Mississippi.

Skip had just handed her a paper cup filled with cold beer when Hallie saw Casey coming up the front steps, his arm draped around a tall slender blonde. It was easy to spot a Memphis girl – they all had big hair – and this one was no exception. But Casey seemingly didn't notice anyone as he and the blonde had made their way through the crowd and into the house. Earlier Skip had estimated that there were at least a hundred people at the party.

Older by five years, handsome, golden-haired and green-eyed, Casey Prescott was sought after by almost every girl on campus. It gave Hallie a curious feeling to know that she could watch him unobserved from her perch on the porch railing, admire his good looks, hate the way the big-haired blonde was hanging all over him, and love the way he was ignoring her.

Skip had been inside when later in the evening Hallie, with her back turned toward the noisy crowd, heard a voice behind her then felt two arms resting lightly on her shoulders. 'Tomorrow night, eight o'clock. Yes or no.'

Hallie had whirled around, her eyes wide. 'I don't. . .'

'No explanations. Just yes or no.' It was Casey Prescott, his green eyes glittering with amusement.

Her heart raced for a moment, then she realized this must be some kind of prank. 'No,' she had replied with a knowing smile.

'Damn!' Casey had grinned and shook his head in mock exasperation. Taking Hallie's arm he had turned her toward him and led her through the crowd to a dark corner of the porch. 'Just what is it you don't like about me?' he had asked, tilting his head back to take a drink of his beer from a long-necked bottle while his green eyes remained fixed on her.

'Nothing,' she had answered. 'It's just that tomorrow night I don't get off work until eleven.' Casey had continued to hold Hallie's arm, running his thumb back and forth over her skin, his touch sending small electrical shocks through her.

'Call in sick,' he had said persuasively, but she shook her head. Casey studied her closely then. He wasn't used to being turned down, especially by a beautiful girl with hair the color of copper, and nicely filled out in all the places he was interested in.

'Maybe another time,' she had said, reasonably certain that this invitation had sprung from some ulterior motive.

'Yeah, sure. Well, see you around.' Casey Prescott

grinned and shook his head as if he couldn't believe what had just happened. The girls he dated were always the most popular and in demand socially. Usually they had been crowned or voted Miss Somebody, Fraternity Sweetheart, or Princess of Some-Big-Event. And here he had just asked out this nobody, and the stupid little redneck had turned him down. He gave her arm a parting squeeze and moved away from her toward the front door of the frat house.

'What did Prescott want?' Skip asked later when they were leaving the party. He took Hallie's arm as they made their way through the thinning crowd, then down the porch steps to the sidewalk.

'He asked me out,' Hallie had confided with a self-conscious dip of her head as they walked the distance to his car. Skip was her friend. They had known each other since elementary school and she could tell him anything.

'Why did he ask *you* out?'

'Well, thank you, Skip. Why shouldn't he ask *me* out?' Her voice was teasing.

'Look, Hallie, that sounded bad. I didn't mean it that way. It's just that Prescott can have just about anybody he wants and . . .' Skip had turned toward Hallie, his expression apologetic. 'I did it again. What I'm trying to tell you, Hallie, is that Prescott plays in a different league. He's a few years older than most of the guys and when he takes a girl out he expects more than a kiss at the front door. He expects to get laid,' Skip had finished bluntly.

'Don't all guys expect that?' Hallie asked sarcastically.

'Geez, Hallie . . .' protested Skip, suddenly embarrassed.

She turned toward him as they reached his car. 'I can take care of myself, Skip, I promise. But thanks for the warning.'

Skip had leaned down and opened the car door for her. He hoped she would heed his warning. Prescott thrived on the challenge and the chase, and the more popular the girl was, the better. But Hallie didn't fit into that category at all, and Skip was afraid that Prescott was only looking to amuse himself with someone new. He never dated the same girl for long, and Skip knew that for many girls this only added to the mystique.

In the beginning Hallie had been flattered and amused by Casey's attention, but for weeks she had refused to take him seriously. When he stopped dating everyone else she began to believe that maybe his interest in her was genuine. Six months after they met he had asked her to marry him and Hallie couldn't believe her good fortune.

Together, they had planned their future with the enthusiasm of youth who live in a world where things so easily fall into place. Casey, with his undergraduate degree in journalism, wanted to be a writer, while Hallie wanted to design clothes.

Hallie sighed deeply, putting aside her thoughts of how they had met and the events that had brought them here to Los Angeles, to this capricious paradise where each day thousands of people arrived in pursuit of fortune and fame. Casey had his shot at fame with the publication of his book. Now, with the movie, he was getting another. While she was thrilled at his success, she only hoped it would not be at her expense.

The excitement of Los Angeles faded after the first month. Hallie was through playing tourist and tired of spending so much time alone. Casey was fully involved in writing the screenplay now, often working into the night and straight through the weekends.

By the second month she was ready to climb the walls. In spite of the sunshine and the outdoor lifestyle, she had not made friends here. It seemed everyone except her had something exciting to do. The energy was there, in the air, so palatable she could almost taste it. And that was part of the problem. Everyone in Los Angeles seemed to have a quest, or a dream, or a mission. Everyone, that is, except her.

One morning on impulse she called the admissions office at UCLA and was told that there would be time for her to enroll for two classes before the next semester began. She reasoned that these classes, both in costume design, would help her fill the long empty days, but by the end of the second week of school Hallie was completely engrossed in her studies. Her resentment at the late hours that Casey kept all but disappeared and she felt renewed. She had not given up on the idea of her own business, but merely postponed it until they returned home to Memphis.

As Hallie's outlook improved, Casey's worsened. Writing a screenplay was vastly different from writing a novel. In *Journey to Fear* he had been able to give substance to his characters by way of their thoughts and emotions. He knew who they were. First, he had created them in his mind, giving them body and soul, then he captured their essence on paper. But the characters in this screenplay had become nothing more than lifeless cardboard replicas. They lacked form and substance.

'Do you realize that this is the first time we have been out together for weeks?' asked Hallie as she tasted the sinfully rich cheesecake she had just ordered.

'You know how it's been.' Casey drank from his wine glass. 'Maybe this is all a huge mistake. Maybe I should stick to writing novels. That's what I seem to do best. According to Ted, I certainly don't know anything about writing screenplays.' Casey's frustration with the whole process was evident in his voice. He leaned forward, so focused on his dissatisfaction that he never noticed the caring concern in Hallie's eyes.

'It's crazy, Hallie,' he continued. 'I realize that the thoughts and emotions in a film are supposed to come from the actors. All I have to do is watch and analyze almost any good film and I see the parallels. But Ted Hinds has ripped *Journey* to shreds, and there doesn't seem to be a damn thing I can do to stop him. I swear, Hallie, there's nothing left. It's almost as if he hates my book.' Or me, he added silently.

'Surely there's something you can do, Casey. Maybe if you sat down with Ted and explained how you feel, it would clear the air,' suggested Hallie.

Casey shook his head. 'I don't think so.'

Daily he had watched his book being hacked into fragments that no longer resembled his powerful and moving story. And whenever he had voiced his objec-

25

tions, Ted would ask him how much experience he had had with screenplays. None, Casey would answer, and he could see the sneering superiority in the way Ted would unconsciously hitch up his pants and stand a little taller.

Each day it became more obvious that Casey was not prepared for Hollywood as it operated behind-the-scenes, where nothing was sacred, and everything was subject to change, or whim, or rewrite.

'In six months it will be all over, then we can go home. Surely you can stay with the project that long. *Journey* will make a wonderful movie, Casey.'

Half of Hallie's statement was true. *Journey* would make a wonderful movie. Maybe she was right, he thought. He was just so worried about the transition to film.

The other part of her statement, the part that wasn't true, troubled him. As far as Hallie knew they would only be here for the six months it took for Casey to work on the screenplay version of his book, then they would return home to Memphis. But Casey had already decided to remain in Los Angeles permanently – a decision he had failed to confide to her.

She would be upset, he was sure – just as she had been upset over every decision he had made during their marriage. He hadn't consulted her then, and he had no intention of doing so now. His ambitions and his career had always come first with him; nothing about that had changed. Hallie would just have to get used to the idea of living in Los Angeles.

For Casey, success had become the driving force in his life. His book had not only earned him an exceptionally large advance for an unknown author, the movie rights had also been sold for an undisclosed amount. The contract his agent had negotiated stipulated that Casey was to write the screenplay, and while the producers had groaned at the thought of having to work with someone from outside who was not in the business of making movies, and who, even worse, also happened to be the author, they finally agreed with the stipulations. Since Casey had never even attempted a screenplay, Ted Hinds, a seasoned writer, had been assigned to work closely with him to act as his editor and consultant.

Journey to Fear, which had climbed to the top of the best-seller list, was the story of a 22-year-old soldier who had been sent to Vietnam where he discovers defective arms shipments are being routinely shipped to his unit, then unloaded, uncrated, and repacked to be returned to the States. To the unobservant, it would seem as if the appropriate action had been taken. After all, it was a bad shipment. But the soldier was extremely observant and what he discovered shocked him. The returned crates contained something extra on their return voyage – heroin.

Probing further, the soldier learns that the scheme for shipping heroin into the United States was far more complicated than he had ever dreamed, involving high-ranking military officers and influential politicians. Before he can substantiate what he knows, he is arrested and, in an obvious frame-up, he is accused of being a part of the smuggling operation. In a bizarre turn of events, others testify at the trial, twisting and distorting the soldier's defense and he is found guilty of a crime he did not commit.

The book stirred up a great deal of controversy as to the real identity of the characters, especially the men who controlled the smuggling operation from behind a seemingly legitimate façade. Casey and his publishers insisted it was a work of fiction, a product of his imagination and nothing more. Still, privately it made more than a few people nervous. All this speculation over the book was a publicist's dream come true. The movie was the icing on the cake.

Casey straightened in his chair and smiled at Hallie. 'No more talk about my problems. Now what do you want to do for the rest of the evening? I promise I will devote all my attention to you.'

Hallie smiled, relieved to see Casey shifting into a happier frame of mind. 'How about a romantic drive along the beach?' she suggested.

'And then?' he asked, with a studied innocence.

'It could lead to other things,' she replied with a teasing smile.

But Casey's good mood was short-lived. Each day he seemed to become more withdrawn, and continued to be disturbed by the direction the screenplay had taken. Hallie sensed the change in him and had repeatedly tried to get him to talk to her, but he refused, saying only that he was too tired. By now he was having trouble sleeping and he would lie awake all night, then fall into a deep sleep only a few hours before he had to be at the studio.

Along with the erosion of the story, the constant criticism from Ted was wearing Casey down. Their writing styles were not compatible, and the starkness of the screenplay format was difficult for Casey to work with.

Besides the technical stumbling blocks, Ted made it no secret that he outwardly resented Casey's youth and his phenomenal success. For years Ted Hinds had worked in Hollywood but, in spite of the importance of the projects he had worked on and the money he had made, real fame and the coveted awards that went with it had eluded him.

This project should have been his. Now he was nothing more than a glorified baby sitter. While it paid well, he still spent his days holding the hand of this so-called literary prodigy. Every time he thought about Casey Prescott and the phenomenal opportunity that had been handed to him, Ted wanted to puke. Where was the reward for his years of diligence, hard work, and that most important ingredient, talent?

Each night Casey would go home drained, angry with Ted for dissecting every line he wrote and challenging every idea he had. When sleep wouldn't come, Casey began to drink steadily, but it wasn't enough.

Ironically, while Casey was becoming increasingly disillusioned with Hollywood, it was an invitation to a Hollywood party that provided him with the hope that he could rescue his screenplay. It would be an opportunity to meet with Irwin Turner, the producer, on a more personal level.

CHAPTER 3

The Turner house was both bizarre and magnificent and, as Casey led her her inside the huge edifice, Hallie thought it was everything a Hollywood producer's home should be. Slender white marble pillars gilded with veins of pale pink separated white carpeted rooms from each other. As she stepped up into the living room, Hallie, unaware that she was as beautiful in her midnight blue gown as any woman there, was dazzled by the glitter and opulence of the guests.

Never had she seen so many perfumed, pampered and pomaded people in one room. Before the night was over she would have studied each of the dresses the women wore and attempted to identify the designer. Casey was equally awed, not by the glitter, but by the power. Its presence was so real that he felt as if he could reach out and touch it.

'Casey, it's so nice to see you again.'

He turned in surprise. The smooth, sultry voice matched the sleek blonde in the black beaded dress who stood at his elbow.

'Hello, uh . . .' He stumbled over his words. He recognized Jasmine Turner from a brief meeting at her husband's office. Clearing his throat, he said, 'This is my wife, Hallie. Hallie, this is Jasmine Turner, our hostess.'

Hallie smiled and nodded and made all the appropriate replies. At the time she thought it was very gracious of Mrs Turner to seek them out.

According to the Hollywood chronicles, Jasmine Turner had arrived in Hollywood from Rapid City, South Dakota, three years ago, broke and believing she was pretty and talented enough to be a star. It took a year of near-starvation while working at a series of minimum-wage jobs for her to realize that Los Angeles was full of girls just like her, only prettier and with more talent.

It was then that she began to plan her future. If she couldn't be rich and famous, she would marry rich and famous. After some skillful maneuvering, and moving from one man to another, she later caught the eye and heart of Irwin Turner, one of the wealthiest and influential men in the motion-picture industry. Privately, the gossips had tagged Jasmine for what she really was, but publicly they held their tongues. Irwin was a man who wielded enormous power; as his wife, Jasmine was someone to reckon with.

Most of Jasmine's story was true; at least, the part about her nearly starving to death and using any man who served her purpose. But Jasmine Turner had never set foot in South Dakota. Her real name was Janice Porter, and she had been scared and running for her life when she arrived in Los Angeles from Washington, DC. Scared that Edwin Mathews, a ruthless multi-millionaire businessman with strong political influ-

31

ence, would find her and the evidence she had that would tie him to the murder of Senator Hugh Rawlins, her former lover.

Now, three years later, she wasn't scared any more. With several plastic surgeries behind her, and more money than she had ever dreamed of, Jasmine was confident that she no longer bore any resemblance to the frightened girl she had once been.

In the beginning of their marriage Jasmine had wished that Irwin had been a younger man, but the endless supply of beautiful clothes and jewels helped to make up for that. Besides, at sixty-eight, he was easily satisfied by his young and beautiful third wife. Sometimes Jasmine believed that Irwin's work kept him more sexually stimulated than she did.

Her sexual appetites, however, were not so easily satisfied, so she had tapped into what seemed to be an endless supply of young and virile men to share her bed. They were waiters, bartenders, and parking attendants, all aspiring actors whom she had promised to help in their search for stardom. If Irwin suspected anything, he never mentioned it to her, and two of the young men had actually landed parts in films that Irwin had produced.

While screenwriters in Hollywood were commonplace, young and dazzling best-selling novelists, it seemed, were not. That night Casey garnered a lot of attention while Hallie stood proudly by, but the opportunity to speak with Irwin Turner at length about the screenplay did not materialize.

Later in the evening, Jasmine returned, plucking a smiling Casey from his audience and from Hallie's side.

32

While not pleased at being left alone in a roomful of strangers, Hallie managed to smile and converse with the other guests, confident Casey would return to her side shortly.

Earlier she thought it was very gracious of Mrs Turner to seek them out, but when Casey disappeared with Jasmine and didn't return for a very long time, Hallie thought she knew exactly why the bitch had been so attentive.

After a half-hour she became panicky, suddenly unsure of what to do and what to say to the other guests. Casey was a celebrity in his own right, a role that he relished, but she was only his wife, a small-town girl from rural Mississippi whose biggest ambition in life was to design clothes. Fighting an attack of shyness, she made her way outside where carefully placed lanterns bathed the patio and pool in soft light.

How strange she felt here among all these famous people. While fascinated with the thought of her husband's book being turned into a movie, Hallie still longed for the security of home and the company of friends and relatives. She tried to picture her Aunt Billie in this setting and the thought brought a smile to her face. By now Billie would have asked their hostess for the recipe for her wonderful lobster salad. Somehow Hallie couldn't see Jasmine Turner being at all flattered by a request that implied that she had actually had anything to do with the preparation of all this food.

'What's so funny?'

Hallie jumped. She hadn't heard anyone approach. The dark-haired, dark-eyed young woman stepped closer, smiling. 'Sorry,' she said. 'I didn't mean to startle you. I'm Dana Gordon.'

Hallie introduced herself and said, 'I was thinking about my Aunt Billie back home and what she'd think of this party,'

'And what would she think?' asked Dana.

'That she could have accomplished the very same thing by inviting everyone over for a backyard barbecue. Half the fuss and a lot more fun. It's difficult to be snotty and aloof when you're busy licking barbecue sauce off your fingers.'

Dana laughed out loud. 'I would agree with your aunt, but I'm afraid that's not Jasmine's style.'

'Do you know her well?' asked Hallie.

Dana shook her head. 'Jasmine is not the sort of person that one can know, or even be friends with. My father and Irwin have known each other for years, though.'

'Well, she certainly seems to like my husband. She whisked him away a while back and I haven't seen him since,' said Hallie with a nervous laugh.

'Umm. Not a good sign, Hallie. Jasmine has a thing for young good-looking guys. If I were you I'd go find him.'

Hallie waited for the smile that would signal that Dana was teasing her, but it didn't appear. 'That's probably very good advice,' she said after a minute, then set off to look for him.

'Where have you been?' Hallie asked angrily a few minutes later when she found Casey, as she noted his rumpled appearance and the glazed look in his eyes. 'You've been gone for over an hour.'

'Just talking business,' he replied. 'I didn't think you would mind.'

'Well, I do. How could you do that to me? You know I don't know anyone here.'

Casey shrugged his shoulders and ran his hands through his golden hair to smooth it down. 'You need to be more outgoing. Talk to people, make friends, Hallie. It's important for my career.' He flashed a smile at a passing couple that they had met earlier. 'He's supposed to be well connected at Boulevard Productions. The young woman with him has just completed her first film for Boulevard.'

'Can we leave now?' asked Hallie, agitated. Purposely, she ignored Casey's attempt to change the subject.

'It's early. It would look bad if we left now. Come on, honey,' said Casey in an effort to soothe her temper.

'Then you stay, Casey. By all means, don't insult your hostess, especially after she has made you feel so welcome. But I'm leaving and I'm almost positive I won't be missed,' she announced.

'Don't do this, Hallie,' he whispered urgently, looking around to see if anyone had heard her. 'This night could be important. There are some things I want to solidify about the screenplay.'

When Hallie spoke, there was no mistaking her message. 'It looks like you've already made a start in the right direction,' she said sarcastically, glaring at Jasmine who was walking towards them. 'Getting cozy with the producer's wife should get you booted right off this picture.'

She turned and walked away. Unconsciously, Casey shrugged his shoulders and smoothed his jacket, dismissing Hallie's actions as a whim. There were some things in life that were more important than his wife's criticism. And so what if Jasmine surprised him by coming on to him? He had enjoyed it. Besides, she had promised that he would have the opportunity to talk to Irwin about the screenplay.

Right now he felt confident and energized. Whatever had been in that little pill Jasmine had given him earlier when he had complained of being tired was certainly working.

Hallie had tried to wake Casey the next morning before she left for class, but it was like trying to wake the dead. After repeated attempts, she gave up. The shrill ring of the phone finally woke him at noon. Clumsily he reached for it.

'I bet you feel just awful,' said the soft voice on the other end. Coming from Jasmine it sounded almost like a caress.

Casey mumbled a reply, while trying to focus his eyes. His head felt about three times its normal size.

'I've got just the thing to perk you up. Jasmine always has the cure for what ails you, honey,' she teased. And she did: pills, coke, sex, or an introduction to the right person. It was a game she played to relieve the terrible boredom that being married to a man more than twice her age could produce.

'Meet me for lunch,' she suggested, her voice low. 'I've got exactly what you need to get you through the day.'

Casey grinned. 'What time is it?' he asked.

'Noon.'

'Oh, my God! I've got to get to work.' He threw the sheet aside and sat up on the side of the bed.

Jasmine smiled into the phone as she heard the click and stretched lazily against the jumble of pillows on her bed. 'Maybe next time,' she whispered as she imagined his hard, golden body.

An hour later Casey showed up for work then wished he hadn't. For fifteen minutes he endured a lecture from Ted on Hollywood parties, and how only the stars could afford the luxury of sleeping until noon while the rest of the people in the industry were expected to show up for work on schedule. It was the longest day of Casey's life. Ted wouldn't lay off him and Casey couldn't concentrate. In spite of the aspirin he had taken at intervals during the afternoon, his head still throbbed with the kind of pain that only imbibing too much alcohol could produce. At six he walked out without saying anything to anyone.

The restaurant was trendy and crowded, and Casey suspected that on his own he could not have gotten a table, but the magic of Jasmine's name had gotten them a choice table overlooking the beautifully groomed gardens to the rear.

'I should have taken you up on your invitation to lunch yesterday,' said Casey. 'It was a wasted day, anyway. I was wasted.'

'So I gathered,' said Jasmine, smiling. Her blonde hair hung straight, then curved inward to cup her jaw line.

'Jasmine,' began Casey, 'you said the other night that

you could help me set up a meeting with Irwin. I really want a chance to talk with him. *Journey to Fear* is not going well, and I'm worried about what's happening to it. No one seems to understand the basic concept of the story.'

Jasmine laughed, dismissing his concern. 'Casey, darling, this is Hollywood. Nothing stays the way it's supposed to be. Not even a best-seller. Look at what they did to John Crawford's book, *Danger Ahead*. They changed the ending. Nobody gives a damn about the way things are supposed to be. They only care about the way they want things to be. Besides, as long as you're getting paid to write the screenplay, what do you care? Millions of people who have never read a book from cover to cover in their lives will stand in line at the nearest theater to see the movie version of *Journey*.'

'But you don't understand, Jasmine. *Journey to Fear* is something I created. It consumed two years of my life. I don't want to see it destroyed. That's why I need to talk to Irwin, to tell him how I see the transition from print to film.' Casey leaned forward earnestly.

'Relax, Casey,' urged Jasmine. 'Here,' she said, reaching into her purse. 'I've brought you something to make you feel better, just like I promised.'

Casey looked at the small white pills she held out to him like candy. It was the same kind she had given him at the party. He reached out and took them from her, put them in his mouth, then washed them down with his glass of wine. By the time their lunch was served, he was already feeling better.

Jasmine Turner was the most fascinating woman Casey had ever met. There was an aura of power about her, and her sensuality seemed to reach out and wind itself around him. With just a look she turned him on more than any woman he had ever known, including Hallie.

'I can do things for you, Casey,' Jasmine whispered as she brushed her hand lightly across his thigh. 'I admire your ambition and your drive. Let me show you how to direct that energy and make it work to your advantage.'

Casey smiled in reply, confident that Jasmine understood him as Hallie never had. With her, he never had to explain his motivation; she knew how consuming the drive for power could be. Besides, he was certain that in him Jasmine recognized a kindred spirit.

The meetings between Casey and Jasmine increased in frequency, and with them, his need for her and the pills she carefully doled out to him. There were never any extra, just enough to last two or three days, until they could meet again.

After each meeting, Jasmine would mentally review their progress. She was orchestrating this seduction very carefully so as not to rush into things. Soon, he would be dependent on her for the drugs she could give him, then he would become addicted to the sex. She had decided the first time she had seen him that Casey Prescott could be easily manipulated. And, with his golden good looks, he would make an excellent lover.

The constant stream of partners she had had lately had tired her. Some were good, but most were bad, and so vain and self-centered. Casey was young and pliable, smart and successful in his own right. If she handled things right, he would be around for as long as she wanted him. Briefly, Jasmine thought about his wife, then shrugged. She was too young and inexperienced to present any kind of stumbling block. Hallie Prescott could have her husband back when Jasmine was through with him.

'Where are you going so early?' mumbled Casey as he rolled over in bed and raised his head off the pillow. It was Saturday morning and for the first time in several weeks he had the weekend off.

'I've got a few things to pick up at the grocery for tonight,' Hallie said as she pulled a sweatshirt over her head, then brushed her hair back and secured it with a rubber band.

'Tonight?' Casey sat up.

Hallie turned away from the mirror to face him and groaned. 'Oh, Casey! Please, don't tell me you've forgotten that we invited the Channings for dinner tonight.'

He rubbed at his eyes with his fingertips then stared at her, his expression blank. 'Who are the Channings?'

'Damn. I knew you'd do this. They are our neighbors and they'll be here at seven tonight for dinner. Casey, you remember, Kate and Charlie?'

He did. The old people. 'Hell, Hallie, do you think they're still alive? It's been more than a week since you've seen them and I think I heard an ambulance go by here yesterday.'

'Casey! Don't say that! They're very spry even though they are in their seventies. Besides I think they are an interesting couple. And nice. Charlie was

40

with Waltham-Zenith studios for years, and Kate is an attorney.'

'Retired, I assume,' said Casey sarcastically.

Hallie leaned over and kissed him quickly. 'Not at all. She still practises law. Now, please be nice tonight. See you later.'

Casey stood, and ran his hands through his hair. He was feeling a little shaky, but some coffee and one of those pills would take the edge off. He supposed it didn't matter who they had dinner with tonight.

Hallie breathed a sigh of relief when Kate and Charlie complimented her on dinner. Even though cooking was not one of her talents, she could, when called upon, put together a nice meal. Of course, Billie helped by giving her several recipes that didn't exceed her culinary skills.

Kate and Charlie are a charming couple, thought Hallie, as she served dessert and coffee, then slipped into her place next to Casey.

'I finished your book a few days ago, Casey, and found it very thought-provoking,' announced Kate. Of the couple, she was the more outspoken. Her husband was good-natured and congenial, but it was clear that Kate Channing was a woman with many opinions, all of them her own.

'Well, *Journey* has had a lot of reviews,' replied Casey, fixing Kate with his best smile, 'but they usually don't stop there. Is there something else you'd like to add to that, Kate?'

'No, not yet. I'm still digesting what I read. Now, tell us which actors you would cast in what part.'

41

After a lively discussion over their collective choices, Charlie turned to Hallie and asked if she, too, had career ambitions.

'Well, right now I'm taking some classes at UCLA,' she replied, 'but when we go back to Memphis I plan. . .'

'Hallie wants to be a seamstress,' announced Casey abruptly. With precision, he managed to cut off any opportunity that Charlie might have had to politely pursue the subject of Hallie's career.

Hallie's reaction to her husband's rudeness was involuntary. First her head jerked in his direction, then a hot flush of embarrassment rushed over her.

Without missing a beat or even sparing a glance for his wife, Casey pointedly returned to the subject of casting the characters in *Journey* and asked Charlie, 'Now, what would you think about Denzel Washington in the role of Captain D'Angelo and Brad Pitt as Private Lawrence?'

Hallie bit at her lower lip to keep it from trembling. She was stunned at Casey's rotten remark and his blatant rudeness to her, and embarrassed by the sympathetic look that Kate sent her direction. There was absolutely nothing wrong with being a seamstress, but it was her ambition to be a designer. They were two completely different things. Casey knew what her ambitions were – they had talked about them many, many times. He was her husband and he should have been proud of her talent. Why had he felt it necessary to belittle her in front of their guests?

'I'll . . . I'll get more coffee,' she murmured, rising quickly. In the kitchen she stood facing the coffee pot, both hands gripping the counter on either side of her until her knuckles were white. She breathed deeply, struggling for control and forcing the hurt down. All the while her throat ached with the need to cry.

Later, when the Channings had left, Hallie retreated to the kitchen to clean up the dishes.

'Want some help?' asked Casey from the doorway.

'No.'

'You were right about the Channings. They are an interesting couple. Did you know he was involved in making propaganda movies for the Navy during World War II?'

'No.' Hallie kept her back turned toward him and began loading the dishwasher. The only sounds in the kitchen were the clatter of dishes mingled with that of running water.

'So what the hell's wrong with you?' Casey asked defensively after a few minutes, when it became obvious that Hallie was giving him the silent treatment.

She straightened then and turned to face him. 'Why did you put me down like that in front of the Channings? You embarrassed me. Did it make you feel superior? You are already successful, Casey. What's wrong with my wanting to be successful also?'

Slowly and scornfully, Casey ran his eyes over his wife, then brought his gaze back to meet hers. 'Isn't that what you want to do, Hallie? Sew?'

'You know I want to design clothes. There's a big difference, Casey. Tell me, is your ego so overblown that you can't acknowledge that I have talent also?'

Casey shook his head, dismissing Hallie's question. 'It's not a question of whether or not I think you have any talent – it's a question of whether or not you have what it takes to succeed. And I don't see it, Hallie. I just don't see it.' He leaned against the doorway, his hands in his pockets, his feet crossed.

'Well, then you don't know me very well. You under-estimate me, Casey. You always have. And once more you have managed to dismiss my dreams as insignif-icant. And right now all I can think about is how much longer I'm going to put up with your selfishness.'

A coldness settled in his eyes as once more he mentally compared Hallie to Jasmine, then he shrugged and turned away.

Hallie returned to the task she had started, only now tears spilled onto her cheeks. She took a quick swipe at them with her trembling hand, then reached for a tissue.

It has always been this way between us.

It wasn't her intention to drag up all the times when Casey had put himself and what he wanted ahead of her, but now she couldn't help it. Memories rushed back, intensifying the hurt she already felt.

The first incident took place a few weeks after their marriage, over dinner at his parents' house. Casey had announced he was going on to graduate school. It had come as a complete surprise to Hallie.

'Tom, won't you please at least listen to Casey and give him a chance to tell you his plans?' pleaded Ruth Prescott, Casey's mother, as she slid into her chair and laid her plump hand protectively on her son's shoulder. They had just finished dinner and Ruth had just served dessert.

44

Tom Prescott had leaned back in his chair and surveyed his wife and son. They had always been a team, and he had always been the heavy in the family. If Casey had told his mother he wanted to go to Mars, Ruthie would have moved heaven and earth just to make it possible. Maybe that's what happens when you wait too late to have children, he had thought. At sixty-six, he felt more like he should be Casey's grandfather rather than his father. Not that we had any choice in the matter, he thought.

Tom and Ruth Prescott had been in their late thirties when they had met, each of them having had a prior marriage, but neither of them having children. A baby was all Ruth had talked about so they were delighted when Casey was born. But the bonding Tom had hoped for between him and his son had never materialized. Instead, it was Ruth that Casey had seemed most comfortable with.

'Go ahead,' Tom had directed as he glanced first at his new daughter-in-law, then at his handsome son. Hallie had made no effort to hide her surprise at Casey's announcement. It was obvious that this was not something that the two of them had discussed.

Then there was Ruthie, who would expect Tom to give Casey whatever it was he wanted. She always did. It had been a pattern that had repeated itself for years. But Casey had graduated from college, and at twenty-six it was time for him to start earning a living and paying his way. He had a wife now, and that meant responsibilities.

Tom Prescott had listened patiently as Casey had outlined his plan to continue his education by working toward his master's degree in English. Tom couldn't help but notice that Hallie had seemed as upset at this news as he did. While Tom admitted that Casey was a good student, he could not reconcile the fact that if Casey had his way, it would mean another year or more without his help in the family business.

'Our agreement was that you would come to work for me as soon as you graduated, or had you forgotten?'

Casey had stretched his legs out before him and ran his hands through his thick blond hair. Arguing with his father was like arguing with a tape recorder. He said the same things over and over. 'This is important,' Casey had explained. I don't have an interest in the business, Dad. You know that. You know I want to be a writer, and having this advanced degree will help me. I can always combine teaching with writing if I have to.'

Hallie had looked from father to son. It had been clear they were at odds, but as of right now, so were she and Casey.

This was the first that she had heard about Casey's plans, and she was upset that he hadn't even discussed it with her. This was not what they had talked about. Maybe Casey had forgotten that they were a couple now, and this wasn't the kind of decision he should have made without first talking it over with her.

Tom had straightened in his chair, intent on choosing his words carefully, not wanting to instigate a family argument that would linger between Ruthie and him long after Casey and Hallie had left. Instinctively, almost as if she could read her husband's thoughts, Ruth had leaned closer to Casey, her mouth forming a straight line, her expression tense.

46

Tom had breathed deeply. There it was. The look that warned him that this was going to escalate into more than a disagreement between him and his son. Once more the battle lines between him and his wife had been drawn. 'I admire your goals and your ambition, Casey,' his father began. 'And I know that if you want it bad enough you will somehow manage to get your master's degree, but exactly two weeks from now, I'll expect you to show up for work at Prescott Castings.'

Casey had stood, almost knocking over his chair. He was angry. 'All you can think about is that damn business of yours. Don't you care what I want?'

Hallie had stood also, reaching out to touch his arm, silently entreating him to calm down.

'Tom,' Ruthie pleaded, 'won't you please reconsider? This is important to Casey.' She hesitated for a moment then added, 'And to me.'

Tom Prescott had risen also.

'Forget it, Mom,' Casey had said sarcastically, as he grabbed Hallie's hand, then turned and departed the dining room through the kitchen. 'Let's go, Hallie. I'll figure out how to do it without any help from him,' he spat, slamming the door behind him.

Hallie had turned back helplessly toward her new in-laws who stood at the doorway as Casey pulled her down the driveway toward the car.

When the argument between Casey and his father had erupted at the dinner table, Hallie had been stunned. She had had no idea that Casey had made an agreement with his father to join the family business after graduation. Nor did she know about his plans for graduate school.

On the drive home she wrestled silently with her feelings. Casey's announcement of his plan to pursue graduate studies had upset her. She had plans to take her small savings and put them into her clothing designs. She had spent the last year learning all the things she needed to know about starting a business, and how to market her creations. She would begin on a shoestring, but she was sure that as her sales grew she would be able to add to the line.

But starting a business while Casey was in school was out of the question. Didn't he realize that his plans would affect her own? Casey had agreed later, on the way home, that starting her business would be impossible, seemingly not bothered by the fact that he had just undermined her ambitions with his untimely announcement, and leaving her no choice but to continue her job waiting tables at The Pepper Seed.

Putting her ambitions to design her own line of clothing on hold had been the most difficult thing Casey had asked of her. Hallie, who had learned to sew when she was twelve, had a natural talent for design and clothing construction and was anxious to put her abilities to work.

Now, almost four years later, she was still waiting.

CHAPTER 4

It had started to rain when Hallie, with time to kill between classes, dashed into the small corner restaurant near the campus. Inside, she barely avoided a collision with a customer standing near the door. 'Sorry, I almost didn't see you,' she said, brushing the raindrops from her jacket.

'That's okay,' answered the dark-haired girl as she turned and looked up. 'Hi! Hallie? Do you remember me? We met at the Turners' party.'

For a moment Hallie scanned the face before her. 'Dana! Of course I do. What are you doing here?'

'I just stopped in to get some coffee. I have another class today, but not until later.'

'Me, too. Look, there's an empty table in the corner. Unless you're meeting someone?' asked Hallie.

'Nope. Let's get to it before someone else does.'

After they placed their order Hallie and Dana began to talk like old friends. They had a lot in common since Dana was also a student at UCLA studying film.

'I didn't grow up in Hollywood,' Dana explained, 'but I did spend my summers here visiting my father.

49

It's because of him that I became interested in making movies.'

'Your father is in the business, then,' said Hallie, so glad to have someone to chat with. 'Oh, that's right,' she said remembering their conversation that night at the party. 'He's a friend of the Turners.'

Dana nodded, not bothering to clarify that her father was Neil Gordon. Obviously Hallie didn't realize that her father was a major star, and had been for the past twenty years. It was nice to visit with someone who wanted to share a coffee break and talk about school. She was tired of people who were nice to her only because they thought she could influence her father to give them a chance to audition for a part in his next movie.

'I read your husband's book right after the Turners' party,' announced Dana.

'What did you think?' asked Hallie with interest.

'It is very good. Handled right, it will be great movie. Handled wrong, it will be an expensive bomb.'

'That's what Casey is worried about,' volunteered Hallie. 'He feels as if the book's soul is missing.'

Dana nodded, knowingly. 'It's that way with screenplays. Only the dialogue and the bare necessities remain. The rest of it comes together during the filming. Tell him not to worry. I've seen miracles happen on film.'

'I hope so,' said Hallie.

When it was time to leave for class, Hallie and Dana walked back to the campus together and agreed to meet again in a few days. As she hurried toward her design class, Hallie was more cheerful than she had been in a while. She was almost positive she had made a friend.

★ ★ ★

A week later Hallie was still buoyant. Next week was Billie's birthday, and for the first time in her life Hallie was going to go shopping for a present without having to worry about how much money she could spend. It was such a liberating feeling.

Billie Dean Barrett deserved something wonderful. It wasn't an attempt to pay her aunt back, because there wasn't enough money in the world to repay Billie, but Hallie wanted to share some of her good fortune.

When Hallie was three, her parents had been killed in an auto accident and she had gone to live with her Aunt Billie, her father's only sister. Sometimes she was certain she remembered her father and mother, and if they were not exactly memories but only impressions, they provided at least a sense of familiarity and security.

But it was Billie who had held her in her arms when she would awake in the middle of the night, crying because she had had a bad dream; and it was Billie who had promised her that she would always take care of her; and it was Billie who had been a mother to her all these years.

Sometimes it troubled Hallie to think that maybe it was because of her that Billie had never married, but then she remembered that through the years Billie had had many offers of marriage, all of them declined. In college she had been engaged to Farell Rogers, a second-year law student at the University of Mississippi, but Farell had been killed in Vietnam.

After that, Billie, who had been in her early twenties at the time, had never again considered marrying anyone. Hallie wondered if it was because Billie and Farell had been so perfectly matched that there could never be anyone else, or if it was simply a matter of Billie never meeting the right man. Either way, it was a shame, Hallie thought, because Billie, who was now in her early fifties, was still a beautiful woman.

'I don't know what to get her,' Hallie had said to Dana. 'Something frivolous, but something she will use. I don't want her to put it away in a drawer. Oh, and one more thing,' she added excitedly, 'it has to be sinfully expensive. I don't believe that Billie has ever owned anything really expensive in her entire life except maybe her silver-blue Cadillac, but even that she bought second-hand from Doctor Campbell when he was ready to trade it up for a newer model.'

'Then we'll go shopping on Rodeo Drive,' announced Dana. 'If you can't find something sinfully expensive there, Hallie, it simply doesn't exist.'

'Quit being so friendly,' said Dana as they emerged from a shop that sold beautiful designer dresses.

'Why?' asked Hallie wide-eyed.

'Because it's just not done,' teased Dana. 'If you don't act like a snot, you'll never be taken seriously. On this street, the snottier, the better,' she added. 'Now try it,' she said as she pulled Hallie into the next doorway.

Hallie did.

'No, no, no!' Dana said, laughing at the ridiculous expression pasted on Hallie's face. 'Look, it's more like this.' Dana hoisted up her chin and placed her sunglasses on the bridge of her nose. 'Never remove your glasses, especially in the store. At any moment you could be blinded by the price tags. Now watch me. And remember, it's the attitude that counts.'

After going from one shop to another, and repeatedly dissolving into fits of laughter, Hallie finally made a decision. 'I can't believe I'm doing this,' she whispered to Dana as she handed over her credit card to pay for a Chanel purse, 'but Billie will love it.' As long as I don't tell her how much it cost, she added privately.

With her purchase in hand, Hallie followed Dana outside into the bright sunlight.

'How about some lunch? I know a place nearby,' suggested Dana.

Hallie was bursting to share her impressions of Rodeo Drive with her friend as they walked the few short blocks to the restaurant.

'It's like shopping on Mars,' Hallie explained. 'I mean, where I come from everyone drives to Memphis or to Jackson for the really important shopping. I don't think they have stuff like this in either one of those places, and if they do, I've never seen it.

'Just look at this!' she exclaimed gleefully, digging once more into the shopping bag she carried and pulling out her tissue-wrapped prize. 'Billie will be the talk of the Piggly Wiggly when she slings this baby over her shoulder.'

Dana giggled, intrigued by Hallie's unabashed enjoyment of this shopping expedition. 'Hallie, what in the world is a Piggly Wiggly?'

'Oh, that's our grocery store back home in Mimosa,' she answered with a grin.

Dana looked toward her left as they approached the corner and saw a white Mercedes approach, then slow for a pedestrian before speeding up. Behind her dark glasses Dana squinted, then stumbled, nearly missing the curb.

'Are you okay?' asked Hallie, turning.

'Yes, I'm fine,' Dana mumbled, and a worried look crossed her face as her eyes followed the Mercedes. The personalized license plates identified the car as belonging to Jasmine Turner, and Dana could have sworn on a stack of bibles that the handsome man seated beside Jasmine was Hallie's husband.

A few days later Hallie studied the announcement taped to the door of the classroom. Her design class had been cancelled. Shifting the portfolio case that contained the projects for this class from one arm to the other, she contemplated the best way to spend the next two hours. She turned and made her way back through the group of students that had gathered behind her.

At the south entrance of the building Hallie stopped at the pay phone. Balancing the portfolio against her knee and the tip of her shoe, she dug into her purse for change, then dialed Casey's number at work, but the line was busy. After trying once more with the same result, she decided to drive over to his office. It was a pretty day, and she was hoping he could have lunch with her.

'Oh, hello, Ted,' she said when she arrived fifteen minutes later. 'How are things going?'

'Good, Hallie,' lied Ted Hinds. As much as he disliked Casey, he would not take it out on his wife. The truth was that things were falling apart. Prescott simply refused to listen to anyone about this screenplay. If things continued as they were, *Journey* was going to be one lousy picture. It was a shame to ruin a good story because of an author whose ego was out of control.

'My class was cancelled,' she said, 'and I was hoping that Casey could join me for lunch.'

'Ahh . . . lunch.' Ted Hinds leaned back in his chair and studied the woman before him. He had only seen her a few times, but each time he was surprised by her. She was certainly beautiful, but there was more to her than that. Prescott didn't deserve her any more than he deserved his phenomenal success. 'Well, I'm sorry, Hallie, but he's in a meeting and it's scheduled to go on for a couple of hours.'

Disappointment was reflected in Hallie's eyes. 'Oh. Well, it was a spur-of-the-moment thing. I tried to call, but the line was busy.' Hallie shrugged. 'Tell him I came by, will you, Ted?'

'Of course, Hallie.'

A few minutes later Ted watched from the window as Hallie Prescott crossed the parking lot to her car. He shook his head, and wondered if he had done the right thing. There was no meeting. Casey had left for lunch over an hour ago with Jasmine Turner. It was the third time this week. Usually when Casey returned he was in a better mood, but it hadn't taken Ted long to figure out that the reason for this was too much wine at lunch. As a result, the work was moving at a snail's pace, and Ted was forced to do more than he was supposed to do just to keep the project together.

Maybe he should have been happy to have more

control over the screenplay, but he deeply resented the fact that Prescott was out playing with the boss's wife while the responsibility for the project's success fell on his shoulders.

Ted shoved his hands in his pockets, shrugged his shoulders, then turned back toward his desk. Too bad he hadn't had the guts to tell Prescott's wife the truth. He wondered how long it would be before she wised up.

In the parking lot Hallie drove past Casey's car and contemplated leaving him a note, then decided against it. After she had gone a few blocks she pulled into McDonald's and went inside. A few minutes later she came back out into the bright sunshine carrying a sack. This wasn't exactly what she had had in mind, she thought, as she sat at one of the outdoor tables and spread her lunch out before her.

Nearby two little boys who appeared to be about three years old squealed as they came down the tunneled playground slide. For an instant Hallie felt her heart constrict. Sometimes, when she least expected it, she was overcome with a very real longing to have a child of her own, but Casey . . . Hallie sighed. It had been a long time since they had even talked about having a baby.

When she had finished eating, she sipped her drink slowly, willing the time to pass until it was time to return to school. It was too bad Casey had been unavailable. She wanted them to start spending more time together, and she had wanted to tell him about the grade she had received on her mid-term project. Not only had she received an *A* for all her hard work, but the instructor had deemed her renderings worthy of display.

While it was nothing so grand as what Casey was involved in, it meant a lot to her and she wanted him to be proud of her accomplishments. Lately, all their conversations seemed to revolve around the screenplay. Some days she was almost positive that Casey had completely forgotten that she was even taking classes at the university.

That afternoon Casey was already at home when she arrived.

'Hi!' she called, passing the bathroom where he was showering. She grabbed her jeans from the closet and began to change clothes. When she heard the shower shut off she called again, then knocked lightly on the door.

'How was your day?'

'Long and painful,' came the reply.

Hallie winced. That had become Casey's standard answer. Why couldn't he lie once in a while, or at least attempt to relate the humorous side of things?

'Want me to start dinner,' she asked, 'or would you rather go out to eat?'

Casey jerked the door open and moved past her in a cloud of steam. 'Let's go out.'

He suggested a small neighborhood restaurant that specialized in pizza cooked in a wood-burning oven. Tonight he was attentive and once they had left the house his mood improved. Hallie thought he was more like his old self.

'We should get out together more often,' she remarked after they had eaten and the waiter had brought them each a cappucino.

'We haven't had a lot of time for each other lately, have we?' asked Casey as his eyes drifted over the crowd then settled analytically on his wife. There was no denying that Hallie was beautiful. There was a softness to her that he had once found very intriguing. But now – now, whatever had once attracted him to her was overshadowed by a much stronger force. Jasmine Turner was compelling, and privately he would readily admit that he couldn't seem to put her out of his mind. It was this spell, this silken web that Jasmine had woven around him, that kept him coming back to her.

'No, we haven't,' answered Hallie with a small smile, 'but maybe that will change. Especially since things seem to be going better on the screenplay.'

'Who told you that?' Casey asked abruptly, turning his attention back to Hallie.

'Why, Ted did. I stopped by your office today to see if you wanted to go to lunch. My class was cancelled and . . .'

'What time?' he interrupted.

'Well, I think it was a little after noon. Didn't Ted tell you I was there?'

'No. Sorry I missed you,' he lied, wondering if Ted had told Hallie that he was having lunch with Jasmine.

'Yeah, me too. He said you were in a meeting,' she replied, reaching for his hand. 'But this is much better.'

Casey squeezed her hand quickly, then released it. Score one for good old Ted, he thought. He might be a bastard to work with, but at least he had covered for him.

That night in bed Hallie turned to Casey, longing for the physical intimacy they had once shared. In response he reached out for her, pulling her close and even kissing her. But even in the darkness she sensed his silent message that this was as far as he wanted things to go. Reluctantly, she closed her eyes, willing herself to be satisfied with this much. Tonight had been the most pleasant time they had spent together in a long while. It was a step in the right direction.

In the weeks that followed, she wasn't so sure. The agreeable Casey had been replaced by an irritable, easily agitated Casey who challenged everything she said or did. In each of these exchanges, she did her best not to provoke an argument. Instead, she tried to smooth things over, telling herself that he was under a lot of stress and that it was this stress that was was responsible for his irritability. But finally, one evening Hallie's patience reached its limits.

With her head tucked down against the early-evening downpour, Hallie dashed from her car to the porch. In each arm she cradled a sack of groceries. By the time she put one sack down on the stoop and fumbled for the door key she was drenched.

Inside, it was dark but a light glowed dimly in the hallway, its source the small room at the rear of the living room that served as Casey's study. Hallie made her way to the kitchen, then set the sodden paper sacks on the kitchen counter. When she glanced at the contents of the stainless steel sink, she made a face that mirrored her disgust at finding this morning's dirty dishes exactly where she had left them. She

would have to clean up first before she could start **dinner**.

'Casey?' she called as she went into the bathroom.

'In here, Hallie,' he answered from the study.

She peeled out of her wet clothes and reached for her robe on the back of the door.

'Didn't you hear me trying to get in?' she asked irritably through the partially closed door as she secured the tie belt around her slender waist, then rubbed her thick hair dry with a towel.

'I was working,' replied Casey who had not moved from his desk.

Hallie clenched her jaw and squeezed her eyes tight in frustration. 'I got drenched trying to get the door open with two sacks of groceries in my arms. You could have at least opened the door for me.'

'I didn't hear you drive up,' he offered. She could hear the scraping sound of his chair as it moved against the tile floor.

'Don't bother with the excuses, Casey.'

'Sorry,' he said as he appeared in the doorway, lifting his arms in a lazy stretch. 'I had some ideas that I wanted to get down on paper, and I guess I was preoccupied. What are we having for dinner?'

Hallie thought about the sink filled with dirty dishes and wanted to scream. What had happened to the times when they would share the household chores, when one of them would surprise the other by cleaning the house or fixing a special meal, when they couldn't wait to make love as soon as they were together, then later, when they remembered that they were hungry, order a pizza?

'Casey, the sink still has the dishes in it from this morning. Couldn't you have loaded the dishwasher?'

'I've been busy since I got home,' he said, turning his broad shoulders away from her. 'If you can't keep up with the house, Hallie, consider dropping those classes you're taking. Or hire a maid. I don't care which, but don't expect me to do your work.

'And when did all this become "my work"?' Hallie inquired with a wave of her hand.

Casey straightened and tilted his head as if he was assessing her question. The light which radiated from behind him cast his face in shadow and his green eyes appeared nearly black. 'Since I've been able to provide you with this kind of lifestyle, Hallie, and since I no longer have to listen to you whine about every penny I spend. Considering what I've accomplished, taking care of the house is the very least you can do.'

The words, laced with hurtful sarcasm, caused her to stiffen.

'And I've been going since seven this morning,' Hallie reminded him plaintively, pushing the mass of damp hair behind her ears with both hands. 'I finished up my design project before going to class, dropped your clothes at the cleaners this afternoon, had the oil changed in the car, then stopped at the grocery on the way home tonight.' She took a breath and waited for some kind words of sympathy or some sign of appreciation for her efforts, but Casey, who by now had retreated to the study, was silent.

'I do a lot more around here than you give me credit for,' she added loudly, shaking her head.

Casey appeared once more in the doorway. 'Hell,

Hallie. We've only been in LA a few months and already you've turned into a bitch.' He walked past her slowly, then took his car keys from the counter. 'Just lay off me,' he said, passing her in the narrow kitchen, then slammed the back door behind him.

Wearily, Hallie put the groceries away then loaded the dishwasher. The overflowing hamper in the bathroom reminded her that she had planned to do laundry tonight, but she was in no mood to spend her evening doing another chore that Casey should be helping her with.

After ironing a blouse to wear to class the next day, she stuck a frozen pizza in the oven, and ate her solitary meal in the living room while watching television. It was the noise that she craved, not the entertainment, so that the sound of being alone wasn't as pronounced.

If she hadn't been so tired tonight she might have cried over Casey's treatment of her, but all that would have gotten her was puffy eyes, blotchy complexion and a headache. Right now she wasn't sure her husband was worth suffering any of those.

Later, alone in their queen-size bed, Hallie closed her eyes. She was tired; tired of Casey's moods, and tired of coming home to a messy house. It was only the fact Casey would be finished with the screenplay in a few months that kept her going. That, and the satisfaction that she derived from the classes she was taking. Then they could go home. Then maybe things would return to normal.

She thought about the years she had worked at her aunt's café in her home town of Mimosa while she had been in high school, saving every penny just so she could escape the stifling monotony of life in the small Mississippi town. Yet it was this same town that gave her a sense of belonging, of permanence.

Nothing ever changed in Mimosa. People took care of one another there, like family, sometimes for generations. It was ironic that the very things that Hallie had strived to leave behind were the same things she treasured when she felt alone and uncertain, like she did right now.

CHAPTER 5

It rained again the following Sunday afternoon. Hallie was in the living room reading while Casey was in the adjoining study paying bills. 'What is this?' he asked from the arched doorway that separated the two rooms.

Hallie looked up from her book and tried to focus on the sheet of paper he was waving in the air. 'What is it?'

'It's our credit card bill, and there's a charge here that has to be a mistake.'

Hallie sat up straight. 'Let me see,' she said, scanning the bill when he handed it to her.

'Right there.'

'Oh, no, that's not a mistake,' she said, smiling up at him. 'That was Billie's birthday present. And she loved it.'

'If I didn't know better, Hallie, I would have thought it was a plane ticket to Europe, but right here it says merchandise. What the hell kind of merchandise might that be?'

'No need to be sarcastic, Casey. It was a purse,' she answered defensively, handing the bill back to him, 'and it's nothing compared to the kind of money you spend.'

'It's my money, Hallie, and I'll spend it however I see fit.'

As he intended, his words stung. So much so that Hallie snatched the bill from his hands and began to read out loud the list of charges and the dates on which they were incurred in an accusatory tone. When she finished she said, 'Don't ever say that to me again, Casey. Have you forgotten that I was the one who supported us while you sat at home on your butt for two years?'

Casey shrugged and turned away. 'Believe whatever you want, Hallie, but just look at where you are today. If it wasn't for me you'd still be at that second-rate restaurant working for tips.'

Hallie tossed the bill back at him. 'You know, Casey. sometimes I don't even know who you are!' she shouted as she grabbed her book and left the room.

Much later that night as she replayed that scene in her mind Hallie tried to pinpoint exactly what it was about that exchange that nagged at her. It was more than his hurtful words, even though there had been far too many of those lately. Most of the time his barbs were more subtle. What nagged at her was something else, something that she couldn't quite identify.

Quietly she slipped from their bed and made her way to the study. The slender candlestick lamp on the desk cast a small circle of light around her. With its terracotta tile floor, stucco walls and the deep windows whose sills were also lined in terracotta, this was one of Hallie's favorite rooms. It had once been a porch, but at some point the previous owners had enclosed it to make a study.

In the beginning, they had both envisioned that Casey would use this room for writing since it had been his plan to begin a new book while he was still working on the screenplay. But he had never imagined the emotional toll that *Journey* would exact on him. So in spite of the urgings of his agent to begin a new project, Casey procrastinated. Most of the time he hardly used the office except for occasions like this afternoon. In spite of this, Hallie spent very little time in here. Casey had claimed it as his territory.

Hallie flipped through the stack of papers in the basket, then opened the top drawer of the desk. There she found the bill that had caused their earlier dispute. She shivered as she read it again. Most of the itemized charges were from restaurants – restaurants she had never been to – and the amounts were such that they clearly indicated they were for more than one person.

When she located the item she had been looking for, she almost wished she hadn't. It was a restaurant charge for the same day that her class had been cancelled and she had gone to Casey's office looking for him. In a flash she knew that Ted had lied to her. Casey hadn't been in a meeting; he had gone out to lunch with someone.

Hallie sat back in the chair, feeling as if she had just been punched. Ted had lied to keep her from finding out that Casey wasn't there. But why? Then the thought came – unwelcome and unbidden – Casey was seeing another woman. Immediately she felt shame for having it, and for her lack of trust. But it explained so much.

A few minutes later she went back to bed, but sleep

eluded her. She tried to put her suspicion aside, reasoning that it was unfounded and surely there could be other reasons for Ted's action. But no matter how hard she tried, the thought wouldn't go away.

Hallie wasn't sure when she first realized that the woman Casey was seeing was Jasmine Turner. For more than a week now she had wrestled with her suspicions, wondering how to bring up the subject. What if it was all in her imagination? Unable to put it off any longer, she tried to talk to Casey about it on Saturday morning.

'Casey, let's do something together today. Maybe we could go for a drive up the coast and have lunch. I hardly see you any more, and we need to talk.' Hallie had brought their coffee out on the patio overlooking the pool. It was quiet and cool this morning and everything was still fresh and covered with dew. In another hour it would be hot.

'About what?' he asked.

'About us. You seem to go your way and I seem to go mine and the only thing we have in common any more is this house. We both sleep here – in the same bed – but we're like strangers. We don't even make love any more. I want us to try to change things, Casey.' Hallie said earnestly, reaching across the table to lay her hand on his arm.

Casey shook her hand off as he reached for his coffee. 'You're in school and I work all the time, Hallie. What do you want from me?' he asked irritably.

Hallie took a deep breath. This was the opening she had been waiting for. 'I want you to stop seeing Jasmine

Turner.' The words hung there in the crystal morning air.

After a moment he said, 'I'm not "seeing" Jasmine, Hallie.'

'Then what do you call it? That day I came to take you to lunch Ted lied to me. You were out to lunch. With her.'

'Last time I heard, there was no law against taking a business associate out to lunch.'

'She is not a "business associate". She is the wife of the producer. The credit card statement is full of charges from restaurants and I called your office several times last week, Casey, and they told me you were having lunch with her.'

'That's right. I was having lunch with her. To talk about the screenplay,' he said, refusing to let her put him on the defensive.

'There's more to it than that. Things that have to do with the screenplay can be handled at work. I'm asking you not to see her any more.'

'Is that an ultimatum?' he asked.

'It's anything you want, but it's from your wife,' she answered evenly, her blue eyes fixed on his.

'Go to hell.' Casey stood and went inside, grabbing his car keys from the counter. He couldn't stop seeing Jasmine, even if he wanted to. Without the pills she had been giving him, he wouldn't be able to get by at work. Besides, he was completely captivated by her. She was the most sexual person he had ever met. Nothing had happened between them yet, but it would. It was just a matter of time.

Each time he saw Jasmine he wanted her. Only the

fact that she was the producer's wife had held him back. But each time they met, their conversation became a little more intimate, her touches a little more familiar, until finally yesterday she had openly admitted that her relationship with Irwin left her sexually unfulfilled.

Hallie followed him into the house. 'Casey!'

He never looked back. Hallie slumped against the kitchen counter, at that moment hating Los Angeles and the lifestyle they had assumed, wondering if she was in real danger of losing her husband. She covered her face with her hands, feeling helpless and alone.

The following Monday evening when Casey was leaving work, he was surprised to see Jasmine parked across the street.

'What are you doing here?' he asked with a wide smile as he approached her car. Bracing his arms over the door of the white Mercedes, he bent over until he was face to face with her.

'Follow me,' she said with a secretive smile. 'I have a surprise for you.'

Casey followed her for several miles until he realized that she was leading him in the direction of her house. 'You arranged the meeting with Irwin,' he stated, clearly pleased, when they pulled up in front of the house.

'No,' she answered as she ran up the steps. At the door she turned. 'Irwin is out of town. We're having dinner here tonight.' The words were simple but, combined with look in Jasmine's eyes, the invitation was unmistakable.

Casey nodded in reply and followed her into the cool marble interior.

Later, he would remember very little about the evening except Jasmine's face when she brought out a small silver tray of white powder.

He raised his eyes to hers.

She smiled seductively. 'I'll show you how, darling.'

With a flourish Jasmine picked up a small silver knife and began expertly dividing the cocaine into rails.

Briefly Casey recalled the guys he had known who had used this stuff. He had smoked a few joints occasionally but had never wanted to mess with anything stronger. But somehow, here, in this palatial Beverly Hills mansion, the cocaine before him didn't seem as sinister as it had before. How could it? In a town where a good dealer could be as important as a good agent, many people in the movie industry seemed to use coke with the same ease they used sugar in their coffee.

Casey leaned back and watched as Jasmine finished her ritual with an almost apostolic fervor, and he had to stifle the impulse to ask himself why he was doing this? Why the pills and now the coke? But down deep in his gut he knew. Jasmine had the power and the connections to get him where he wanted to be. He would do whatever she wanted him to.

The image of Hallie flashed across his mind and he shut it out. Hallie couldn't do for him what Jasmine Turner could. And if the price for his success was to entertain this polished and pampered Hollywood wife, he was ready to pay it.

Fate was handing him another opportunity. It wasn't greed, he assured himself, but ambition. One was ugly, the other admirable. Being the author of a best-selling novel wasn't enough. Casey Prescott wanted more. He wanted power, the same power he could feel all around him, and nothing was going to get in his way.

Several hours later, Casey drove along the beach, too wired to sleep. He kept seeing Jasmine's face, the way she had looked when she was naked; the way the tiny beads of perspiration had gathered along her upper lip, framing her full red mouth while she had hovered above him and worked her sensual magic.

He could never remember sex with Hallie being that good. Tonight it was as if every sensation, every touch and every smell, had been magnified. He closed his eyes, recalling the sleek body that had slithered all over his. Jasmine was the most erotic woman he had ever met.

It was strange how easily Hallie and Casey had settled into their separate lives. Hallie saw so little of Casey now that it was almost as if she had no husband. He came and went as he wished, and it was rare that they were home at the same time. Since that Saturday morning two months ago when she had confronted Casey about Jasmine Turner, Hallie had not mentioned her name to Casey again. Fear of the learning the truth had paralyzed her into silence. Once she acknowledged how distant she and Casey had become, she would have to acknowledge that she was a failure, that their marriage had ceased to exist.

In December Hallie began to notice precisely how much Casey had changed. Since he would have the week off between Christmas and New Year, she had suggested that they go home to visit their families, but

Casey declined. Then she suggested that they have both sets of families out to California.

'Damn it, Hallie,' he said impatiently as they sat in the kitchen. 'It's the first time I've had any days off, and you want me to spend them entertaining my family and yours?' He jumped up from the table and began to pace the length of the kitchen. In frustration he ran both hands through his blond hair.

'I'm sorry, Casey. I just . . . I thought it would be nice to have everyone together. But I understand.' Hallie reached out to touch him as she stood, hoping this wouldn't escalate into an argument. 'We can enjoy being together for the holidays. It will be fun.'

Casey was forced to stop pacing as Hallie wrapped her arms around his neck. 'It will be like old times, you and me, lazy mornings in bed . . .' she said, attempting a playfulness she didn't really feel, but desperately longing to recapture the closeness they had once shared.

Casey was nervous. His agent had been harassing him to start another book. Even though he had some ideas, he was having difficulty getting anything on paper. This, his first case of writer's block, he attributed to the difficulty he was having with the screenplay. But his private and very real fear was that he would never be able to create another book, especially one as successful as *Journey*.

Right now he felt smothered. He had to see Jasmine soon. These days he lived with the constant fear that she wouldn't be available when he needed another hit. It wasn't in his head, even though Jasmine insisted it was. His need was real. Physical. Without it he was dull and lethargic; with it he could accomplish anything he desired.

His fear that Jasmine would cut him off from his supply of drugs was also real. She was a woman who lived by whims. He had to find another source, but it wasn't as easy as he had thought it would be. He had been trying to connect, but it was as though Jasmine had made sure that he wouldn't be supplied by anyone other than her.

In the beginning he had considered the time he spent with her payment for the stature and power she possessed, and her willingness to use her influence on his behalf. Then he realized that there was more to it than that. He was addicted to her just as surely as he was addicted to the fine white powder she continued to give him.

When Casey finally realized what Hallie had said, and what she was alluding to, he smiled derisively. 'I can't think of anything more boring,' he said cruelly as he reached up, pulled her arms from around his neck, giving her a slight shove back, then stepped away from her. His green-eyed gaze that once could have turned her knees weak was cold and contemptuous. Without any sign of remorse for his cutting words, he turned and left the room.

For months now Hallie had tried to lay the blame for the problems between her and Casey on the hours that he spent at work and the hours she spent on her projects for school. But as she stood alone in the middle of the kitchen with a hurt that rose from deep inside she knew that wasn't an excuse any more. She knew that Casey was sleeping with Jasmine Turner. She guessed she'd known it for a long time, and just refused to act on it. The truth was too painful. Weakly, she sank into a chair, not knowing what to do, or how to stop the terrible pain that ripped so deeply into her heart.

During the next several weeks Hallie wavered between wanting to run home to Billie for comfort, and wanting to ride this out until Casey came to his senses. She clung to the hope that the break at Christmas would give her time to work things out with him. They had too much invested in each other and in their marriage to throw it all away. Maybe . . . maybe they could salvage something and start again. She had to try.

Ironically, the week she had waited for turned out to be a nightmare.

'What are you doing?' Casey asked sharply one morning as he opened the bathroom door and walked into their bedroom, finding Hallie there. Since that morning a few weeks before she had abandoned this room and the bed they had once shared and, as far as she could tell, that suited Casey just fine.

Hallie straightened up from the dresser drawer she had been rearranging. She couldn't help but notice that Casey's body, which had always been lean, appeared lean almost to the point of emaciation. His skin had lost its luster and had been replaced by a blue-tinged pallor. It was the look of someone in bad health. 'You should eat more, Casey,' she said quietly as she let her eyes roam upward over his face, then she turned back to her task.

Without warning, Casey was beside her, his hand gripping her upper arm, forcing her away from the dresser. Hallie stumbled at the rough treatment, unprepared for the sudden attack.

'Stay the hell out of my stuff,' he said angrily.

Hallie looked at him bewildered. 'I was just . . .'

'You heard me. Keep your goddamn hands off my things.'

'But, Casey . . .' she began, then bit her lip. This was not the first time he had lashed out at her over something she had done. These days she tried to gage his mood on those rare occasions when they were together. The slightest thing seemed to throw him into a rage.

Casey had thrown on some clothes and was reaching for his car keys and his wallet when she asked, 'Where are you going? It's the day before Christmas Eve. Can't we spend it together? Go shopping, then have a late lunch? Let's at least try to work things out,' she pleaded, not caring that she had put her pride aside by begging him to spend time with her.

He turned and let his eyes travel over her as though what she had suggested was slimy and repulsive, then crossed the room, passing her by like she didn't exist. Within seconds she heard the kitchen door slam.

Hallie sank down on the bed, her legs too weak to support her and felt her world breaking apart, one chunk at a time. She didn't matter to him at all. He acted as if he was over and done with her, and, having made that decision, he could no longer stand to be around her.

As bad as the previous day had been, Christmas Eve was worse. That morning Casey's mood seemed to be better and he offered an apology for the events of the previous day. Hallie felt a small leap of hope when he left at noon and promised to be home by five so they could spend the evening together.

That afternoon, she had taken special care to look her best. Dressed in a pair of ivory silk pants and a matching shirt that brought out the copper sheen of her hair, Hallie felt that she looked better than she had in a long time.

In the living room, she finished wrapping the gifts she had bought for Casey and placed them under the tree. What he had done to her, his reckless and hurtful disregard for her, still rankled. But it was Christmas and she was going to do her best to make it pleasant. She glanced at her watch and wished Casey would hurry home.

At six, she decided that he was just running late, and she began preparing dinner. By the time he arrived everything would be almost ready. Sheer will power prevented her from becoming edgy and giving into the doubts that nagged at her. He had promised her he would be home to spend Christmas Eve with her and he wouldn't disappoint her. Not tonight.

At seven she turned on the TV, unable to stand either the mocking sound of Christmas music or the overwhelming silence. He has been delayed, she thought.

By what? came the mocking reply.

In the kitchen she washed the dishes in the sink, then reached for the phone, intent on calling Billie, desperately needing to hear a familiar voice. With shaking hands she dialed the number, but before she finished she slowly replaced the receiver. Billie would insist on wishing Casey a Merry Christmas, too. And when she found out that Casey wasn't there with her, it would only ruin her aunt's celebration.

At midnight Hallie turned out the lights and went to bed in the spare bedroom. Under the darkened tree lay the unopened presents. The table was still set with the sparkling china and crystal and candles that had never been lit. Dinner was dried beyond recognition in the now cold oven.

It was almost dawn when Hallie woke. She had cried most of the night and her eyes felt swollen and unnatural, her face puffy. For a while she lay in the stillness and considered staying in bed, but she knew she would only be more depressed than she already was. Slipping on her robe, she made her way quietly down the hall and stopped at the door of the bedroom she and Casey had once shared. He had come home sometime during the early hours of Christmas morning.

She swallowed hard. Last night she had cried enough, and today she was determined she would not shed another tear over a man who cared so little for her. Silently she continued toward the kitchen. This was a Christmas she was never going to forget. She had no friends or family here to turn to, and the only man she had ever loved had abandoned her for another woman.

Accompanied by the tune of the coffee maker as it bubbled then dribbled into the pot, she ventured into the dining room, but she couldn't bear the sight of the table, still festive and waiting for a celebration that would never come. In the kitchen she perched on a stool she had drawn up to the counter. Clutching an empty cup with both hands, Hallie leaned forward and rested her forehead against the edge of the overhead cabinet.

For the first time in her life she felt as if she was drowning in despair. She had no idea what to do about Casey, or herself, or their situation.

Several hours later Casey sauntered into the kitchen. He glanced briefly at Hallie as he reached for a cup and poured some coffee. The silence between them grew until Hallie couldn't stand it any longer.

'Where were you last night?' she asked, her voice low. 'I waited for you until midnight.'

Casey raised his bloodshot eyes to meet hers over the rim of the steaming cup. What had he ever seen in her? he wondered idly as he assessed her oval face with its delicate features, her dark blue eyes and her mass of copper hair. In comparison to a woman like Jasmine, Hallie was nothing more than a young, inexperienced, small-town girl who no longer interested him.

'I was out,' he replied after a moment.

'Out *where*, for God's sake? Casey, it's Christmas.'

He ignored the question and turned to leave.

'Don't walk away from me,' Hallie commanded with trembling anger. 'I deserve an answer.'

His stance deceptively relaxed, Casey turned back to face her. 'I was at a party.'

'What about our plans? Didn't they mean anything? Don't I mean anything to you?' Her eyes were dark and pleading.

His green eyes glittered for a moment, then turned unnaturally cold and hard. He raised his shoulders in a slight shrug before he answered. 'No.'

CHAPTER 6

It occurred to Hallie that afternoon as she drove along the deserted highway that followed the shoreline of the Pacific Ocean that there was something irreverent about southern California on Christmas Day. All the imagery of the season was lost here. Even the decorations and music seemed to be at odds with the bright sunshine and palm trees.

Never would she be able to forget the look in Casey's eyes, or the betrayal she had felt when she realized her husband no longer loved or wanted her. How naive she had been. The signs had been there all along, but she had been too blind and too trusting to heed them. Even when she had realized that Casey was seeing Jasmine she had held out hope that they could still work things out. She had thought that maybe, with counseling, they could salvage their relationship. Until today. In the past few months he had changed so much. He was no longer the same man she had married.

It was nighttime when she pulled into the driveway of their stucco house. Grabbing her sweater from the seat beside her, Hallie hurried inside, never noticing the blue van parked down the street.

In the living room the scent of pine from the unlit Christmas tree was pungent. She inhaled deeply as she turned on a small lamp, then made her way past the bright red and green of the wrapped gifts that lay scattered around the tree. The sight of them seemed to be mocking her. She hurried toward the bedroom. In the years to come she would always associate the smell of Christmas with sadness. It would be a day to dread, an anniversary of pain and heartbreak.

With her head bowed, Hallie opened the door to the bedroom where Casey now slept alone, intent only on gathering some of her clothes. Silently, the door swung open. Hallie stood there frozen, helpless at the sight before her while her mind, acting like a camera, recorded every detail.

Later she would recall that the smell of sex had been all around her – hot, sweaty and sour. The scene before her seemed to grind down to slow motion. From one corner of the bed the covers hung down in a jumbled heap, but the rumpled bed was empty. Clothes were scattered across the room. On the floor in front of the French doors that led to the patio were two people, naked, entwined, and glittering with sweat. The guttural sounds that came from their throats were harsh and primitive.

Hallie couldn't move, couldn't scream; she was a captive bystander enduring the ultimate humiliation.

The look on Jasmine's face as she met Casey's thrusts was a mixture of triumph and evil. Her eyes glittered with power while her full breasts swayed from the motion of flesh meeting flesh.

It was Jasmine who noticed her first. Then Casey, his

green eyes glassy, turned his head slightly, his eyes following Jasmine's. Dimly, it registered that someone was watching them. It only made it more exciting. He had always heard that coke made for great sex and now he knew it was true. He had never been better than he was now.

As he began to climax, Casey turned his head toward the voyeur in the doorway and realized it was Hallie who stood there. With his final thrust the look he sent her was glazed and triumphant.

Blindly, Hallie turned and ran from the house, unaware of the photographer who stood at the edge of the patio, concealed by the shrubs there. Nor did she hear the muted sounds of the camera as it clicked and whined and captured her fleeing image on film, then made itself ready for the next frame.

From his outdoor hiding place, the photographer shifted his attention from the fleeing woman back to the scene beyond the French doors. Prior to the second woman's appearance, he had already taken about a dozen shots of the couple when suddenly his fingers couldn't move fast enough and the camera couldn't record the scene before him with sufficient speed.

After years of hiding and waiting for a chance to photograph the controversial, the rich and the beautiful that populated Hollywood, working at all hours of the day and night, sleeping in his car, drinking cold coffee and smoking one cigarette after another just to get pictures he could sell to the tabloids, Nick Hardister had hit the jackpot. He would never have to work again.

What he was recording was a familiar scene, no different than hundreds of others. The little wife catching hubby doing it with another woman. What made this one so right was that the other woman was his old friend, Jasmine Turner – the beautiful Jasmine, now the wife of one of the most powerful men in Hollywood – screwing her brains out.

The glow of the red light from the makeshift darkroom cast an eerie pallor over Nick's swarthy skin. Carefully he reached for the photos he had just developed, then hung them with clothes pins on the cord that was strung the width of the room. In black and white they were even more shocking than what he had witnessed earlier outside the Prescott house.

Satisfied with what he had, Nick left the darkroom and went to the phone. Not only was he going to collect the rest of his fee from the guy who hired him to take these photos, he was going to retire on what he could get from a certain wealthy and influential husband who would be interested in keeping these photos out of circulation.

'I'll sign for it,' said Irwin Turner's secretary the following day as she held her hand out for the envelope.

'I'm sorry,' said the messenger, 'but it says that it's personal and confidential on the outside, and my instructions are not to leave it without Mr Turner's signature.'

The secretary sighed. She had worked here for fifteen years and each year things seemed to get weirder. The manilla envelope probably contained a screenplay from an unknown writer. Last week someone had faxed Irwin an entire screenplay.

'Come this way,' she said as she rounded her desk and led the messenger through the double-paneled walnut doors.

'Irwin, there's a messenger with an envelope for you. He needs your signature.'

Irwin motioned for the messenger to hand him the envelope while he continued his phone conversation. With a quick look at the front, he signed the delivery slip. Then he threw it on the stack of mail already on his desk. He would get to it later.

The building was dark and everyone had left for the night before Irwin leaned back in his chair and reached for the day's mail. The first envelope contained a proposal from a writer who had written his first successful screenplay about two years before and was still looking for his second success. He placed the envelope to the side of the desk. It was worth a look.

Beneath the screenplay was an invitation to a charity ball. Wearily, he rubbed the back of his neck. He could hardly avoid this one. Not only was it a worthwhile cause, but he was also on the board of directors. As he absently reached for the envelope the messenger had delivered earlier in the day and pulled out the contents, Irwin made a mental note to make sure Jasmine had nothing planned for the date on the invitation.

What the hell! Abruptly he dropped the envelope and the photo on his desk and stood, pushing his chair away. First, he raised his hand to his mouth in shock, then he covered his eyes in despair. The bitch has finally done it, he concluded. From far away came the thought that he shouldn't be shocked or outraged, but he was.

Slowly he eased himself back down in his chair and reached for the photo once more. Even though he couldn't identify the man who was with her, there was no doubt that the woman was Jasmine. His wife. He sat still for a long while; then, with the tips of his fingers, as though he was afraid that the ugliness before him would contaminate him also, he gingerly flipped the glossy black-and-white print over. On the back was a phone number.

Wearily, Irwin pinched the bridge of his nose between his thumb and forefinger. When had his life become so complicated? Since Janie had left him fifteen years ago, taking their three children with her, he admitted. He ought to be going home to her at night, or someone like her. Someone who would comfort him and understand that while most of the time he loved what he did, there were other times he despised it.

It was ironic that he and Janie had stayed together during the bad times, and that in retrospect those times were the ones he cherished most. But when his driving desire for success had become a reality, that success had become the wedge that had finally driven his wife and children away. His children were adults now and had children of their own. He hardly knew them.

A second marriage, short and regrettable, had followed the divorce from Janie. After that, he never considered marriage again until Jasmine had worked her way into his life. He wouldn't deny he had been lonely, but he would never admit that he had been afraid of being old and alone. Somehow he had hoped that Jasmine, with her beauty, youth and energy, would

84

help him stay youthful also. Money and power no longer seemed to be enough.

Irwin shook his head slightly as if to rid himself of the oppressive feeling, like a heavy weight, that had settled over him. He should have known this, or something like this, was inevitable. Jasmine was so much younger and her sexual appetites were more than he was prepared for. He had never loved anyone deeply since Janie. Yet, confronted by the blatant evidence of Jasmine's adultery, he couldn't help but be hurt.

In a shallow society where dignity had little value, he had maintained his. Others might cheat and swindle under the guise of business, but he never had. In a city where hustle was a byword, he had never hustled or allowed himself to be hustled. Except for now. Deliberately, Irwin reached for the phone and dialed the number that was written on the back of the photo.

'I received your package,' he said when the phone was answered, not bothering to identify himself.

'I have more,' volunteered Nick Hardister.

Irwin remained silent, forcing the man to continue.

'I'll bet you didn't know your wife had all that talent,' Hardister snickered.

'What do you want?' asked Irwin, his voice even and unemotional.

There was a pause as Nick took a deep breath. 'A hundred thousand.'

'I see,' replied Irwin. 'And what do I get for that?'

Nick grinned. This was it. He had finally hit the jackpot. 'You get the pictures, all of them, with the negatives.'

'I want to see them first,' said Irwin. 'But that is no guarantee I'm buying,' he added.

'Where do you want to meet?' asked Nick, confident that he was on his way to transferring that hundred thou from Turner's pockets to his.

Irwin named a small bar two blocks from his office. They would meet in an hour. After he hung up he sat staring into space, his mind just now absorbing the full impact of what he saw in the photo before him. He reviewed his options. He could buy the photos and hope that this wouldn't turn into a case of continued blackmail, or he could refuse. If he did refuse, Irwin was sure the man he was meeting would peddle them elsewhere. If the rest of the pictures were like the one he was looking at now, even the tabloids would back off, but they wouldn't back off the story.

In spite of his earlier elation at Turner's phone call, Nick Hardister was nervous. He hadn't expected Turner to move so fast. What if he didn't buy the pictures? But he would. What man in his right mind would want those kinds of pictures of his wife circulating or, worse yet, published? As soon as he had his money Nick would make sure that Jasmine knew that he had been the one to take the pictures. He wanted her to know that he had been the one to expose her.

When he had taken this job, he had no idea it would prove so lucrative. Not only would he sell the photos to the guy who hired him as well as to Turner, he would have his revenge against Jasmine for the way she had treated him.

She had been a few years younger when he knew her,

and new to Hollywood, but cunning and greedy. He hadn't been able to see past his fascination for her until she used him, then dumped him, taking all his money. A week after she had left he heard she had moved in with an agent he had introduced her to at a party. For several years he had watched her climb to the top, using one man after another.

For a long time after she had left him, he had wanted revenge. In fact, he had been obsessed by it. Jasmine had been different from the other women in his life. He had made the mistake of falling in love with her.

The lights inside the small bar were dim and tonight it seemed they were tinged with an eerie shade of green. Hardister, who was seated in the farthest corner opposite the bar, was not difficult to recognize. He looked exactly as Irwin anticipated: dark and sleazy and covered with greed.

Hardister looked up expectantly at Turner's approach.

'Let me see them,' said Turner without preamble. A few moments later he asked, 'Is this all of them?' Without allowing himself to study each one closely, Irwin removed the photos from the envelope one by one. They were ugly and sordid. By the time he had pulled the last one he knew that his wife's lover was Casey Prescott. Slowly he replaced each one of them in the envelope and pushed his chair away from the small round table. He felt old and tired and beaten.

Nick watched nervously, and when Turner stood he also stood. He licked his thick lips and fought the impulse to ask when he would have his money. Too much was riding on this meeting for him to appear anxious.

'I don't want them.' Irwin said, tossing the envelope on the table, then turned away from him.

Nick glanced down at the manilla envelope. His heart thundered against his shirt. Surely he had misunderstood Turner. When he spoke his voice betrayed his uneasiness. 'Look, man, if you're trying to get the price down you can just forget it. I know what I've got here. The price is still the same.'

Irwin stepped away from the table then paused, looking back at Nick Hardister, hating everything he saw. A snake, he thought, as he took in the dark greasy hair, the ill-fitting jacket and tight jeans. How stupid of Jasmine to have placed herself in this position. 'I'm not buying,' he repeated. 'Not now, not ever.'

For a minute Nick was stunned, his mind refusing to process Turner's refusal. When he spoke the words tumbled out in a rush. 'I'll peddle these, Turner. See how you like it then when everyone in town knows your wife is screwing another man.'

Irwin shrugged, then straightened his drooping shoulders as he considered Nick's words. His dignity would suffer, and his pride. What Jasmine had done made him angry and strangely sad, but he would survive. He refused to be hustled by this low-life piece of scum.

Hardly able to believe what he was hearing, Nick grabbed for the photos. 'I won't let you or that bitch you're married to cheat me, Turner,' he shouted, as Irwin turned and walked away. 'You'll be sorry!'

Jasmine was asleep when Irwin arrived home. He walked past the bedroom through the house, stopping only long enough to pour himself a Scotch. As an afterthought, he carried the decanter with him to the pool. The sight of the water was peaceful and soothing, just like the Scotch he sipped. He needed time to reflect upon the decision he had to make.

Of all the pictures he had seen, only one had been able to stir him from his distant, unemotional perusal. It was one of a young woman running from the house where Jasmine and Prescott had been photographed. She was obviously crying, bent over and clutching at her stomach as if she were in great pain. It was Prescott's wife. He remembered her from the party she had attended at his home a few months ago. A pretty girl, he had thought at the time, with a freshness that belongs only to the young, and a sweetness that could not possibly survive in this jaded environment.

Irwin sank heavily into a chair, never taking his eyes from the water. He should be feeling sorry for himself, he thought. Instead he felt sorry for her.

He lost track of the hours and the number of times he had refilled his glass, but before it became too late and his thoughts too blurred, Irwin made the decision he could no longer put off.

The following morning he placed two calls. The first was to his attorney. The second was to Ted Hinds, the screenwriter who was editing *Journey to Fear*.

CHAPTER 7

His dismissal the Tuesday following Christmas Day had come as a complete shock to Casey. What was even more insulting was that bastard Ted Hinds, who had enjoyed every minute of it. In fact, gloated over it. But the last laugh will be mine, thought Casey, as he adjusted his sunglasses, then ran his hands through his hair. Within the next few days his attorney would file suit against TPL, Irwin Turner's production company.

He had been driving aimlessly for hours, unsure of what to do or where to go. As he turned sharply toward the freeway exit he thought about Jasmine. The other night with her he had felt invincible. He had never been better, never had better sex. Right this moment he was shaken and insecure, but Jasmine would be able to fix all that.

Casey had reached the point where he could no longer be without cocaine. For insurance, in case Jasmine should suddenly decide to cut off his supply of the drug, he had found a dealer. In addition to what she was giving him, he was also buying on the side. He needed the way it made him feel. Sure and powerful, confident. He had other insurance, too. Today he was meeting with the photographer he had hired to take the pictures of Jasmine and him. With those in his possession she would think twice about dumping him for anyone else.

Jasmine described herself as a creature of the night, staying up very late, then sleeping late in the mornings. It was noon when she stepped from her bath, dried off, then wrapped herself in a vivid pink silk robe. She had just lit a cigarette and poured her first cup of coffee when the maid appeared on the patio to announce that she had a visitor.

'Bring him out,' she instructed as she ran her hands through her hair, fluffing it, 'and bring more coffee.'

Arthur Green was an attractive man, younger looking than his fifty-two years, and always charming and witty. He was also Irwin's attorney.

'Hello, Jasmine.' His expression was serious as he joined her at the table.

'Arthur, how are you?' she asked brightly, tilting her head to one side. It was unusual for Arthur to stop by the house, but maybe Irwin had asked him to drop off some papers.

He didn't answer. In spite of all his success this was the part of his job he hated most, but he could hardly refuse to carry out Irwin's orders. Irwin Turner was one of his most important and powerful clients, and he knew Irwin would never ask him to do something this distasteful unless it was absolutely necessary.

'Jasmine,' began Arthur slowly as his eyes met hers,

'this is a very unpleasant task that I have been called upon to do.' He cleared his throat.

She looked at him with raised brows. What could possibly have prompted this seriousness? She felt a distant prickle of fear at his words. 'Come now, Arthur. How can you be so serious on such a beautiful day? Besides, I haven't seen you for quite a while. The last time was at Jared Blake's party, I believe.'

The maid returned with fresh coffee and Arthur cleared his throat, waiting for her departure before he continued. From his briefcase he withdrew some papers and handed them to Jasmine. She extended her slender hand with its perfectly manicured red nails and read the first few lines. A sudden panic gripped her. As she read further down the page the words danced before her eyes. Her heart began to beat erratically. Surely there must be some mistake. These papers were not for her. They didn't make sense.

'I'll see that Irwin gets these, Arthur,' she said, setting them casually aside in an attempt to disguise her panic.

'No, Jasmine,' said Arthur firmly, wishing he could make this easier. 'These papers are for you. Irwin is filing for divorce and he wants you out of the house by tomorrow.'

Jasmine smiled vaguely and looked out toward the pool and the gardens beyond, pretending she hadn't heard a word of what Arthur Green had just told her.

He leaned closer now, his voice earnest, almost pleading. 'Listen to me, Jasmine, please. Don't you understand what I just said?'

She turned to face him, her blonde hair swinging

against her face. This couldn't be happening. Not to her. Damn it, she had worked too hard to be dumped like this. She raised her eyes to the man across from her, her eyes suddenly focused and sharp. She put her cigarette out and quickly lit another. Then she nodded. 'I heard what you said, Arthur, although I wish I hadn't. But why?'

'Irwin didn't say. Have you, uh, done anything . . .?'

Jasmine threw her head back and laughed bitterly. 'Indiscreet? Get the hell out of here, Arthur, and tell that rotten son of a bitch you work for that a real man would have had the balls to do his own dirty work.'

Arthur rose with a slight bow of apology, anxious now to be on his way before things got really nasty.

When he had gone Jasmine rushed to the bar in the den and poured herself a drink. She could feel the panic rising within, then receding when the burning sensation of the whisky forced it down. It was the same feeling she had had when she ran from the police after the death of Senator Rawlins; and when she had first realized that in spite of everything she was never going to make it as an actress. But she had survived then, and she would survive now.

She could only speculate that Irwin had had her followed and found out about her affair with Casey. Except for enjoying the power and prestige that came with being Mrs Irwin Turner, she had never felt much of anything for Irwin. He wasn't worth fighting for, but his money was. She would vacate this goddamn mausoleum he called a house, but he was going to pay dearly to be rid of her.

* * *

93

When Hallie awakened she was disoriented. At first she couldn't remember where she was or even what day it was, but after a few minutes it all came rushing back. Every slimy, sordid detail of that terrible night paraded itself through her mind. In an effort to block the painful images, she squeezed her eyes tightly shut. But it was a wasted gesture, and now she was feeling battered and hurt. The desire to simply curl up and cry was almost overwhelming. But she had given in to that urge long enough. Finally she forced herself to get out of bed, shower and leave the motel where she had been staying for the past two days. There were things she needed to do.

Dana met her at noon, and over lunch Hallie told Dana what had happened. Together they scanned the paper for an apartment for Hallie.

'Hallie, please reconsider this. You can move in with me until you get your bearings. You've been through a terrible time. Why didn't you call me right away?' Dana's dark eyes were full of concern for her friend.

Hallie looked up from the Classifieds. Her face still showed traces of puffiness from crying. Her dark blue eyes appeared stark against her pale skin. 'I was shocked and hurt . . .' Hallie paused, looking away as she swallowed down a sudden urge to cry again. 'I . . . I was so embarrassed, Dana. I feel like such a failure as a woman and as a wife, and the funny thing is that I'm not even sure what I did wrong.'

'You did nothing wrong, Hallie. You don't deserve to be treated this way. I'm not sure anyone deserves this. I only wish you would have called me.'

'I wasn't thinking. All I knew was that I had to get out

of there fast. The shock was so . . .' Hallie let the thought drift away, still unable to cope with what she had witnessed. It was so dirty. After a pause she continued. 'Besides, it was Christmas night and I was much too ashamed to call anyone. For some reason, I feel almost as if everything that has happened *is* my fault. I keep saying to myself, "If only I had tried harder to be a better wife."'

Hallie sighed and her voice quivered when she spoke again. 'I don't even know what went wrong, or at what point in our marriage I ceased to matter to Casey.'

'Well, the least I can do is help you find a place to live, and then I'll help you move your things.'

That afternoon after looking at several apartments, Hallie finally settled on a spacious studio apartment in Brentwood. It was far enough from the house she had shared with Casey to insure she wouldn't constantly run into him. Dana assured her it was a good area and worth the rent, which was reasonable by Brentwood standards, but which Hallie considered outrageous.

'Don't worry about the rent,' Dana said. 'Casey has made a pile of money so far, and stands to make a lot more with this movie. He can afford to keep you in style.'

Hallie nodded uneasily. When Casey first received the advance from his publisher for *Journey to Fear*, he had insisted on taking complete control of their finances. And Hallie, weary of scrimping and fighting with him about never having enough money for anything other than their rent and bills, had readily agreed to hand over all financial responsibility to him. She was tired of being the sole breadwinner, tired of budgeting every last dime, and tired of being the bad guy, always saying no, whenever Casey wanted to buy something they couldn't afford.

And since that time she had not kept track of their finances, but, as Dana had pointed out, Casey could afford to keep her in style. If the divorce lawyers didn't get all of it, she added silently, reminding herself of the difficult time that lay ahead.

That same afternoon Hallie went to the bank, intent on withdrawing enough money to last her for a while. When she asked for a balance at the drive-up window she had been shocked to find out how little was left in the account. Surely there had been a mistake! She parked the car and went inside the bank, where she stared glassy-eyed, as if in a trance, as the teller placed a closed sign at her window and led her aside to a desk, then pointed to page after page of a print-out of the account's activity over the past three months.

Where had it all gone? What had seemed like an enormous advance had almost disappeared. Casey couldn't have possibly spent that much money that fast unless he was gambling or spending it on drugs, she thought, then froze.

In a flash of insight, all the pieces of the puzzle fit together: the change in his personality, the mood swings, his weight loss, the excess energy and the sleepless nights.

How could things unravel so quickly without her knowing it? How could she have missed all the signs? But there was nothing in Hallie's background that would have prepared her to recognize what was happening to Casey.

She fought for control, resisting the urge to bury her face in her hands and cry out in complete despair. Instead Hallie struggled to her feet, clutching the printout in her shaking hands and mumbling a hurried thank-you to the teller, then left. Outside she leaned against the car door, suddenly incapable of moving any farther. They were nearly broke.

Nick Hardister stood in front of the open refrigerator holding the cold can of beer against his sweating forehead. God, it was hot in here. It must be at least a hundred degrees outside and the air conditioner wasn't working. Slowly he pushed the door closed, shutting off the flow of cool air, then leaned back against the counter and let his eyes roam over his apartment as if he was seeing it for the first time.

He was tired of living in dumps like this, and paying outrageous rent for the privilege. He had spent way too much of his adult life in places that looked just like this one – dirty gray linoleum floors that no amount of scrubbing would clean, sinks permanently stained with rust, and shabby furniture that belonged to someone else. But soon he would be able to change all that.

Irwin Turner's refusal to buy the pictures of his wife had forced Nick to alter his plans, but only for a while. It had taken him several days after the news of Jasmine's impending divorce had been splattered across the tabloids to find her. But now that he had found her, all he had to do was confront her. The money he had been paid by that Prescott dude who had hired him in the very beginning to take those picture hadn't lasted long. At first he wondered why the guy wanted the pictures, but then he figured he probably got off on that kind of stuff.

Maybe he had sold out too cheap to Prescott. What was it the man had told him when he had handed them over? That they were his 'insurance'. The amount they had agreed upon in the beginning seemed like a lot at the time, but that was when he had believed that Turner would pay any price to keep his wife's affair out of the public eye. Man, had he been wrong about that. But now he was sure that things would work out for him. Just as soon as he paid Jasmine a long-overdue visit.

The Turners' separation and upcoming divorce had been fodder for everyone interested in Hollywood gossip. No one actually knew the real reason for the split, but those who had spent any time at all around Jasmine speculated that Irwin had finally found out about one, or possibly several, of her many affairs.

Nick knew for a fact that Jasmine, who had no knowledge of the existence of the pictures, could not afford to have them surface in a divorce hearing. Even if Irwin Turner hadn't wanted to buy them, he would certainly benefit from them in court. The existence of the photos would severely reduce Jasmine's chances of a healthy settlement.

Nick checked his reflection in the cloudy, pitted bathroom mirror, then ran his hand along his black stubbled jaw. Jasmine would be forced to buy those photos, just to keep them out of someone else's hands.

He smiled as he reached into the medicine cabinet for

the can of shaving cream and wondered why he hadn't thought of that before. He only wished he could bring his camera with him when he went to see her. He would give anything to capture the expression on her face when she saw him again.

Jasmine would have slammed the door in his face the following day except that Nick was faster, wedging his shoulder between the door and the frame. 'What's the matter, honey? Aren't you glad to see an old friend?'

'Get out,' demanded Jasmine.

'Not before we talk.'

'We have nothing to talk about, Nick.' Jasmine stepped back and surveyed the man in front of her. If anything, he was seedier than she remembered. Jasmine shivered. She had been so scared and desperate when she had first come to Los Angeles, and by the time she hooked up with Nick Hardister she was willing to overlook what a sleaze he was.

After the murder of her lover, Senator Hugh Rawlins, the fear that Edwin Mathews would track her down and kill her had overridden everything else. It had been her intention to cooperate with the FBI and testify that Mathews had had the Senator killed; she even had proof. But a lot of good it had done her. She realized that the minute she agreed to cooperate with the FBI she would be signing her own death certificate. Mathews had made sure she knew that.

The FBI had talked at length about the witness protection program, promising her safety, including a new identity and a new life in another city. But by then Jasmine was too jittery. Besides, she had ambition.

What if they stuck her in some small, out-of-the-way place? She would wither and die. No, she had always lived by her wits and trusted in her gut instinct, and she wasn't about to change.

It had been a long time since she had thought about Hugh Rawlins. He had been a handsome man and, in spite of the difference in their ages, they had shared many common interests. She had never met a man like him before. His power had been an aphrodisiac. He seemingly did nothing, yet he did everything. With a deceptively simple discussion he could change the outcome of a vote, shift the balance in his favor, control the actions of other influential men.

What she hadn't known up until the end was that Hugh Rawlins was nothing more than a pawn. Edwin Mathews was the real power. It was he who controlled men of influence like Hugh. It was also he who ordered Hugh's murder, when Hugh refused to do his bidding.

The FBI had come to talk to her then, and in the beginning she was willing to talk to them, to turn over the evidence she had that would link Mathews to the Senator's murder. But when Mathews had discovered where she was being held in protective custody, he sent his men after her. And they would have killed her if she hadn't run.

'Sure we do,' said Nick smoothly as he reached out to caress her hair. 'You're a little blonder, a little thinner, and a whole bunch richer than you were when we were together.'

Jasmine jerked away from his touch.

'I see you don't remember me with the same fondness I have for you. But you're going to like what I have in the envelope. It's something you want, Jasmine. Something you need.'

'There is nothing I want from you, Nick. Now get out of here.'

'Don't be so anxious to get rid of me, honey, not until you look at these.'

Jasmine took another step back as he handed her a large envelope. Nick had been a tactical error. Their relationship hadn't lasted long, maybe four months. Always, there had been that uncertainty about him. For as long as she had been with him, he always seemed to be edgy, ready to explode. There had been several times when she could have sworn that he walked that fine line between sanity and uncontrollable rage. She had seen it in his eyes.

Without taking her eyes from his face, she opened the envelope. When she looked down she drew her breath in sharply. 'Where did you get these?' She would not panic.

'I took them. You and that boyfriend of yours are quite a treat to watch.'

'What do you want me to say, Nick? That you obviously are talented at your work and therefore you love what you do?' The venom in her voice was unmistakable.

Jasmine squeezed her eyes shut, clenching the photos tightly in her hand.

'It's what I do for a living,' Nick continued, ignoring her. 'I follow important people and catch them at their worst. Only in your case, at your best. Isn't that what you do best, Jasmine? Screw people? Especially people who care about you.'

'Shut up, Nick. Why did you bring me these?'

'They're for sale. I figured you and the boyfriend would want to put them in an album or something. Or maybe you wouldn't want your soon-to-be ex to get a hold of them. Especially not until after you had negotiated your divorce settlement.'

He is slime, thought Jasmine, and he'll never be anything else.

'What do you want, Nick? Money? What's your price?'

Nick reached out and took the photos from her hand. With a studied casualness he placed them back in the envelope. 'A hundred thousand.'

Jasmine laughed bitterly. 'You've come to the wrong place, Nicky boy. I don't have that kind of money. I'm broke.'

'You're bluffing.' Nick's eyes glazed over as he stepped toward her.

'No, no, I'm not, Nick. I . . .' She took a faltering step backwards, hating the fear she felt, hating the look in his eyes, terrified of what he might do. He was on the verge of rage. She could feel it. And he didn't believe she was broke, but it was the truth.

Suddenly Nick's big hands shot out and fastened around her throat. 'I want the money, Jasmine. You cheated me when you walked out on me, but you're not going to cheat me again.'

'Nick, stop!' choked Jasmine, reaching up to pry his hands away from her throat. 'Don't do this. I can't breathe.' Jasmine swallowed her panic. Would he actually kill her or was he just trying to scare her?

'I'll be back for the money tomorrow. You had better

have it. You are not going to cheat me this time.' Roughly Nick released her, giving her a shove at the same time. Jasmine fell to her knees, pressing her hands to the base of her throat as she inhaled raggedly. Across the room Nick retrieved the envelope. 'Tomorrow,' he repeated looking down at her, then he slammed the door behind him.

Slowly Jasmine crawled to the nearest chair, certain that Nick was going to kill her if she didn't give him the money. But she didn't have it to give and there was no one she could ask, not even Casey. He might have been able to help her at one time, but not now. Not with the kind of cocaine habit he had. If he had any money left at all, it would soon be gone. And soon, so would she, she mused. But she had one last plan – to cash in on the tape. For that she was going to need Casey.

His dependency was smothering, and it had gone much further than she had ever intended. He was supposed to be an amusement, but now he was addicted to cocaine and to her.

Sex with him had lost its thrill, and the past few times he had been unable to perform, blaming his inadequacy on stress. After Irwin had fired him, all the doors in Hollywood had silently closed to Casey Prescott. He couldn't find work, and when he tried to write, to begin a new book, the words that rumbled in his head refused to flow onto paper. Whatever money he might have stashed away would soon disappear now that his wife had filed for divorce.

Casey could make all the excuses he wanted about the disappearance of his sexual prowess, but Jasmine knew that his impotency was caused by the large quantity of cocaine he was using each day. He had ceased to be important to her. Letting him hang around this long had been a mistake, one she would rectify just as soon as she was through with him. Especially now, since he didn't have a hundred thousand dollars to give her.

She ran her hands through her hair in frustration, biting nervously on her lower lip. Where was she going to get that kind of money? In the time since she had moved out of the house, Jasmine had spent every dime that Irwin had given her. Somehow she had to find a way to get those pictures from Nick.

For Jasmine, the climber of the ladder of success, the user of men, the powerful Hollywood First Wife, it appeared that luck had run out. No, she screamed silently. I'll think of something. I always do.

Hours later she wasn't so sure. She was desperate. After phoning everyone she knew to try and borrow money, she knew exactly what it was like to fall from grace. Most of her so-called friends wouldn't even take her calls. She had considered hocking her jewelry, but she realized that would not bring anything close to what it was worth. Still, it was a beginning.

Finally, she did the one thing she hated most. She called Irwin. Surely he would not want those pictures circulating, would he? 'Kathy? This is Jasmine. Is he in?'

'Oh, Jasmine, he's . . . well, he's . . .'

'I know, Kathy. He doesn't want to talk to me and he's probably instructed you not to put me through, but this is important. It's a matter of life and death.'

Kathy winced. She could hear the desperation in Jasmine's voice, the shallow, rapid breathing. In spite of all the gossip, no one had any idea as to the real reason for the breakup, but dammit, it wasn't fair for Irwin to put her in this position. She was only his secretary. 'Just a minute, Jasmine. I'll see what I can do.'

Jasmine held her breath and listened for a series of clicks.

'Turner,' the voice on the other end of the line answered.

CHAPTER 8

'Irwin, I need your help. Before you hang up please listen. I have no one else to turn to . . .' Jasmine waited, certain that the line would go dead at any minute. When it didn't she rushed on. 'I need some money, Irwin.'

There was a weary sigh, then Irwin answered. 'My lawyers give you plenty of money, Jasmine.'

'I know, but this is different. I . . . someone is trying to blackmail me, Irwin. If I don't give him what he wants he says he's going to . . . to kill me. He's got pictures of me, Irwin. Surely you wouldn't want the press to . . .?'

'I know about the pictures and I don't give a damn who sees them. I gave you everything in the world, Jasmine, including my trust and my respect. You're a slut. Everyone always thought that about you. Everyone, that is, except me. Now they'll know it for a fact.'

She could feel the sweat trickle between her breasts; her mind raced. She needed a hook, something that would make Irwin squirm. 'But what if I told the press that you were the one who paid to have those pictures taken? That you liked to watch me with another man? That that was the only way you could . . .' She hadn't finished the sentence before she heard the click followed by a dial tone.

She sat, her mind blank for a few moments. Jasmine shook her head, almost laughing, close to hysteria. She had worked for years to get this far. The divorce was unfortunate, but it didn't mean much in this town. People divorced every day. But she refused to consider losing her stature in the elite society in which she reigned. Somehow she had to get those pictures from Nick.

She reached for a cigarette, then swore when she realized the pack was empty. She rose and went to the kitchen for a new package. There had to be another way to get what she wanted. She returned to the living room and went to her desk, flipping through the contents of a drawer until she found a file folder. Quickly she scanned several sheets of paper, then found the information she needed. Jotting it on the tablet next to the phone, she smiled.

It was all so simple, really, when it came right down to it. Jasmine wondered why she hadn't thought of this before. Didn't everyone have things they wanted to hide? And if it was bad enough, they would do anything, even pay dearly to keep their secrets from being revealed. She brought the cigarette to her lips and inhaled deeply, then reached for the phone and dialed.

Not so long ago she was at the pinnacle of Hollywood society and she would be again, but not if anyone got hold of those pictures. If that happened she would be ruined. She would be no different than all those others who had come to Hollywood to make their fortunes and failed. She would once more be a nobody named Janice Porter.

The conversation with the person on the other end of the line was brief. A meeting had been arranged. Of course, Jasmine knew it would take some time before she could get her hands on the money, but it would all work out. She had, finally, with just that one phone call, shaken the right cage. Not only would she take possession of those damaging pictures, she would have enough money to last her for quite a while.

She smiled, congratulating herself for being shrewd enough to play all the angles. She glanced at her watch. It would soon be time for her meeting. She would deal with Nick later. Right now it was money she was after.

'You must be out of your mind! Surely you wouldn't do this. I would be ruined. You know that, Jasmine.' The beautiful dark-haired woman who had spoken cast nervous glances over both shoulders, desperately hoping that no one in the restaurant was sitting close enough to listen in on this conversation.

Jasmine shrugged. 'You should have considered the consequences. You knew that some day someone would find out.'

'How could you be so cruel? Do you have any idea how many people's lives will be ruined by this? For God's sake, I beg of you, think of what this will do to my children.'

'That's what I'm asking you to do, Deidre. Think of your children.' Jasmine said calmly. 'Hmm, how old are they now?'

'What do you want from me, Jasmine?' In contrast to the impassioned plea she had just made, Deidre's question was now cold and without emotion, as if she knew she had already been beaten by a stronger adversary.

'Money, Deidre, what else? I need two hundred thousand dollars by tomorrow.' There. That was easy. That sum will do me nicely, thought Jasmine, as she watched her victim turn pale. For a while, anyway.

'I . . . I don't think I can get my hands on that kind of money that fast, not . . . not without Carl suspecting something. Maybe I could manage a hundred thousand.' Her voice faded while fear hovered in the depths of her dark eyes.

Jasmine knew exactly what it was to feel fear like that.

Deidre de Morea was a respected actress in her late forties. She had always been regarded as very beautiful, distant and mysterious. Legions of men had not only beat a path to her door, they practically killed one another to get her attention. When she married for the first time at the advanced age of thirty-nine to a man twenty years her senior, then proceeded to bear two children, the movie-going public was in shock. Their woman of mystery had suddenly become quite ordinary. After taking several years off to be with her children, Deidre had returned to acting. Her first film after her return was critically acclaimed, but had done poorly at the box office. Her latest film was a huge success and there was talk that she might be nominated for an Oscar.

'Surely you've confided in Carl about your past,' said Jasmine as she studied the people around them. 'Haven't you?'

Deidre's upper lip trembled while she fought to regain control. One glance told Jasmine that she hadn't.

'Please, Jasmine, please think about what you're doing,' pleaded Deidre.

'You have connections, Deidre, old clients with plenty of money. There are other ways to get the money if you don't want your husband to know about it.' Jasmine stood. 'Call me tomorrow. Let me know where to meet you.' She turned, never letting the shattered woman she had left at the table see the satisfaction that settled over her.

She had known about Deidre's past for quite some time. Digging into people's backgrounds with the help of private investigators was something she amused herself with. Like Jasmine, Deidre had come to Hollywood to re-invent herself. Too bad she had left a trail that could so easily be followed.

Now it was time to cash in on what she knew. Jasmine smiled, knowing that she would get the money she had demanded. Deidre de Morea could not afford to let her husband and her children know that before she had become an acclaimed actress she had once been a highly paid prostitute.

In her car Jasmine pulled a piece of paper from the pocket of her white slacks and dialed the number she had written down earlier. She had forgotten how powerful she felt when she could make someone sweat. And there was one special person at the top of her list who deserved to be knocked off her holier-than-thou pedestal. She cursed when she reached an answering machine. While she waited for the message to play through and the beep that would follow, she tapped her scarlet nails impatiently against the console.

'*This is Hallie. I'm sorry I can't take your call now, but please leave a message.*'

'This is Jasmine,' she said. 'I have something I think might interest you. Stop by my apartment tomorrow evening.' Jasmine hung up, then checked her hair and makeup in the lighted mirror on the sun visor, clearly pleased at her cleverness.

It wasn't money she was after now, it was the satisfaction of seeing that little bitch's reaction when she told her about the pictures. Jasmine prided herself on always getting even, and she had never forgotten how Hallie had looked at her that night at the party after she had discovered that Casey had been with her. Like she was beneath her. And Hallie Prescott *would* show up. She would bet her life on it. Curiosity was a powerful motivator.

Down the block, Nick Hardister had watched as Jasmine left the restaurant with none other than Deidre de Morea. Since they had never been friends, Nick could only assume that Jasmine had something on Deidre. He knew for a fact that from time to time Jasmine had hired private investigators, but he had never known her to actually use the information that she had gathered. This time, though, might be different. It had been a long time since Jasmine had had to be concerned about her future.

Just as Jasmine had expected, Deidre had called the next day to tell her that she could only raise half the money, and that it would be that night before she could get it to her. The second half would have to wait for a while. Jasmine acted distraught and threatened to call

111

Deidre's husband, then relented. She would take the hundred thousand. Deidre was too scared not to follow though with the rest. Besides, she held all the cards. At any time she could threaten to reveal Deidre's past.

That evening at her apartment, seated at the tall, stately, antique writing-desk in her living room, Jasmine pulled open one of the drawers. Carefully she took the small, almost dainty object in her hand. The gray metal felt cold yet strangely reassuring as she studied the gun with its ornate mother-of-pearl handle. Swiftly she loaded it, then slipped it into the pocket of the green silk slacks she wore, tugging at her matching shirt to make sure the fabric would conceal the gun. It would be her salvation.

It was strange, thought Jasmine, as she sat by the window that overlooked the tree-lined street below. I should be nervous and scared, maybe even shocked by what I'm about to do, but I'm not. It wasn't frightening in the least.

She ran down her checklist, double-checking to see that the scene was set correctly – the overturned furniture, the vanity swept clean, its contents strewn over the bedroom carpet, the bedcovers in disarray.

This was just something she had to do to survive. And Jasmine knew all about survival. For a few months she would have to be very careful about what she did and who she saw, but she had her plans in place. In a short while she would regain the power and stature she craved.

Last night had been a sleepless one for Jasmine as she wrestled with the story she would tell the police about the murder of Nick Hardister. It was believable, even logical, she thought, as she rehearsed it once more. Nick was nothing more than filth; if she didn't get rid of him, he would never leave her alone.

She would tell them he was a lover from her past who had come after her when he heard she had left her wealthy husband. He wanted to resume their relationship. She refused, of course, but he was a violent, obsessive man. In a rage he pushed her into the bedroom, threatening to kill her. She struggled (she already had the bruises on her throat from their previous encounter to prove it), but she was able to break free of him. It was then in the midst of her terror that she remembered the small loaded handgun she kept in the nightstand next to the bed for protection. She grabbed it and when Nick lunged for her again, she fired. In self-defense.

A good lawyer would be able to build a credible case of self-defense for her and she was satisfied that she could live with the publicity that would follow. She could live with anything that would give her possession of the incriminating photos of her and Casey.

It was dark now and through the window Jasmine could see the headlights of a car turning the corner. She stood. She was ready. But when she heard the knock on the door, she was suddenly gripped by unexpected fear and panic. Forcing her fear down, she went to the door, the gun concealed in the pocket of her green silk pants. With shaking fingers she touched it, hoping to gain reassurance from it.

'I've been waiting for you,' she said with apparent calm, as she opened the door.

CHAPTER 9

Later that same night Casey knocked at the door of Jasmine's apartment. When there was no answer he tried the knob, surprised to find it unlocked. He called out to her. The silence that answered him made him suddenly uneasy. He took a few steps then stopped. His skin prickled. In the living room, a chair lay on its side, a lamp shattered. Tentatively, he called out to Jasmine again as he made his way down the hall toward the bedroom. Fear clung to him, making each step more difficult.

At the door he halted. Every piece of furniture in the room except the bed was overturned. Broken glass covered the floor. Casey turned, certain he was about to be sick. On the bed was Jasmine, dressed in deep green silk, lifeless and sprawled across the pale pink satin coverlet that she had so artfully rumpled earlier in the day. Her head hung limply off the side of the bed, strands of her blonde hair brushing the muted rose and green carpet that was now stained scarlet with blood. Her carefully made-up face registered a look of surprise.

Casey's first impulse had been to run like hell.

114

Fighting for control, he stumbled backwards from the bedroom, unable to take his eyes off Jasmine. Her lifeless eyes seemed to be staring straight at him. In the hallway he turned, and hurried to the living room. At the front door he suddenly stopped, remembering the tape and Jasmine's scheme for blackmail. Frantically he searched, trying to remember what she had told him. With shaking hands he tore through the bookshelves that lined either side of the marble fireplace. Then he ransacked the desk. There, held in place by a wide band to the backside of a drawer, was the tape.

He hadn't even known of its existence until Irwin had kicked Jasmine out. What he paid her every month was a fortune, but not to Jasmine. She needed more. But she had a contingency plan. Together, she had confided to Casey, they could tap into vast sums of money. All they had to do was to get in touch with Edwin Mathews. He would pay just to keep her from turning the tape she had over to the police.

He grabbed it, ready to run. But he knew he couldn't just leave Jasmine like this. He had to call the police. With trembling hands he lifted the phone and dialed 911. All around him was the smell of blood. Soon it would seep into the pores of his skin. Satisfied that he had done the right thing, Casey, who had deliberately refrained from giving his name to the 911 operator, ran from the building to his car.

Miles away, he pulled the car over to the side of the road and shut off the ignition. He couldn't think clearly. In spite of the cool night air, glistening beads of sweat ran profusely down his face and into his eyes.

He couldn't put the image of her wide open, startled eyes and her lifeless body out of his mind.

Why hadn't he wiped his fingerprints off the phone? Who had killed Jasmine? Why did he have to be the one to find her? Would the police suspect him? Of course they would. He was her lover. They always suspected those closest to the victim. Besides, his fingerprints were all over the apartment and the phone. And the blood. He could still smell the goddamn blood!

Control yourself, he cautioned. He had to think about what he would do and what he would say when he was questioned. He hadn't done anything wrong. But someone had either hated Jasmine enough to kill her, or wanted something she had bad enough to kill her.

And now that the tape was in his possession, would they come after him also? He had to think; so much was at stake.

When the police arrived at the crime scene minutes after Casey's departure from Jasmine Turner's apartment, it was evident that there had been a struggle prior to the shooting. Sam Harris, the lanky, youthful detective who was in charge of the investigation, glanced around the pink-draped bedroom and swallowed the bile that always rose in his throat when he was called to a murder scene. This one was not as messy as some, but violent death was still difficult to deal with. After ten years on the force he should have been immune to it.

Sam turned back toward the living room, knowing he would have to get ready to confront the crowd of neighbors and members of the media that had already gathered outside. Given the identity of the victim, he supposed that this murder would provide fodder for the press for days. He would begin his questioning with the neighbors. Statistics showed that most murders were committed by someone the victim knew. He wondered if that would hold true in this case.

'Okay, guys, let's get going in here,' he directed. Behind him the forensic team moved into the blood-stained bedroom to begin their work.

Diedre de Morea's husband had left the house early the next morning. After seeing her children off to school, Diedre poured herself another cup of coffee and reached for the front page of the paper, intending only to scan the headlines before settling down to read some scripts that had been sent over to her.

Seeing the news of Jasmine's death splattered across the paper, she stood suddenly, knocking her coffee cup across the table. As the brown liquid crawled rapidly across the table, Diedre stared helplessly. Last night she had gone to Jasmine's apartment, prepared to give her whatever was necessary to keep her quiet, but when she arrived the police were swarming all over the place. Deidre had hurried away before anyone had recognized her.

Now she would be forced to deal with the police, for she knew they would come around asking questions. The restaurant where she had met with Jasmine two days ago had been crowded, and she was certain they had both been recognized.

Moving as if in a trance, Diedre reached for the

phone and dialed the number for her husband's office. When he answered, she asked him to come home immediately.

'Diedre, are you all right? You sound so strange,' said Carl.

'Just come quickly,' she pleaded in a strangled whisper. 'There's something I must tell you.'

Hallie stared in horror at the pictures on the front page of the *Los Angeles Times* and wondered where Casey fit into all this. Months ago she would never have believed that she could have even entertained the thought that he might have played a part in a murder, but that was months ago, before she discovered she hardly knew the man she had married.

Most unsettling was the phone call she had received from Jasmine the night before she had been murdered. Hallie had erased the message after listening to it, wanting nothing to do with Jasmine and her devious games. Now she couldn't help but wonder if whatever it was that Jasmine had wanted to tell her had had anything to do with her death.

When the phone had rung again on the night of the murder, Hallie had nearly jumped out of her skin. Jasmine again, she thought, as she had jerked the phone to her ear. But it wasn't Jasmine. The voice at the other end had been deep and hurried and the connection was bad, full of static and cutting some of the words out. 'I want . . . husband to . . .' Then the connection was broken.

Hallie had stared at the phone in her hand, replayed the cryptic message in her mind, then shook her head.

Should she have called the police? What could she have told them? That she had had a strange call that made no sense? It must have been a prank or a wrong number, she reasoned.

All the rest of that day, Hallie was uneasy, reading the headlines over and over, unable to believe them. She had never before been so close to violent death. And Casey? Where was he? What in God's name had happened to him?

That afternoon she called Billie and told her what had happened. 'I wanted you to know before you read about it in the newspapers,' explained Hallie in a shaky voice.

'Oh, honey. How terrible! I should be there with you. What's going to happen next?'

'I don't know, Billie. I just don't know.'

The next night, fresh from the shower, Hallie wrapped a thick towel around her head, anchoring the ends with one hand as she reached to answer the phone. At the sound of Casey's voice she jumped, both fearful and concerned. His voice, normally arrogant, was full of terror.

It had been two days since Jasmine's murder and Casey was calling from a pay phone. 'Where have you been?' asked Hallie. Things were not going well, he explained, he had been hiding out and he was nervous. He was certain he was being followed. This was the first time in over two months they had spoken directly to each other without their lawyers present.

'Somebody killed Jasmine and now they're coming after me.' Casey's voice faded as he turned his face away from the receiver to glance nervously at the traffic on the busy street behind him.

Hallie sank to the edge of the bed, her knees suddenly weak. 'Casey? Who? What are you talking about?' she asked. 'Are you all right?' It was habit. She couldn't keep from voicing her concern in spite of his sins against her.

'I was the one who found her dead, shot to death in her apartment. I called the police, then ran. I've been hiding out for the past two days, but they know who I am. My fingerprints are all over the place and now they're following me.'

'The police are following you?' asked Hallie.

'No I don't think so. It's not the cops. It's someone else. It's only a matter of time before they find me. You have to help me, Hallie.' His speech was rapid and disjointed, interrupted only by his breathing, as if he had been running and was trying to catch his breath.

Hallie's felt a twisting tension in her stomach. She had despised Jasmine Turner for what she did, but she would never wish her dead. She wanted to scream at Casey and tell him that she didn't give a damn about him; why she didn't, she would never know. But somewhere down deep she still remembered how things had been between them in the beginning. She still mourned what they had lost.

'I need a place to hide for a while, Hallie, just until I can sort things out. I've got to have time to think. Can I stay at your place?'

'Casey, I . . .'

'Oh God, Hallie, don't desert me now. Please!' Casey

jerked his head to the side, checking the parking lot. His right eye began to twitch. Sweat blurred his vision.

'You have to go to the police, Casey. Just tell them exactly what happened and . . .'

'I can't, Hallie, not now. But I will, I promise. I just need time to think. Please!'

'Calm down, Casey. You can't stay here and you can't keep running. You have to go to the police now. Tonight. Tell them the truth.'

When Hallie hung up the phone a few minutes later she buried her face in her hands, hating herself for turning him away. Had she done the right thing? In spite of everything she was still concerned for him. He had been in trouble for a long, long time, and now he was a murder suspect.

She dressed in a T-shirt and a pair of sweats that she had cut off into shorts, then went to the kitchen and made a pot of coffee. Nervously she paced the floor of her apartment, fearful that Casey would suddenly appear. When she couldn't stand it any longer, she stepped out on to the small patio off her living room that faced the street, searching for Casey's car. Each time a car turned the corner her heart jumped. When after an hour he still hadn't appeared, she was relieved. He had sounded so desperate. Had he taken her advice and gone to the police instead? She desperately hoped so.

Anxiously, Casey jammed the phone down and ran toward his car. He was scared and he was crashing, coming off a high into the worst time he had ever experienced. He had first felt its onset before he had pulled over to call Hallie. Depression seemed to blanket him, smothering him. He had nowhere to hide! He struggled to breathe. Panic had set in, closing its fingers around his throat, rendering him nearly helpless. Jerking and thrashing, as if he was fighting an invisible assailant, Casey struggled to regain control of his mind and his body. His breathing was erratic, coming in rapid gulps, sweat dripped into his eyes, distorting his vision.

Jasmine was dead. How could she leave him alone like this? Who had killed her? He had been there in her apartment and found her dead. Had the killer seen him? Had he followed him? No, no, the killer would have run. But the police would come for him. Frantically, his eyes darted from place to place. Were they already here? No. He was confused. Things kept getting mixed up. It wasn't the police that were after him, it was someone else. Following him. He squeezed his eyes shut for a moment. He had to concentrate, to try and figure what he should do next. Concentrate, dammit!

In desperation he ran for the car, then fumbled to open the glove compartment, searching for the Valium he knew was there. Jasmine had insisted he keep it with him. It would help ease the crash until he could get more coke. He had to have more. Without it he would never make it through the night. Reality clashed with his imagined terrors and Casey perceived shadows and danger all around him, closing in, slashing at his sanity, choking him.

In the rear-view mirror he saw a car pull up close behind him. Now paranoia kicked in. The dark-colored auto that occupied the space in his rear-view mirror became, in his mind, the enemy. They had found him!

From the other side of the car he saw a shadowy figure making its way between the two cars toward him. He had to get away. No one would believe that he hadn't killed Jasmine. He had been there and found her. Now they were going to kill him!

He had to get out of here. He had to get to Hallie. He could hide and she would help him figure out what to do. Casey shoved open the door, stumbled from his car, and began to run. The lights of the cars on the busy street blinded him, causing his perception of light to become distorted, rendering him unable to judge the speed of the oncoming cars. Now the headlights became a continuous stream of bright, blinding light.

They would never find him, he thought, as he ran toward the stream of light, consumed by fear and panic. Once he was able to cross through the light and into darkness he could hide until he could find his way back to Hallie. He looked back over his shoulder. There! He knew it! Someone was chasing him. A man. They had found him! Deliberately he darted into the path of an oncoming car. The man followed. Suddenly there was the scream of brakes, of metal hitting metal, then a scream like nothing he had ever heard before and then a terrifying silence.

If anyone in the group that gathered in the street had been able to describe what they had seen unfolding before their eyes they would have said the accident happened so fast, in less time than it took them to snap their fingers. Yet in the same breath they would talk of how the scene and the accompanying sounds seemed to play out as if in slow motion: the oncoming headlights of the car, the man who ran from the darkness as if he were being chased by demons, the second man that followed, the gut-wrenching sound of metal impacting on flesh and bones. And the scream. That unearthly, ungodly sound that would replay itself in their minds for weeks and months or maybe years. Then the litany of the driver as he bolted from his car screaming, 'Oh my God, oh my God,' over and over.

Like a rag doll, the victim was flipped off the hood and into the air at the impact, landing thirty feet away. Another car swerved at the last moment, just missing the already-broken body. All around brakes squealed. Stunned, people climbed from their cars and gathered.

One of them, a man who emerged from the dark fringes of the crowd, walked toward the body and, with zombie-like motions, fell to the pavement. Then he bent over and his hands splayed over the victim's chest, feeling for some sign of life. Finding none, he began a methodical search of the man's pockets, as if he was looking for identification. He hovered almost protectively over the victim, shielding him with his body from the view of the crowd.

From the stunned group of onlookers someone roused and shouted, 'Hey! What are you doing?' Slowly the man stood and took a few faltering steps backward while a near-hysterical woman begged in a tearful voice for someone to call an ambulance. Without another glance, he turned and walked slowly through the distraught group and beyond, disappearing into the night.

The woman sobbed while she bowed her head and touched her fingers to her forehead, her breast and each shoulder in the Sign of the Cross, then silently began to pray for the battered and unrecognizable man who lay lifeless in the street before her.

When the doorbell rang later that night, Hallie jumped with fright. Her nerves were like live electrical wires. It had been almost three hours since Casey had called. It must be him. She hurried to the door, peering anxiously though the peephole, her hand on the safety bar.

'Mrs Prescott? Police.' A distorted badge was waved in her line of sight. 'We need to talk to you about your husband, Casey Prescott. There's been an accident.'

The overhead light was harsh and glaring, and even though it hurt her eyes Hallie couldn't blink. In her hand she clenched an empty cup of coffee that she never remembered drinking. The two young policemen who had driven her to the hospital had been kind, and had done their best to prepare her for what had to be done. Now that it was all over, she couldn't put it out of her mind. But shocking though this night had been, it still didn't seem real.

Hallie shivered with the kind of chill that had nothing to do with the temperature in the hospital waiting room, and clutched at the blanket that someone had thrown over her shoulders. Had that really been Casey's body that she had seen? She had told them it was, but the injuries were massive. The driver's licence the police had found on the body said it was her husband, but it wasn't until they pulled a watch from a plastic zip lock bag that she was sure. Engraved inside the watch was Casey's birth date, a gift from his parents.

'Is there someone we can call to come and get you, Mrs Prescott? A relative or a friend?' The voice belonged to one of the officers that had escorted her here.

She shook her head.

'We don't want you to go home alone. You can stay here until we can locate someone to come for you.'

Hallie didn't remember how long she had sat there, but she did remember Dana and her father coming to get her and taking her to their home.

The next few days were a blur. Billie arrived in Los Angeles and so did Casey's parents. The police asked Hallie more questions about Casey, then about Jasmine Turner. Hallie didn't remember what she told them.

She did her best to block it out. All of it.

CHAPTER 10

It was cold and raining when the friends and family of Casey William Prescott gathered at Oaklawn Cemetery in East Memphis to mourn his tragic and untimely death. It was almost over, Hallie reminded herself, as she studied the faces of those around her. Today her thoughts were as gray and heavy as the Memphis skies. No one, not even his mother and father, knew the truth about what Casey had become over the months that preceded his death.

For all the world to see, Hallie grieved as befitted the widow of such a young and vibrant man. Inwardly, she cried for Casey and the terrible way things had ended for them. At the same time she cursed at the role she was now forced to play.

Now she was torn between the need to console his loving parents, and the need to confess that the only thing that had kept their marriage from being fully dissolved was the divorce that had been pending at the time of Casey's death. Casey's parents had only learned of their separation several days ago, and it had been Hallie's duty to tell them, as gently as possible, sparing them the real reasons.

The marriage had been dissolved long ago, eroded by the ugly choices Casey had made, but she couldn't tell them the truth. Technically, Hallie was a widow. And out of respect for Tom and Ruth Prescott, she acted the part. But didn't that imply that there had been a lasting bond of love and honor and trust between a husband and wife?

The words of the minister faded in the dampness, and he moved toward her, his hands outstretched in sympathy. Fighting the ridiculous urge to hide her hands behind her back so that she wouldn't have to participate in this farce, she extended them, and immersed herself in the role she had to play. With a few words and a brief squeeze of her hands, the minister let go of her, moving on toward Tom and Ruth.

Beside her Billie wrapped her arms around Hallie, gathering her in their warmth, and Hallie was grateful. Billie had been with her in Los Angeles and now she was here to help her get through this terrible day. For as long as Hallie could remember Billie had been her safe haven.

Tom Prescott stood next to his wife, his shoulders bowed as if the burden placed there was more than he could handle. Ruth, her eyes swollen and her skin tinged with gray, had aged ten years in the few days since her son's death. They would look to her now, Hallie knew, to take Casey's place, to act in his stead as their daughter, the only living link to their son. She would do what she could, and would carefully hide the bitterness she felt. She hated the deceitful role she was forced to play, but how could she tell them the truth about their only son?

* * *

The day following the funeral Hallie left to return to Los Angeles. Tom and Ruth had tried to get her to stay longer, and even Billie had suggested that maybe it was too soon to leave, maybe Hallie should go home with her for a few days until she felt better. But Hallie knew she had to get away, before the sickening smell of death permeated her pores, before the smothering sorrow that hung in the air stole her spirit away. If she stayed any longer she knew her soul would shrivel up and die, too.

Ruth kept her distance while Tom awkwardly wrapped Hallie in a bear hug, knowing that once she left their only link to their son would be severed. After a few moments Tom pulled away, understanding that it was time for Hallie to leave.

Tears gathered and spilled onto Hallie's cheeks, in spite of her efforts to blink them away. She wished she didn't feel like such a fraud. As she turned away she had to remind herself that in the end Casey had not wanted her. Truthfully, he had succeeded in killing anything she might have felt for him that terrible Christmas night. Her sorrow now was for the devastating loss his parents had suffered.

She closed her eyes tightly against the scene that seemed to replay itself over and over. That part of her life was over. For Hallie, it was time to exorcise the memories. She turned and walked toward the car where Billie waited to drive her to the airport.

Each day following his son's funeral Tom Prescott felt a little stronger and better able to cope with his wrenching grief, but he was greatly concerned for Ruthie. With each day she seemed to grow more bitter than the day before. And protective, refusing to let Tom out of her sight, insisting on accompanying him wherever he went. He felt like he was being smothered.

One afternoon they were sitting side by side on the patio when Tom broached the subject. 'Ruthie, I think you should start seeing your friends again. Get out some during the day. You don't need to be with me all the time. I'm going back to work on Monday.'

'I can't leave you. You never know what can happen. I should be here with you.' Ruthie's concern was genuine.

'No,' he answered with a frown on his face. 'We need to start living like normal people again.'

'I worry, Tom.'

'That I'm going to die?'

Ruth sobbed, nodding her head.

'And leave you like Casey did.' Gently, Tom reached out and caressed her face. He didn't need her to answer. 'Casey's death was an accident, Ruthie,' Tom said softly. 'It wasn't anyone's fault.'

Ruth was silent for a minute then she voiced the thought she had carried with her since the moment she had heard that her son was dead. 'It was her fault,' she whispered bitterly.

'Whose fault? Hallie's?' asked Tom.

Ruth nodded.

'No, it wasn't, honey. Hallie had nothing to do with Casey's death. It was an accident. A terrible, terrible accident.' Tom spoke quickly, but it was as if a storm had been unleashed within his wife.

'She left him when he needed her the most,' she

sobbed. 'What kind of woman leaves her husband when he needs her? She could have helped him. She should have insisted that they go to counseling. There are places . . .' Ruth reached for a tissue.

'You can't know what happens privately between two people, Ruthie. Maybe Casey didn't want to work things out. I can't believe Hallie would have left him if she had thought there was any hope for them.'

Ruth looked up. Her eyes were a softer shade of green than Casey's, but now they glittered with anger. 'You always did take her side, and now you've absolved her of all guilt. But I haven't and I never will. I've lost my only child, Tom.'

'Oh, Ruthie. Please, please, let go of this. You are going to be devoured by your own bitterness if you continue to blame Hallie. Casey was old enough to know what he was doing. He made some bad choices.'

Ruthie sighed, dabbing at her eyes. Tom could believe what he wanted, but she knew better. She had not wanted her son to marry Hallie in the first place. Casey had always been sensitive and high strung. She had known since he was very young that he was destined to be someone special. He had needed a strong woman to guide him, not some child like Hallie. One of these days Tom would come to his senses and realize that Hallie was the reason their son wasn't alive today.

Finally the tears had ceased and Ruthie stood stiffly, putting a hand out to steady herself on the chair back. It was getting a little cool, she decided, and Tom would need a sweater.

* * *

131

Instead of going straight from the airport to her apartment, Hallie stopped at a pay phone and called Dana.

'Hallie! Where are you?' asked Dana.

'Just got back. I'm trying to decide what to do now that I'm here.'

'Come on over,' suggested Dana, 'or I'll meet you somewhere. We can have a drink.'

Hallie sighed, wishing she could just put everything aside. Why did life have to be so hard, and why did she feel so responsible for tying up all the loose ends?

'Thanks, Dana, but not just yet. There are some things I need to take care of first.'

'Can I help you, Hallie? If you'd rather be alone, I understand. But if you want some company . . .' Dana's voice trailed off, not wanting to pressure Hallie.

'I . . . I think I want some time alone, Dana. I'll give you a call tomorrow.' Hallie hung up, dreading what she still had to face.

A half-hour later she pulled into the driveway of the beige stucco house that she and Casey had shared. From the moment she stepped onto the porch, she could feel the memories crowding in on her. How long had it been since she had left there? Three months? It seemed so much longer than that.

She reached into her purse for the keys.

'Hallie?'

She jumped at the sound of her name and the keys slipped from her hand and landed with a clatter against the concrete porch.

'I'm sorry. I didn't mean to frighten you.'

Hallie swung around and raised her hand to her throat. 'Oh, Kate, no, I'm okay. Still just a little shaky. How have you been? And how's Charlie?' After she had moved out, it had been Hallie's intention to call Kate and Charlie and invite them to dinner at her apartment, but she just never got around to it.

'Charlie is fine and so am I, dear. We are so sorry to hear about Casey. Such a tragedy. Is there anything you need, anything we can do to help?'

Hallie shook her head, unable to speak for a moment. 'Thank you, Kate. It's kind of you to offer, but I have someone to help. I . . . I moved out a while back,' Hallie added quietly.

'I gathered as much.'

'I'll be closing up the house soon.'

Kate nodded sympathetically. 'Oh, I forgot to tell you. Several days ago there was a man here. Charlie and I saw him just as he came from around the back of the house.'

Hallie looked at the older woman, confused. 'A man?' Who?

'Well, Charlie didn't ask his name, but from a distance they look so much alike, except his hair was darker, so we assumed it must be Casey's brother.'

Casey's brother?

'Oh, no, Kate. You must have been mistaken. You see –' Hallie replied with a worried frown.

'Well, it was nearly dark. I keep telling Charlie he needs new glasses, but he won't go and have his eyes checked. I really didn't see him, until he was well past the driveway. Then I only saw him from behind. Perhaps we were mistaken. And we certainly have no

133

business adding to your worries, Hallie. I'm so sorry.'

'Kate, it's okay. It could have been any number of people.'

Inside the house a few minutes later, Hallie leaned back against the closed door, shutting her eyes. Her pulse was racing and her breath was coming in shallow pants. What should she do? Call the police? And report what? That two elderly neighbors thought they had seen her husband's brother? There was only one big problem with that – Casey didn't have a brother. So who did they see?

Vowing not to panic, Hallie took a quick tour through each of the rooms, opening the closets and cupboards as she went. Nothing seemed to be disturbed. Maybe it had been someone from the police? Or the utility company? Or the water department? Or was it someone who had come looking for Casey, someone he knew?

Resolutely, Hallie made her way back to the living room. It was obvious that whoever the Channings had seen had not been inside the house. She looked around and began to make a mental list of what had to be done in order to vacate the house before another month's rent came due.

This job had fallen to her. If she didn't do it, who would? She only had a few days to sort through Casey's things. Her original intent had been to sweep every thing into boxes so they could be shipped to Tom and Ruth, but she realized that would never do. What if there were things that his parents shouldn't see? No, she would have to go through his things one by one, box them, then send them on. The furniture she would donate to charity. There wasn't anything here that she wanted.

But an hour later she knew that wasn't true when she found their wedding picture. She studied the couple in the ornate white ceramic frame, remembering how happy they had been that day. From behind the glass her smile radiated toward him, lighting her face. Next to her was Casey. Funny, she had never noticed before that although he, too, was smiling, his gaze seemed to be focused not on her, but on something far beyond the camera lens.

A chill ran through her. This was not the first time she had sensed that once they were together Casey had deliberately distanced himself from her, almost as if she had no longer mattered. From the time she had left him, she had been trying to pinpoint exactly when their relationship had begun to unravel. Certainly the turning point in their lives had been their move to Los Angeles, but in her heart Hallie knew that Casey had begun to change soon after their marriage.

She sank down in the nearest chair and rested her head in her hands, the wedding photo still resting in her lap. Without warning, old memories washed over her. How many times had she made excuses for him, until his selfishness had finally driven a wedge between them?

They had never had a real honeymoon. Not until Casey had finished graduate school. But then they had never had a real wedding either since they had eloped, promising each other that they didn't need all the

trimmings. They only needed each other. As a graduation gift Tom and Ruth had generously arranged to
send them on a week-long trip to Jamaica.

Once they had arrived on the island, they spent their
days laying in the sun drinking tropical concoctions of
fruit and rum, and their nights making love. Hallie
thought of it as a prelude to a new beginning. Now that
Casey was out of school her days of waiting tables
would finally be over. He had been on a number of
job interviews during the last two months while he was
completing his studies, and it looked like he would get
an offer from at least two companies.

'It's been a wonderful week, hasn't it?' Hallie had
asked as she idly ran her fingers over Casey's arm.
Around the pool candles flickered at every table. It was
their last night on the island and she was wearing a tea-
length white eyelet dress that showed off her newly
acquired tan.

'I almost hate to go home. Casey, let's promise
ourselves that we'll come back here next year. Let's
see,' she had said, pretending to count on her fingers,
'by that time I should be making tons of money and my
designs will be in constant demand, I'll be a household
name, then we can reward ourselves with another trip.'

She had smiled then, secretly admiring this handsome husband of hers with his golden tan and his green
eyes. For the past week they had behaved like newlyweds. Silly, giddy, carefree honeymooners. It had been
like falling in love all over again. Casey had been
attentive, relaxed and charming. And for the first time
since their marriage, Hallie had felt free of stress. The
hours they had spent together had rekindled their

romance, reminding them of what brought them together in the first place.

Casey glanced away.

Hallie leaned forward, searching his face for some response to her suggestion. 'So what do you think? Next year, same time, same place?'

He fiddled with his wine glass, casting his eyes toward the pool, looking uncomfortable. 'Uh, Hallie, there's something we need to talk about.'

She frowned at the unexpected seriousness in his voice. 'Please, don't say anything that will spoil our last night here,' she had pleaded, suddenly uneasy.

'I . . .' Casey had cleared his throat and started again. 'I know you're excited about starting your business, and I am too, but we are going to have to put it off for at least another year.'

A stunned expression had appeared on her face as her mind frantically searched for a reason for this request. 'Another year? But why?' she had whispered.

'My novel. It's time for me to begin. These things don't happen overnight. I think it will take me about a year. I've already made some notes and done some research, but I can't do it if you don't keep working. It's what I've dreamed of doing.'

She had been silent, still reeling from the shock of his words. 'What about me, Casey? I know you want to write, but why can't you work days and write at night and on weekends? Other people do it. I'm ready to get on with my career.'

She took a deep breath then hurried on. 'I've found a building on Madison. The second floor is empty. It's in pretty bad shape, but the rent is cheap. With some

137

cleanup and some paint I could make it work.' Even to her own ears, she sounded panicky, like someone who desperately needs victory, but knows they have already lost the battle.

'There were some days this past year when my dreams of what I would do once you were out of school were all that kept me going.' When Hallie finished her blue eyes glistened with tears. *He had to understand. Surely he knew how hard she had worked, and how much she wanted this.*

'I know, I really do, Hallie,' he said. 'But this is something I have to do. It's so important to me. It's taken me five years of college to get to this point; five years to get ready to write this book. I know I can do it, Hallie.'

Pushing away from the table, she stood. In the moonlight her tears glistened as they spilled down her cheeks. 'More important than me?'

'Honey . . .'

She turned away. 'Never mind, Casey. I think I know the answer to that.'

He stood and watched her walk away. Then signaled the waiter for another drink.

Hallie didn't know how long she had been gone or how far she had walked along the beach. She had been stunned by Casey's announcement. This was not the way they had planned their future. Her dreams kept taking a back seat to his. But they had talked about the future, and now it was her turn. Casey would just have to make things work.

Hallie had stopped and sat for a while on a low wall that ran along the beach in front of one of the hotels. All that week, she had believed that she and Casey were off to a new start, that their days of struggling were almost over. Instead he had asked her, for the second time in their brief marriage, to put off her dreams so he could pursue his.

She had stared blindly at the glistening moonlit water. How could he be so self-centered? So callous and uncaring? She could have asked herself these questions all night long, but she had known she would never find the answers, unless she was willing to recognize her husband's glaring selfishness. She stood, brushing off the skirt of her dress and began to walk again.

Several hours later she had returned to their room.

'Where have you been?' Casey demanded.

Hallie had pushed her way past him. A delicate white sandal dangled from each hand. 'Walking on the beach.'

'Hallie, I want you to understand . . .'

'I don't,' she had replied, her voice quiet but cold. 'I don't understand how you can be so selfish.'

'It's just that I have to . . .'

The hurt and the anger that had welled inside her made it difficult to talk to him. 'No, it's not, Casey,' she interrupted. 'It's just that you want to. And you always get exactly what you want, don't you? I don't feel like talking any more. I'm tired and I'm going to bed.'

By the time they had arrived home the following day Hallie was calm, but the hurt had refused to go away. That night in bed Casey had gathered her in his arms and pulled her toward him. 'Honey, I know you're disappointed, but we can't go on like this.'

'Of course we can, Casey. You're doing just fine because you're doing exactly what you want, while I'm not able to do anything I want to do.'

He had pulled her closer and stroked her hair. 'I wish this could be different.'

Hallie had pulled away. 'Do you? Then why don't we consider some alternatives? You could work part-time and write the rest of the time, and I could work part-time and at least get things started for my business. Then we'd both be able to do what we want.'

Casey's hand had stilled. 'No,' he said, his voice low. 'No, I'm not willing to do that.'

'You're not willing?' Hallie had been close to shouting as she sat straight up in bed. 'Well, I'm not willing to keep on working.'

There was nothing wrong with being a waitress; she had certainly done it long enough, but she was ready for a change. Casey's plans, though, would force her to stay at her job. With the job market glutted with new graduates, Hallie was smart enough to know that the money she brought home from her job at the restaurant was better than what many of her former classmates were making.

She had jumped out of bed, pulling the comforter behind her along with her pillow. Without another word she went to the living room, leaving Casey to spend the night alone.

For the next week they were like strangers sharing the same apartment. Casey had begun to write, and in the end it was Hallie who had succumbed, hating herself for giving in, trying to bury her disappoint-ment. But in her heart she had doubted that she could ever fully put this episode of selfishness behind her.

One year had stretched into two while Hallie struggled with her job and the resentment she felt toward Casey each time she walked in the door of their apartment, her feet hurting, her patience exhausted, and saw Casey seated at the computer. Often he worked late into the night and woke up in the morning long after Hallie had left for work.

Some days they barely spoke to one another and on those occasions when they had made love, it lacked the intensity and the passion they had shared in the beginning.

Hallie raised her head, then closed her eyes for another moment. Slowly she stood, suddenly feeling more tired than she had ever been. They had had so much together, so much to look forward to. When had he stopped loving her? She clasped the wedding picture against her breast. She wasn't exactly sure what she would do with it. Burn it? That had crossed her mind. But that still wouldn't eradicate the memories of her marriage.

In the end she took the picture with her and left the rest of the house undisturbed. She would be back another time to tend to details. Now it was time to tend to her wounds.

CHAPTER 11

March 1997, Washington DC

'What do you want, Anderson?' Grant Keeler didn't
bother with the greeting ritual as he took a seat.

The balding man beside him nodded as he smoothed
his striped tie, almost as if he knew how distasteful
Keeler found his presence. 'I want you to look into
something.'

'I don't work for you any more.' Grant's voice was
taut.

'Yeah, I know. But I thought you might have a
personal interest in this one, Keeler.'

'What makes this one different?' Anderson had been
trying to get him involved again with the FBI for a long
time, but Grant had always declined.

Anderson cast a sideways look at the rugged profile of
the dark-haired man beside him. When he spoke his
words were carefully measured, precisely delivered. 'It
has something to do with your wife.'

Inwardly Grant flinched. Even after all this time it
hurt to talk about Libby. 'I don't have a wife,' he
answered, a warning in his voice.

'You did,' challenged Anderson.

Grant drew his breath in sharply, once more caught off guard by the unexpected pain that still haunted him. For a moment his cool gray eyes threatened to blur as he thought of Libby. They had had so little time together. And with that thought a flood of memories came rushing back, each fighting for his attention.

They had met at a party hosted by Libby and her roommate. Steve Heller, a friend at the Bureau, knew the roommate. It was one of those bring-along-a-friend affairs, Steve had said. Grant declined. Washington parties where throngs of government workers gathered in the darkness and spent hours discussing the jobs they did during the daylight hours were not the least bit appealing. But Steve had insisted, and finally Grant agreed to put in an appearance.

He hadn't been inside the apartment for more than sixty seconds when he spotted Libby. She was tall and slim with shoulder-length blonde hair and a face that proclaimed an innocence that drew him like a magnet. Later he remembered thinking that she should have been a model instead of working in a congressman's office. Not more than a dozen words were exchanged between them that night, but every time Libby looked up she met Grant's eyes. So it came as no surprise when he called her the following day. She was, in fact, expecting to hear from him.

Six months later they were married, and it was a perfect blending that inspired in both of them a certain awe at their good fortune in finding each other. When Libby became pregnant that following year their happiness only increased. Then three months later, in the few seconds it took a speeding car to jump the curb where Libby was waiting to cross the street, everything that mattered to Grant Keeler was destroyed. His wife and his unborn baby were dead, his dreams shattered.

Realizing suddenly that Anderson was watching him, waiting for his reaction, Grant ran his hand through his thick dark hair, his agitation openly showing. 'You're running out of time here, Anderson. Get to the point.'

Anderson studied the toes of his scuffed wing-tip shoes. 'The wife of an important movie producer was murdered recently in Los Angeles. Her boyfriend died a few nights later. Hit by a car. Maybe it was a coincidence. The police are still searching for the woman's killer. We want you to look into it. You'll be working with an old buddy of yours in Los Angeles, Sam Harris.

Grant's eyes narrowed. 'And what exactly would I be looking for?' He knew this was about more than finding a killer.

'The murdered woman, Jasmine Turner, was a former girlfriend of Senator Hugh Rawlins before she married the producer. When he was killed several years ago, she had agreed to tell us what she knew about his murder and his connection with Edwin Mathews. But then she got scared and ran.' Anderson paused on purpose, waiting for the full impact of his words to have their effect on Grant.

Edwin Mathews was a man who arranged to have anyone who got in his way removed. Not by his hand, but by the hands of others. Mathews was much too fastidious to be involved in the actual murder, and he traveled in social circles that would overlook almost everything except the soiling of one's own hands.

Everyone at the Bureau knew he had ordered the Senator's death, yet no one had been able to gather enough evidence to put him behind bars. No one, that is, except Grant Keeler. Three years earlier he had closed in on Mathews, but even then, he was not able to bring the powerful man to trial.

'And I'm sure you remember, Grant,' continued Anderson, 'at the time Senator Rawlins was murdered, the lady – her name was Janice Porter then, instead of Jasmine Turner – said she had a taped phone conversation that would put Mathews in prison, but she disappeared along with the evidence before Mathews could be indicted.' Anderson paused, waiting for Grant to respond.

'So you think Mathews finally found her and had her murdered?' asked Grant, remembering all the months he had spent building a case against one of the most influential men in Washington.

'I don't know. We searched for months and couldn't find her, so we assume Mathews couldn't either. She just disappeared. Vanished. She changed her identity, and her appearance. That was three years ago. The one thing she couldn't change, though, was her fingerprints.' Anderson shook his head in amazement. 'Who would have ever thought that she was right there, mingling with all those movie stars, right in front of our eyes?'

'Then who killed her?' asked Grant.

Anderson shook his head. 'We don't know. Truthfully, we don't much care. What we do care about is finding the evidence she had that will convict Mathews.'

'And what do I get out of all this?' Grant stared straight ahead, without seeing anything except Libby's face.

Anderson stood, hitching up his pants. 'You might get to see the man who was responsible for your wife's death behind bars.'

The words sliced the air. Grant had always known that Mathews was responsible for Libby's death, but he could never prove it, or even get anyone at the FBI to acknowledge that it was even a possibility. But he had known.

The threats against Grant began when he was closing in on Mathews. When it became apparent that he would not back off, they had gone after Libby. And one day she just happened to be standing on the wrong corner when a speeding car jumped the curb and struck her, killing her instantly.

'What do I have to do?' Grant stood.

'Find the tape that the Turner woman had. We want Mathews,' answered Anderson.

So do I, thought Grant. So do I.

'Detective Harris,' said Sam as he absentmindedly answered the phone. With the back of his free hand he mopped the beads of sweat that had gathered on his forehead. The air conditioning must be on the blink again today, thought Harris. With all the money the city had, it didn't seem too much to hope for a police building with an air conditioning system that worked.

'This is Grant,' announced the voice on the phone.

Sam had been expecting his call. 'Grant, are you in LA?'

'No,' he answered. 'I'm still in Washington. I'm winding up some things here and I should be there tomorrow. I was hoping you could fill me in and fax me copies of the reports on the Turner case.'

'Be glad to. Give me a call when you get in,' Sam said with a grin. 'We've got some catching up to do, buddy.'

It had been five years since they had seen each other but, hanging up the phone, it seemed to Sam as if it had been yesterday. They had met when they were in the Air Force and had remained friends through the years. Standing, Sam stretched, then walked over to the coffee pot in the corner of the room. He reached for a cup, picked up the pot of dark, overcooked brew, then put it down. It was too damn hot for coffee.

By the time he located the report that Grant had asked for it was late that evening. He had been advised that he would be working with Grant on special assignment, but this was the first chance he had had to actually read the full report on Jasmine Turner's murder without interruption. He had been there at the scene, and it was still vivid in his mind. Hell, they were all vivid in his mind. Murder, in any shape or form, was not an easy image to dismiss.

He leaned back in his chair and began to read. After a few minutes he frowned unconsciously. A name there in the report bothered him, and halfway through the second page he shouted across the room. 'Hey, Charlie! You ever hear the name Casey Prescott?'

Charlie looked up surprised. He never figured Sam Harris had ever read a book from cover to cover in his life. Especially one without pictures of naked women. 'Sure,' answered Charlie. 'He wrote *Journey to Fear*.

It's been on the best-seller list for a long time. Supposed to have been made into a movie, but that was before the dude up and died.'

Sam sat up straight. 'Died? How?'

Charlie swiveled in his chair and propped his feet on an open bottom desk-drawer. 'Man, where have you been? The report is here somewhere. I just saw it today. Accident. Hit by a car, I think.'

'Did you know he was screwing the lovely, but now dead, Jasmine Turner?' asked Sam.

'No kidding,' said Charlie, sitting up straight also.

'No kidding,' Sam confirmed.

Grant Keeler stood, stretching to his full six feet, when he spotted Sam Harris at the entrance to the hotel lounge. After shaking hands, Sam followed Grant's lead, settling his wiry frame in the chair. With his sandy hair and smattering of freckles across the bridge of his nose, Sam Harris looked more like an overgrown choirboy than a law enforcement officer.

'Did you find anything interesting in the report I faxed you?' asked Sam after they had ordered drinks.

'A lot of unanswered questions. Do you have any suspects?'

Sam laughed. 'Sure we do. One is dead and the other is alive, but we can't find him. His name is Nick Hardister, small-time con man turned freelance photographer and one of Jasmine Turner's ex-boyfriends.

'Who's dead?'

'Casey Prescott, a writer, and up until a short time ago, the current boyfriend. It appears to be an accident. He was hit by a car, two days after Mrs Turner was killed.'

'Was there any connection between the boyfriend and the photographer?'

Sam shook his head. 'Not that we know of.'

'What was the motive?'

'Jealousy, possibly. It seems the lovely Jasmine had an itch and there was no shortage of men to take care of it.

'What about her husband?'

'We brought him in for questioning. He and Jasmine had been separated for several months, and Turner seemed genuinely distraught over her death even though the divorce was almost final. Nevertheless, if it was a crime of passion, the husband qualifies. Seems he found out about about his wife's affair and threw her out of the house.'

'Doesn't Prescott's death strike you as odd?' prompted Grant.

'It does, but right now it appears to be just a coincidence.' Sam reached for his drink.

Grant probed. 'Were there drugs involved?'

'I don't know,' answered Sam truthfully. 'I haven't checked to see what the autopsy report said. Jasmine Turner was a user, but high-style and strictly gourmet stuff. According to the grapevine she never used the stuff around her husband, only with the string of men she had on the side.'

'Users, too?'

'Some were, some weren't. At least at the beginning. When she tired of them, most of them couldn't afford it. The drugs were Jasmine Turner's way of controlling her lovers.'

Sam leaned forward, studying the rugged features of

149

his friend's face. 'Grant, why the interest in this case? How did Anderson manage to get you involved again?'

Grant looked uncomfortable for a moment then answered. 'It's just an assignment, Sam. Somebody got curious and wants a few facts.'

'So Anderson decided to look you up.'

'Uh huh. For old times' sake.' Grant nodded affirmatively.

Sam, who didn't believe a word of what Grant had just said, raised his glass in a toast. 'Well, here's to the old jackass. At least he gave you a good reason to come out to California.'

By the end of that evening Grant had found another reason to be glad he had come to California. She was wearing a sleek black dress and had hair the color of polished copper and the most beautiful blue eyes he had ever seen. The minute he saw Hallie Prescott, he felt alive again, charged by the sexual tension that traveled the distance across the smoky club to where she stood.

From the first moment he touched her, she had never hesitated in her response to him. Except once, at the door to his hotel room. There was something in her eyes – regret? resignation? – but it was fleeting, and the night they spent together was something he couldn't put out of his mind.

At odd, unexpected times over the next few days her image would drift into his thoughts, disturbing him, frustrating him. Why in God's name had he let her leave without asking her name, or anything about her?

* * *

The following day there was a message waiting for Grant when he returned to his hotel. It was from Sam. After unlocking the door he threw his wallet and keys on the table next to the bed, then reached for the phone and dialed the number Sam had left, but it was busy.

Grant stood and stretched, his body muscular and lean from his years of conditioning. In the bathroom he looked in the mirror and found the reflection tired. The stubble on his chin was barely visible, but there nevertheless. His eyes, usually a startling clear gray, were clouded with fatigue. The one thing he hadn't anticipated when he had agreed to work on this case was the emotional involvement it would exact. Too many things about Libby and their life together were beginning to resurface. Things he thought he had already set aside, things he hadn't thought of in a long time.

When he stepped out of the shower ten minutes later, the phone rang. Grant wrapped a towel around his hips and crossed the room. The change of temperature from the steamy bathroom to the air conditioned bedroom made the dark hairs on his powerful arms stand up. 'This is Keeler,' he answered.

'Grant, I've got a copy of the autopsies on Turner and Prescott. Cocaine showed up in hers. But him, what a mess! The guy was a walking pharmacy – a little of everything.'

'How long had he known Jasmine Turner?' Grant asked with interest.

'About six months. Prescott and his wife met the Turners when they were invited to a party at the Turner house,' answered Sam.

'Wife?' repeated Grant startled. 'You didn't say

151

anything yesterday about Prescott being married. There was no mention of her in the report.'

'Yeah, I know. Somebody left that bit of information out of the report, Grant. Stuff like this sometimes happens here in LA, or hadn't you heard? He had identification on him when he was hit and later at the hospital morgue, the wife confirmed his identity. Ramirez said it was tough on her. The body was in bad shape with severe trauma to the head.

'Evidently Prescott had called his wife several days after the murder from a pay phone at the accident scene. Said he freaked out after he discovered Jasmine's body and ran. At least that's what she told us. Anyway, she refused to help him hide out, but she said she still expected that he would come to her apartment anyway. He never showed up.'

'Was she brought in for questioning on the Turner case?'

'Yeah. Ramirez talked to her. Ms Prescott said that she had been at home all evening. No way to confirm that,' observed Sam.

'Anything else?'

'Uh huh. Ramirez thinks she's holding something back.'

Grant leaned forward. 'Based on what?'

'Just a hunch,' replied Sam. 'We found plenty of fingerprints at the crime scene, some we were able to identify as belonging to Prescott and Hardister.

'Anything to tie Prescott's wife to the murder?'

'Just a piece of paper we found in Jasmine Turner's pocket. It had the wife's phone number written on it,' said Sam.

Who but the scorned wife had a better motive for killing Jasmine Turner? Without voicing the thought that crossed both men's minds about Prescott's wife and the numerous loose ends on this case, Grant suggested that someone be assigned to watch Hallie Prescott. 'At least for the next few days. I want to know how she spends her days, and nights, for that matter. If she does anything at all unusual or tries to leave town, I want to know about it immediately. By the way, did she know her husband was screwing around on her?'

'She and Prescott were separated,' said Sam. 'I assume that was the reason.'

After a few more questions Grant hung up the phone, puzzled now that there was a wife in the picture. From his briefcase he removed a picture of Jasmine Turner, taken before her death, that Sam had sent along with the report. She was blonde and pretty, but the eyes were a dead giveaway – cold and tough. Maybe Prescott's wife had decided that hubby's affair had gone too far and decided to do something about it. And maybe she had the evidence Grant was looking for.

'How did Mrs Prescott escape all the notoriety that accompanied this case?' asked Grant the following day. They were seated on either side of Sam's desk.

Sam shrugged and shook his head. 'After the initial scandal about Jasmine Turner, when her husband first threw her out, and then the murder, the press wasn't too interested in the death of the boyfriend. Authors don't have the same high-profile appeal as movie people.'

Grant raised his brows. 'Come on, Sam. Don't you find it strange that the Turner woman and her lover die

153

within days of each other? Someone let a few important details go unnoticed.'

Sam leaned forward and pinned his friend's eyes with his own. 'Grant, what are you looking for, and why the interest in this case?'

'Let's get out of here,' said Grant, pushing his chair back and standing suddenly. 'I need some fresh air.'

Sam followed his lead and when they were outside Grant turned to him, knowing that he could trust his friend with the truth. 'A few years before she became Jasmine Turner, the lady was Senator Hugh Rawlins' girlfriend. She was supposed to testify against Edwin Mathews, said she had evidence, a tape, that would link him to Senator Rawlin's death. But she disappeared and the Bureau couldn't find her or the evidence to indict Mathews. Now they want the tape.'

'But why are you involved?' asked Sam. 'I know you worked on the case, but that was a few years back, before Libby . . .' Sam let his words trail off. It was the first time her name had been mentioned between them and now he wished to God he hadn't reminded Grant of his loss.

Grant looked away and swallowed hard before he spoke. 'There were threats, first against me, then against Libby. I ignored them. I was so damn close to getting Mathews that I couldn't stop. It had almost become an obsession. I should have known that a man like Mathews would follow through, And he did, Sam. Libby was standing on a street corner two blocks from home when she was hit by a speeding car.' Grant hesitated, buying time so that his voice wouldn't betray the emotion he was feeling, and reached into his shirt pocket for a cigarette before he remembered that he didn't smoke any more.

He took a deep breath. 'Libby was three months pregnant when she was killed,' he added absently, looking up at the sky as if he had lost track of where he was. Then he snapped back. 'I tried to get the Bureau to investigate. I knew Mathews was responsible but no one would listen. Now, Anderson has dangled this plum in front of me, the opportunity to nail the man who caused Libby's death.'

'And what you want is not Jasmine Turner's killer, but the evidence Jasmine claimed she had.'

'She had it alright, Sam, and I'm sure Mathews lost a lot of sleep over Jasmine, especially since he didn't know exactly what she had or where she was.'

'Do you think there really is a tape?'

Grant nodded. 'It's our only hope of tying Mathews to the Senator's murder. She told the FBI she had it. Later she changed her story, saying she lied because she was scared, that she had no evidence at all, then she disappeared.'

Sam was silent for a while then asked, 'Did you ever meet her? Jasmine, I mean.'

'No,' Grant replied. 'Anderson handled the deal with her.'

Something about the black and white photos bothered Grant, but it took several minutes for him to realize exactly what it was. When he did, he went to question the detective who had taken the surveillance photos of Hallie Prescott.

'Ramirez, were these taken outside Mrs Prescott's

apartment?' Grant indicated the glossy prints. Ramirez shook his head. 'Yeah. She and Prescott rented a house in the same area when they were together, but now she lives in this apartment in Brentwood.' The photos showed Hallie in jeans and a T-shirt walking toward the front door of a two-story yellow brick building that housed possibly ten or twelve rental units.

'Kind of modest, isn't it, for the wife of a famous author?'

Ramirez shrugged. 'Brentwood is a classy part of town, lots of movie stars live there, but it doesn't exactly look like she's living it up, does it? This area is a mix of small bungalows, apartment buildings like this one, neighborhood stores and small ethnic restaurants.'

Grant was on the verge of asking himself why she would live this way, then he remembered Prescott's drug addiction. Supporting a habit wouldn't take long to rip through a large amount of money. He studied the photos, curious about the woman there. He had expected someone older. The image before him was more of a girl than a woman; the features of the face too blurred to reveal the sadness in the eyes.

That afternoon, Grant had just returned to the furnished apartment he had moved into the day before when the phone rang. Sam sounded excited. 'Ramirez just called and it seems Mrs Prescott has decided to take a trip.'

'So?'

'So someone's tailing her and it's not us.'

CHAPTER 12

If asked, Grant wouldn't be able to say what made his heart race as he drove to the airport to meet Sam Harris and go after the Prescott woman. Instinct possibly, or just an overblown curiosity, but his gut told him something was about to happen. As of right now there was really nothing to link Hallie Prescott to this case. Nothing except her phone number which they had found at the crime scene, and the fact that Hallie's husband had had an intimate relationship with the murdered woman. And that's enough motive for almost anything, he thought.

Grant slammed the door of his rental car and ran toward the Northwest Airlines terminal. Once inside the glass doors, he scanned the area, his gray eyes darting, skimming the crowds before him. Finally he spotted Sam Harris.

'Where is she?'

Sam never answered, but instead nodded his head toward a security clearance area. 'Let's go. I'll fill you in when we're in the air.'

Grant's eyes narrowed. Through the crowd he could see the woman they were following. She was dressed in a navy jacket and a pair of khaki slacks. Her hair was pulled back in a loose pony tail looped high off her neck, and she was wearing sunglasses.

'Let me guess,' said Grant. 'Could it be that someone from Mathews's camp is also interested in what this woman has?'

'It appears that way.'

When they boarded the plane and found their seats Sam indicated that he would take the window seat.

'Where exactly are we going?' Grant asked.

Sam laughed. 'Why, we're going to Memphis, good buddy. And if things fizzle and we find out this is a wild goose chase, then maybe we'll go spend an afternoon at Graceland.'

'Swell,' replied Grant sarcastically, as he located the men Sam had pointed out only minutes ago. One was seated a row ahead of Hallie Prescott and the other was directly across the aisle.

Grant studied Hallie from his place across the aisle as she stood and reached into the overhead compartment, but her face was angled away from him. Distantly, he registered something familiar, then just as quickly put it aside. Of course there was something familiar about her. Over the past few days he had seen dozens of photos of her taken by the surveillance crew.

The conversation between Sam and Grant was fragmented over the next four hours, and Grant caught only brief glimpses of the woman they were following. Theirs was a wait-and-watch game. Before they did anything, they wanted to know what Mathews's men were going to do.

As soon as they were on the ground in Memphis, Sam moved into the aisle so that he could be closer to Hallie. Grant followed, a few paces behind. Once they were in the terminal they separated even further, but this time Grant was in the lead. Hallie stopped on the concourse only once to shift her bag from one shoulder to the other. As soon as she rejoined the moving crowd, Mathews's men began to close in. Sam looked worried, but he knew Grant was in position to move in quickly.

Suddenly, and without warning, the larger of the two men following her pushed his way through the travelers. Sam saw it just as Grant did, but Grant moved in faster from the opposite side and took the offensive. 'Hallie!' Grant called across the heads of the crowd. 'Hallie! Over here!' Now there were only two people between Grant and Hallie.

At the sound of her name Hallie had stopped and looked around in confusion. It was all the time Grant needed. He approached from her left, caught her by the arm and swung her around to face him. At that moment a look of incredulous disbelief crossed her face, but before she could utter a protest, Grant pulled her tightly against him and lowered his lips to her parted ones in a searching and intimate kiss. All around them passengers smiled at the scene, a little embarrassed, but forgiving, certain that this man and woman were lovers reunited after a long separation.

In spite of the gravity of the situation, it was all Sam Harris could do to keep from laughing out loud. His mother would have clucked her tongue and commented loudly to anyone who would listen that what he had just witnessed was a shocking public display of intimacy and bad taste. And for the first time in years, Sam would have had to agree with her. It was, he thought. It most definitely was.

As soon as Grant had reached for Hallie, Mathews's man had faded into the crowd and disappeared. It didn't mean the two men were gone, only that they would wait for another opportunity to catch Hallie alone.

Hallie's heart was beating rapidly and her breathing was labored and shallow as though she had been running for miles, but it wasn't much different from what the usually unflappable Grant Keeler was experiencing.

In the split second between the time he had pulled Hallie toward him and kissed her, he had recognized her as the woman he had made love to his first night in Los Angeles.

Along with his surprise came a strong physical response that he was completely unprepared for. Even though she was in danger, it didn't for a moment interfere with the pleasure of having her slender body against him and her lips moist and open beneath his. When he pulled away from her slightly he deliberately pushed her face into his broad chest and whispered harshly into her ear, 'Your life could depend on what you do next. Do exactly what I say until we get out of here. You're being followed.'

Hallie raised her head and opened her mouth to protest just as Grant took her bag off her shoulder with one hand. With his other hand he grabbed her bottom. It was a crude diversion, but it worked. She may have been sputtering, but she was also speechless. As he pulled her along with him hurriedly through the airport he leaned down and warned her, 'I can do worse if necessary.'

She glared at him, her eyes radiating the fury she felt. 'I'm sure you can,' she said. 'Your crudeness defies the imagination.'

Grant bestowed his most charming smile on her. It was the same smile he had practiced for years, beginning with his twelfth birthday and perfected every year since. Hallie wanted to turn and raise her knee between his legs and hope that she would do some serious damage, but her instincts cautioned her. What if she really was in danger? There had been several times in the past few days that she had felt a prickling sensation as if someone was watching her, but she thought it was nothing more than an overactive imagination. Since she had returned from Casey's funeral she had been jumpy and on edge.

Outside the airport the night air was warm and heavy with humidity. As soon as they had cleared the doors Grant and Hallie were met by Sam, who indicated a car parked only a few feet away. Grant had to remember to thank Sam and to ask him how in the hell he managed to arrange for a car that fast.

'Let's go,' Grant said as he took Hallie's arm.

'No, thanks.' Hallie planted her feet in a stance that clearly said this was the end of the line for her.

While Sam slid into the driver's seat, Grant rounded the car and put Hallie's bag into the trunk. Then without a word, he opened the rear door and pushed a protesting Hallie into the back seat. Swiftly he slid in beside her and slammed the door. At the sound of her protests a policeman, directing airport traffic, had decided to see if everything was okay.

Sam started the engine.

'Wave,' commanded Grant.

'What?' asked Hallie.

'I said, "wave,"' he repeated as he took her hand firmly and along with his wiggled it at the officer.

'You could have smiled, too,' he added with a grin.

As Sam pulled away from the curb Hallie shouted, 'What the hell is going on here?'

When Grant didn't answer she shouted at Sam, 'Who are you?' Then, with a searing look at Grant, she threatened, 'If you don't let me go I'm going to start screaming! I'll turn you both over to the police!'

Sam sighed as he reached into his jacket pocket and pulled out his badge, flipping it open for Hallie to see. In the rear-view mirror he watched the changing expressions on her face.

Grant smiled broadly. He hadn't expected to enjoy this, but once he recognized Hallie he knew that this was going to be a trip worth remembering.

Hallie was furious. 'How dare you!' she said to Grant. 'And just who the hell are *you*? The FBI?' she asked sarcastically. She couldn't wait to scratch that insulting grin off his face. That face, that night . . . Suddenly she was awash with memories of that night, and she could feel her face flush with embarrassment.

Slowly, indolently, Grant reached into his jacket and produced a wallet. Inside was his ID and badge. It identified him as Grant Keeler, special agent for the FBI. More than anything Hallie wanted to spit in his smug face. Instead she turned back to Sam. 'What is all this about?'

'We'll tell you later, Mrs Prescott,' he answered as his eyes met hers in the rear-view mirror. Then he accelerated, turning his attention toward the road ahead.

Frustrated, Hallie turned her face toward the window, seeing nothing but the darkness, and resigned herself to going with these men. It didn't seem as if she had much choice, and not even the fact that they were law enforcement officers alleviated her apprehension. If anything, that made her even more nervous, that and the fact that she and the sexy dark-haired man beside her had once spent an entire night making love.

Oh, why hadn't she told Ruth what time to expect her? Instead she had merely left a message at the hospital that she would be there as soon as she could. Tom had had a heart attack and was now in the intensive care unit. Somehow she had to get to the hospital. Ruth would be too worried about Tom to give any thought to Hallie's whereabouts.

They rode in silence, neither man speaking. After what seemed like hours, Sam turned off the highway and onto a side street, then into the parking lot of a motel. The blinking light on the bright yellow neon sign lit up the car's dark interior. For a moment no one moved. Then Sam and Grant checked to see if they had been followed. It was Sam Harris who spoke first. 'I'll go in.'

Hallie looked toward Grant, his rugged profile clearly outlined in the light, and started to speak, then thought better of it. How many times had she thought of meeting him again, dreamed about it? But never had she imagined it would happen like this. For once in her life she had absolutely no idea what to say.

Her skin grew hot at the memory of that night, and she was grateful for the shadows that hid her from his watchful eyes. Now that there was just the two of them she wondered how long it would be before he reminded her of their night together.

When Sam returned he started the car and drove to the rear of the motel. 'Look,' said Hallie, as Sam shut the engine off, 'I don't know what all this is about, but I've got someplace to be.'

'The only place you're going to be tonight is here with us,' stated Grant tersely.

'You don't understand. I have to get to the hospital. My father-in-law is in intensive care. He's had a heart attack.'

'I'm not sure you understand. You were being followed. Those men nearly snatched you at the airport. Any idea who they are and what they want?'

'Isn't that your job to find that out? For all I know, you are making this whole thing up. I didn't see anybody at the airport.' Hallie pushed the loose strands of hair from her face. 'Look, I need to get to St Francis Hospital as soon as possible.'

'Maybe tomorrow, if everything looks okay.' Grant turned to Sam. 'Let's go,' he said as he took Hallie's hand and pulled her from the back seat of the car, up the outside stairway and into room 210.

Inside, Hallie stood in the middle of the room and shivered. The air conditioner hummed noisily as it blew an icy stream of air across the room. Sam checked the bathroom and the closet, then turned to Grant. 'I'm going outside to check things out.'

Grant nodded and put Hallie's bag in the closet. Hallie was alarmed at the thought of being alone with Grant. 'You can't leave me here with him,' she protested, scurrying around Grant to face Sam.

'Don't worry, Mrs Prescott. You'll be safe with Keeler here.' Sam grinned even as he said the words and with a wave he was out the door.

Safe? She thought about the way he had kissed her in the airport and the way his long legs felt as they touched hers in the car and she knew she would never be safe in his presence. With her eyes shut tight, she held her breath, waiting. Any moment now Grant would bring up their first meeting. And oh, it was some meeting, all right.

'Do you want something to drink?' Grant asked.

Hallie's eyes flew open in surprise. Her expression was less tense. 'Sure.'

With the room key in his hand, Grant paused at the door. 'Don't open this to anyone,' he cautioned.

Hallie stood, indecisively biting at her lower lip, then crossed the room. Cautiously, she opened the door a few inches and peered out. When she was sure that Grant was nowhere around she ran to the closet and grabbed her bag. Outside she half-skipped, half-ran past the row of dark green doors that lined the outside of the building, then scampered down the black metal stairs to the ground. She turned toward the parking lot and never saw the hand that reached out from the archway behind her to grab her solidly by the belt at her waist, lifting her off the ground.

'Going somewhere, Ms Prescott?' The voice was quiet and deep.

Her surprise at being so roughly apprehended left Hallie speechless. Instead, she kicked at him unsuccessfully.

Grant put her down without releasing his grip on her belt then began pushing her back up the stairs. 'You can't leave yet,' he said in a patronizing voice. 'You haven't had any refreshments.'

Once inside the room Grant gave Hallie a shove that sent her flying across the room to land on the bed. She sat up indignantly. Her copper hair had tumbled from its loop and was now wildly arranged around her small face. She had no idea of the enticing picture she made. Grant faced her, intent on remaining impersonal, ready to tell her what a stupid thing she had just tried, but his desire to pin her to the bed with his body and make love to her kept getting in the way.

With an attempt at indifference he set down the two cans of coke, pulled the chair away from the built-in dresser and turned it so it faced the bed. He opened both cans and handed her one; then he straddled the chair, studying her intently. When Hallie raised the cold sweating can to her lips, Grant raised his can in a mock salute. She almost choked as she pictured him that night at the club. It was a silent reminder. He was deliberately taunting her. Any moment now he would ask her about that night.

'Tell me about Edwin Mathews,' he said quietly.

The question took Hallie by surprise. 'I don't know anyone by that name,' she answered, then countered, 'Tell me why you kidnapped me.'

166

'You are being followed by two men known to be employed by Edwin Mathews. It was either you go with them, or you go with us, and we're the good guys.'

Hallie shot him a look that carried all the animosity she felt. 'My relatives are expecting me at the hospital. When I don't show up they'll worry and call the police.' This last was an exaggeration, but it was worth a try.

After digesting this latest bit of information, Grant rose from his chair and walked to the table beside the bed. He picked up the phone and handed it to Hallie. 'Call them,' he ordered.

She raised her blue eyes to meet his.

'Call them,' he repeated, 'and since you won't want to worry them you won't want to mention your, ah, accommodations for the night. It would undoubtedly upset them to think that the young widow had replaced her husband so quickly, and not with one man but two.' The anger Hallie felt at Grant's words was written all over her face, but she took the receiver from his outstretched hand. 'Tell them your flight from Los Angeles was cancelled and you'll arrive tomorrow.'

After Hallie had completed her call, she asked Grant if she would be able to go to the hospital tomorrow. It was difficult to keep the uncertainty she felt from showing. Why would anyone follow her?

'If Mathews's men don't try anything, you can.' Grant returned to his chair.

'I don't know why anyone would follow me. I haven't done anything. I don't even know who this Mathews guy is.'

'Not important,' said Grant as he drank from the can,

then held it out straight in front of him, his arm propped on the chair back between them.

For a moment he seemed to study the can intently, then added, 'What *is* important is that Mathews thinks *you* know, or have something and he's not going to give up until he has you.' He paused, taking a deep breath. 'Three years ago Mathews arranged to have a US senator killed. He wouldn't worry for a minute about knocking off someone like you. Now, Ms Prescott . . .' he began, his steely gray eyes boring into hers.

'Will you stop calling me "Ms Prescott"!'

Grant raised an eyebrow at her outburst.

'My name is Hallie, but you know that already,' she continued in a quieter tone and wondered how long he would wait before he brought up their previous encounter.

'Did you know Jasmine Turner?' Grant studied her face as he waited for her answer.

Hallie winced at the name, then a sadness seemed to cloud her expressive blue eyes. Finally she nodded. 'I met her once.'

'When?'

'About six months ago when we first moved to Los Angeles.'

'What about Nick Hardister?'

Hallie bit her bottom lip to keep it from trembling when she realized where this questioning was going to lead. With her eyes averted from Grant's probing gaze, she shook her head from side to side, then pulled her knees up to her chin and rested her forehead against them. 'I don't know anyone by that name.'

'Where were you when –?' Grant began, but Hallie

cut him off before he could complete his question.

'Look, I don't want to talk about this.' Her voice was muffled.

'You have to,' Grant answered in a firm tone. 'The police are looking for Hardister. He's a suspect in the murder of Jasmine Turner. They haven't been able to find him. But I'll bet my last dollar that Edwin Mathews is looking for him also, just like he's looking for you.'

'But why is he after me? I don't know anything.' There was genuine bewilderment in the question.

'It doesn't matter,' said Grant. 'Mathews doesn't know that.' And neither do we, he added silently. 'Hallie, you have to tell me the whole story from the beginning.'

Hallie shook her head.

'Could your husband have killed Jasmine Turner? You have to tell me about your husband's involvement with her and anything you know about Nick Hardister.'

She raised her head this time, her chin jutting forward slightly, defiantly. Her eyes locked with his. 'No, not tonight, not ever.'

Determination was written all over her face, and Grant knew that even if he threatened her with all the legal ramifications her refusal could bring down on her, he would get nowhere tonight. Tomorrow would be soon enough.

Hallie turned away from him then, and Grant couldn't help but wonder how many other men besides him she had sought out to ease her grief since the recent death of her husband. Was her refusal to talk prompted by her love for her husband? Or maybe loyalty to his family? Or was it simply too painful for her to admit that he had preferred another woman to his own wife?

His reverie was interrupted by a light knock at the door. Hallie jumped nervously. Grant motioned for her to go into the bathroom, while he positioned himself behind the door. Then he heard Sam's call. Relieved, Grant unlocked the door.

When Sam sauntered in, Grant almost laughed out loud. His arms were loaded with two large pizzas and a six-pack of beer. 'Well,' he said defensively, 'detectives do get hungry.' As he set the pizzas down he looked around. 'Where's Ms Prescott?'

Grant nodded toward the bathroom. 'And her name is not Ms Prescott,' he announced loudly. 'It's Hallie.'

'There was no sign that we were followed. What about her?' asked Sam.

'She refuses to talk. Says she doesn't know Mathews or Hardister. I'll try again tomorrow.'

'Well, whether she knows them or not, she may be the one person that can get them to come out in the open, especially if she has the tape.'

After Grant opened the bathroom door and told Hallie that it was okay to come out, the three of them sat in the blue-carpeted motel room eating pepperoni pizza with a gusto that surprised them all. In the past half-hour the atmosphere had changed and everyone had relaxed, acting as if they were three old friends.

This camaraderie vanished an hour and a half later when Sam announced that he had taken the room two doors down and Hallie was to stay here in this room with Grant. At this announcement Hallie's eyes flew wide open and she looked at Sam disbelievingly. 'You can't . . .' she began. 'I can't –'

'Sorry, Hallie, but this is the way it has to be,' Sam interrupted as he put the empty cardboard pizza boxes on the floor next to the trash can. Neither Grant nor Hallie could see the grin that crossed Sam's face as he bent over at his task. Any idiot could sense the sparks between these two.

Hallie opened her mouth to argue, then realized that she would just be wasting her time. I can't do this, she thought, while her breath came in short spurts and her heart rate accelerated. She could not be alone in this room with this man and not want what she had wanted before.

Through the partially opened door she could hear their voices, low and serious. Then Grant stepped inside and locked the door behind him. Hallie panicked and jumped up from the side of the bed where she had been sitting. With a studied nonchalance Grant sauntered toward Hallie, and before she was able to do anything more than murmur a protest, he pulled her toward him, wrapping his arms around her, her arms pinned at her sides. Her breath was shallow, and she was incapable of any movement except to moisten her lips with her tongue.

In frozen fascination, coupled with anticipation, she watched as Grant lowered his face to hers. Just as his lips brushed hers she heard a click and her eyes flew wide open. Grant stepped back and Hallie, horrified and unbelieving, stared at her hand. She was hand-cuffed to Grant Keeler!

Before she could call him every dirty name she knew

or could ever remember hearing, Grant pulled her along with him toward the bed. With his free hand he reached down and pulled back the covers. 'You can lay down or sit up, whatever you want,' he said as he sat down on the side of the bed and single-handedly removed his shoes. Pulling her with him, he stretched out his long frame on the bed. 'I need some sleep,' he said, reaching out with his free hand to turn out the lamp on the night stand.

Hallie had no choice. No matter if she sat up or laid down she was still going to be in bed with him. Reluctantly she too laid down, keeping as much distance between them as possible. 'You bastard,' she spit out between clenched teeth, as she thought of the last time they had shared a bed.

In the darkness, Grant smiled briefly and resigned himself to spending what he knew would be a sleepless night. His body had already reminded him of how much he wanted her.

With an attempt at reasoning, Hallie turned toward him. 'This really isn't necessary, you know. Actually, it's a little theatrical, the handcuffs and all.' This last was accompanied by a nervous little laugh.

'Not to me,' Grant replied.

'I won't try to get away. You can take them off,' she assured him.

'And you'd be gone in a flash. You have no idea of the danger you're in and not enough sense to realize that you're better off with us.'

Hallie was silent for a few minutes then asked, 'Can't we at least watch TV?'

'Why?'

'Because I'm wide awake,' she answered.

'Well, I'm not.'

'You are too,' Hallie protested. 'I can hear your breathing and I know you're not asleep.'

'I would be if you would shut up,' Grant replied, fighting hard to keep from pulling her toward him. 'We could talk instead,' he suggested.

'No,' she answered quickly.

'Why not? Are you afraid I'll ask you again about your husband and Jasmine Turner?'

'No,' she answered in a rush. 'I'm afraid you'll ask me about that night in Los Angeles.' Hallie waited, afraid to move, afraid to breathe.

Grant was silent. He hadn't expected this.

The continuous hum of the air conditioner provided the only sound in the room.

'I hadn't intended to bring it up,' Grant said quietly.

'Oh,' she murmured in a small voice. She was feeling very foolish.

'But since you did, let's talk about it. What were you looking for that night Hallie?'

She swallowed. 'I'm not sure I can talk about that either, Grant.'

Grant rolled onto his side. His face was inches away from Hallie's, so close that she could feel his breath against her temple. With a slight tug he pulled Hallie to him so that her face was now nestled in the hollow of his shoulder. The kiss he placed on her hair was so light that she might almost have imagined it. To Grant the fragrance and feel of her hair was just as he had remembered. With his free hand he touched her cheek then let his hand trail down to her breast.

Hallie couldn't help herself. In the darkness her lips went in search of his while her body seemed to align itself with him so that they were touching in all the right places. Once more she found herself far beyond where she intended to be. What was it about this man, this stranger that caused her to throw caution to the wind just for the chance to be near him? Freely, he explored her mouth with his tongue and when he pulled back finally, she lay breathless, needing more, yet afraid of what would follow.

In a husky voice Grant repeated the question that had been nagging at him since he had first recognized her in the airport only a few hours ago. 'What were you looking for that night, Hallie?'

She moved against him, then looked up at him. 'I was looking for you,' she whispered truthfully.

'Not me, Hallie. Someone like me, maybe. Tell me, just how many other men have you gone looking for like that?' As soon as he voiced the question he knew it was irrational for him to ask, or even to want to know, but it had nagged at him since that morning in his Los Angeles hotel room when he had awakened to find her gone.

Hallie jerked away from him and managed to scoot back up against the headboard, furious that she had allowed herself to be so vulnerable. 'What are you talking about?' she asked angrily.

Grant raised his shoulders in a shrug. 'You weren't exactly shy that night, Hallie. Actually, you were quite good.'

'At what?' she asked incredulously.

'Everything.'

'Leave me alone,' she cried, turning away from him. 'I don't have to put up with this.'

Grant obliged by rolling over on his back and throwing his free arm up to cover his eyes, meanwhile cursing that part of his anatomy that seemed to work independently of his mind.

'Undo these damned handcuffs!' she demanded.

'Tomorrow,' he promised in a low voice. 'I'll let you go tomorrow.' And Grant knew this would be one of the longest nights of his life.

CHAPTER 13

This time when Grant awoke he was positive that Hallie would still be there. She was, already sitting up in bed rubbing her wrist.

'Undo these,' she said in a rush.

Grant groaned. It had been near dawn before he had fallen asleep and he felt like hell.

'I, um, I have to go to the bathroom,' said Hallie.

He smiled like he didn't believe her. Hallie reached out with her free hand and punched him on the shoulder. 'Now!'

'Okay, okay,' he said, reaching to unlock the handcuffs that still bound them together.

As soon as she could, Hallie raced to the bathroom and flipped on all the switches, then ran the water in the sink so he couldn't hear her.

In front of the mirror that hung over the dresser Grant ran his hand over his face, wincing at the night's growth of beard. When Sam knocked at the door, he moaned. He was greeted by a cheerful Sam, showered and shaved, and carrying a white paper sack in each hand.

Sam took one look at Grant and grinned. 'Rough night, huh?'

Grant was going to answer, then thought better of it. 'I need about a gallon of black coffee.'

'What did you find out?' Sam set the sacks containing coffee and doughnuts on the dresser.

'I don't think I'm going to get any information out of her. Let's turn her loose.'

'What about the guys from last night?'

Grant knew he was about to use Hallie as bait and he felt bad about it. 'We'll watch her. If they make another move, we'll be right there. Let's see if they're interested enough to come after her again. If they still think she's got the tape, they will.'

'Do you think she has it?' asked Sam.

'I don't know.'

Just then Hallie opened the bathroom door and gave both men a look that clearly indicated she was not looking forward to another minute of their company.

'Where do you want to go, Hallie?' asked Sam in an apologetic voice.

Hallie felt awful and a night without sleep had done nothing to improve her disposition. 'St Francis Hospital,' she answered, glaring at Grant. 'And the sooner the better.'

The only sound in Tom Prescott's hospital room was the occasional beep that accompanied the hum of the computerized monitoring equipment. After meeting her in the corridor, Ruth Prescott had ushered Hallie into the room and then left. Hallie hadn't asked her where she was going and Ruth hadn't volunteered anything.

Since Casey's death there had been a strained truce

between the two women, a fact that made Hallie uncomfortable, for she was truly fond of her father-in-law, and she had tried her best to nourish a friendship with her mother-in-law. But she had known from the beginning that Ruth Prescott had not approved of her son's choice for a wife. Hallie suspected she lacked the social credentials that Ruth had deemed her future daughter-in-law should have had in order to be worthy of her only son. The right wife, of course, from the right family, would have then been able to provide an economic springboard for whatever career Casey would follow.

Secretly, Hallie had always thought Ruth was a snob, but because she was Casey's mother she had done her best to get along. Casey's father, however, never forgot his humble beginnings and did not share Ruth's social aspirations.

For most of the day, Hallie stayed close by, but Tom was too ill to realize she was there. It was early evening before he roused. Ruth had returned earlier in the day but, knowing how worried and exhausted she must be, Hallie urged her to go home for a while and rest.

Now Hallie stood awkwardly beside Tom's bed. She had been shocked to see how sick he was. Her concern was evident in her eyes. Just then Tom opened his eyes and did his best to smile. He reached for Hallie's hand, tugging her closer.

In those first few hours after his heart attack Tom Prescott decided that he would be truthful with Hallie about his son's death. He grieved deeply for Casey, but he could no longer let Hallie carry the burden of guilt alone. How he loved this girl, this daughter, for trying to protect them from the shocking truth about their wayward son.

'Come here, Hallie,' he whispered as she bent closer. Hallie nodded, unable to speak.

'Drugs . . . he was full of them. I know why you left Casey.' Tom turned his head away for a moment, then continued, 'It's okay, honey. I know you tried to protect Ruthie and me.' His breathing was labored now.

'Tom . . .' began Hallie, but he shook his head.

'It's okay . . . not your fault.'

Now the tears ran freely down Hallie's face. She felt strangely absolved of the guilt that had haunted her since the night of Casey's tragic death. Even though it made no sense, she had somehow felt responsible for what happened to Casey. If she had not left him, she had reasoned, then maybe he would still be alive.

Later, outside the doorway to Tom's room, Hallie paused and wiped away her tears with a tissue. She leaned her head back against the wall and breathed deeply, thankful for Tom's understanding. She wished that Ruth could be as understanding also, but in her heart she knew that forgiveness from Casey's mother would be a long time in coming, if it came at all.

The clock at the nurses' station said that it was six-thirty; she had another hour before Ruth would return. Visits with Tom were limited, so there was nothing she could do for the next half-hour. Deciding that she could use a cup of coffee, Hallie walked down the hall and took the elevator to the lower level of the hospital where the cafeteria was located. She paused as she stepped off the elevator, suddenly apprehensive. This time of the evening, the cafeteria was deserted except for a few people.

She cast an uneasy glance down the corridor to her left. This was not the first time she had felt like someone was watching her. Maybe that whole thing at the airport with Grant and Sam hadn't been so absurd after all.

She looked back over her shoulder as she rounded the corner and stumbled into a man dressed in navy blue scrubs. She raised her arms in an effort to try to keep her balance and cried out in protest just as he placed one hand over her mouth, then turned her around so that she couldn't see his face. Viciously, he twisted her arm behind her and pulled her out of sight into an abandoned hallway. Frantically her eyes darted left and right, searching for help, or an avenue for escape. But the area, which by day would have been teaming with administrative personnel, was deserted. Instinctively she raised her foot and stomped down as hard as she could on his foot. She heard him curse, but the pain she inflicted only resulted in him twisting her arm into a more painful position. She moaned, then tried to bite the hand that covered her mouth, but his grip was firm.

Hallie cringed at the warning that was delivered. 'Listen, bitch. We're not going to wait much longer and next time we won't ask. Just give us the tape and we'll leave you alone.'

Her blue eyes were wide with fright as he released her with a final wrenching twist on her arm before turning and running. She cried out in pain and sank to the floor. Almost immediately the doorway that led to the stairwell slammed open and in a blur Grant Keeler sprinted past her in the same direction her assailant had taken.

A few minutes later he returned, crouching down beside her. Hallie cradled her injured arm against her, powerless to move it.

'Here, let me see,' he said, reaching out and running his fingers over her skin carefully.

She winced at his touch.

'Can you stand?' he asked.

She nodded as he reached out to help her, then placed his arm protectively around her trembling shoulders.

'Let's go upstairs and have someone take a look at this.' This time Hallie didn't protest as he took charge of her care. 'Did you get a look at him?' she asked.

Grant shook his head. 'I was too late.'

Later, after the doctor had determined that her arm was not broken, but merely sprained and bruised, Grant insisted on taking her home and once more Hallie didn't protest.

'You must have been really scared when that man grabbed you,' he remarked later that night when they were seated at the kitchen table inside the Prescott house. Grant had fixed coffee, and Hallie was grateful for the comforting warmth of the cup that she cradled in her hands.

'I was terrified,' she admitted with a wry smile.

'Well, at least now you know that these people are serious. They believe you have something that is very critical to them, Hallie.'

'He asked me for a tape,' she said, her bewilderment evident. 'I didn't know what he was talking about. I don't have a tape. Could it be that he has the wrong person?'

A tape. At least now the existence of what he had been sent to find had been confirmed. Grant shook his head, his gray eyes firmly fixed on hers. 'No, Hallie. They believe they have the right person.' Then he explained where the tape had come from.

'But why would they think I have anything to do with it?' she asked.

'Because they think your husband took it from Jasmine the night she was murdered, and now he's dead. You're next in line.'

'That's absurd!'

Grant shrugged. 'Is it?'

Hallie looked up, startled. 'What do you mean?'

'We know now that a tape exists and it should be enough to put Edwin Mathews behind bars. We've always believed that Jasmine had evidence that we could use against Mathews, but a search of her apartment revealed nothing. We think your husband was the last person in that apartment before the police arrived. He must have known about the tape and taken it. Maybe he had even planned to blackmail Mathews himself. At any rate, he's dead and so now that leaves you.'

'So until you find that tape, these guys are going to keep after me,' concluded Hallie.

'Probably,' said Grant. 'Once we get back to Los Angeles I'll do my best to see that you have police protection. Here, I'm out of luck unless I make this trip to Memphis official, which I'd rather not do. So I think

I'll just stay around and keep an unofficial eye on things,' he offered with a lazy grin.

Hallie sat up straight, suddenly alarmed. 'Stay around where?' she asked.

'Here,' he clarified with a wave of his hand to indicate his surroundings.

'Oh, no, you're not,' Hallie replied quickly. 'This is my in-laws' house and just because they're not home doesn't mean you can stay . . . here.' Hallie waved her index finger in the air to add emphasis to her words, then pointed to the kitchen floor in case there was any doubt in Grant's mind.

'Well, I didn't mean *here* exactly,' Grant explained, chuckling. 'I meant outside. I'll watch the house from the car.'

'Oh.' Hallie digested this information. After a moment's hesitation she said, 'No, you can't do that either. It will upset the neighbors, especially the elderly couple next door. If they see a strange car parked in front of the house all night, they'll call the police.'

Grant stood. 'Well? What's it going to be, Hallie? Inside or out? Because I'm not leaving you alone tonight.'

Hallie rested her head on her crossed arms and wondered when life had gotten so complicated. She was exhausted and the last thing she wanted was to alert the neighbors. How could she begin to explain a strange man who was was watching the house to the Morrisons next door?

She raised her eyes and met Grant's compelling gaze. 'Inside,' she answered with a sigh. 'But for goodness' sake, pull the car in the driveway.'

* * *

183

After what seemed like hours Hallie climbed from her bed and tiptoed through the family room past the sofa where Grant lay. She had been so tired earlier, but when she had gone to bed sleep had eluded her, and her arm had begun to throb. In the dark kitchen she opened the refrigerator looking for the milk. From the cabinet she took a cup, filled it and opened the microwave door. The light glowed brightly while the hum of the oven filled the kitchen as she waited for the milk to heat.

'Aren't you going to offer me something to drink?' asked Grant from behind her.

Hallie jumped as his husky voice cut through the stillness. 'You scared me.'

'Sorry. Why aren't you in bed?'

She shrugged her shoulders, turning away from him at the sound of the ding of the microwave. 'I couldn't sleep.'

'Me neither.'

'I kept thinking about that man who grabbed me tonight,' she said. 'Want some?' she asked, indicating the milk.

'Got a beer in there?' Grant asked, nodding his head toward the refrigerator.

Hallie put the milk away and handed him a can. Together they leaned against the kitchen counter in silence. 'What kept you awake?' she asked, turning her head to study his profile.

Grant took a drink, then turned to her. 'You,' he answered and his gray eyes held hers.

Hallie shifted suddenly, pushing herself away from the counter. 'Look, maybe this isn't such a good idea, your staying here, I mean. Last night was . . .'

But she never finished the sentence. Without moving from his position against the counter Grant reached out and pulled Hallie against him. 'Honey, this is the best idea I've had all day,' he said, then he kissed her.

She was too tired to argue and too lonely to object. Instead she let herself enjoy the play of his mouth against hers, responding readily to his touch the way she had the night they first met. It was only when he pulled away that she remembered where she was.

'I must be out of my mind, acting this way.'

'Why?' he whispered in her ear. 'Do you think the neighbors are watching?'

'Probably,' she answered, giggling against his chest. 'I have to get some sleep,' she said. 'I'm going home tomorrow.' Then she looked up at him, remembering his role and the reason she had come face to face with him again. 'But you already know that, don't you? You probably even know which flight I'm taking.'

Grant nodded.

Hallie moaned and tried to pull away from him, but he held tight then led her to the sofa, pushing aside the blanket that had earlier covered him so she could sit beside him. 'Stay here for a while,' he said.

'I'm having a difficult time with this watchdog act of yours,' she admitted. 'There's more to it than finding a tape, isn't it? Am I a suspect in Jasmine's murder, also?'

Grant looked into her wide blue eyes and wanted to soothe her fears. He, more than anyone, wanted to believe that she had nothing to do with Jasmine's murder, but the truth was that she was indeed a prime suspect. Maybe the best one they had. 'Everyone who knew Jasmine is a suspect,' he explained.

'And I'm high on your list,' she surmised with a sigh.

'At the top,' he admitted, 'right along with Irwin Turner.'

'You have a lousy job, do you know that?' she asked more with resignation than malice.

Grant nodded and smiled. 'Just think of it as a good excuse for us to spend time together.'

Hallie leaned her head against his shoulder, and he reached out and pulled the blanket over her. 'Tell me what you thought about the night we first met,' she whispered after a few minutes.

Grant smoothed her hair gently. 'I felt your presence before I actually saw you,' he said thoughtfully. 'You were sending out some really strong signals. It was a damn good thing I was there to save you.'

Hallie straightened, looking up at him. With help of the moonlight that seeped into the room through the double set of French doors, she could see the strength that was there in his shadowed features. 'Save me? From what?'

'From that guy that was hot on your trail, and from making a mistake by going home with the wrong kind of guy.'

'You mean the kind of man who would have sex with me then never call me afterwards?' she asked with studied innocence.

Grant nodded seriously. 'Yeah, that kind of guy.'

'And who would never even ask me any questions? Not even my name?' Even in the darkness she could see him wince.

'Tactical error,' he admitted.

She leaned back against the cushions, then elbowed

him playfully. 'Boy, I was one lucky girl. Now tell me what you really thought.'

'I thought I was about to get lucky.'

'Grant!' Hallie scrambled away from him, suddenly uncomfortable with his teasing candor.

'Come back here,' he commanded.

'Only if you tell the truth,' she said.

He pulled her toward him and settled her in the curve of his arms. 'I thought you were too beautiful to be real,' he whispered.

'Really?' she asked, unaware of the wistfulness that accompanied her question.

'Really,' he replied in a husky voice, wishing he was anywhere else but here and desperately wanting to make love to her.

They sat in silence until Hallie fell asleep against his shoulder. Carefully, he eased from beside her, gathered her into his arms and carried her into the bedroom where he gently laid her on the bed. Then he leaned down and kissed her forehead and pulled the covers over her.

Back in the family room, he stretched out on the comfortable sofa and thought about the night they had made love. It was only a matter of time, he assured himself, until he would make love to her again.

The steady ring in Hallie's head wouldn't go away even though she turned on her side and pulled the pillow over her head. With a crash, reality hit and she realized that the ring was caused by the doorbell, and whoever was out there wasn't going away. Just about that time, she remembered Grant. Springing from bed, she stumbled and nearly fell headfirst into the closed door. Blindly she pushed her hair out of her eyes and grabbed the doorknob. She was halfway out the door when she ran back into the room and scooped up a pair of sweatpants from the floor to go with the T-shirt she had slept in. Frantically, she shoved one leg into the pants and was hopping down the hall and across the family room, trying to get the second leg on when she encountered Mrs Morrison, her in-laws' neighbor, and Grant in the entry.

'Ah, Mrs Prescott. Good morning. I trust you slept well,' Grant said quite formally.

Hallie looked from Grant to Mrs Morrison. 'Huh?'

'Mrs Morrison came over to investigate the strange car parked in the driveway all night,' Grant announced calmly.

The elderly woman's mouth was set in a tight straight line, and it was obvious that she disapproved of Hallie's appearance as well as what she imagined had gone on here in Tom and Ruth's house during the night.

Hallie looked down. In her haste to answer the door, she had neglected to finish putting on the sweatpants and it was nearly impossible to tell whether she had been caught in the act of putting them on, or taking them off. Her face flamed.

'Really, Mrs Morrison, this is not what you think. Grant, uh, Mr Keeler here was just . . .'

'Actually, I was in the middle of telling Mrs Morrison what we did last night.' Grant smiled politely.

'Oh!' Hallie looked past the neighbor at Grant, wondering how in the world he was going to convince the elderly woman that they didn't . . . they hadn't . . .

From over Mrs Morrison's head he winked at her.

'Well, then, Mr Keeler, please continue,' said Hallie with attempted dignity, 'with, uh, what we did.' Resolutely, she stuffed her other leg into her pants and pulled them up around her waist. Then straightened her shoulders as if everything was perfectly normal.

Velma Morrison continued to look suspiciously through her silver wire-rimmed glasses first at Hallie, then at Grant.

Well, thought Hallie, if Grant was looking to charm this old bird, he was clearly out of luck.

'You see,' said Grant in a husky voice as he stepped closer to the elderly woman as if what he was about to say was extremely confidential, 'I'm Mrs Prescott's personal bodyguard. Someone is stalking her and it's my job to protect her.' Then he paused and pretended to study the older woman before he continued. 'You know, you are still a very attractive woman, Mrs Morrison. If I were you, I'd be very careful. These types, like the ones that are after Mrs Prescott, they like women like you. Kind of a challenge. Know what I mean?' Grant flashed her a big smile.

For the first time since she had entered the house, Velma Morrison appeared flustered and she actually blushed. 'Well, really, Mr Keeler, I hardly think that a woman my age . . .'

'Oh, please, Mrs Morrison, for a woman like you with your charm, age has absolutely nothing to do with it. It's . . . hmm, how can I describe it? It's an aura that only women of a certain age have that seems to say – well, I can't really put it into words,' murmured Grant confidentially, then he leaned close to her ear and whispered, 'But it just drives men wild.'

Velma nodded in complete understanding, and Grant was certain he had just confirmed something that the woman had known about herself all along.

'You be careful now, Mrs Morrison, you hear?' Grant called a few minutes later to the departing woman. Hallie stood next to him, dumbfounded.

He had managed to charm the neighborhood no-nonsense busybody into thinking she was some kind of senior sex goddess. It could have been her imagination, but Hallie could swear that Mrs Morrison, who was at least seventy-five if she was a day, had a certain swing to her hips and a bounce to her walk that hadn't been there fifteen minutes earlier.

Hallie collapsed onto the marble floor of the entry. 'How do you do it?' she giggled. 'Poor Mr Morrison. I wonder if he will be able to keep up with her now?'

Grant grinned, then said with a shrug, 'All I did was tell her something she always wanted to hear.' He leaned down and offered both hands to Hallie.

She placed her hands in his and allowed him to pull her to her feet. 'Can you cook?' she asked.

'I'm a great cook.'

'Good,' said Hallie. 'You can fix us breakfast while I shower.'

'Why don't we go out for breakfast instead?' suggested Grant. 'That way we can shower together.' He smiled that teasing, heartstopping smile.

Hallie skipped down the hall, feeling better about herself than she had since the night she first met Grant. Now that she thought about it, she couldn't much blame Mrs Morrison for being taken in by Grant's charm. It was almost impossible to resist him.

'Breakfast out sounds great,' she called as she went into the bedroom.

'Hey, what about the shower?'

'Oh, that sounds great, too, but I'm already in enough hot water.' She giggled at her silly reply as she shut the door behind her.

'I'm going to stop by the hospital on my way to the airport,' announced Hallie at the restaurant as she poured maple syrup over her stack of pancakes. The waitress refilled their coffee.

'I'll be right behind you.' Grant had ordered the biggest breakfast on the menu.

'I don't think so. By the time you finish all that you won't be able to move,' Hallie said teasingly.

'Hey, being a personal bodyguard is hard work. Take today, for instance. I had to fend off Mrs Morrison. Now, not only do I have to go with you to the hospital, I have to go to the airport to make sure you get on the plane safely.'

'What about you? Aren't you taking the same flight?'

'No, I'll be on the next one. I want to hang around the airport to see if anyone comes looking for you. I'll see you later tonight. Meanwhile, if you need anything when you get back, call Sam.'

'But what about the man who was following me?'

'Oh, he'll be back, but now that he's warned you, he will probably wait to see what you do next. We'll just wait and watch.'

When they had finished their meal Grant drove

Hallie back to the Prescott home to collect her things. He carried them out and put them in the car. Hallie checked the house once more, making sure to leave everything as she found it.

Grant joined her in the kitchen. 'This is your last chance, you know.'

'For what?' she asked with a playful smile. 'Let's see, I've had my shower and I've had breakfast. What could I have missed?'

'This,' he answered and he took her by the shoulders and kissed her long and hard. At first, Hallie's knees nearly buckled, but she was caught up in the kiss, transported momentarily back to the first time he kissed her. Suddenly he released her and she wanted to protest that it was too soon, she wasn't ready to give up the pleasure of his warm lips against hers, or that warm languid feeling that was slowly washing over her. But before she could say anything he took her by the arm and propelled her out the door.

CHAPTER 14

Nick Hardister had disguised himself well, and because of that he had been able to hide out since Jasmine's death. He didn't kill Jasmine, but his fingerprints were there in her apartment and he knew the police wanted him for questioning.

He took great pride in his cleverness. One morning shortly after the murder he had looked in the cracked mirror of the dingy hotel where he had taken a room and was shocked at his reflection. He looked like one of those street people who roamed near the beach in Santa Monica.

That was when the idea first hit. Unless provoked, the police rarely did more than prod those people to move along. And, he reasoned, most of them wore enough clothes to make it difficult to discern a shape or size. With a few days' growth of beard, he could look fifteen, maybe twenty years older.

It was the perfect solution. He could move about freely without the risk of being recognized. Unless he grew careless, he would be relatively safe from the police.

Nick patted the envelope inside his shirt. This

information was his insurance. So valuable, in fact, that tomorrow he would exchange these papers for a big fat check. He had found a buyer. He did feel bad about Jasmine, though, but only when he thought about their good times together, before she had dumped him and moved on.

She had promised him she would have the money, but once more she had managed to cheat him. He had shown up at her apartment that night just like he said he would, but someone had been there before him. When he found her dead in the bedroom he knew he had better get the hell out of there before one of the neighbors saw him. After a quick search of the apartment he had found her secret file which contained a lot of nasty information on some very important Hollywood people. It hadn't been difficult to find. He had given Jasmine credit for being smarter.

The infamous file. When they had been together she had gone on and on about how she had hired a private investigator so that she could collect dirt on celebrities. He had asked her just how valuable this information really was. Almost anyone would pay big bucks to keep her quiet, she told him. But when he would ask her what was in the file, she would just laugh. It was her insurance, she told him. Just in case.

It wasn't until Nick read through it and made a few calls that he realized exactly what he had hold of. Now he was about to collect. This afternoon he was to meet with Deidre de Morea, one of the people on Jasmine's list.

As it turned out, Nick Hardister didn't have to wait to meet the two men that Deidre's husband sent to collect the file. They found him first, outside his hotel, long before the scheduled meeting, and did a damn good job of scaring the hell out of him. Not to mention that they almost killed him, stopping just short of the actual deed.

Nick groaned as one of the men kicked him again. 'Filth like you don't deserve to live, Hardister. Now we're going back and tell Ms de Morea that she will never ever hear from you again.'

The two men had made it clear that they would be back to finish him off if he ever tried anything like this again. But Nick had never put all his eggs in one basket. Jasmine's file had been taken from him and destroyed, but he was armed with other potentially profitable goods. He still had the pictures of her and Prescott.

All during the flight back to California, Hallie kept looking behind her, wondering if the man who had attacked her in Memphis the day before had followed her back to California, but she never saw him. Since the incident in the hospital her awareness of her personal safety was heightened, and as she made her way through the airport parking lot toward her car she was careful, walking briskly and purposefully, keys in hand, looking from side to side. When she was seated safely in her car with the doors locked, she breathed a sigh of relief.

That evening she climbed the stairs to her apartment slowly. It felt good to be back, she thought, as she put her bag down in the hallway then unlocked the door. She was never sure if she sensed something was wrong before she saw it, or if it all hit her at once. She stood as if paralyzed as the door swung open to reveal the destruction before her.

Every piece of furniture had been overturned, every drawer pulled out and its contents spilled onto the floor. Multi-colored glass shards glittered from every corner like candy sprinkles on a cake. When she was able to move she rushed forward a few steps, then faltered, backing toward the door. In the hall she turned and ran to the apartment next to hers. She knocked frantically, the sound echoing through the empty hallway.

Cautiously, Nora Johnson opened her door a few inches. 'Oh, Hallie, it's you. What's wrong?' she asked when she saw the distress on Hallie's face.

'I . . . someone's broken into my apartment. I have to call the police.' Hallie's chin quivered and her voice shook as she looked back toward the open door to her apartment. All her things were destroyed. Someone had had their hands on everything she owned.

Mrs Johnson gestured for Hallie to follow her. When she reached the phone she dialed, then held the receiver out to Hallie. With shaking hands Hallie held the receiver to her ear. She was about to tell the officer on the other end of the line what had happened when she thought of Sam Harris. Could this have anything to do with the men who had followed her? 'I need to talk to Sam Harris, please.'

'Please hold.'

'Detective Harris.'

'Sam, this is Hallie Prescott,' she said in a rush.

'Hallie? Are you okay?' Sam sat up straighter. He had

left Grant in Memphis to keep tabs on Hallie, and he assumed that Grant would not be far away.

'Yes. No. Someone broke into my apartment.'

'I'll be right there.' Sam dispatched a car to the address Hallie had given him, then he called Grant's apartment and left a message when there was no answer. In his gut, Sam knew this was no ordinary burglary. This had something to do with Mathews.

When he arrived at the apartment fifteen minutes later, he was sure he was right. Someone had done a thorough search. But did they find what they were looking for?

Hallie had sworn she had no idea why she was being followed. Was that true? Or was she doing a damn good job of acting? Her husband could have gotten the tape from Jasmine and she could have found it and decided to use it to her advantage. Mathews would pay dearly for that tape. And Hallie Prescott was almost out of money. Sam shook his head and went next door to find her.

He nodded to Mrs Johnson, then took Hallie's arm and led her out into the hall. In a daze she followed him. Sam dropped his hand from her arm then leaned back against the wall, stretching as he did so. He looked tired. 'Hallie, this is a dangerous situation. Whoever was in your apartment was looking for something. This wasn't a routine break-in. But you know that, don't you? I don't know if they got what they were looking for, but if they didn't, they'll be back. Next time, for you.'

Hallie's blue eyes widened as she listened to him. Her hair had slipped from its ribbon and much of it hung loose and curled around her face. When she spoke, she tried her best to sound defiant, but instead she only sounded tired. 'I don't have what they're looking for, Sam.'

She had been through so much in the past few months. Her life, which she had thought was wonderful when she and Casey had moved to California, had gone down the toilet. Casey was gone. Why couldn't everyone leave her alone so she could get on with putting her life back together?

'We'll have to find you a place to stay,' said Sam. 'I'll take care of it.'

'No,' replied Hallie. 'I can stay with a friend. I . . . I'll call her to come and get me.'

Sam was about to protest, concerned about her safety, when Grant appeared at the top of the stairs. His dark hair was slightly ruffled as if he had just run his hands through it. She cursed inwardly when her heart skipped a beat at the sight of him. She had been determined from their first night together to forget him, but she hadn't been able to put him out of her mind. It was, if anything, worse now that she had seen him again. And that night when she had been accosted at the hospital he had been so gentle.

'Don't bother. You can stay with me,' he said in a tone that was clearly a command.

Surprise registered on Hallie's face as well as Sam's.

'I got your message,' Grant said as he walked toward Sam, passing Hallie without speaking. Instead his eyes locked with hers, daring her to disagree with him.

She fully intended to, then abruptly changed her mind. She was too tired to argue. Grant took her arm and guided her back toward her apartment. When he reached the doorway he let out a low whistle. 'Thorough, weren't they? Is anything missing?'

Hallie bit her lip as she surveyed her only possessions, broken and torn. 'I don't know,' she whispered. 'How can I tell?'

Suddenly a look of panic appeared on her face. 'My portfolio! I've got to find it!' Breaking away from Grant, she ran through the apartment to a large closet. There, she began to pull out all the drawers that were built into the wall for storage.

'Just tell me what we're looking for and I'll help you,' offered Grant.

'It's a leather portfolio full of drawings, things I've done for class.'

'Is this what you're looking for, ma'am?' A young policeman in uniform held out the leather case.

'Oh, yes, thank you,' replied Hallie, relieved that it had not been damaged.

Grant turned toward her and his shoulders seemed to fill the space around her. He put his arm around her in a protective gesture. 'How long will your men be here?' he asked Sam.

'It'll take us a while,' Sam replied as he surveyed the apartment.

'Hallie will be at my place, if you need her.'

In the hallway Hallie, still clutching her portfolio, paused. 'Wait. I have to check my mailbox.'

Grant held out his hand. 'Give me your key. I'll do it.'

Hallie reached into her purse and handed over her key with a shaky smile. 'Snooping?' she asked.

'Can't help it,' replied Grant with a wry smile as he turned away. With her key he unlocked the brass mailbox and withdrew its contents, flipping through the assorted envelopes and junk mail. But it was a small brown window envelope that was addressed to Casey Prescott that held his interest. The return address was a Los Angeles post-office box number and the bottom-left corner was covered by a yellow label indicating that it had been forwarded from Casey's address to Hallie's. Quickly, he glanced down the hallway. Hallie's back was turned toward him as she spoke with a uniformed officer. With a practiced touch Grant ran his thumb over the envelope then slipped it inside his jacket.

A look of speculation appeared on Sam's face as he watched Grant and Hallie leave the building. It was that gut instinct of his again. He would bet his entire paycheck that the other night in Memphis was not the first time those two had met.

CHAPTER 15

Grant put Hallie's bag along with the portfolio in the back seat of the car, then slid behind the wheel and turned the key in the ignition. 'Are you okay?' he asked as he pulled away from the curb.

'Just lovely,' she answered sarcastically, her gaze fixed somewhere on the street ahead. 'My husband is dead, my mother-in-law barely speaks to me, someone has trashed my apartment and everything I own and, according to you, I'm being followed by a couple of mobsters right out of a B movie. Everything is wonderful, Grant. Just wonderful,' she finished bitterly.

Grant laughed loudly at her summary and reached over to pull her against him. When she was nestled in the circle of his arm, he kissed the top of her head. 'Things could get worse,' he said jovially.

Hallie straightened and shot him a look that said they'd better not.

At the front door to his furnished apartment, Hallie waited while Grant went ahead of her to turn on the lights. 'It's temporary,' he said with a wave of his hand toward the beige contemporary furniture, 'but the decor does make a statement.' She paused, suddenly reminded of the night they made love. He had gone into the room ahead of her then, as if to make sure all was ready.

Hallie made her way toward the sofa and stretched out, resting her head against the sofa cushions. Grant set her bag near the sofa and her portfolio on the coffee table.

'So,' he said with a smile as he pointed toward the leather case, 'are you going to show me what you have in here?'

Hallie blushed, suddenly self-conscious. 'It's just some costume designs. I'm taking a couple of classes at the university.'

Grant nodded, and waved his hand for her to open the case.

Hallie did, hesitantly turning the clear acetate pages and offering a brief explanation of each drawing and the time period it represented.

After she came to the end of the class projects she reached over and began to zip up the case, but Grant stopped her.

'What are these?' he asked, pointing to several more acetate pages at the back.

'Nothing,' she answered quickly. 'Just some dresses. My designs,' she mumbled.

'Yours? Can I see them?'

'They're not that good,' she explained, 'just things I've done on my own.'

'Would you show them to me?' His eyes met hers, sincere and steady.

Hallie hesitated. These were things she had been working on since she started classes, and she had never shown them to anyone. Not even Casey. She had wanted to, but something held her back. Down deep, she was afraid he would make fun of her or belittle her talent. The few times she had tried to show him drawings from her class assignments, he had barely spared them a glance. At best she had gotten the equivalent of 'that's nice', like a token pat on the head.

His lack of appreciation for her work had hurt. Perhaps she should have expected it, but because she had shared an interest in his writing, and had helped whenever he asked, she thought he should reciprocate.

Sensing her reluctance, Grant said, 'I'd really like to see them.'

Encouraged, Hallie smiled shyly and began to turn the pages, briefly explaining what she had rendered. When she had finished, he complimented her on her work. Hallie, pleased at his words, closed the portfolio, then set the case on the floor next to the sofa.

'Why didn't you continue with classes?' asked Grant.

Hallie sighed. How could she explain that her failed marriage had robbed her of all her energy and ambition. It sounded too much like she had taken the easy way out.

'I planned to, but it didn't work out. There were the obvious complications. School seemed suddenly insignificant. Actually, the classes were just something to do in the beginning, to fill the time and hopefully to make friends. Casey was working long hours and I was alone with nothing to do. I didn't know anyone here. But then I found that I really enjoyed having a place to go where people had the same interests.'

After a few moments she asked with a half-smile,

'Where do you live when you're not following me?'

Grant had just returned from the small galley kitchen with two glasses of wine. She took one from his outstretched hand and watched him over the rim while he seated himself next to her.

'In Virginia, just outside Washington DC. I have an apartment there that looks a lot like this one.' He leaned forward to set his glass on the table in front of them. Their eyes met. He thought Hallie looked exhausted, but there were some questions he had to ask her. Now, while her guard was down.

'Tell me about your marriage.'

Hallie frowned. She hadn't expected this. She shrugged, knowing that sooner or later she would have to answer him. 'It was . . . okay. There's nothing to tell, really. Casey and I were married almost four years.'

'Marriages are not okay,' he remarked absently as if he was lost in his own thoughts. 'They are either wonderful, or boring, or suffocating, but not "okay".'

'How would you know?' Hallie asked sharply.

'Because mine was wonderful,' he answered in a husky voice.

'Oh.' Hallie was silent for a moment as a small shock shot through her. She waited to see if he would elaborate and when he didn't she said, 'I . . . I didn't know you were married.' She had not even considered that possibility. 'We . . . uh, we didn't talk much that night,' she added lamely, referring to their one night together.

'Would it have made a difference?' he asked.

It was on the tip of her tongue to say 'of course'. What kind of a woman went to bed with a married man? Then she thought about that night, and how much she had needed him. She answered him truthfully in a hushed voice, 'No.'

That night it wouldn't have made a difference. She would have put all her principles, all her values, and all moral judgements aside. She had been desperate to know that she was still desirable, that she was alive, that she could feel something other than guilt and shame. Nothing would have mattered to her then. But tonight it would.

'I'm not married now and I haven't been for quite a while,' he volunteered, reaching for his wine and shifting to a more comfortable position.

'Divorced?' she asked quietly, wanting a clarification of his status.

'I'm no longer married,' Grant repeated firmly as if that was his final word on the subject. 'What about you and Casey? What kind of relationship did you have?'

Hallie had wanted to ask him more about his marriage, but her opportunity had passed. She looked toward the ceiling as if searching for answers. 'In the beginning, things were simple. I worked and Casey wrote. It was the pattern of our life. There were no highs and lows. I was always tired and he was always busy.'

'What about children? Did you want a family?' Grant asked.

Hallie nodded, then looked away, unable to meet his steady gaze. How she had longed for a baby! During their marriage, they had discussed the subject of children many times. At least Hallie had discussed it many times. Casey had always used their financial situation as his excuse not to start a family. 'Not until I'm able to support a family,' he had said in the beginning.

'But you can take a teaching job,' Hallie had argued.

'My writing is too important right now, Hallie. We'll discuss this later when the time is right. We have plenty of time before taking on that kind of responsibility. I'm afraid you aren't really prepared for that kind of commitment. I know I'm not.'

Hallie had brought up the subject again right after he had sold *Journey*. This time Casey wouldn't even consider it, saying that the sale of his book was his big break. He was just beginning his career and he wanted to be free to travel and enjoy his celebrity.

After that Hallie had avoided the subject entirely. How could they have even talked about babies when they had rarely made love?

Instinctively she had known that their relationship was in jeopardy. Too often people in an unstable relationship mistakenly believe that a baby can solidify things between them. The results are usually just the opposite, and in the end it is the child that suffers. She had never again broached the subject while she and Casey were together. Now she was a widow and having a child was not an option any longer. What a crooked path her life had followed.

Still, at unexpected times, in the mall or in the grocery, the sight of a mother and baby brought pain to her heart, and once more she would feel a desperate longing to experience that kind of love and caring. But somewhere deep inside, she had known that it would have been a terrible and selfish mistake to have brought a baby into their marriage.

'We had talked about a family,' she admitted, bringing her eyes back to his. The small bitter laugh that escaped her lips revealed so much more than her words. 'Then things became . . . complicated.'

'When Casey became a celebrity? When you moved to Los Angeles? When he began the affair with Jasmine Turner?' he prodded.

'Does the whole world know my husband was cheating on me, or just the LA police department and the FBI?' Her pain was evident.

Grant's eyes narrowed. 'It was in all the newspapers. Irwin Turner is a big name, a legend in Hollywood. It only stands to reason the media would sensationalize their divorce and then the murder of his wife. Everyone knew she was seeing Casey, Hallie. His fingerprints were all over her apartment. And then there was Casey's death. For some reason, your name was kept out of that report. I only found out about you by accident.'

'Too bad,' she said with attempted sarcasm.

Grant ignored her. 'Tell me about Casey and Jasmine,' he prompted again.

Agitated, Hallie stood and began to pace. Her heartbeat accelerated.

'Sit down,' Grant commanded quietly. 'I didn't mean to upset you.'

'The hell you didn't.' She hurled the accusation back at him. 'Everything you've done since I first saw you has upset me. Well, you're not doing it again – not ever. The subject of my husband's relationship with Jasmine Turner is closed.' Hallie turned away.

Grant wondered if that affair was the reason that Hallie had left the club with him that night, and when he voiced that thought Hallie, with her back to him, replied, 'There were a lot of reasons for that night, Grant. None of which I want to discuss. Neither of us had a spouse that would be hurt by what we did that night. In your own words you were "not married" at the time and I was very recently widowed.'

Hallie took a deep breath. 'Please, Grant, don't ever bring up my husband's relationship with Jasmine Turner again,' she warned him.

Grant remained calm as he purposely continued to provoke her. Now that he was involved in this case, he was determined to get the evidence he needed. He owed that much to Libby. 'How long had the affair been going on before you found out about it?'

Hallie's breathing was rapid now. 'Didn't you hear me? I refuse to talk about it!' She turned to face him, her hands clenched at her sides. Suddenly tears formed in her vivid blue eyes, then rolled from the corners onto her flushed cheeks.

Grant went to her. 'Hallie, Hallie, I didn't mean to hurt you,' he whispered as he reached for her arms, but she jerked away from his touch.

'Leave me alone,' she said. 'It was a mistake to come here in the first place. You made me believe you were concerned for me, but you're not. All you want is to know how badly I got screwed over by my husband.' Hallie reached for her purse and hurried toward the front door.

Just as she reached it Grant's hand shot out and held the door, preventing her from leaving. 'Don't, Hallie.

You can't go home tonight. Please, stay here with me.'
His voice was low now and soothing. His hands moved
from the door to Hallie's shoulders as he gently turned
her toward him, pulling her back into the room.

Traces of tears lingered on her cheeks. With her
fingertips she attempted to brush them away. She
raised her blue eyes to his, imploring him not to hurt
her, silently begging him to let her trust in him.

Grant felt his gut twist. No woman had looked at him
in just that way since Libby. It struck a cord of
protectiveness that he thought had died right along
with Libby.

With one hand he pulled Hallie toward the apartment's only bedroom, then folded back the coverlet on
the bed. He swallowed, knowing that this was what he
should do, but wanting instead to pull her close, to feel
her body pressed against his. At this moment all he
wanted was to make love to her like he had that night
they met.

With great effort Grant said, 'You can sleep here. I'll
take the couch.' He almost winced at the gratitude he
saw in her tired eyes as he pulled the door closed behind
him.

In the kitchen he refilled his wine glass. What was it
about this woman that touched him so? Why did he feel
so protective of her? And why did he desperately need
to know the secrets of her marriage? It was more than
the investigation, that he knew. What had happened
that was so painful for her to remember? Was her loss
that great? Had she loved her husband more than she
admitted?

From the linen closet in the hall he took a blanket,

then stretched out on the sofa, pulling the blanket over him. In the darkness he remembered his grief after Libby's senseless death and the death of their unborn child. At first it had been a white-hot rage, then a pain that would not be relieved. Finally, it was replaced by a deep and lingering sadness. But through it all he remembered Libby, her smile, the happiness that always seemed to radiate from her, the joy she brought to his life.

His image of her was not as sharp and clear now as it had once been, but he had been told it would be like that after a while. He supposed it was a part of healing.

But Hallie's pain was different somehow. He could see it in her eyes whenever he questioned her about her husband. It was more than the pain of losing someone. Maybe it was the pain of being betrayed by someone she trusted.

Grant finished his wine and hoped he could sleep, but just knowing Hallie was in the next room was enough to keep him awake. He couldn't help but think about making love to her. Given the time they had been together, there should have been an easy intimacy between them by now, but instead it was as if they were complete strangers. Gone was the camaraderie of the previous night. The secrets between them had become a barrier.

Hallie blinked first at the sound of the phone ringing, then at the sunlight that invaded the bedroom. Automatically she reached out and answered it.

'Hallie? It's Sam. I need to to talk to Grant.'

Hallie made a groaning sound into the phone and

slowly sat up and swung her feet to the floor. Her reflection in the mirror across the room told her she was decent – barely. The T-shirt she was wearing just barely covered her panties. It would have to do, she thought, as she ran her hands through the tousled copper curls that framed her sleepy face. With a yawn she padded barefoot into the living room.

Grant was still asleep. So many times she had wondered how it would be to wake up beside him, and cursed herself for not being brave enough that first night to stay the entire night with him to find out what the morning would have brought. And that night at the motel in Memphis sure didn't count.

Carefully she perched next to him on the edge of the sofa, intending only to study his relaxed, unguarded face closer before she woke him. Without meaning to she raised her hand to touch him, but before she could do more than caress his cheek a hand shot out, cupping her bottom. With very little effort he pulled her toward him with one arm while the other reached up and pulled her head down so that her lips met his.

It was the morning kiss of lovers who remembered the uneasiness of the night before and were willing to forgive. Hallie returned his kiss, enjoying the lazy exploration of his tongue. Their scents mingled, hers young and fresh, his unmistakably masculine. Sometime during their prolonged kiss Grant's other hand had moved from her neck down her back and up underneath her T-shirt. She groaned when he turned the hand that cupped her breast and ran his knuckles over her nipple.

'This is the way I like to start the day,' he whispered against her lips, his breath mingling with hers.

A wave of pleasure surged through her. 'Oh my God,' she said, suddenly pulling away from him. 'Sam . . . I forgot! Sam is on the phone for you.'

With a groan Grant ran his hand over the lower half of his face. 'Sam's timing stinks,' he said, grinning, then kissed Hallie lightly. With one hand he pushed her toward the edge of the sofa so he could sit up. 'We can finish this later.'

Hallie went to the bedroom to hang up the receiver just as Grant picked up the phone in the kitchen. 'Sam?' he said, wondering if he was still there after all this time.

Sam laughed. 'Don't bother to explain what took so long. Something interesting turned up. It appears that Hallie's apartment had another visitor. Can you and Hallie meet me at the apartment in an hour?'

Grant sighed inwardly as he watched Hallie stretch to reach the coffee cups in the cabinet. The enticing view he had when her T-shirt rode up to reveal her shapely bottom made him wish he could ignore Sam's request. 'We'll be there,' he promised reluctantly. It was a shame business had to intrude on a morning that held such promise.

If anything, Hallie's apartment looked worse in the harsh glare of day. She shivered as she followed Sam and Grant through each room. It was impossible to tell if anything was missing.

'Okay,' said Sam, thinking out loud as he tugged at his ear. 'We are assuming the first visitor to take a tour through here had to be from Edwin Mathews. Definitely looking for something that Hallie has, or that they think she has. The second intruder was an amateur by comparison.'

'How can you tell?' asked Hallie, looking over the trashed apartment.

'We had a team watching the place from outside,' answered Sam, 'but the guy got away from them.'

'But I don't have anything. What could they possibly want?' asked Hallie 'Money? I keep some cash for emergencies in the kitchen. I forgot all about it.'

Sam groaned. 'Couldn't you think of a better hiding place than that?' he asked as she rushed toward the cabinet over the refrigerator.

'Look, it's still here,' she said in amazement.

'I think they're all looking for the same thing, Hallie,' said Sam.

'Maybe not,' replied Grant.

At a signal from Grant, Sam followed him outside. 'Let's get this checked out,' said Grant as he handed over the envelope he had removed from Hallie's mailbox the night before. 'See what you can find out.'

Dana came over later after Hallie had called her to tell her about the break-in. And in spite of Dana's presence, it was difficult to keep her emotions in check as she sifted through her things, but she kept at it, knowing that the sooner she sorted through her possessions, the better off she would be.

'There are so many things that will have to be replaced,' Hallie observed. After Dana had arrived, Hallie had wandered from one thing to another, not knowing what to do. Dana, realizing that Hallie was not thinking clearly, had organized the cleanup effort.

'What is it they want?' she asked Hallie as she swept the splintered china from the kitchen floor.

'I don't know, Dana. I just don't know. I've racked my brain, trying to remember if Casey had anything that I might have picked up by mistake, but I haven't come up with anything. It has to be a mistake. I am worried though.' She wished that she could tell Dana the whole truth, that she knew now why her apartment had been destroyed, but Grant had sworn her to secrecy about the tape.

Dana leaned on the broom and faced Hallie. 'Geez, Hallie, if someone had done this to my place, I'd be worried sick. Why don't you stay with me for a while?'

'I can't. I can't risk endangering you. I'm being followed. I didn't realize it when I left for Memphis to see my father-in-law, but I've felt strange several times, as if someone was watching me.'

'Do you still think you're being watched?'

Hallie looked up from the papers she was sorting. 'I'm not sure.' Once more she avoided confiding in Dana about the attack at the hospital. 'There have been several times in the car when I was sure I was being followed. I would see the same car in my rear-view mirror.'

'You shouldn't be here alone tonight,' said Dana.

'Sam is going to have a patrol car outside. I'll be okay.'

'Have you told your aunt about this?' With a sweep of her hand Dana indicated the trashed apartment.

'No, it would only worry her. She would want me to come home immediately, or she would insist on coming out here to stay with me, and I'm just not ready for that. Besides . . .' she paused as her voice cracked '. . . the police are looking for Jasmine Turner's murderer. Because of Casey, they think I have a motive. Jealousy. A crime of passion.'

'That's absurd!'

'I know, Dana, but until I have all this sordid mess behind me, I can't go home to Mississippi, no matter how much I want to.'

With the kitchen floor cleared, Dana went into the living room to help Hallie. She grabbed a box, picking up whatever could be salvaged in one piece and carried it over to the kitchen counter.

It was then that Dana noticed the picture of Hallie and Casey. She shook her head, but refrained from expressing her thoughts out loud. Casey was a good-looking man, there was no doubt about that, but no woman in her right mind should trust someone like him. Of course, Hallie hadn't had the benefit of growing up in LA, where hoards of predators like Casey roamed the streets. Ambitious and ruthless, with glistening smiles and hard, golden bodies. In search of their moment in the sun. Men who discarded women with the same ease they discarded their underwear.

She picked up the white ceramic frame that held the photo, studying it closely, then shook her head in a sympathetic gesture. With both hands, she cradled the frame, then carefully set it down on the counter. It was then that her fingers brushed something strange. Turning the frame over, she saw that it was a key that had been taped to the back.

'Hallie, do you know what this is for?' she asked.

Hallie turned. 'What is it?'

'A key – taped to the back of your wedding picture.' Dana pulled the key loose and held it up for closer inspection. 'It looks like a key to a safe-deposit box.'

Hallie shrugged, too exhausted to care. 'Just put it in that little box of junk on the counter. I'll sort though that stuff tomorrow.'

It was dark outside when Dana left. The apartment was at least livable. Dana had offered to stay longer, but Hallie had insisted that she wanted to be alone, and with the police right outside, nothing could happen to her.

It wasn't until later, when Hallie remembered the photo of her and Casey taken on their wedding day, that she began to cry in earnest. Tears blurred her vision as she hugged the picture against her heart. *How could you hurt me like you did, Casey? We deserved better. I deserved a husband who cared about me and you deserve to be alive. How did we get so screwed up?*

Hallie didn't hear Grant as he knocked, then unlocked the door to her apartment. He was barely inside when he saw her sitting in the middle of the living-room floor, a picture frame resting in her lap. Great heaving sobs rocked her body.

His first impulse was to go to her, to ease her through this, but he recognized the pain. It was the same pain that had caused him to weep bitterly over Libby's death. To him, it came late in the healing process, unexpectedly stealing over him long after he was sure he was once more in control of his grief. His had been the cry of anger, an unreasonable anger, directed first at God for taking his wife and child away, then at Libby for leaving him alone.

Grant had no way of knowing how great Hallie's grief was, that added to her anger was the pain of betrayal. It was something that each person had to face alone. He turned, closing the door silently behind him as he left the apartment. He knew with certainty this was not a time that could be shared.

Hallie spent most of the next morning cleaning what she had left from the night before. She felt weak and vulnerable, and when the phone rang she jumped.

'I'm coming over,' Dana announced.

'Don't you have class today?' asked Hallie.

'Yeah, but I'm going to skip it. I thought I'd help you, then we can go to lunch. This afternoon we can shop for whatever you need.'

A few hours later, Hallie had to admit she was beginning to feel better. With Dana's help she had made a list of the things she needed immediately. The apartment was shaping up, and Hallie had been grateful to see an unmarked police car parked across the street.

When they were seated at the outdoor patio at Florentina's, Dana asked, 'How do you distinguish the good guys from the bad guys?'

Hallie laughed. 'It isn't easy, but I think the good guys just sit and watch for the bad guys to do something.'

Dana considered her answer for a moment, then said, 'Don't look now, but I think that sometimes the bad guys just sit and watch, too.'

Immediately, Hallie swiveled in her chair and looked behind her.

'I told you not to look!' hissed Dana.

'Which guys?' asked Hallie, leaning forward.

Just then the waiter arrived with their lunch. When he had left, Dana described the location of two men who were seated several tables away.

'Umm. I don't know. The faces keep changing.' When the men in question were joined by a woman a short while later, Dana and Hallie concluded that they had made a mistake.

'This business makes you paranoid, doesn't it?' observed Dana after they left the restaurant. 'Who do you think killed Jasmine?'

Hallie shrugged. 'I don't know. It wasn't Casey. I know that for certain. He could never abide physical violence. Oh, he could write about it, but it wasn't part of his character.'

'My father thinks it may have been one of Jasmine's ex-boyfriends. There were quite a few of them, you know. Everyone knew about her affairs, it seemed, except for poor Irwin.'

'But why would they want to kill her?' asked Hallie.

'For the same motive the police believe you have – jealousy.'

They made three stops that afternoon before Dana announced that she thought they were being followed.

'You are worse than I am,' teased Hallie.

'Yeah? Well, I haven't had much experience, but I could swear the two men following us are the same ones from the restaurant.'

'Did they ditch the woman?' asked Hallie with a grin. 'They probably stuck her with the lunch tab.'

'See that black Lexus behind us? That's the car.'

Hallie looked over her shoulder. Dana was right, It was the two men from the restaurant, but so far, nothing had happened. 'They just want me to know they're there,' said Hallie.

'You sound so calm! You, we, should be screaming our heads off for the police.'

'But they haven't done anything.' Yet, thought Hallie, knowing that these men were only biding their time. 'Besides, I'm sure the police are close by,' she said with more confidence than she was feeling.

When they pulled into the parking lot at Fowler's, Hallie and Dana hurried from the car into the store. Inside they hurried down the aisles, picking up the items that were on their list.

'Oops!' exclaimed Hallie as she pushed their cart around the end of an aisle. 'They're here! In the store.'

'I know how to keep them from following us,' said Dana quickly. 'Let's head on over to Electronics.'

'What good will that do?' asked Hallie.

'You'll see.'

When they reached the department that carried televisions, stereos, CD players and cameras, Dana went down one aisle and directed Hallie to go in a different direction. After a few minutes Dana rejoined Hallie. 'Are you ready to check out?'

Hallie nodded. When she had paid for her purchases they walked toward the exit. The two men were close behind them.

'Now just act normal,' Dana instructed, 'and when we get out the door get to the car as fast as you can.'

Hallie and Dana had just passed through the exit

door when a loud shrieking alarm went off right behind them. Hallie turned in time to see that the two men who had been following them had been prevented from leaving the premises by the store's security guards.

'Run!' ordered Dana.

When they were safely inside the car, Dana pulled out of the crowded parking lot into the busy street. At the corner Hallie ventured a look back, but saw no signs that the two men had followed.

She slid down in the seat and closed her eyes. 'It's okay. You can slow down.'

'But I was just getting good at this cloak-and-dagger stuff,' said Dana, giggling.

'Exactly what did you do back there? And what caused that alarm to go off like that?' asked Hallie.

'Umm . . . did I ever tell you about the time I got caught shoplifting?' asked Dana, grinning.

'You?'

'Sad,' said Dana, 'but true. I was in junior high school. Only I didn't steal anything, but one of my friends did, and I was with her. Of course, I had no idea what she had done, but it didn't matter. The security people came after us. Anyway, that's what gave me the idea. I picked up a couple of small items while we were in the electronics department, then I found a couple of guys and told them I wanted to play a joke on my friends. I gave them twenty dollars to slip the items in the coat pockets of the men who were following us. So when they went to leave the store – bingo! The alarms would go off.'

'That was a brilliant strategy.'

'Yeah,' agreed Dana.

'You know,' observed Hallie, 'I don't think I'm the kind of friend you ought to be hanging out with.'

Dana giggled with sheer relief. Now it seemed funny. A few minutes ago she had been terrified at the prospect of being accosted by the two men.

'This doesn't have anything to do with Jasmine's murder, does it?'

Hallie sighed. Promise or no promise, she was going to tell Dana the truth. She deserved to know, and if Grant didn't like it, well, that was just too bad.

'Yes, it does,' Hallie answered.

The clock on the stove said it was midnight when Grant pushed his chair away from the table and began stacking the files he had gathered over the past two days. He stood, stretching. On impulse, Grant reached for the phone and dialed Sam's number. Sam's breathing sounded labored when he finally answered.

'Sam, did you ever ask –?' began Grant hurriedly.

'Can I call you back?' asked Sam in a choked voice.

'Why?' asked Grant with a sly grin as he heard a woman's voice in the background.

'Because I can't talk right now.' Sam's whisper was laced with embarrassment.

'This is important,' Grant stated with mock seriousness.

'So is this, Grant, and just so you'll know, I do have a life aside from the department, so go away.'

Grant laughed out loud as he hung up the phone. His questions could wait until tomorrow, but he was satisfied that he had gotten even with Sam for interrupting him and Hallie the other morning.

Over and over he had reviewed the facts of Jasmine Turner's murder and the missing pieces nagged at him. Who really murdered Jasmine? All the suspects seemed to have a motive. Certainly Nick Hardister did, and Casey Prescott and Irwin Turner. But the thought that bothered him most was that Hallie perhaps had the strongest motive. She was, after all, the wronged wife. A woman scorned.

Hallie invaded his thoughts frequently, sometimes getting in the way of his work. Grant had not seen her since the night he had accidently found her crying in her apartment. That incident had triggered some feelings he hadn't been able to deal with. Without a doubt he wanted to make love to her, but he wasn't ready to get emotionally involved with anyone. Especially Hallie.

With Libby, he had laid bare his heart and soul and look what it got him. He had lost her and their baby and, for a while, he was certain that he was going to lose his sanity. He had been positive that he could never again care for another woman until Hallie came along. He wasn't sure he had ever wanted to give that much of himself to anyone. But with Libby, it had been so easy. And now, as he stretched out on the bed and waited for sleep to come on, it seemed as if it had been a lifetime ago.

Grant inhaled raggedly, forcing himself to end his reverie. He never wanted to care that much about anyone again – especially not about Hallie Prescott. Besides, there was no harmony between them, not like there had been with Libby.

With Hallie there was only friction. And fireworks.

CHAPTER 16

'It's just a hunch,' Grant said the following morning, grimacing as he swallowed bitter black coffee from a plastic cup. 'But it's worth checking it out.'

'There's no record in the file of a check of the victim's or any of the suspects' phone calls. I'll take care of it,' said Sam as he turned and walked back toward his desk.

Grant finished the last of the bitter liquid, then wished he hadn't. 'Sam, wait just a minute. Make sure to check Hallie's phone calls, too.'

'What are you looking for?'

'I'm not looking for anything. Let's just hope we don't accidently find something we wish we hadn't.'

'What's the matter?' teased Sam. 'What happened to "round 'em up, bring 'em in" Special Agent Grant Keeler, FBI tough guy?'

'Cut it out,' he replied with a grin. 'You know what I mean.'

'Yeah,' replied Sam. On paper Hallie might be a logical suspect, but neither he nor Grant believed that she was capable of committing murder. Besides, he liked Hallie and he thought that she was just what Grant needed in his life.

The next evening Grant was waiting there at the small neighborhood café when Hallie arrived. 'Have you been getting any sleep?' he asked after they were seated in the corner booth. But he already knew the answer. In spite of the carefully applied makeup he could see the dark smudges under her eyes. He reached for her hand. 'You're worried that there will be another break-in.'

Hallie nodded.

'So you've been staying up as late as you can.'

Once more Hallie nodded.

'You can't do that much longer.'

'I know. It's foolish of me to be so nervous, but I can't seem to get it out of my mind,' Hallie said with a nervous laugh.

'Would you like to stay with me?'

'Not in a million years,' she answered, her voice suddenly brighter.

'Why not?' asked Grant, pretending his feelings were hurt.

'Because you'd try to take advantage of me,' she answered with a smile.

'I didn't the other night,' he replied seriously.

Hallie considered his answer for a moment, then she shot back, 'What about the next morning? If I hadn't suddenly remembered that Sam was on the phone . . .' She stopped then, suddenly embarrassed at the memory of just how far things had progressed before she remembered Sam.

'You were saying?' prompted Grant.

'Forget it.'

Hallie was feeling better now. What was it about Grant that made her feel so protected?

All through dinner Grant had watched Hallie's mood improve. The sparkle returned to her eyes. He hated to change that, but he feared that what he needed to discuss with Hallie would alter her mood. When he had paid the check and he and Hallie left the restaurant, Grant hesitated, suddenly unsure of the best way to handle things. Before he could speak, Hallie gave him the opening he was looking for.

'Have you found out anything more about the case?' she asked as they walked slowly toward her apartment.

Grant nodded. 'This morning I realized that the police had neglected a routine procedure. Sam took care of it and came up with some interesting information.

'Important?' asked Hallie.

'It could be. Your husband knew Nick Hardister.' Grant waited for Hallie's reaction to his announcement.

'But I don't remember . . .'

'That's possible, Hallie. Your husband may have known a lot of people you didn't know. Friends other than Jasmine Turner.'

Hallie was silent as they approached her apartment. Once they had reached the entrance she turned. 'How do you know?'

'Phone calls between Casey and Nick. Several over a two-week period. Nick also called Irwin Turner. Turner told us that Nick had taken pornographic pictures of Jasmine and your husband and was trying to sell them to him. We think Casey hired Nick to take those pictures.'

Confusion was reflected in her blue eyes, then resignation. Since his death, she had been bombarded with the details of Casey's other life. She wasn't sure she could be shocked any more. 'But why?' she asked.

'Blackmail, most likely. Maybe Jasmine was tiring of him.'

For a moment Hallie was incapable of speech. Deeply humiliated that Casey would sink so low, she asked, 'Is that why you keep coming around, Grant, so you can dig up more dirt about Casey, then taunt me with it? Casey is dead. Why can't you leave him alone?' she cried as she ran inside the building. She stopped in front of her door and fumbled in her purse for her keys. Just as her shaking fingers found them, she felt Grant's strong arms turning her, pulling her against him.

'Listen to me, Hallie. I have to ask you these questions. It's why I was asked to get involved in this case. So the answer is, yes, I am here to find out all I can about this murder. Do you know what else your husband was involved with? Cocai –'

Before Grant could complete the word Hallie raised her hand and slapped him across the face. The sound echoed in the empty hallway.

Grant was silent for a moment, then took a step back. 'I forgot that you don't want to know what kind of man you were married to.'

'Not from you I don't,' she hissed.

'Then from who, Hallie? Who is going to remind you what he really was?' Grant reached out to her, taking hold of her arms, gripping them firmly. 'Never mind that he was sleeping around on you, or that he was so high on cocaine that he didn't know who you were most of the time, or that he was doing business with unsavory people. Instead, let us remember the wonderful Casey Prescott as he really was. Let's see, best-selling writer, unfaithful husband . . .'

Hallie tried to push away from Grant, but his grip on her arms remained strong.

'Was that why you came looking for me that first night? Because your husband was dead, and even when he was alive he wasn't much of a lover? How long had it been, Hallie, since your husband had made love to you?'

She tried to twist out of his grasp and might have succeeded if Grant had not seen the glimmer of unshed tears in her eyes. Still holding her with one hand, he unlocked the door to her apartment.

Inside he held her, gently this time, and kissed her. Slowly he could feel the tension leave her. Against her ear he whispered, 'Remember how it was that night?'

Hallie nodded. While common sense told her she was making a mistake with Grant, her heart told her differently. How she craved his lovemaking. Once more she wanted to feel the wild, nearly primitive passion that he had stirred in her. This time, she promised herself, there would be no ulterior motive, no quest for revenge. She could set aside the past.

'We can have that again,' he promised in a whisper and Hallie felt all her defenses slipping away.

Slowly, Grant led her through the apartment, undressing her as he went, covering every inch of soft flesh with his lips. In the bedroom, moonlight danced slowly

227

over them, casting their shadows on the wall, as they began the ritual of lovers. All over, Hallie's skin burned from his touch. Inside, hot liquid raced through her veins and when she thought she could stand no more she begged Grant for release.

But he hesitated for a moment, delaying the joining that would bring them together, looking deeply into her eyes. What he saw was a glimpse of her soul, filled with guilt and a desperate need to exorcise the past. It was the same look he had seen in her eyes the night they met. When she reached out to pull him to her, he was filled with a sudden sadness.

Sweat covered his chest, giving it a slick sheen that glistened in the moonlight as he began to move inside her, his thrust rhythmic and hard, carrying them both to a shattering pleasure.

Grant lay still, and Hallie, reluctant to let go of the moment, treasured the feel of his weight upon her. When finally he rolled to his side, he reached toward Hallie and stroked her face in a soft, protective gesture.

Hallie closed her eyes and fell into a light sleep, waking only as she felt Grant get out of bed. When she realized he was getting dressed, she sat up. 'Grant? Where are you going?'

'Back to my place,' he answered quietly.

'Oh.' The sound escaped her lips. 'Don't . . . don't you want to stay?'

With his steely gray eyes fixed on hers he said, 'Yeah, I want to, but not until you're ready to have me here. I can't stay in your bed as long as there's three of us, Hallie. Each time we've made love I know you're remembering your husband. I'm not going to do that again. When you can make love and not feel guilty about it, then give me a call. I can't compete with a dead man.' Grant reached for his wallet and slipped it into his back pocket.

Hallie sat up a little straighter, pulling the sheet up with her. 'And what about your wife, Grant?' she asked defensively. 'Are you entirely free of her, or have there been more ghosts in this room than you care to admit?'

Grant stood motionless, frozen by her words. He could deny it, of course, but what would be the point? 'You're right, Hallie. It got very crowded in here tonight and I'm not sure either one of us has the right to criticize the other. I'm sorry. It won't happen again.'

Grant straightened, and wished he had never gotten involved in this mess. He was at war with himself. Professionally, he had taken on an assignment and his duties were clear. He should have remained aloof and objective. Instead, he had let himself get bogged down with emotions and an involvement he neither wanted nor needed.

In the bedroom Hallie heard the soft click of the front door closing behind him. A tear seeped from the corner of her eye and rolled slowly toward her temple. Sadness filled her heart.

The following day Sam called Hallie and arranged for her to meet with Grant and him that afternoon at police headquarters. She agreed readily, knowing that if she had to face Grant again after last night, it would be easier in a public place with other people around. She dressed carefully, taking longer than usual to apply her makeup and fix her hair. It was important that he detect no sign of the havoc his parting words had caused.

A few hours later, with her head high and a forced smile on her face, Hallie sat in the small office. Across the battered tan metal desk, Sam smiled at her. Grant, who was leaning against the window frame, his arms crossed in front of him, nodded to her but made no attempt to relax the scowl that marked his dark features.

'Hallie, did you arrange for your husband's mail to be forwarded to you?' asked Sam.

'Yes, I did. I was going to have it sent to his parents, but then I realized that much of that mail might also concern me since we were not yet divorced. Why?' Her blue eyes darted from Sam to Grant and back.

'There was an envelope addressed to your husband. We intercepted it yesterday. It was from a bank. What do you know about a safe-deposit box at Hampton Guaranty Bank?'

Hallie frowned, tilting her head. 'Nothing. We didn't have a safe-deposit box. Our accounts were at a different bank.'

'Well, well,' muttered Grant, speaking for the first time.

Hallie glared at him, then turned her attention back to Sam's friendly face. 'Wait,' she said suddenly, sitting straighter. 'I . . . I do remember Casey saying something about needing a place to keep his contracts on the book and the movie . . .' Her voice trailed off as she tried to recall that conversation. 'There was so much paperwork when we moved out here. So many letters between his agent, the publisher and the movie studio. Casey handled all that.'

Grant straightened and walked toward the desk, stopping at Sam's side. Behind him the sun streamed into the office, casting a glare that nearly hid his features. He reached out and pulled a chair up to the desk.

'Did you ever sign a card that entitled you to access the box?' asked Grant as leaned back.

'I don't remember. I signed a lot of papers. There were so many things . . .'

'And you let Prescott handle everything,' he observed sarcastically.

Hallie swung to face him, her cool blue eyes meeting his icy gray stare. 'He was my husband,' she replied, her tone warning him that she had had enough of his sarcasm. 'I trusted him.'

Grant shook his head, unable to hide his feelings. 'Too bad he wasn't deserving of all that trust.'

'Grant . . .' warned Sam, leaning forward.

Hallie jumped to her feet. 'I've had it with you, Grant Keeler.'

'Not quite yet, you haven't,' he replied, not taking his eyes from her. 'There is the matter of the safe-deposit box. We want to know what's in it.'

'I don't suppose you have a key, do you, Hallie?' inquired Sam calmly. He, too had risen, hoping to diffuse the situation.

'No, I don't have a key. I didn't even know that box existed until just now.' Suddenly she remembered the key that Dana had found taped to the back of the framed wedding picture. Could Casey have hidden the key

231

there? Had he ever mentioned it to her? Or had he purposefully kept it from her like so many other things in his life?

Well, she would find out soon enough, but she sure as hell wasn't going to tell Grant Keeler or Sam Harris anything about it. Whatever was in that box was none of their business.

'Get out,' Sam turned and shouted to one of his co-workers who had just come through the door of the men's bathroom in the police building. 'Go find another place to piss.' The officer looked up in surprise, then turned and hurried through the door.

'What the hell is wrong with you?' Sam shouted at Grant. 'You did everything possible to antagonize Hallie in there. What purpose does that serve? Right now she's the only link we have to Mathews. You're the one that's looking for him. You are the one that has this . . . this vendetta.'

Grant raised his head sharply. 'I'm taking myself off this investigation,' he announced.

'You can't quit now,' Sam shouted at Grant.

'Forget it, Sam. I've had enough of LA and this case. We're getting nowhere.' The echo of their voices bounced from the porcelain sinks to the black-and-white porcelain tile floor and back again to the urinals.

'Why don't you just admit that Hallie Prescott is at the bottom of all this? It's not for professional reasons at all, is it? You've been sniffing around her since you met her.'

Taking a guess, Sam continued, 'That time in the Memphis Airport was not the first time you two had met, was it?'

The look that Grant gave Sam was a warning that he had overstepped his bounds.

Sam ignored it and stood his ground. 'What's the matter? Can't you make it with Hallie? You seemed pretty chummy the morning after the break-in at her apartment, and she did spend the night at your place. Tell me, Grant, are you still mourning your wife? Or –'

'Cut it out, Sam.'

'Or,' resumed Sam, unwilling to back down now, 'is she still grieving for the pretty boy she was married to? Maybe you just don't measure . . .'

Sam never got a chance to finish the sentence. Like lightning Grant's fist shot out, connecting with Sam's jaw, sending him to his knees.

With almost the same lightning speed, Grant reached out for him and hauled him to his feet. Instantly, he was filled with remorse. Sam was his friend.

Sam bent over, breathing heavily. When he straightened he rubbed his jaw experimentally. 'That was some punch, Keeler. Took me by surprise.' Sam rubbed his jaw.

'Hell, I didn't mean . . .'

Sam held up his hand. 'I asked for it. I just don't want you to bail out on me in the middle of this investigation.'

'Damn it, Sam, I can't hang around here that much longer.'

From the doorway Jim Perkins called out, 'Hey, Harris! You in here? Keeler? Where the hell are you? There's some guy on the phone who said he was stopped by a bum peddling porno on the Santa Monica pier.'

233

'So what else is new?' Sam said sarcastically as he pushed past Jim into the hallway.

'This one could be,' said Perkins as he reached his desk and held the phone out to Sam. 'Says they're pictures of the producer's wife that was just murdered.'

Sam grabbed the phone from Perkins and reached for a pen. A few minutes later Sam hung up, grabbed his jacked and nodded toward Grant. 'You want in on this?'

Grant nodded and followed Sam out the door toward the car. Fifteen minutes later they pulled up in front of a small white single-story house. Bright red geraniums spilled over from the planter boxes that lined the porch. Brightly colored plastic toys dotted the neatly trimmed lawn and a white Chevrolet pickup was parked in the driveway.

'Mr Ross? I'm Detective Harris and this is Agent Keeler.' Both men produced their identification.

Wayne Ross had taken his grandson to the pier that morning to fish when he was approached by a man who was obviously down on his luck. 'I reached in my pocket for some money. There have been times when I was laid off from my job, so I understand hard times,' he explained. 'But instead of asking for money this guy reached into his coat and extracted an envelope. He told me he had some pictures he wanted to sell and that they were worth a lot of money. Said I could sell them to a newspaper. Told him I wasn't interested, but he pulled one of the pictures out anyway. It was a man and woman having sex. I grabbed my grandson and our fishing gear and got the hell outta there. Then he started yelling at me that I was passing up an opportunity to make some big money. He said it was a picture of some producer's wife.'

'Did he identify the woman?' asked Sam.

'No,' answered Ross, shaking his head.

'Can you describe the man who stopped you?'

'He looked dirty. His hair was dark and his clothes looked like they had been slept in more than once, but I couldn't tell you how old he was, or how much he weighed. I wouldn't have even bothered to call the police but my wife insisted. She said she read all about a producer's wife who was murdered a short while ago.' Wayne Ross shrugged. 'It was easier to call than to listen to her go on and on; besides, somebody ought to get that guy off the streets.'

Later in the car Grant asked, 'If it was Hardister, why was he trying to peddle the pictures to someone like Ross?'

'Maybe he needed the money.'

'Then why wouldn't he try to sell them to one of those magazines himself?'

'Maybe it wasn't Hardister.' Sam shrugged as he pulled out into traffic.

'But what if it was? He knows that we're after him and maybe we're not the only ones looking for him. Maybe Mathews knows that Hardister saw Jasmine the night of the murder. Maybe he thinks he has the tape.'

Sam swung the steering wheel to the left as far as it would go and made a sharp U-turn. 'When was the last time you went sightseeing down on the Santa Monica pier?'

* * *

235

By the time Sam and Grant caught up with Nick Hardister his luck had run out. He had been stabbed to death.

'Do you think it was Mathews?' asked Sam.

Grant shook his head. 'Not his style. Mathews's men would have taken the photos. It would have been a nice clean job. This is too messy. My guess is that Hardister was talking around about these pictures and how much they could be worth and someone down here took him at his word, killed him, then took the pictures and was trying to sell them to anyone who would buy them.

At the Santa Monica Police Department Grant dumped the set of pictures that had been found sewn inside the lining of Hardister's coat onto the desk and spread them out. They were all of Casey and Jasmine except one, which was to Grant the most startling of all. It was of Hallie, running from the house she shared with Casey. Her arms were wrapped protectively over her stomach as if she was in pain.

Grant wondered if she had known all along about the existence of these photos. Yet the other night when he had told her about Casey and Nick she had seemed genuinely surprised. He tried to survey the pictures before him impartially and professionally, but it was impossible not to be moved by the picture of Hallie. And while he fought the feelings of sympathy for what she had been through, he couldn't help but wonder if he wasn't looking at the picture of a woman who had the strongest motive of all for murder.

CHAPTER 17

Hallie barely remembered the drive from the police building to her apartment. Inside she raced to the box where she had asked Dana to put the key she had found. But the box contained eight other keys. Two she could identify as extra car keys. What the devil did a safe-deposit key look like? Wait . . . this one. It had a weird shape and it had a number on it. She slipped the key in her pocket. At the front door she turned, retraced her steps to the counter, grabbing the phone book, then the box with the unidentified keys. For insurance, she decided, then headed for her car.

A quick check of the phone book told her that Hampton Guaranty Bank had branches all over the city. It could be any one of a dozen locations. She drove to the branch nearest to their house.

'No,' the manager advised her when Hallie showed her the key. 'This key doesn't belong to a box at this bank. Try one of our larger branches.'

Bewildered, Hallie looked down at the key, then back at the manager. 'How . . .?' she asked.

Smiling, the manager explained, 'Your key number is 517. We only have three hundred boxes here at this

237

branch. Here, I'll get you a list with our locations.'
By the time Hallie left the bank it was almost closing
time.

The next morning, working on a hunch, she chose the
bank closest to the studio where Casey had spent his
days working.

'Good morning. May I help you?' asked the dark-
haired receptionist.

Hallie looked past her nervously, then said, 'Yes,
please. I . . . uh . . . my safe-deposit box. I'd like to
open it.'

'Certainly. If you'll just have a seat I'll call
Mr Kavanaugh to help you. He's the manager.'

Hallie looked around anxiously. What if this wasn't
the right bank? What if this wasn't the right key? She
knew absolutely nothing about safe-deposit boxes.
Why hadn't Casey told her about this?

The young man who approached looked friendly
enough. His smile was welcoming. Still, she fidgeted
nervously while he checked his records and verified her
identification.

'I'm sorry for the delay,' he said apologetically,
looking up at Hallie briefly.

Hallie held her breath.

'Ah . . . yes. Here we are. Well, Mrs Prescott, it
seems you are not listed as a joint box-holder.'

Her hopes plummeted.

'But,' continued the manager, 'you are listed as a
deputy, which means that as long as you have the key,
you are authorized not only to open the box, but to
remove any of the contents.'

Hallie nodded, but didn't breathe again until the keys, hers and the manager's, had turned in the lock.

Immediately, the manager stepped back. 'Please, Mrs Prescott, take as long as you like. When you are ready to leave, just ring this bell.'

Hallie nodded, and when he had left her she slowly pulled the box out. With shaking hands she reached inside and extracted several thick brown envelopes. What she discovered caused her knees to buckle. Each envelope contained large amounts of cash – more money than she had ever seen in one place at one time. She groped blindly for the edge of the desk and, finding it, slid into the chair.

Where had all this money come from?

In slow motion she continued to explore the other contents of the box. The contracts were there, just as she had expected they would be. She scanned them and found the answer she was searching for. On the last page of the movie contract was an addendum that provided for a cash buy-out of Casey's contract if he failed to complete the screenplay. When he was fired from the picture the studio must have decided to pay him off rather than go through the hassle of defending a lawsuit.

Hallie leaned back in her chair. Casey never told her about that provision or the money. All along he had intended to keep that a secret. Were there any more surprises? she wondered as she pulled a small plastic case from the box. She removed the lid and this time her gasp was audible. Inside the case was an audio tape.

Dear God, was there no end to this?

Quickly she replaced the money and the papers in the

box, then slipped the tape back in the case and dropped it into the zippered compartment of her purse. The money could wait until later, until she decided what to do with it. But the tape? Instinctively she knew this was the tape that Grant, that everybody, was searching for. Jasmine's tape.

At that moment she also knew that if anyone had followed her here, they would be waiting outside for her to leave.

She rang the small bell that was mounted on the desk and waited for the manager. After the box had been returned to its slot and secured she said, 'Mr Kavanaugh, is there another exit besides the front door?'

When it was obvious that he found her request somewhat strange, she hurried on. 'You see, I parked my car around the corner. I . . . I thought there was another entrance. Closer.'

Not good enough, thought Hallie, noting his raised brows, so she hurried on. 'Ah, I'm . . . I'm not feeling well.' She fanned her face with her hand and fixed her eyes on the ceiling. 'It's . . . you see, Mr Kavanaugh, I have this unfortunate tendency toward claustrophobia. I tend to pass out no matter where I am. So if I can just get some fresh . . .'

From the rear door usually reserved for bank employees, Hallie exited cautiously, then dashed toward her car. She had the door open and was about to slide inside when she saw him sitting in the passenger seat.

'Did you get it?' Grant asked with a conspiratorial grin.

'Get what? And what are you doing in my car?' Hallie demanded as she got into the driver's seat.

240

'You neglected to lock it.'

'I did not. I always lock my car. You broke into it,' she accused.

'Not me,' he replied innocently. 'It must have been Sam.'

'Sam? Fine. Same difference. Don't you people have any scruples?' she asked irritably.

'I don't,' Grant admitted. 'It's part of my FBI training. But Sam does.'

'Really?' she asked sarcastically. 'How can you tell?'

'He was worried about messing up your door locks. Now get in and drive, honey. I think we've got company.'

The car, a gray Mercedes, tailed them until they turned off the freeway twenty-five minutes later. 'Wow! What was that all about?' asked Hallie.

Grant turned to look behind them. 'That was to let us know that they're tailing you. They'll be back.'

'How do you know?' she asked, suddenly shaky.

'Because now they know you have the tape, Hallie.'

'But how do they know that?'

Grant shook his head. 'Honey, don't you ever watch any gangster movies? They know it because we know it. Now you're in real danger.'

'What am I supposed to do now?' she asked, turning into her driveway.

'Give me the tape,' he commanded. 'We need to know what's on it. It's our only hope of nailing Mathews. We'll make a copy and then you can put the original back in your safe-deposit box.'

Hallie dug into her purse and handed the cassette to Grant. 'And then what?' she asked as he got out and walked around to her side of the car. 'What happens to me?'

He leaned down, propping his hands on the window frame and his gray eyes glinted with humor. 'I'll have to get back to you on that.'

'Hey!' protested Hallie, laughing in spite of her apprehension, but her protest was cut short by a hard fast kiss.

'Did you get it?' asked Sam later that afternoon. Grant handed the tape over to him. 'You're sure this is it?'

Grant nodded. 'It makes sense, doesn't it? Jasmine's husband kicks her out because he finds out about her and Prescott. He might have tried to ignore her infidelity except for Hardister, who has pictures of the wife and the boyfriend and is ready to peddle them to anyone that has the cash.

'Now Jasmine is on her own, and the money she's getting from her husband for temporary maintenance won't quite support her lavish lifestyle. A neighbor identified Hardister as one of the men who came to her apartment the day before the murder. If he couldn't get Turner to bite, why wouldn't he try and peddle the pictures to Jasmine? She would do anything to see that they didn't get into the wrong hands. So now she needs more than extra spending money. She desperately needs cash. What better place to get it than from Mathews?'

'Exactly where does Prescott fit in?' asked Sam. 'He was the one who hired Hardister to take the photos in the first place.'

'Prescott paid off Hardister for the pictures, not

realizing that Hardister had kept a set of prints for himself. Jasmine, not knowing that Prescott was the one who hired Hardister, was much too shrewd to dump Prescott until she was through using him. She must have told Prescott about the tape and her plans to blackmail Mathews.

'When he finds Jasmine dead, Prescott takes the tape and hides it in the safest place he can think of – his safe-deposit box – until he can formulate a plan to blackmail Mathews himself.'

'So where did the key to the safe-deposit box come from?' Sam asked. 'Hallie said she didn't know anything about it.'

'From someone who needed Hallie to retrieve the tape. Think about it, Sam. The second break-in. What if the whole purpose was to *leave* something in her apartment, not take something?'

'The key,' said Sam, reaching the same conclusion as Grant. 'But who?'

Grant shook his head. 'I don't know. That's what we have to find out.' Grant paused and checked his watch. 'What time do the banks close here?'

'Five. Why?' asked Sam.

'Let's backtrack.'

Bruce Kavanaugh had recently been promoted to branch manager at Hampton Guaranty. If it hadn't been for Jim Franklin's retirement the previous month, he would still be a manager trainee down at the main office. He knew it and so did everyone else, so he was determined to make the best of this opportunity. His broad, welcoming smile disappeared, however, when

243

Sam and Grant showed him their identification. He was visibly flustered. At their insistence he pulled the card from the file that recorded the signatures and dates for each occasion Casey Prescott's safe-deposit box had been opened.

'We'd like a copy, said Grant.'

Small beads of perspiration began to gather above his upper lip. 'Oh, I really can't do that, sir . . . without calling my supervisor, that is . . . uh, I don't think I'm supposed to . . .'

'Call him, then,' said Sam. 'We'll wait.'

The last thing Bruce Kavanaugh wanted was to call any attention to himself at the main office. Managers were supposed to manage, not run to their supervisors every time there was a problem. Especially one that he hadn't encountered in training. 'But it's almost time to close. I have to –'

'Uncooperative,' mumbled Grant. 'Make a note of that, Detective Harris.'

As instructed, Sam pulled a small black note pad and a pen from his jacket pocket, looked up briefly at Kavanaugh as if memorizing his features, then hastily scribbled a few words on the pad.

'You are going have to give us the information one way or another. If necessary we can get court order, Mr Kavanaugh. Although I have to advise you that can get real sticky. Once we get the court involved . . .' Grant shook his head from side to side, then looked once more toward Sam.

'Irregularities . . .' said Sam in a confidential tone, also shaking his head.

'Remember that manager over at . . .? Grant waved a

hand as if pulling a name from the air, then turned and started toward the main entrance. Kavanaugh followed.

'Valley National,' supplied Sam quickly, falling into line behind Kavanaugh. 'Umm . . . messy situation,' agreed Sam. 'I really don't think the poor guy knew anything about it, do you?'

'Naw,' replied Grant, turning. 'He was new . . . just trying to do his job. Too bad, though. It sure cut short his career in high finance.'

'Wait,' Kavanaugh said hastily, looking from Grant to Sam. 'Maybe . . . maybe I misunderstood. After all, it is only a copy of the signature card you want.' He laughed nervously. 'I mean, it's not like you want access to the box itself.'

'No,' said Sam quickly. 'We would never ask you to do anything that would jeopardize your position with the bank.'

'Does this mean what I think it does?' asked Grant a few minutes later as he and Sam studied the signature card.

'I'm afraid so,' said Sam incredulously.

'There could have been a mistake,' suggested Grant.

'Nope,' answered Sam. 'Banks are very careful when it comes to record keeping.' He paused, shaking his head in amazement. 'This would certainly explain who it was that wanted Hallie to have the key,' he volunteered.

'Hell,' muttered Grant as he read the copy of the card once more, just to be sure his eyes hadn't deceived him.

Casey Prescott had accessed his safe-deposit box seven times since he had first rented it.

The last time was two days after he died.

★ ★ ★

Later that same evening Hallie drove a few blocks to the neighborhood market. Ordinarily, she would have walked there and back, but after being followed from the bank this afternoon, she wasn't about to take any chances. As a precaution she drove several blocks out of her way then doubled back. When she was satisfied that no one had followed her she made a left into the grocery store parking lot. After pulling into a parking space near the front of the store she sat for a moment, unable to throw off the feeling that her life was a complete mess.

In spite of the events that precipitated her separation from Casey, in spite of his shabby treatment of her, she was still haunted by guilt. Of course, it hadn't helped matters when she had gone to Memphis and Casey's mother had been so condemning.

Now there was the matter of the tape and the money. How could she have been married to Casey all that time and not realize that he lived a separate life? The things he had done, the secrets he had kept . . . When would this nightmare end?

And then there was Grant Keeler. Hallie sighed. He was never supposed to be anything more than a one-night stand, a desperate attempt to prove to herself that she was still attractive and desirable. An exorcism of bad memories. But things had backfired, and now she wasn't sure she would ever be able to put Grant out of her mind and her heart.

He made her feel alive. He also made her face up to the glaring problems that had existed between her and Casey – problems that she had tried to ignore in the beginning, and now still tried to put aside.

Giving herself a mental shake, she got out of the car, locked it and went inside the market. When she emerged ten minutes later with a single brown bag filled with groceries, she paused and scanned the parking lot, a habit she had developed since her frightening encounter that time at the hospital.

She had shifted the bag of groceries from one arm to the other, when she sensed rather than heard the two men behind her. Her heart raced, her hands trembled. No need to panic, she thought. There are plenty of people around. It isn't quite dark yet and the parking lot is brightly lit. This is just a coincidence. But her instincts told her better.

With her free hand she reached into the pocket of her jeans and pulled out her keys. Damn, why couldn't she stop shaking long enough to get the doors unlocked? Just as she did one of the men moved in beside her. The other stood a few feet away. Both were dressed in knit shirts and wore sunglasses in spite of the waning daylight.

'What do you want?' she demanded. She was almost positive that these were the same two men that had followed her and Dana

'No need to panic, Mrs Prescott,' the one who stood closest to her assured her.

'How do you know my name?' Hallie asked in a controlled voice.

The second man took a few steps toward her. 'You have something we want, Mrs Prescott.' His voice was smooth, almost oily. 'It belongs to us. A package that found its way to you by mistake. Mr Mathews wants it back.'

'I don't know what you're talking about.'

'Sure you do.'

'No.' Her voice quavered in spite of her attempts to sound strong. 'I don't know anyone by that name.'

'We searched your apartment a while back, Mrs Prescott, but we didn't find it. Today you made a trip to Hampton Guaranty Bank to your safe-deposit box. Now we're wondering if you were foolish enough to turn it over to the police. That would be very unwise.'

'No, no,' she protested.

'Well, maybe you have it on you.' He leaned closer to her, causing her to flinch. Later she would remember the sickening, sweet smell of his cologne as it combined with the waves of heat that rose from the pavement beneath her feet.

Hallie shook her head, her eyes wide. Her fear was genuine. 'Look, I don't know what it is you're looking for.'

'Now, Mrs Prescott, we've been real patient, just waiting for you to lead us to the tape, but now we're running out of time.'

The man who stood next to her moved closer. Hallie took a step back. 'You have until tomorrow to turn the tape over to us. Mr Mathews will not tolerate any more delays.'

'Please,' Hallie said, her voice pleading, 'you have this all wrong. I never had a tape. And I don't know anyone named Mathews!'

'But you'll find it for us, won't you? By tomorrow.' The grins that appeared on both their faces sent shivers along her spine.

Hallie took another step backward, her bag of groceries still clutched protectively in front of her. 'And if I'm telling the truth and I don't have it?'

'That would be too bad.' The man shook his head as if to commiserate over such an unlikely event, then reached in his pocket for a cigarette and nodded to his companion. 'In that case we would have to personally conduct another search for the tape. Our employer is insistent that we find it.' Both men turned and walked away. 'Better get on home now, Mrs Prescott. You haven't got much time.'

Hallie threw the bag of groceries across the seat, scrambled into the car and locked the door. With quick, jerky movements, she looked over her shoulder, but the men who had accosted her had disappeared. A man with two children came out of the market and got into the mini-van that was parked next to her.

For a moment she rested her forehead against the steering wheel. She could feel her whole body beginning to shake. Those men had done nothing to hurt her, she thought as she frantically searched her rear-view mirror for any sign of them, but she knew they could.

With trembling fingers, Hallie started the car. A few minutes later she pulled into her parking space and after locking her car ran for the safety of her apartment.

Inside she grabbed for the phone. 'Sam Harris,' she said after she had dialed the number.

'Please hold.'

'Detective Cooper.'

'I'm trying to reach Sam Harris,' she said breathlessly.

'Harris is not here. Can I help you?'

'What about Grant Keeler?'

'Not here either. Who is this?'

'Hallie Prescott. Look, I need to talk to one of them. It's urgent. Tell them I was stopped by two men. They want the tape. By tomorrow. I don't know what to do.'

'I'll see what I can do,' Cooper promised.

Where the hell were Sam and Grant when she needed them?

The taped phone conversation between Edward Mathews and Senator Rawlins did indeed contain threats against Rawlins, although veiled and presented in a civilized, strangely cultured manner. If Senator Rawlins refused to change his vote on a bill that would be adverse to Mathews's oil interests, Mathews would see the Senator eliminated from the equation.

The message was certainly clear, thought Grant later, as he drank from the cold can of beer he had taken from the refrigerator, it should have been enough.

But the problem, the Justice Department had concluded earlier today when they evaluated the contents of the tape, was that the threat was only implied, couched in language that was not only ambiguous, but ridiculously polite.

We need more, Justice had concluded, and that son-of-a-bitch Anderson, who was responsible for getting Grant involved in this in the first place, had agreed. Then he had taken it even further.

Anderson had a plan and Grant was to be the key player. That wouldn't have bothered Grant nearly as much if the other key player was to be someone other than Hallie Prescott. The difference was that Grant knew what the setup was and the danger involved.

Hallie, on the other hand, had no idea she was about to become a pawn in the game of gathering enough evidence to finally put Edwin Mathews behind bars.

She jumped when there was a knock at her door. It had been only an hour or so since she had called for help, but it seemed so much longer.

Through the peephole she could see Grant.

'I've been so frightened,' she confessed as she unlocked the door. 'There were these two men and they threatened . . .'

Grant pulled her toward him and folded his arms around her. 'It's okay, honey,' he said soothingly. 'I won't let anything happen to you, I promise.'

'But those men, they were so nasty. And they didn't care who saw them. They want the tape, Grant. What am I going to do?'

Grant held her away from him, his hands firmly gripping her arms. 'You're going to give them the tape,' he said, his voice firm and reassuring.

Hallie almost sagged with relief as she looked into his steady gray eyes. Grant was here. He would help her through this ordeal. He was someone she could count on.

After he had poured her a glass of wine, he brought it to her and sat down.

'Here's the tape, Hallie,' he said reaching into his jacket pocket and holding it out to her. 'Now there's something I need you to do.'

'No!' she cried when he had outlined the plan and her role in it. 'I can't do that!'

'We'll be right there, honey, listening to every word. Close by. We can get to you within seconds if we have to, but no harm will come to you. Not as long as you give them what they want. And this,' he said, fingering the plastic case, 'is what they are desperate for.'

'That's what worries me, Grant. These men are desperate. People like that do crazy things. They've already broken into my apartment and come after me at St Francis and here, right in my neighborhood. It wasn't even dark yet. What happens after I give them the tape? What will happen then?' she asked worriedly. She could feel a nervous twitch in her stomach – the first sign of panic.

'Hallie, Hallie,' Grant said soothingly, 'as soon as we get what we need on tape, we'll get you out of there. You have my word. I won't let anything happen to you.'

'But what if something goes wrong?' she asked in a small voice, hating herself for being such a coward. Grant needed her to make this work, and all she could think about was that she would be at risk.

'Nothing will, honey, I promise,' he assured her. 'I'll stay here with you tonight for as long as I can.' *Damn*. He hated doing this. He could see that she was beginning to weaken as he continued to work her. Most of the time it had never bothered him to cajole and manipulate people until they gave him what he wanted. It was what he had been trained to do. But this time was different. This was Hallie. And no matter what he promised, she would be in danger.

* * *

'Hallie, honey, it's time,' he said a few hours later. 'Take off your shirt.'

Not even the feel of his warm, strong hands against her skin as he taped the wires to her could stop her fear. The whole time he talked to her, his voice low and calm, telling her exactly how things worked and how close he would be. He had stayed with her most of the night, leaving just before daylight. While he was satisfied that she understood how the wire worked and what her role in this scheme was, he was troubled by what he knew.

CHAPTER 18

From where Grant sat in the front seat of the surveillance van he had a clear view of the entrance to Hallie's apartment and the parking lot that wrapped around one side of the building. He shifted for perhaps the hundredth time since daybreak this morning when he and Sam and the rest of the team had set up their equipment.

Every bone in his body ached. Aside from the physical discomfort he was experiencing, he was also the victim of mental discomfort. It had been a difficult night, spent first convincing, then reassuring Hallie that their plan was sound.

After he had left her it had been all he could do to keep from rushing back inside to tell her that she didn't have to do this for him or for anyone else. But he also knew that if he got anywhere near her his heart would interfere with his job. He would tell her to run, and warn her that she was only being used to lead them to Mathews. And while they were reasonably sure that this plan would work, there were no guarantees.

Grant Keeler, who was always supposed to remain cool and composed under pressure, had just managed to place another woman he loved in jeopardy. That in itself was enough to drive him crazy. In the overall plan, nobody gave a damn about Hallie Prescott. Nobody except him.

When Hallie awoke after falling unto an uneasy and uncomfortable sleep, the sun was shining brightly. She had only a few moments before recalling everything that had happened yesterday. What would these men do to her if things didn't go right? She shuddered, then forced herself to get up and go into the kitchen where she made a pot of coffee.

A few minutes later, she filled her cup. With unsteady hands she reached for it, her fingers brushing the handle. The cup skidded sideways across the counter and over the edge shattering as it hit the floor. Hot brown liquid followed its path, spreading over the counter top and dripping onto the floor.

It was one thing too many. Hallie began to shake as she stooped to gather the broken pieces of china. She knew that Grant was outside the apartment along with Sam, and that he wouldn't let anything happen to her. Even though he had remained with her through most of the night, making every effort to ease her apprehension, and making sure she knew exactly what to do, she was still scared. She didn't want to be heroic or brave. She just wanted to go home – to Mississippi and to her Aunt Billie, where she knew she would be safe.

While her first impulse this morning had been to listen to the cassette, Hallie knew better. Right now all she wanted to do was to turn it over to Mathews. If she didn't know anything, she couldn't get hurt, she reasoned, as she quickly traded her loose-fitting gray sweat pants and sweat shirt for a pair of jeans, a T-shirt, and a long-sleeve shirt. Over that she put on a light-weight jacket. In the mirror she pulled both shirts up to her chin, then twisted and checked the transmitting equipment that was taped tight against her skin. It had been in place long enough to make her itch.

'Exactly what am I supposed to do?' she had asked Grant during the early-morning hours as she had sat cradled in his arms. 'Sit here and wait for them to come and get me?'

'No, we want them to go after you,' he explained.

'That's not a very consoling thought,' she had replied, scrunching her chin in the palm of her hand.

'When you get up in the morning you are to drive back to the bank. If they don't pick you up when you leave here, they'll be waiting for you there.'

'How can you be so sure?'

'Because, doll,' he explained in his best gangster voice, 'they have figured out that, one, you either have the tape on you, or, two, you're going back to the bank to get it.'

Hallie glanced at her watch. It was time. From the kitchen counter she grabbed her purse and her car keys, flipped open the flap of her purse intending to drop the casette inside, then thought better of it. She shoved it instead into the pocket of her jacket. Her heart, she calculated, was beating at least ninety miles an hour.

Breathlessly, she hurried through the hallway outside her apartment, then burst through the exit intent upon reaching the safety of her car which was only a few feet away. But she never made it. Outside the door she was grabbed by two fleshy hands and slammed roughly against the brick wall.

'You're in a big hurry, Mrs Prescott. You weren't going to leave with our tape now, were you?' asked the bigger of the two men.

Hallie's blue eyes were wide with fear and she bent from the waist fighting to catch her breath. She hadn't expected to see these two again, especially right outside her apartment. And she had never even considered that she would be manhandled like this. But why not? Grant and Sam had told her these men were thugs.

Before Hallie had recovered enough to protest this treatment, the shorter of the two men grabbed her arm with one hand, pulling her upright while he attempted to run his other hand down the length of her from her throat to her breast and finally to her pelvis. She struggled, not only to avoid his touch, but to keep his hands from discovering that she was wired, but his grip only tightened. The look in his eyes told her that she had every right to be scared. This one wanted more than just a tape from her.

When the second man gave a signal, Hallie was pulled toward the gray Mercedes that blocked the alley that led to the street. She opened her mouth to scream, but a hand was clamped over it, muffling the sound as she was roughly shoved into the back seat.

If there was anything to be thankful for at that moment, Hallie supposed she should be grateful that the man who had pawed her only a few short minutes ago was now driving instead of sitting in the back seat with her. 'Look,' she said, trying to control the terror that she felt, 'I'll give you the tape if you'll just let me go.'

The driver turned toward her. 'We can't let you go.' His eyes slid over her again and she felt her skin crawl. 'You know what's on the tape.'

'No, no!' she protested, wildly shaking her head. 'I never listened to it, I swear. I don't know anything about it. I found it . . . in my husband's safe-deposit box.'

'What did you tell the police?' he asked.

'Nothing, she replied. 'I didn't tell them anything.'

'They why have they been watching you?'

'My husband left me for Jasmine Turner. They think I had a motive for killing her. It's the truth, I swear!'

Neither man responded to her declaration as the driver pulled out onto the narrow side street. 'Please,' she pleaded. 'You've got to believe me. I never listened to the tape.' Once again there was silence in the car and Hallie realized that no matter what she told them they would never believe her.

Minutes passed before she remembered that there were questions she was supposed to ask. 'Where are we going?'

She really didn't expect them to answer so she was surprised when the man sitting next to her spoke for the first time. 'We're taking you to Mr Mathews.'

I ought to be able to scream for help, thought Hallie, but I'm here because I stupidly agreed to help the police. I must be out of my mind. But her fear gave over to the irrational as she remembered what Grant had told her about Edward Mathews. He was a powerful man and nothing got in his way.

Hello, Mr Mathews. How nice to see you. Yes, it is a lovely day for a murder. Especially mine. Had I known, I would have dressed better.

Hallie stifled a wild desire to laugh, but her runaway monolog did little to calm her. If Edward Mathews could have a United States senator killed, he wouldn't blink an eye at killing her.

Well, Grant Keeler could take his grand scheme and stuff it! It all sounded plausible at three this morning, but it sure didn't right now. Wire or no wire, she was getting the hell out of this situation any way she could.

From the back seat she considered her options as she tried to memorize the route they traveled. All the doors and windows were locked and could only be opened by the driver. It appeared that her only chance to make a run for it would come when they arrived at their destination.

'Aren't you afraid I'll be able to tell the police where you're taking me?' she asked the man next to her.

'No,' he answered without adding any explanation.

Of course not, she thought. Dead people don't lead the police anywhere. They have no intention of letting me go.

The tinted windows made it almost impossible for anyone to see inside the car, but Hallie had no difficulty seeing the winding canyon road they traveled. Even though the area was residential, the traffic was still heavy. They had gone about two miles when the driver suddenly made a sharp right. The road ahead curved, climbing even higher. Mentally she recorded their trip with her own coded series of numbers and letters. Two left turns followed. In a short while they were high enough that she could catch a glimpse of the city in the distance. The urge to look behind her, to see if Grant was tailing them, was powerful. But she was afraid to look. Last night he had warned her not to do that.

The car finally slowed in front of an ornate set of iron gates just long enough for the driver to open them with a remote control. Inside the walled property the trees and shrubs were dense, but Hallie could see patches of white and red in the distance and she rightly assumed it was Mathews's house. In less than a minute the car pulled up in front of the imposing façade of stark white stucco topped by a dark-red tile roof. A row of slender Palladian windows spread across the front of the house, their half-moon tops capping the rectangular panes like inquisitive eyebrows.

Hallie sat still in the back seat, her adrenalin pumping in overdrive, her heartbeat rapid. Now, she thought, now is my chance to make a run for it. She was ready. From behind the steering wheel, the driver released the door locks. Just as both men leaned to open their doors Hallie lunged from hers.

In seconds she was free of the car and running down the drive. She had succeeded in surprising her two guards and now all she had to do was get through the gates. There was plenty of dense foliage to hide her once she was off the estate. She turned once to look back over her shoulder and as she did she lost her balance, sliding on loose gravel. She stumbled and nearly fell. Scrambling, she fought to regain her balance and ran harder than ever. By now her lungs felt like they were about to burst and her insides felt like they were on fire. In spite of her near fall she still had outdistanced the heavier of the two men.

I'm going to make it, she reassured herself just seconds before her feet were knocked out from underneath her. The ground seemed to rise up to meet her as she slammed into it face down, then rolled onto her side. She gasped for air, but her burning lungs refused to accept it. Roughly, she was hauled to her feet and came face to face with a man she had never seen before. Undoubtedly, he was the one responsible for her fall. Without giving her a chance to catch her breath he hauled her to her feet and dragged her toward the house. He was soon joined by the man who had driven the car.

Hallie thought then there was no need for them to kill her. She was about to die right now for lack of oxygen. But by the time they had reached the massive front doors of the house she was at least able to draw shallow breaths.

Inside the van that was parked outside the gates to the estate, Grant and Sam cursed. There had been silence, then static, and now the voices of several men, but nothing from Hallie.

'What the hell is she up to?' asked Vince West, one of the young electronics technicians who were now an integral part of law enforcement. 'I thought you said she knew exactly what she was supposed to be doing. What happened to the questions she was supposed to be asking? And what about the key word, the one that would let us know that she was inside the house? I told you this wasn't going to . . .'

'Shut up, Vince. Something's happened,' warned Sam.

'Damn right something's happened,' Vince shot back. 'That dumb-ass broad can't even . . .'

The words were barely out of his mouth, when Grant had scrambled from the front of the van to the back where Vince was seated. In one swift, unbroken motion he hauled the technician out of his seat and threw him against the van's metal-skeleton interior and pinned him there.

Sam winced.

'Not one more goddamn word from you except to tell me what's going on with Hallie, do you hear me?'

Vince nodded, and when Grant released him he silently slid to the floor of the van.

Inside the cool, marbled entry, Hallie once more became aware of the driver's scrutiny. Even in her weakened state she could feel her skin crawl as his eyes slid over her. She didn't think she could stand it if he put his hands on her again.

'You really messed yourself up, Mrs Prescott,' he said, reaching out to smooth her hair away from her face.

She jerked away before he was able to touch her. 'Keep . . . away . . . from me.' Her voice was raspy, the words disconnected.

Her captor shrugged. 'Suit yourself, but it won't be long before you'll be begging me to be nice to you.' His eyes, which had always appeared to be black and flat, now gleamed with malice. The anticipation in his voice was unmistakable as he continued, 'Only now, you had better be prepared to do more than beg.'

Hallie shuddered, remembering how he had tried to run his hands over her, attempting to touch her intimately. Suddenly, a set of heavy, intricately carved double doors that looked strangely out of place in this sleek entry opened at the far end of the hall and she was pushed toward them. The room beyond was full of white, as stark and rigid as the impeccable man in the dark gray suit who watched her entrance from a few feet away.

His hair, which was short and wavy, was the color of steel. The smile showed an expanse of perfect white teeth. 'How nice of you to bring me the tape in person, Mrs Prescott. Unfortunately, our mutual friend, Jasmine Turner, was unable to deliver it herself, and, instead, your husband Casey Prescott chose to place it in your care. He assured us that you would deliver it.'

The pale amber eyes studied Hallie like a predator might study his victim, prepared to toy with it in order to weaken its defenses, and prolong the torture before going in for the final kill. His intense scrutiny sent alarm signals shrieking in Hallie's brain. Edwin Mathews, the man who stood before her, poised and immaculately groomed, was more than dangerous. He was deadly.

'I don't know what you want from me.' protested Hallie, desperately trying to hide her fear. 'And I don't know any reason why my husband would have been involved with people like you.'

Besides the short repulsive man who had shoved her into this room, Hallie was now aware that they had been joined by the man who had sat next to her in the back seat of the car and the man who had kept her from escaping. All together, they were an unsavory group, thought Hallie. In spite of the expensive clothes they wore, they could not hide their coarseness.

'I believe you have a tape for me?' asked Mathews. The voice was cultured and silky, but Hallie could sense the evil that lay just behind the polished façade. Mathews nodded, and Hallie cringed as she saw the repulsive driver move toward her. Before he could touch her Hallie stepped back and reached into the pocket of her jacket for the tape.

She could only pray that Grant was recording all this and would get his butt up here now and get her away from this pack of vicious animals.

The driver took the tape from her extended hand, making sure his hand fully covered hers as he did so, a gesture that was not missed by Mathews. 'I see that Paul has taken a liking to you, Mrs Prescott.'

Hallie felt her skin crawl.

'I always thought you had a preference for blondes, Paul,' continued Mathews conversationally as Paul approached the cabinet that housed the tape player, then pushed the necessary buttons to start the tape.

The only set of eyes in the room that was not focused on the tape player belonged to Edwin Mathews. He had the tape in his possession now, and he was immensely relieved. Jasmine had posed a serious threat to him.

After a few seconds of silence, Mathews turned toward Paul, his brows raised inquiringly. Nervously, Paul punched the buttons and rewound the tape. The soft whirring was the only sound in the room, followed by the click of the stop and play buttons.

Silence followed. The four men and one woman waited, certain that at any moment they would hear voices. After a full minute Mathews nodded toward Paul to fast-forward the tape. Again the whirring sound filled the room, followed by a click as Paul pressed the play button.

Panic gripped Hallie, stealing her breath away. Had the police given her the wrong tape? Surely they wouldn't send her in with the wrong tape!

When the tape failed to produce any sound, Paul looked expectantly toward Mathews, waiting for a signal. Mathews nodded in response and Paul left his post, covering the space between him and Hallie in seconds.

The look in his eyes was her first warning. Hallie's eyes widened.

'You lyin' bitch!' He spat out the words just as his hand connected with her face, the force of the open-handed blow sending her to her knees. There was a moment when she couldn't feel anything, then a wave of pain sent her crashing down to the floor. The other two men had positioned themselves on either side of Hallie and, at Mathews's command, they hauled her upright to a standing position. Paul waited, smiling, eager to repeat his punishment.

Finally, Mathews spoke, slowly, wearily, as if he had tired of this game. 'Where is the tape, Mrs Prescott? Did you think you could fool me with this? That was very stupid of you.'

At Mathews's almost imperceptible nod, Paul struck Hallie a second time, sending her to the floor once more. Hallie swallowed, certain that she was about to throw up. The second blow, combined with her earlier fall, had left her weak and momentarily disoriented.

'I . . . don't know anything,' she gasped, struggling to her feet. 'I don't even know what's supposed to be on this tape.'

With the fingers of both hands held together in front

of his face in a gesture of prayer, Mathews stared at Hallie for a few long moments. Then he adjusted the direction of his hands until all ten fingers were pointing at her. This time she sensed rather than saw Paul moving toward her, and she braced for the hit. But it was interrupted by Mathews.

'Bring him here,' directed Mathews, his attention suddenly focused elsewhere. Paul moved immediately, leaving the room.

Hallie looked over her shoulder, her eyes following Paul's retreating figure. The involuntary movement made her dizzy.

Within seconds Paul reappeared with another man at his side.

'Is there a problem, Mr Mathews?' asked the man who had accompanied Paul as far as the doorway.

At the sound of the voice Hallie spun around, her face suddenly bloodless, as cold and as white as her surroundings. In shock, she stared.

Before her stood her dead husband.

This time Hallie slumped to the floor on her own, hitting her head on a nearby table.

Again rough hands hauled her upright, this time not releasing their grip.

'Shake her,' commanded Mathews.

Hallie moaned, and her eyes fluttered open.

'My God,' she whispered. 'Oh, my God. Casey?'

'Alive and well,' he replied in a bored tone.

'But how . . .? The accident? I . . . I saw you . . . there . . . in the morgue.'

Casey shrugged. 'It was someone else. I ran and he came after me. I thought he was after me because of

Jasmine's murder. I don't know where he came from, or why he was chasing me. I was coming down hard off the drugs, crashing, and I panicked and ran. Nothing seemed real. He must have followed me – maybe he intended to kill me. Who knows? At any rate the car that barely missed me got him.

'Then, when I saw him lying there on the pavement like that, I knew I had the answer to all my problems. He was so messed up, it would be hard to identify him, so after making sure he didn't have any ID on him, I left my wallet on his body.'

'And your watch,' she murmured raggedly, but Casey just kept talking.

'The rest was easy, and it kept the police from coming after me for Jasmine's murder. I hid out until after the funeral. Jasmine had plans to blackmail Mr Mathews with the tape, but she was scared of him. She planned to use me as a go-between. When I found her dead I simply took the tape and used a different approach.' He nodded toward Edwin Mathews. 'Ours is a business deal.'

'Did you kill her?' asked Hallie in a choked voice, staring at the man before her, still in shock.

'Jasmine? I know you'd like to believe I did, but someone else had already done the honors before I arrived that night. She was dead when I got there.' Casey shrugged his shoulders, dismissing the tragedy of Jasmine's murder.

'But why involve me?' she whispered shakily, still not fully believing what she was hearing. 'Why couldn't you have given them the tape? It was in your safe-deposit box.'

'I tried that once,' he explained smoothly, 'when I first placed the tape in the box at the bank for safe-keeping, but it was too risky to go back for it after that. I was afraid someone had read of my death in the paper, or seen the news on TV. I didn't know if you remembered the box, and I was afraid you would have notified the bank of my recent demise. That's why I needed you, Hallie. I even broke into your apartment behind these guys and left the key where I knew you would be sure to find it.'

'Our wedding picture,' she gasped.

'You are so predictable, Hallie. I knew that was the one thing you would never get rid of.'

'But I didn't know about the safe-deposit box. What if I hadn't gone after the tape?'

'One way or another, I would have made sure that you retrieved the tape.'

Hallie stared at Casey, struggling with the reality of his presence. He was still glittering and golden, but there was a hardness in his eyes. He was so . . . unaffected by all this. Her distress over his death and now the danger she was in meant nothing to him. He was cold and composed, unemotional and completely lacking in remorse for his sins against her and his family.

She shook her head hopelessly, as tears that had nothing to do with her fear, or the pain and bruises she had suffered, spilled down her cheeks. The man who stood before her was a stranger. 'What happened to you, Casey?'

He came toward her, ignoring her question, intent only on getting what he wanted. 'Mr Mathews is willing to pay me a great deal of money as soon as you hand over the tape. More than enough to start another life somewhere else. Don't screw this up. They'll hurt you, Hallie.'

'Would you care, Casey? Would you try and stop them?' she cried.

'Just tell them where to find the tape,' he commanded.

'This is all very touching,' interrupted Mathews, 'but we have a problem. This is not the tape. Without it there will be no deal.'

'No!' protested Casey, his golden smile quickly fading.

'The tape is blank, Prescott. I don't like people who lie to me.'

'No, wait,' pleaded Casey. 'Wait. There's been some mistake. Give me a chance . . . You can't . . .?' Beads of sweat suddenly dotted his forehead. Fear replaced the coldness in his green eyes.

'Ah, you misjudge me, Casey, but perhaps your wife here doesn't fully understand how important this tape is to me. Or to you.' Mathews's smile was evil, menacing. 'It seems that Janice – ah, Jasmine, I believe she called herself, conveniently got herself killed by someone else. You see, Jasmine recorded a telephone conversation of mine and heard me making certain arrangements as to the disposal of an important political figure.'

'Murder, you mean! You had Senator Rawlins murdered!' Hallie cried out, convinced now that it was only a matter of time before he would give the order to have her killed. She knew too much. They

269

would never let her go. Grant would never be able to save her now.

'Precisely,' said Mathews with a small smile. 'I had Hugh Rawlins killed because he failed to cooperate. This whole episode has created a certain amount of discomfort for me for a very long time, and now I'm ready to put an end to it. If you fail to tell me what you have done with the tape, you could suffer the same unfortunate consequences as our mutual friend, Jasmine.'

'Hallie,' pleaded Casey.

Hallie turned toward Casey. 'You bastard! How could you do something so demented . . . so sick?'

'Give it to them, Hallie. Please. You don't know these people.'

'I don't have it,' she screamed. 'Don't you understand? I don't have it!'

'For chrissake, Hallie, they're going to kill me. Give them the . . .' Casey looked around him. Fear and panic had replaced his earlier calmness.

From the corner of her eye Hallie saw Mathews nod once more. This time to a man whose presence she hadn't noticed before. He pulled a gun and aimed it at Casey.

Hallie's cry of denial died in her throat when she heard the sharp crack of the gun as it was fired. A look of disbelief crossed Casey's face as he was spun around by the force of the bullet; then he crumpled on the floor. She screamed again, then stared in horror as a pool of blood seeped from beneath Casey's body and ran toward her feet. This time she was certain Casey hadn't escaped death.

Suddenly there was terse cry of 'Police!'

Hallie glimpsed the flash of metal as Paul jerked his gun from his jacket. The sound of another gunshot rang in her head and Hallie watched in horror as Paul's stocky body careened into the glass table next to him, then hit the floor. Hallie frantically scrambled away. Horrified, she watched helplessly as blood spurted from his neck.

Behind her a uniformed officer stood in the doorway, his legs spread, pivoting, his gun pointed with both hands. Suddenly the room was filled with commands and activity as several uniformed officers moved to handcuff Mathews and his men.

'You have no right –' began Mathews, but his protest was cut short by Grant Keeler.

'You're under arrest, Mathews, for conspiracy to murder Senator Rawlins, the murder of Casey Prescott and the kidnapping of Hallie Prescott.'

At the sound of Grant's voice Hallie sagged in relief.

Sam Harris signaled the uniformed officer to take Mathews out of the house. Simultaneously, the officer began to read Mathews his rights. But Mathews wasn't listening. 'I want to call my lawyer,' he shouted. 'This is an outrage!'

'Get him out of here,' ordered Grant as he reached down to gently help Hallie to her feet. With his arm wrapped protectively around her shoulders he led her outside, away from the scene of carnage and betrayal, to an unmarked car. Carefully, he helped her into the front seat.

She smiled crookedly, then winced in pain. The swelling around her mouth and eye was just beginning

271

to show. Her lip was cut. 'Are you okay, babe?' he asked tenderly, all the while feeling guilty that he had been a part of this whole setup. He had known from the beginning that Hallie would be at risk. 'We know about Casey,' he said, his voice unexpectedly gentle.

She nodded. It was all she could do. If she tried to talk, she would only cry.

Sam climbed into the back seat and reached across the back of her seat to touch Hallie's shoulder, to reassure her that she was safe. 'That's going to be some shiner, kid,' he said with a feeble attempt at humor. He felt terrible just looking at her delicate face. It would only be a matter of minutes before it became discolored with bruises and distorted with swelling.

Hallie fixed her eyes on Grant as they drove away in an attempt to reassure herself that everything was going to be okay now that he was here beside her. He looked over at her, his concern evident in his eyes. 'I'm taking Hallie to the hospital,' announced Grant over his shoulder. From the back seat Sam nodded his approval.

'I don't want –' protested Hallie, but the effort seemed futile when Sam interrupted.

'You have to, Hallie.'

At the emergency-room entrance, they left Sam, assuring him that they would take a cab after Hallie had been treated.

Grant remained at Hallie's side while the doctor examined her. 'Were you hit anywhere else beside the face?'

'No,' Hallie replied. The doctor reached for her hands, turning them palms up to reveal cuts and scrapes. 'I fell when I tried to escape,' she explained, looking down at her hands as if remembering for the first time that she had hurt them when she fell. 'My knees are pretty messed up, too.'

The doctor instructed an assistant to clean the cuts and Hallie winced when the antiseptic was applied.

'You tried to escape?' asked Grant with a quick smile.

'Yes,' she answered, not missing the surprise in his voice. 'Oh, Grant, I was so scared. I forgot everything you told me. I knew they were going to kill me. And then Casey . . . Casey was there! It was such a terrible shock. And to see him murdered . . .' her voice trailed off.

In that moment Grant wanted to take her in his arms and tell her how very, very sorry he was that he hadn't protected her from all this. But he knew that Hallie would never understand all the reasons why he had allowed her to risk her life.

'Where were you all that time?' she asked with a little cry as the assistant applied a salve to her hand. 'I thought any minute you would come through the door and get me out of there.'

Grant looked away uneasily. 'We had no idea that things would escalate that quickly,' he replied, hating the lie.

'Okay, Mrs Prescott,' interrupted the doctor. 'We're all done here. You should be fine other than being very sore and bruised.' With one finger under her chin, he looked her face over again. 'And if I were you, I wouldn't schedule a screen test for at least a month,' he quipped.

Hallie wanted to smile, but it hurt too much.

CHAPTER 19

So far Grant had not asked Hallie to recount anything that had happened to her that day. She would have to make a statement, but tomorrow would be soon enough. He had insisted on taking her back to his apartment, and she was too exhausted to protest. Once there, he made sure she had everything she needed within reach, then he left to catch up with Sam at headquarters.

A half-hour later Hallie stepped gingerly out of the shower. The spray of water had hurt her face and it had been difficult to keep her bandaged hand dry, but the hot water had felt good everywhere else. Wrapped in a fluffy towel, she lay down on Grant's bed. It was now late afternoon but she felt as if it was the middle of the night. Within minutes she was sound asleep.

When she awoke two hours later it was dark. Disoriented, she sat on the side of the bed for a moment, then went into the bathroom in search of her clothes. They were there, right where she had left them in a heap, still soggy from the shower spray. She would just have to borrow something of Grant's.

As she pushed the hangers in the closet from one direction to the other she was reminded of that day before Christmas when she had been straightening Casey's clothes. His behavior that day, just like so many other times, should have been a clue. But she had missed it. Missed them all. It was true that he had always been particular about his clothes, but his behavior that day had been bizarre.

When her search of the closet yielded nothing suitable, Hallie moved to the dresser. In the bottom drawer she found a white T-shirt and a pair of sweat pants. Holding up the sweat pants, she realized they would be much too large, but she could make them work by tightening them and rolling the waist band over several times.

Hallie looked at herself in the mirror and made a face. She looked like a clown with her rumpled hair and baggy pants. Then she giggled. All she needed to complete the picture was one of those fake flowers that squirted water. It would complement her red puffy nose and her purple bruises.

She turned and began to search the top drawer of the dresser for a pair of socks. She might as well have big floppy feet also. Toward the back of the drawer she found a pair of white socks. She grabbed them and was about to shove the drawer closed when something familiar caught her eye. It was her phone number, her old phone number, from the house she and Casey had shared, and it was written boldly on the outside of a large, wrinkled manilla envelope. But why would Grant have her old phone number?

Hallie pulled the envelope from the drawer and

unfastened the clasp. She reached inside and what she saw next caused a deep, searing pain to rip through her. Her legs gave way and she stumbled backwards until she reached the edge of the bed. In the glow of the light from the lamp Hallie removed the contents from the envelope, spreading them one by one across the pillows. The pictures were of Jasmine and Casey, each one more graphic and disturbing than the one before it. The last was a picture of her, running from their house. Christmas night – the night she had discovered Jasmine and Casey together.

Hallie swallowed several times, then ran to the bathroom and fell to her bruised knees in front of the toilet. Over and over again she threw up as if she was trying to purge herself of the filth and betrayal she had just seen.

She had known about the pictures. Grant had told her of their existence that night at the restaurant. He had also told her that he believed that Casey had hired Nick Hardister. But seeing the pictures laid out before her somehow made what he did a thousand times worse. There had, at least, been room for doubt. But now, just as she had begun to come to terms with Casey's betrayal and his death, she was once again confronted with the ugly, sordid truth.

It was here in black and white: a stark testimonial to the world that he had not loved her, that she had not been enough for him; that he had resorted to depravities and deceit of a magnitude that she would never have believed him capable of.

Hallie had no idea how long she sat on the cold tile floor, her hand gripping the rim of the toilet. Finally she pulled herself up and washed her face in cold water, then reached into the medicine cabinet for the green bottle of mouthwash she found there.

A half-hour later she was seated on the bed, the pictures scattered around her when she heard Grant come in. By now her shock and disgust had been replaced by a white-hot rage.

'Hallie?'

She didn't answer. She could hear the jingle of his keys as he placed them along with his pocket change on the kitchen counter. The cool mint taste of the mouthwash still lingered in her mouth, but the rest of her seemed to be on fire.

'Hallie?' he repeated softly at the doorway to the bedroom. 'Are you . . .?' Grant stopped. Hallie sat on the bed, her back toward him. Something is wrong, he thought, moving toward the side of the bed. Then he saw the envelope clutched to her breasts and the pictures scattered around her. 'Oh, God,' he whispered.

He had known at some time he would have to tell her about the pictures but never, *never*, had he considered showing them to her. If he and Sam had not spent the last twenty-four hours watching over her, the pictures would have been safely locked away at the station.

She looked up at him and his heart ached at the sight of her now-purple bruises. 'How long have you had these?' she asked.

Grant reached for her, intending to hold her in his arms, but she jerked away from his outstretched hands. 'Answer me,' she demanded.

'I got them two days ago from the Santa Monica

police. Nick Hardister was found on the beach there. He was murdered.'

'Why didn't you tell me you had these?'

'I didn't want to, Hallie. I hoped you would never have to see them.'

'What were you going to do with them, Grant? Keep them and every once in a while drag them out just to remind yourself what a bastard I married?'

'They belong to the police, Hallie,' he answered quietly, desperately wanting to ease the punishment she was inflicting on herself.

'He was alive that whole time, you know. He faked his death.' Hallie paused and breathed deeply. 'Did you know that?' she whispered, almost as if this was the first time she could actually bring herself to acknowledge the truth.

'I didn't know for certain, not before we went in after Mathews,' he said quietly, 'but I began to suspect something like that a few days ago. The dates on the signature card that recorded the number of entries to Casey's safe-deposit didn't match up. The last one was two days after his death. We were in the process of verifying the signature.

'Oh.' The small sound escaped her and she was silent for a moment. 'Now you know about me and all about Casey. All the terrible things I never wanted to think about again, things he did that I never wanted anyone to know.'

'These have nothing to do with you, honey,' he said as he gathered the photos, stuffed them back into the envelope and put them out of sight. Then he took her by the arms and brought her close to him.

'Don't they?' she asked bitterly. 'Why do you think I set out to find a man the night I found you, Grant? It really wouldn't have mattered much who I left with that night, as long as he was willing to take me with him and make love to me. I was out to get revenge on a dead man. I needed to know that I was still desirable. I had to stop feeling like I was dead, too.'

'Hallie, baby, you are a very beautiful, very desirable woman,' Grant whispered softly.

Hallie turned away. 'Stop! I can't stand any more lies in my life. My marriage turned into a hateful lie and the funny thing was that everyone else in Hollywood seemed to know about it before I did. And now this.'

She swept her hand broadly to indicate the envelope he had just removed. 'How long have you been feeling sorry for the poor little widow, Grant? So sorry, in fact, that you took her to bed when all you were supposed to do was investigate the murder of her husband's lover. What a fraud you are!'

'You're the one that's a fraud,' Grant shot back at her, 'for refusing to admit that you were married to a man who lied and cheated. And now he's still causing you pain. And the irony of it is that you're still letting him get away with it. It's time to get on with your life, Hallie. But you can't do that until you admit that your husband was a rotten bastard who didn't deserve you!'

Hallie turned suddenly, pushing past him. 'I'm leaving.'

'It's late, Hallie, and you're upset and hurting. Stay here and I'll take you home in the morning.'

'No,' she said as she headed for the front door.

Grant reached for the car keys. 'Then I'll take you.'

Hallie pulled the front door wide and was surprised to see Sam standing there, his hand raised to knock.

'Hello.' When no one returned his greeting Sam's crooked smile faded and he added, 'Uh, I think I may have arrived at a bad time.' When his attempt at humor failed, he peered around Hallie and said to Grant, 'I'll call you in the morning.'

Grant rushed to the door. 'Actually, your timing couldn't be better.' Sam looked from Grant to Hallie. 'Hallie was just leaving. Will you take her home?'

'Well, uh, sure,' said Sam uncertainly. He wasn't sure what he had stumbled into, but he would be relieved to get out of the crossfire.

'I gather things are not going smoothly between you and Grant,' Sam said a few minutes later in the car.

Hallie didn't answer. She was too tired to do anything but nod her head. Sam was a nice man, he didn't deserve her wrath.

'I'm really sorry for everything you had to endure yesterday and today, Hallie,' Sam said sincerely. 'But I have to admit Grant was right. Letting Mathews's men come to you was certainly the way to handle things. I have to tell you that I was against it at first, putting you at risk like that, especially when we gave you a blank tape. But Grant . . .'

Hallie jerked her head toward Sam, struggling to sit up. 'What did you say?'

Too late Sam realized his mistake. He had assumed that by now Grant had told Hallie all about . . . *Damn.* Would he never learn to keep his mouth shut?

'We . . . uh . . . nothing, actually.'

'You and Grant knew that the tape was blank? You sent me into that hellhole with a blank tape? You knew I was in danger and still you delayed coming after me? Did you know that I was scared out of my mind? I thought they were going to kill me at any minute. Are you telling me that you knew they would come after me like that?' By now Hallie was near hysteria. 'You let me go through this when you could have stopped it?'

Sam nodded miserably, and feebly tried to defend their action in the face of Hallie's incredulous interrogation. 'We didn't know for sure that they would rough you up like that, Hallie, but we did hope that the blank tape would provoke Mathews into revealing his involvement in Senator Rawlins's murder.'

'Boy, you two are certainly a pair. Anything for law and order, and screw anyone or anything that gets in your way. Is that it, Sam?'

Before Sam could explain, Hallie ordered him to stop the car. He slammed on the brakes, coming to a stop just as the car door swung open.

'Hallie, wait!' called Sam, but she was already out of the car and hurrying down the street toward her apartment. 'Hell!' exclaimed Sam. Why the hell hadn't he kept his mouth shut? Hallie would have never been the wiser, but he honestly thought that Grant had explained why they had deliberately put off coming after her.

Once inside her apartment Hallie threw herself on the bed. The tears that followed were accompanied by hard, racking sobs. Finally she gave into the confusion, bitterness and betrayal she felt. The harder she cried, the more mixed up things became in her mind.

How could Casey do the terrible things he had done? Did he ever consider what his affair with Jasmine and his cocaine addiction would do to their marriage? How could he have faked his death? Didn't he realize the anguish he would cause?

Didn't he care? Had he *ever* loved her?

And Grant. How could he have ever agreed to put her in such danger? How could he have set her up like this, and allowed her to get hurt? She could have been killed, but he was willing to risk that just to get to Mathews.

Didn't anyone care what happened to her?

It was early morning before Hallie fell into a troubled sleep, certain that she would never trust another man as long as she lived.

Hallie was not the only one that sleep eluded that night. In his apartment Grant cursed the fact that Hallie had found those pictures. He had never intended for her to see them. In fact, if they hadn't been related to Nick Hardister's death, he would have burned them the minute he had gotten his hands on them.

But Grant's restlessness and inability to sleep that night also went beyond that scene with Hallie to Hallie herself. For the most part his work here in Los Angeles was done. It was time to move on. Ordinarily he would have had no problem with that, especially in this instance, except for Hallie. He had absolutely no idea what he was going to do about her. But then, he reasoned, why should he have to do anything about her?

He poured himself a glass of wine and carried it into the bedroom with him. And by the time he was finished with it he knew that walking away from her would be difficult. But to stay would be worse. There were things he needed to resolve – there was still Libby. How could he be in love with another woman when he still loved Libby with all his heart?

Finally, Grant stretched out on the bed, waiting for sleep.

CHAPTER 20

'Hey man, congratulations!'

'Yeah, way to go!

'Guess it isn't every day that you land a fish as big as Edwin Mathews.'

Sam grinned and waved self-consciously at the comments from his co-workers the next morning.

'You're a hero, Sam,' Hallie said, as he escorted her into a large office that faced out toward the parking lot. In the light of morning she had forgiven Sam. He wasn't responsible for putting her in jeopardy.

Sam still had the same silly grin plastered on his face that he had been wearing all morning. No matter how hard he tried he couldn't hide it. 'Bringing Mathews down is definitely a career move in the right direction,' admitted Sam.

After receiving a few more congratulatory handshakes, Sam asked Hallie, 'Have you seen Grant this morning? I know he wanted to talk to you before you gave a statement.'

Hallie shook her head. Just then Grant joined them along with two other men. With the exception of their ties, they were dressed nearly identically in conservative dark gray suits. Hallie looked around in confusion.

'Two groups are represented here,' explained Sam. 'Besides the Los Angeles Police Department – that's me and Detective Ramirez – you remember him? – these two men along with Grant represent the Federal Bureau of Investigation. They, of course, are only interested in your statement about what occurred during the two days that preceded Mathews's arrest. So we'll start with that.'

Ramirez, the detective who had first questioned Hallie about Jasmine's murder, had just joined them. At the introduction he nodded at Hallie just as the two men from the FBI had.

The entire session took less than forty-five minutes. During that time, Hallie watched Grant closely, but his somber expression told her nothing. Whenever possible, she avoided meeting his piercing gray eyes.

When the two men thanked her and stood to leave, Hallie also stood, reaching for her purse, as she too prepared to leave. She turned in surprise when Grant laid a restraining hand on her shoulder.

'We need to ask you a few more questions,' said Grant.

Sam rubbed his jaw as he spoke. 'Hallie, we ran a check of every phone call each of the suspects made the night of Jasmine Turner's murder. Most of what we found, we already knew or suspected. Jasmine called you the night before she was killed. Do you have any idea why?'

'My answering machine picked up the call.'

'Do you have any idea what she wanted?' Ramirez asked.

Hallie fixed an icy stare on him. 'She already had the one thing that was important to me – my husband. Beyond that, I had no reason to speak with her. I never spoke with her except at our first meeting the night of her party.'

Sam fiddled with the pencil in his hand, then looked toward Grant. With obvious discomfort Sam prepared to ask Hallie a question he wished he didn't have to.

'There was another call,' interjected Grant. 'And we almost missed that. It was only when we ran a second check that we remembered to include any calls that were made on cellular phones.'

His eyes were the color of steel and just as cold as he stared at her. 'Hallie, why didn't you tell us about the phone call you received from Irwin Turner the night of the murder?'

Hallie looked from one man to the other, her confusion evident in her blue eyes. 'I don't understand,' she began. 'I didn't . . . Irwin Turner? There must be some mistake.'

'Think back, Hallie, to the night that Jasmine was murdered, that same night. There was another call,' prodded Sam.

Hallie sat back in her chair and closed her eyes. She struggled, now, to remember the details of that night. Nothing.

No! Wait! There had been a call . . .

She sat up very straight now. Her eyes wide at the memory. 'I *do* remember a call. Up until this very minute I had forgotten all about it. At the time I dismissed it as a prank or a wrong number. The connection was bad and the words were disjointed. He said something about my husband.'

Hallie paused for a moment, then raised her hand to cover her lips, looking from one man to another. 'You don't think . . .?'

'How well did you know Irwin Turner?' asked Sam.

'Not well. I met him at a party at his home. The same party where I met Jasmine.'

'Then why do you think he would call you?' asked Grant.

'I don't know,' Hallie answered defensively.

'Sam,' asked Grant, 'could we have a few minutes alone?'

'Huh? Oh, yeah, sure.' Sam stood, looking from Grant to Hallie, obviously surprised by Grant's request. 'Come on, Ramirez, let's, uh, get some coffee.'

When they were alone Grant picked up the same pencil that Sam had discarded minutes ago and tapped it repeatedly against the desk top while he considered his next question. After a moment he asked quietly, 'Hallie, why did you go to see Jasmine Turner the night she was murdered?'

CHAPTER 21

Seconds ticked by, but so far the only sound in the room had been Hallie's involuntary gasp. Now she sat with her eyes closed tightly, her head cradled in her hands.

'How did you know?' she whispered.

Grant raised his hands to his head, rubbing his temples with his fingertips. 'A neighbor who was walking his dog remembered seeing your car. The Tennessee license plates stuck in his mind. Seems he has a brother who lives there. Plus, he was able to pinpoint the time of your visit. Evidently, he is one of these people who adheres to a rather rigid daily schedule.'

Grant searched her face. What he saw there made it difficult to keep his breathing even and his features calm. Her beautiful face may have been covered with nasty bruises, but her eyes were guileless. This was not the face of a murderer.

If he hadn't loved her so much at that moment, then maybe he might have remembered all those textbook cases of crimes so violent and so vicious that they almost defied the imagination, many of which had been committed by the most surprising people – people who had wide guileless eyes, who could lie so convincingly they fooled even the experts. People who had faces like angels.

In a gesture that reflected his inner turmoil, Grant ran his hands though his dark hair, then sighed. Quietly he asked, 'Why, Hallie? Why did you go there that night?'

'Do you think I killed her?' Hallie asked just as quietly as she once more raised her eyes to meet his. She tried, but she could not keep her voice from trembling.

'It doesn't matter what I think. What matters is that the police can now place you at the scene.'

'What you think matters to me, Grant. Do you believe I killed Jasmine?'

Grant leaned forward, wanting to reach out and take her in his arms and tell her everything would be okay. But he couldn't. First he had to hear what she had to say. 'Tell me about that night, Hallie,' he said as gently as possible.

Hallie sighed, feeling both relief and apprehension. Even though it was difficult to talk about, it felt cleansing to tell someone what she had done. Maybe this was how all criminals felt when they finally tired of hiding the truth and confessed their guilt. But what would happen to her now? Would she be arrested? Did they really think that she killed Jasmine?

She took a deep breath then began to speak. 'Jasmine's call the night before was upsetting. I tried to ignore it, but her message and the sound of her voice kept repeating itself in my head. Her voice was . . .

taunting. Almost as if she wanted to keep me informed about what she and Casey were doing; as if she was daring me to meet face to face with her once more.'

Hallie sat up a little straighter. 'I know it sounds trite, but it didn't at the time. I wanted her to know she hadn't gotten the best of me.' Her hands, which had been tightly clasped together in her lap, now began to fold and unfold nervously. 'You see, I lied about having seen Jasmine only once. The second time was in my house, the house where Casey and I lived. He brought her there on . . . on Christmas night. I walked in on them while they . . .' She stopped, biting her lip, then turned her head, and let her eyes roam over the room until she could regain enough control to go on. 'That's when the pictures were taken. That night.'

'Hallie,' whispered Grant, wishing he could make all this go away for her. The sight of her bruises made his heart ache. But he stopped himself from offering the consolation that hovered there on the tip of his tongue. This was an official procedure. Any efforts to console her would have to come later.

'That picture of me running from the house was taken that night. I can't begin to tell you what I was feeling – humiliation, anger, hurt. I was deeply hurt. Betrayed. And I . . . I wanted to see Jasmine again. I was suddenly overcome with an anger that I thought I had gotten over. I wanted to confront her, to tell her how she had destroyed my life and Casey's.

'So that evening I drove to her apartment, and I got out of the car and started across the street. But just then I . . . I heard sirens nearby and, it sounds stupid, but I got scared. Like I was going to get caught doing something wrong. Maybe I just came to my senses, I don't know, but I ran back to my car and drove away.' Hallie raised her eyes to meet his.

'Did you see anything or anyone?' asked Grant.

'No, by then it was dark.'

'Why didn't you tell this to the police when they first questioned you?'

Without taking her eyes from his Hallie answered. 'I was scared,' she confessed, 'and ashamed – ashamed to admit that my anger had finally driven me to the point where I wanted to confront the woman who had taken my husband from me.'

Grant nodded silently. He understood that kind of anger. It was the same kind of consuming anger he had felt after Libby's death.

Hallie watched Grant closely as he assessed her words. While there was understanding in his eyes, and compassion, he had not said that he believed her. Disappointment settled like a lump in her throat. After all they had been to each other, could he really believe she was capable of murder?

Grant stood, indicating that his part of the interview was at an end. When Sam returned a few minutes later he signaled to an officer waiting outside the door and in a low voice issued a series of instructions that Hallie could not hear. After a few more questions Sam told Hallie that she could leave and he summoned another officer to escort her to her car while he and Grant remained in the office.

'This is just the beginning, Sam,' said Grant later as they were leaving the building. 'Not only do we still have a murder to solve, but some very important people are going to be implicated along with Mathews, especially when this goes to trial. There will be lots of noise from some very nervous people. And probably some threats as well. So watch your back.'

Frank Guzman, Sam's immediate supervisor, stopped both men in the parking lot and extended his hand to first to Sam, then to Grant. 'Got to hand it to you, Keeler. We weren't keen on having the FBI here in the beginning, but you and Harris make a good team.'

'Thanks,' replied Grant, but his enthusiasm was dampened by what had happened last night between him and Hallie, and now by the startling discovery that Hallie had actually been at Jasmine's the night of the murder.

So far this morning he hadn't had a chance to speak privately with Sam to find out what Hallie might have said on the way home the previous night. Each time it looked like they would have a few uninterrupted minutes, Sam would excuse himself on the pretense of having something that needed his immediate attention.

By lunchtime it had become obvious to Grant that Sam was deliberately avoiding him except in the company of others. 'What is going on here?' asked Grant finally. 'Why are you avoiding me?'

Sam actually managed to look hurt.

'Cut it out, Harris. Let's go get something to eat. I want to know about last night when you drove Hallie home.'

The two men stopped at the delicatessen a half-block

west of the station. Grant had just taken a bite out of his sandwich when Sam told him about his foolish revelation to Hallie.

Grant nearly choked.

'Son of a bitch,' croaked Grant when he could speak again. 'You actually told her that we had set her up with a blank tape on purpose?'

Sam nodded, and this time he looked genuinely contrite. 'Honestly, I thought you had probably leveled with her and that you two were having a good laugh over the whole thing.'

'It wasn't exactly a laughing matter,' pointed out Grant with a wry smile.

'Well, I found that out,' admitted Sam, 'when Hallie nearly jumped out of the car while it was still moving.'

Grant finished his sandwich and went outside to the nearest pay phone to call Hallie, but there was no answer. Intermittently for the remainder of the day and night, he continued to dial her number with the same results.

It was past nine the next evening before Grant was able to break free and go over to Hallie's apartment. When she answered the door he followed her into the living room.

'Aren't you glad to see me?' he teased, knowing that she had been deliberately avoiding him.

'No,' she answered crossly. At the small counter that separated her living room from her tiny kitchen she halted, crossing her arms over her chest. 'What do you want?'

'I wanted to explain things to you.' When she didn't

respond he continued, 'About the past few days.'

Still nothing.

'You're not going to make this easy on me, are you, Hallie?'

She shook her head.

'We've arrested Jasmine's murderer,' Grant announced softly. Hallie turned, startled, but before her lips could form the question, Grant answered it. 'This afternoon a warrant was issued to search the house and any automobiles belonging to Irwin Turner. Tonight, he was placed under arrest for the murder of his wife. Irwin Turner,' he repeated grimly as though he, too, was having trouble believing that someone of that stature could be a part of something so violent.

'But why? Why would he do something like that?'

'She threatened him with the pictures. We know that Hardister tried in the beginning to sell them to Turner, but he wasn't buying. Unfortunately for her, Jasmine threatened to go even further. She threatened to tell everyone that Turner liked to watch her having sex with other men, so much so that he hired Hardister to take those pictures. Jasmine wanted money from her estranged husband and she was ready to resort to lies and blackmail to get it. It was too much for him. It pushed him over the edge. He drove to her apartment. He had to stop her.'

'But how did you know it was him?' asked Hallie.

'We didn't until you remembered the phone call. He must have seen you there. Maybe his call was meant to be a warning to you, or a threat against Casey. Right now it's only speculation, but it's possible that the man who was actually run over the night that Casey faked his death may have been hired by Turner to go after Casey.

'To kill him?' asked Hallie, still stunned.

'Or to rough him up.' said Grant. 'At any rate, the phone call triggered something else. When he had been questioned about his wife's murder, Turner had told the police that Jasmine had called him at work the day before she was murdered. Turner told us that she was always asking him for more money. There were things that just didn't ring true,' said Grant, then recounted what Turner had told the police.

'And what was the context of that call, Mr Turner?' the police had asked.

Irwin had turned his head, suddenly overcome with grief, even for a wife who had betrayed him. 'We were in the process of divorcing, but you must know that,' he said after a few moments. 'In spite of our recent problems there were some good memories between us, and now . . . now I just can't believe it. Jasmine certainly did not deserve to be murdered.'

'The phone call?' prompted the detective.

'Money,' answered Irwin. 'She always wanted more money. Poor Jasmine. I gave her a great deal of money each month, but . . . she always wanted more.' He smiled sadly now, then looked toward the ceiling as if he was making an attempt to recall some cherished memory for their benefit. 'She was a very beautiful woman, you know.'

The young detective nodded, only half-listening now. Irwin Turner was rambling on like an old man. 'Green was her color. Deep emerald . . .'

'What did you tell her?'

For a moment, Turner's eyes clouded in confusion. Then he continued. 'I told her that I had already given her as much money as she was going to get until the divorce.'

'Was she angry?'

'Of course,' he answered. 'Jasmine was always angry when she couldn't get what she wanted.'

'And what about you? Were you also angry that she was trying to hit you up?'

Irwin sighed. 'Irritated, maybe. But you have to understand how Jasmine was. Since the separation I had become accustomed to her frequent requests for money.'

'On the surface,' explained Grant, 'it sounded plausible. A husband who, fully aware of his wife's shortcomings, accepting the inevitable. Plausible, except for a few curious things. According to the lawyer representing Irwin Turner in the divorce proceedings, Irwin had had absolutely no contact with his wife since the morning she was first notified by the attorney that he would sue for divorce. Until the day before her murder.

'He said something else in the first interrogation that bothered Sam,' Grant continued. 'Turner had said that green was Jasmine's favorite color, that he would always associate that color with her. Sam did some checking. There was nothing green hanging in Jasmine's closet on the night she was murdered. It was only logical that a woman would own several items in a color that was her favorite. But she *was* wearing green silk slacks and a matching shirt the night she was

296

murdered. That particular piece of information was never released to the press. Turner's mention of green seemed to be more than coincidental.'

'But that doesn't prove . . .' interrupted Hallie.

'No, you're right,' Grant said, 'except for one thing. A check of Jasmine's credit card purchases revealed she had purchased that outfit the same day she was killed.'

'But still,' insisted Hallie, 'maybe Turner was only reminiscing when he mentioned the color green.'

'That was a possibility,' agreed Grant, 'but it was enough to set the wheels in motion. A search of Turner's car this afternoon yielded fibers that matched the green silk that Jasmine was wearing. We also found blood samples that matched hers. It was enough to arrest him. Another search of Jasmine's apartment will probably turn up more evidence that will definitely place him in her apartment at the time of the murder.'

'I almost feel sad for him,' murmured Hallie. 'I only met him once at a party at his home, but I thought he was a kind man.'

'So did a lot of other people,' Grant added. 'Maybe he was. Maybe Jasmine pushed him beyond reason.'

Hallie shook her head, finding it hard to believe that a man like Irwin Turner, a man who had everything, would do something so terrible.

'What about Nick Hardister?'

'Hardister was a con man, not a murderer. He had also been in Jasmine's apartment the night of the murder. He was more than ready to threaten blackmail, but he didn't have what it took to commit murder. It was never reported in the newspaper, but there was another 911 call that night besides the one Casey made.

Hardister called us from Jasmine's apartment, then he ran. Murderers don't usually call the police to report what they have done. Jasmine was already dead by the time his call came in.'

'Is this what you came to tell me?' she asked after a few minutes.

'Part of it. Actually I came to talk to you about the role you played in Mathews's arrest and what happens next. The trial will begin in a few months. You will have to testify.'

Hallie wished it would all disappear. 'I know,' she said.

'We want you in protective custody. That way you'll be safe. Not that we really expect anything to happen to you.'

'Good,' she replied, 'because I don't really expect anything to happen either. You can forget about "protective" anything, Grant. I have to get my life back on track, and the idea living in a hotel room at the government's expense with guards around the clock while I wait for this trial to begin doesn't excite me. I need a job, I have bills to pay, and I need to start acting like a normal person again.'

'Hallie . . .' began Grant, hoping to change her mind, but the stubborn look on her face stopped him.

'Okay, you win. But there will be someone to check on you from time to time. We'll try to be inconspicuous, but your safety is important to us.'

'Is it? I know how you used me,' Hallie said accusingly. 'You certainly weren't concerned about my safety then.' Today her face looked even worse than the day before.

Grant wanted to take her in his arms and caress her bruised face, and tell her that he would never let anyone hurt her again. But he knew she wasn't ready for that. 'That part is true, honey, but there wasn't any other way to do it. We have been after Mathews for years. It was important for a lot of different reasons, Hallie.' Grant ran his hand through his hair.

'Important enough to get me killed?'

'I didn't have any choice. Sending you into Mathews's house with a blank tape was not my idea. It was an order. Don't you see, Hallie?'

There was no way she could mistake the regret in his eyes. And faced with it, she looked away.

Grant continued, 'It's not something I'm proud of. I was worried sick about you, worried that something would happen to you before I could get you out of there.'

Hallie let her arms fall to her sides, then she turned toward the kitchen, away from Grant.

'Please understand, Hallie. I would have never hurt you if I could have kept from it. But there are times when my job gets in the way.'

Grant's mind raced. How could he explain that only by putting Mathews behind bars could he feel that he had come to terms with Libby's senseless death? 'We would never have let anything happen on purpose,' insisted Grant.

'Well, there were a few times when you could have fooled me. I was so scared. How could you let me go through that?'

It was the opening he had been waiting for. He moved toward her, but she held up her hand to stop him. 'Explain it to me.'

Grant took a deep breath then, exhaling, he told her of the first time he had investigated Mathews, of Jasmine's involvement and how her disappearance, along with the taped conversation of Mathews ordering the murder of Senator Rawlins, had left the government unable to prosecute.

Finally, he spoke of Libby, the baby she was carrying, her death, and how he had felt so terrible for not protecting her.

'I . . . I had no idea,' whispered Hallie. 'I'm so sorry.'

'You couldn't have known how important this was to me, but I have done the best I could to make things right,' replied Grant.

Now it was Hallie's turn to take a deep breath before voicing the question that was uppermost in her mind. 'And what now, Grant? What about us?'

Gently, Grant reached out to caress Hallie's tender swollen face. But the words he wanted to say would not come. There were still too many memories. He needed more time. 'I don't know.'

Hallie swallowed, hurt by his words. She knew she loved him. What was keeping him from admitting that he felt the same way about her?.

'I have to return to Washington. There's still a lot of work to be done before Mathews's trial can begin here in Los Angeles.'

'Oh.' The small, quiet sound of that word echoed and lingered. It contained all Hallie's hopes for the future. It rang with disappointment.

They were silent for a moment, then Grant asked, 'What about you?'

Hallie bit her lip to keep it from quivering. No matter

what, she would not let him see her cry. This had been something she had thought about often since Casey's funeral, but up until now she had not made a decision. 'After the trial, I . . . I might go home to Mississippi for a visit. To see my aunt. I might stay a while.' Or a lifetime, she added silently.

More than anything Hallie wanted to hear him ask her not to go. She wanted to tell him she would wait for him. But the time was not right, the memories too fresh, and the hurt still hovered too close to the surface.

'I see,' answered Grant. And he did. But right now there wasn't a damn thing he could do about it.

CHAPTER 22

She wasn't exactly sure when Grant left town. It didn't matter. There was nothing left to bind them together. Jasmine's murder had been solved, and soon Mathews's trial would begin. During the past few weeks she had come to count on Grant's presence. He had become a powerful force in her life, but now she was alone.

Maybe, she mused, it was never meant to be anything more than a brief interlude, but in her heart she knew it was so much more than that. She was in love with him, and sadly, she had believed that he felt the same about her.

During the long, lonely days she mulled over her future, taking solitary walks during which she weighed her options, and thought about the twists and turns her life had taken. At night she indulged her broken heart, listening to music that made her sad and watching romantic movies that made her cry. For several miserable days she considered going home to Mimosa until the trial began, but in the end she decided to stay in Los Angeles.

* * *

'Hallie,' Dana Gordon said excitedly a few days later, 'I have a lead on a job for you. I don't know much about it, but my dad said to tell you to check into it.' It was because of Dana, who seemed to know everyone, that Hallie now had a large group of friends.

'Should I call for an appointment first?' Hallie asked.

'No, just get on over there. You know how these jobs always get filled by somebody who knows somebody.'

Two hours later Hallie sat nervously waiting for the man behind the old-fashioned wooden desk to acknowledge her. But the only thing he had said to her so far was, 'Sit down, please.'

His head was bent, revealing the thinning brown hair, as he carefully read her resumé and the application she had filled out minutes ago.

The late-afternoon sun streamed into the drab office of Joseph Aaron, the owner of Aaron Costumes. From beyond the doorway, Hallie could hear the voices of his employees as they prepared to leave for lunch.

After a long silence, so long in fact that Hallie had to keep reminding herself to sit still and not fidget, Joseph Aaron fixed his brown eyes on Hallie. 'What kind of experience have you had, Miss Prescott?'

'None in costume design,' she answered honestly then added, 'but I've taken several classes at UCLA and designed and sewn evening wear for a number of people here in Los Angeles. It's how I've helped support myself while I've been looking for a job.'

Joseph Aaron looked at Hallie with new interest. He was tired of interviewing for this position, but at least this one wasn't another rich kid playing at being a

303

designer. 'Let me see your portfolio,' he said abruptly.

Hallie stood and placed the large leather case on the edge of the desk, then pulled the zipper to open it.

'Talk, talk,' he said with a wave of his hand. 'I don't just want pretty pictures, I want to know why you did this. And this.' His finger moved from one detail to another on the drawings before him.

Hallie took a deep breath, and as she turned the pages her enthusiasm for the work she loved doing most became evident.

'And what if I hire you and teach you the business then you leave me and get famous?' he asked with a sincerity that was surprising.

Just as sincerely Hallie answered, 'If you hire me, I will do the best work I can for you. But I will leave here eventually, and I will use everything I've learned from you. I'll become famous, too. But I'll always say that it was Mr Aaron who made it all possible, who gave me a chance when no one else would.'

Even though he tried, it was difficult to suppress his smile. Joseph Aaron was beginning to like this girl with the hair that almost glowed.

'You're hired,' he said, then named a salary that was far below what she needed.

Hallie shook her head. 'I can't work for that,' she said with more bravado than she felt, then she named a figure that was almost twice that of his offer.

Joseph's eyebrows shot up. 'Too much, too much,' he said with a shake of his head. 'You have no experience.'

'But I have to eat, nevertheless,' replied Hallie. 'If you don't pay me a decent wage, I'll have to keep cleaning my apartment building to make ends meet.'

Knowing that she couldn't afford her apartment for much longer unless she found a job, Hallie had struck a deal with the elderly couple who owned the building. She would clean any of the apartments that were vacated and supervise any necessary painting and repairs in exchange for half of her rent.

Becoming self-supporting had been her choice, but it had not been easy. She had sent the money she had found in Casey's safe-deposit box to his parents, keeping only enough to carry her through for a while. Only last week she had heard from Casey's parents that they planned to set up a scholarship at the University of Memphis in Casey's name. It would be specifically reserved for students who intended to pursue a writing career.

For Joseph Aaron, Hallie's revelation had just struck a chord. 'You clean houses?

Defensively, Hallie raised her chin a little higher. 'Only my apartment building.'

'How do you feel about cleaning up after other people?' he asked kindly.

'I'd rather be doing something else, but I do a good job.'

Joseph Aaron studied Hallie with new interest. For years after his father had died, his mother had supported her seven young children by cleaning houses. It was honorable work.

In the end they struck a bargain. He would pay her one-and-a-half times what he had originally offered. If she did a good job he would give her a raise in three months.

Hallie did some quick math. She could make it work if she was careful. Besides, she had had no other offers. Instinctively, Hallie knew that Mr Aaron's handshake was as good as his word.

That evening Dana and Hallie celebrated her new job with hamburgers at Johnny Rocket's on Melrose. It was one of their late-night favorites with its fifties style, great burgers, fries, and shakes. Hallie was especially impressed with the valet parking.

'Everyone in Los Angeles has valet parking,' Dana had explained seriously the first time she had taken Hallie there. Hallie had dissolved into giggles.

Dana had spent a lot of time in Los Angeles while she was growing up, and the irony of a hamburger stand with valet parking completely escaped her.

The fact of their friendship was also something of a surprise to Hallie. Dana had come from a privileged and sophisticated background, yet she and Hallie had hit it off perfectly from the beginning. In fact, they had known each other for a long time before Dana had revealed that her father was Neil Gordon.

When Hallie said nothing, Dana had repeated, 'Neil Gordon?'

Still Hallie said nothing, only shrugged her shoulders in a questioning gesture as if to say 'Who is that?'

Dana laughed. 'That's why I like hanging out with you, Hallie. Absolutely nothing about Hollywood impresses you.'

Suddenly, what Dana had just revealed registered and Hallie had actually gasped.

306

'Neil Gordon? You're kidding,' she said, at first not believing a word Dana had said. 'You think I just fell off the last turnip truck to cross the Mississippi state line?'

'Did you?' Dana replied, laughing. 'Neil Gordon really is my dad. You do have "talking" movies in Mississippi, don't you? You have seen some of his pictures, haven't you?'

Hallie ignored the jab at her home state and grinned. 'Uh huh. We even have movies in color, too. They change the feature once a week, every Thursday. Of course, if you want to see a first-run film, you have to drive about thirty-five miles to another town.'

This time it was Dana's turn to say, 'You're kidding!'

Hallie's work at Aaron's Costumes proved to be more exciting than the she had anticipated, for much of their business had to do with furnishing costumes for movies. For big-name, big-budget productions, Hallie often met with the film's costume designer, learning exactly what they were looking for, then supplying them. On films with low budgets, she was often given guidelines and it became her job to find or design the clothes they were looking for.

The assignments that involved period costumes were her favorite, though. It was this type of assignment that she had come to love the most, for even though it sometime required extensive research on the clothing of the time period in which the story took place, it also gave her the opportunity to use much of what she had learned in class to either create the clothing, or to comb second-hand stores and thrift shops for exactly the right thing.

In Hallie, Joseph Aaron had found someone who was dedicated and loyal. She was also quick to learn. The friendship that had developed between this somber, balding, middle-aged man and the talented young woman with the honeyed southern accent and the vivid copper hair was based on mutual respect.

Her job had become the focus of her life, edging out, but not quite replacing, the terrible longing that still lingered. It had been two months since she had seen Grant; two tormenting months during which she had vacillated between convincing herself that if she never saw him again it was good riddance – he had done nothing but make her miserable anyway – and telling herself that if she didn't see him again, she would surely die of a broken heart.

The time she had spent with him during the investigation had been the worst and the best time of her life. Lately, though, whenever she recalled that time, she tended to focus more on the time they had shared together, and less on the events that had brought them together. But now she immersed herself in her work, refusing to let her mind entertain fantasies that would never become reality.

In all this time she had not heard from Grant Keeler. Not one word.

Jeff Cousins stuck his head into Hallie's office. 'Are you going to spend the rest of the day in there, or will you be courageous and brave and have lunch with me?'

Hallie turned, surprised at the sound of his voice. So far, Jeff had asked her out every time he had been in Los Angeles, which was every few weeks. He was a manufacturer's representative for several of the smaller Eastern fabric mills.

'You should be taking Mr Aaron to lunch, Jeff.' she said. 'He's your client. Probably your best client.'

Jeff smiled. 'Joseph said he was busy. He also said that today you have no deadlines and nothing urgent that would keep you from having lunch with me.' Jeff, who was in his late twenties, had a boyish face and an engaging smile. His good nature was contagious.

Hallie returned his smile. She was well aware that any one of the single women who worked here would love to go out with him. And, like the others, she wasn't completely immune to his blond good looks. 'Okay. Lunch it is, exactly one hour, no longer, and I pick the place,' she said, reaching for her purse.

'Where to?' he asked once they were outside.

The breeze ruffled her copper hair. 'To my favorite place.'

Less than five minutes later Hallie was pumping catsup from the red plastic dispenser over her mustard-and-relish laden foot-long hot dog. Jeff watched with a grin. The hot-dog stand was on the corner near a small park.

'Be my guest,' Hallie said, as she picked up her coke with her free hand and moved out of his way.

Jeff declined her offer of catsup and followed her to a bench in the shade. 'You know, Hallie,' he said between bites, 'it isn't often that you run across a woman with a true appreciation of fine dining, not to mention the finesse required to eat something this messy.'

'There's an art to it,' she replied, licking her fingers.

'If you're too fussy about the ambiance, you miss out on some of the finest cuisine in the world.'

'I take it you are a regular customer.'

Hallie nodded. 'I like to get outside for lunch. It helps break up the day.'

'Have you ever been to Europe?' he asked.

She shook her head.

'They have wonderful food on the streets,' he declared, then went on to furnish her with colorful descriptions of all the places he had been.

The remainder of their conversation centered around their jobs and Joseph Aaron. During the walk back to work, Jeff stopped suddenly, reaching for Hallie's arm. 'This has been fun, Hallie. I'm going to be here in town for a few more days. Will you have dinner with me on Friday night?'

Hallie hesitated. She had always declined the invitations of men she worked with, saying that she never dated fellow employees. It was easier than explaining she never dated at all. Although this wasn't Jeff's first invitation, it was the first one she had ever considered accepting.

Recognizing her hesitation, Jeff softly assured her. 'It's just dinner. Nothing more.'

'Was I that obvious?' she asked with an embarrassed smile.

'Uh huh. If I didn't know better I might think there was a boyfriend or a husband in the picture. But I know there's not,' Jeff answered with certainty.

'You do?'

'I asked Joseph.'

Fearful of all the questions that might arise, Hallie

had checked the box marked single on her application. She had purposefully omitted the fact that she was a widow from her application. It seemed easier that way. Being single never required an explanation. Being widowed at her age would, and the notoriety that would follow once it was discovered who her husband had been, would be uncomfortable. It had taken a long time to come to terms with her guilt and anger over Casey's death. And, when she least expected it, she was surprised by the pain she still felt.

'Well?' asked Jeff. 'Dinner?'

Hallie studied the man in front of her. His eyes were a clear blue and beneath them his grin engaging and open. Jeff Cousins was a nice man, she thought. 'Dinner would be nice,' she answered.

And it was. Hallie had forgotten how good it felt to laugh and be in the company of a man who thought she was attractive and interesting. There was only one awkward moment when Jeff had innocently asked about what had brought her to Los Angeles.

She had answered with a half-truth about wanting to go to school. How could she have ever explained what her life had been like? How could anyone be expected to understand the sudden success that brought her to Los Angeles, the sordid details of her marriage, then her short and turbulent affair with Grant? While she had finally come to grips with Casey's betrayal, she had not resolved her feelings for Grant. But maybe she would never have to. It had been months now since they had parted, and still she had not heard from him.

Jeff, true to his word, was courteous, attentive and

engaging. At her door that evening, he kissed her lightly, promising to call her when he returned to Los Angeles.

Inside, Hallie kicked off her shoes. She had enjoyed Jeff's company, and she knew he liked her, but she wondered how long it would be before he would expect more from her.

Don't be silly, she thought. It was just a date.

The next few weeks at work were hectic. A new contract with an almost impossible completion date had everyone putting in more hours than before. Hallie worked hard, a fact that didn't go unnoticed by Joseph Aaron. As agreed, he had given Hallie her raise, pleased that he had found someone who was not only talented, but who seemed to enjoy the work as much as he did.

When his marketing director left to take another job, Joseph asked Hallie if she would be interested in the position.

'Do I know enough to handle it?' she asked candidly.

'No,' he answered truthfully, 'but I will teach you.'

'Will I make more money?' Hallie asked.

'Eventually,' he answered, 'but not until you can do the job without any assistance from me.' Once more they shook hands, sealing her new promotion.

It was a Friday night and she had just hung up from talking to Billie when the phone rang again. Hallie grabbed it quickly, certain that it was Billie calling back with something she had forgotten to tell her. 'Talk fast,' she teased, 'I'm dying to get out of these clothes.'

There was a small silence before a male voice said,

'Damn. I'm always in the wrong place at the wrong time.'

It was Jeff. Hallie giggled. 'Oops. Thought you were someone else.'

'I just called to see how you are. So, how are you?'

'Good,' she answered. 'I got a promotion today. Things are looking up.'

'Congratulations! We can celebrate when I get back to Los Angeles. I'll be there on the fifteenth and I'll take you somewhere special,' said Jeff. 'Now what else have you been up to?'

They talked for a half-hour and Hallie had to admit that Jeff was a bright spot in her life. If only she could keep things between them simple. He was intelligent, good-looking, and charming. What woman in her right mind could resist that combination? Hallie certainly couldn't, and she was looking forward to seeing Jeff again.

The 'somewhere special' to celebrate Hallie's promotion turned out to be a day-long outing. The drive from Los Angeles to Santa Barbara was beautiful and once there, they had lunch at a charming tearoom. The owner, who was a self-proclaimed psychic, did a reading for each of them.

'I don't believe in that stuff, do you?' Jeff said with a laugh as they left the tearoom.

Hallie smiled up at him. 'Why not?' she asked.

'Well, how could she know anything about either of us? She's never even seen us before.'

'A lot of things can't be explained,' she replied, unwilling to dismiss the woman's psychic ability. Hallie might have scoffed like Jeff except for one thing. When she had taken the chair across the table from the woman, Hallie had joked, 'I suppose you're going to tell me that I'm destined to meet a tall, dark and handsome man.' The woman had looked up at Hallie quizzically and studied her face for a few moments before she spoke. 'But you've already met him,' she said quietly.

A unexpected chill caused Hallie to shudder.

The woman continued. 'The man with the dark hair is far away. You're waiting for him to come for you.'

Hallie was momentarily shaken. 'Will he come back?' she whispered.

The woman sighed, shaking her head. 'I see him far away. I'm sorry. It's not clear.'

After a while Hallie put the woman's words aside. There was no reason to spoil the day and certainly no reason to give any significance to the words of a stranger. Grant had left her and it was foolish to cling to the hope that he would come back to her.

The rest of the afternoon was spent strolling idly from shop to shop and from one art gallery to another. At one of the galleries Hallie spotted a small watercolor of a child playing in the sand at the beach that stole her heart, but after checking the price, she knew that it was more than she could afford.

The drive home that afternoon proved to be just as enjoyable, and when Jeff suggested a late dinner she accepted. Like him, she was reluctant to have their time together end.

All in all it had been a pleasant day, but Hallie was bothered by what the tearoom owner had told her during her reading. Several times that afternoon, she had tried to put this aside, but it kept echoing in her head and she was sure the woman had been speaking of Grant.

Jeff had laughed later, telling Hallie that maybe what the woman saw was him each time he left to return home. Hallie had smiled at that and nodded. But she knew that Jeff was not the man the psychic had referred to – it was Grant.

A few days later a package for her arrived in the mail, and when she opened it, it took her breath away. It was the watercolor she had so admired that day in Santa Barbara. She knew it was from Jeff, and after calling him to express her surprise and her pleasure, she told him it was much too expensive. He laughed and reminded her that it was rare that something captured your heart the way that painting had. Besides, he had added, it was a gift to remind her of her promotion.

After Hallie had hung up, she continued to admire the watercolor. Jeff was sweet and generous, but she knew the day would come when he would want their friendship to become more, and she dreaded that day. From the beginning she had made it clear that she enjoyed his company, but wanted to remain uninvolved.

Hallie continued to see him whenever he was in town. Often he would call her between trips. She was content with their easy camaraderie, and hoped he was also. But all that changed in the course of one afternoon.

It was Sunday, one of those rare days when the world and everything in it seemed to sparkle. At Manhattan

Beach, the water was bluer, the skies clearer. The air had that wonderful warmth that comforts the mind and soothes the soul. Hallie and Jeff were walking hand in hand when Jeff, who had seemed preoccupied all afternoon, suggested that they sit for a while.

'You look so serious,' Hallie said with a smile.

'I am,' he answered, glancing toward her.

'Is something wrong?' she asked, brushing long, burnished strands of hair out of her eyes. The smile had faded.

'I don't know, Hallie. Is something wrong? With us, I mean. With me? We're not going anywhere, Hallie, you and me. You're content with things as they are between us, and each time I've tried to move our relationship forward physically, I've been rebuffed.'

'Jeff . . .'

He held up his hand as if to stop her. 'You're very gentle about it, Hallie, but you make it very clear that I've overstepped some invisible boundary.'

Hallie pulled her knees up, and wrapped her arms around them. Her hair fell forward, a copper curtain hiding the distress she felt.

'Is it always going to be like this between us?' he asked quietly.

Hallie sighed. Why couldn't things have stayed like they were? She turned to look at Jeff. He deserves better, she thought. He deserves the truth. 'You knew when you first asked me out that I wasn't interested in any kind of a relationship, remember?'

'Yes, but I thought that you were just . . . that maybe your last relationship hadn't worked out and you were just reluctant to begin another.'

Reluctant. Hallie closed her eyes for a minute, hoping to gather the words. Gentle words. The truth. She had no desire to see Jeff hurt. Yet she knew that no matter how carefully she phrased things, he would be hurt. Then he would move along.

'Oh, Jeff,' she began, propping her head on her folded arms as they rested against her knees. 'I don't know where to begin. You see, I haven't been completely honest with you.'

Occasionally Hallie would see an unmarked police car parked in front of her apartment. It was so easy to identify them. They looked like government cars – stripped down and stodgy. No one else would be caught dead driving one. At other times a patrol car would cruise the neighborhood, and Hallie took comfort in their presence. While she had declined the offer of protective custody, she did not take her personal safety for granted. Not any more.

Dana Gordon could hardly contain her excitement as she flew down the stairs, making a sharp U-turn toward the kitchen. Tonight everything had to be perfect. It was a party to celebrate her mother's return from Europe. A family reunion. She wished it had been as easy to explain her parents' unorthodox marriage as it had been to plan this party. But it wasn't.

'It's not exactly a commuter marriage,' she had said to Hallie over coffee several weeks earlier. 'I mean, they don't fly back and forth to see each other like a lot of other couples do. It's more like they're married, but

317

they lead independent lives except for once or twice a year when they're together, like normal.'

Hallie smiled and nodded, pretending to understand.

But Dana could see that she didn't. 'I know it's odd, but Mother prefers living in Europe. Her family is there. She and Daddy met there while he was filming on location. For the most part, his work is here in Los Angeles, although he sometimes does a movie outside the States, then they'll meet somewhere.'

'It's really difficult to explain, Hallie. I don't think it's weird because I grew up with it. The summers I always spent here with my father, the winters with my mother, usually in Spain or Italy.'

But it did seem weird to Hallie. In Mimosa, almost everyone had lived with both their parents except her and Tucker Davis, whose mother had been divorced since Tucker was a baby.

'But that's not important.' Dana rushed on. 'I've told my mother about the beautiful dresses that you design and she wants to see them. If she likes them and decides to wear one to the party, it could launch your career as a designer.'

'That's very kind of your mother, but I'm sure it would take more than her appearance in one of my dresses to make me an overnight success.' Hallie smiled and shrugged her shoulders.

Dana wanted to tell Hallie how wrong she was. Her mother's stamp of approval could insure Hallie's acceptance in the social circle that craved the best, the most expensive and the most innovative.

A quick conference with the caterer assured Dana

318

that everything was under control. Now all she had to do was stop worrying.

This was not the first party she had planned, but it was the first time that she would be responsible for launching a friend's career. If there was one thing that American society loved, it was European society. And Dana's mother reigned, no matter on which side of the Atlantic she happened to be in residence.

The white silk crêpe dress Selena LaBianca Gordon had chosen from the four that Dana had insisted Hallie bring over was the perfect foil to her dark hair and dark eyes. It was simple in the extreme, beautifully cut so that at each movement the fabric flowed. Hallie knew that the very absence of glitter and shine, combined with her exotic beauty, would make Dana's mother the most outstanding woman in the room.

'You look wonderful,' exclaimed Hallie to Dana, when she arrived for the party that evening. And she did. Dana had inherited her mother's dramatic dark looks, but she also had an inner beauty that made her glow.

Dana smiled. 'I've invited someone to the party tonight. A date,' she admitted shyly.

'No! Who?' she asked excitedly. While Dana had many friends, she rarely dated.

'He'll be here in a little while. Come on upstairs with me and I'll check on Mother. I want you to see how absolutely stunning she looks.'

Selena was easily the star of her own party, and Hallie had a feeling that no matter what she wore, Dana's mother would always stand apart. 'Regal' was the word Hallie would use later when describing her to Billie.

Curiously, while that night gave Hallie's career its beginnings, it was also that night that made her realize that it was time to leave Los Angeles.

Hallie was talking with Franklin and Emily Lansing when she felt a tug at her elbow. She turned. Next to Dana stood Sam Harris, and he was grinning from ear to ear.

'Sam! What a surprise? How . . .? What . . .?' Hallie finally realized that whatever she said was going to sound inane, so she waited for Dana to offer some explanation.

'I invited Sam to be my date for the evening,' explained Dana shyly.

'But how? I mean, where . . .?'

'. . . did we meet?' finished Sam.

Hallie nodded, embarrassed that she should be so dumbfounded at the sight of Sam Harris, a Los Angeles police detective, at a society gathering like this.

'I've decided to get my law degree,' Sam said shyly, glancing down at Dana, 'so I've been taking some classes at night.'

'And I have a class on Wednesday evening,' added Dana. 'We actually met at Sharkey's. I was with some friends and he was with some friends. I thought I knew him from somewhere, then he mentioned that he was with the police department and all of a sudden it clicked. I realized who he was and why his name was familiar.' Dana stopped, breathless.

'This is wonderful,' Hallie said. 'How have you been, Sam?'

Before Sam could answer, an elderly woman tapped Dana on the shoulder, and Dana turned, embraced the older woman, then with a smile and a shrug allowed herself to be led away. 'I'll be right back,' she mouthed.

'Good, Hallie, and you?'

'I'm okay, much better, actually.' Feeling suddenly ill at ease, Hallie searched for a topic of conversation, something safe.

'I didn't know . . .' she began

'Are you still . . .?' he blurted at the same time.

Hallie blushed and laughed. 'Sorry, Sam, I was reaching.'

'Yeah, me too,' he said. 'You first.'

Hallie smiled. 'I was going to say that I didn't know you had aspirations of becoming a lawyer.'

'Well, it wasn't like we knew each other socially,' he replied with a grin. 'And I didn't know you had aspirations of becoming a dress designer. Dana told me you designed the beautiful dress her mother is wearing.'

Hallie nodded. 'I have all kinds of talent,' she teased.

'That's what Grant always said about you,' he quipped. Too late Sam realized his mistake.

The mention of Grant hung there in the air between them until Hallie reached out and touched Sam on the arm, lightly rubbing it as if to reassure him that she could handle this.

'How is he?' asked Hallie quietly.

'He's still occupied in Washington, getting ready for the trial,' answered Sam nervously, 'but I did see him.'

'When?'

'A couple of weeks ago. He was here for two days. You know, meetings, stuff like that. I don't suppose he . . .?'

Hallie shook her head, swallowing her disappointment, then took a deep breath before answering. 'No, I didn't hear from him, but I really didn't expect to . . .' She had succeeded in keeping the regret out of her voice.

Liar. She had been waiting to hear from him.

Holding her breath.

Hoping. Praying.

The next step would have been bargaining. A sort of divine version of the old TV game show, Let's Make A Deal.

She had been like this since the day they had parted.

It was at that moment that Hallie realized, with a sudden flash of insight, that her reasons for remaining in Los Angeles had almost nothing to do with her, and everything to do with Grant. She had thought that by remaining here, he would know exactly where to find her when he came back for the trial. When he came back for her.

Well, that theory just got blown all to hell.

Dana reappeared, and Hallie used that opportunity to excuse herself, saying she had to be at work early the next morning.

That night she slept fitfully.

By the next morning she had made a heart-wrenching decision. Los Angeles held too many memories. She could stay here, of course; she had her job and it might even be possible to launch herself as a designer. But she would only end up spending her days waiting for Grant to return; searching for a dark-haired man in the distance whom she thought might be him; turning at the sound of a stranger's voice that reminded her of him.

And she knew it was time to go home.

CHAPTER 23

The trial in Los Angeles commenced two weeks later, but Hallie stayed away from the courthouse until the day before she was to testify. Since she had never been a part of any sort of legal proceeding, she wanted to know in advance exactly where she had to go and what would be expected of her. She had just located the courtroom when she sensed someone close behind her.

'Keep walking.'

Hallie slowed her stride and looked over her shoulder toward the sound of the voice. For this she received a hard shove against her shoulder blade that propelled her forward, nearly causing her to stumble. Several people passed by, casting curious glances her way.

'You're not listening, Ms Prescott. Just keep walking straight ahead like normal.'

Hallie opened her mouth to protest, just as she did she felt the nudge of a gun barrel against her side.

'Just do as I tell you,' the deep voice ordered.

Hallie continued to walk down the corridor. Her heartbeat accelerated rapidly and was now thundering in her ears. She considered screaming for help, then wondered if she could even manage a sound. Her eyes darted from side to side. The corridor that only a few minutes ago had echoed with a crowd of voices was now deathly quiet. The tapping sound of her shoes and the duller thud of the man's beside her provided the only break in the silence.

'What do you want?' she asked after he had guided her to the opening under the stairwell.

'I'll have to discuss what I want later, Ms Prescott – after hours, hmm?' His pale gold eyes ran over her, then he smiled. 'Right now I have a message for you, so pay close attention. It would be beneficial to your health if you were to forget certain things you heard and saw that day at the Mathews estate.'

Gathering her meager courage, Hallie raised her chin and bravely asked, 'And if I don't? What are you going to do then?'

Expecting a threat, she was surprised when he laughed. 'Me? Nothing. I won't even be in the court-room when you testify. But someone else will.' He shifted then and pulled the gun from beneath his jacket. Balancing it in his palm, he held it out for her to inspect. 'And he, or she, will have one of these – pointed straight at you.' He leaned forward, his pupils sharp pinpoints as he closed the distance between them. His voice dropped to a threatening hiss. 'Forget every-thing about that day and you'll live to a ripe old age. Testify and you're a dead woman. Understand?'

'You can't . . . there's security, and guards every-where,' replied Hallie nervously.

'Just like today?' he asked, then laughed at her.

With a sinking feeling Hallie realized he was right. Because of the Mathews trial, security had been stepped up, but he had managed to get a gun past them today. Why would tomorrow be any different? She had thought she would be free of all this once Mathews had been placed under arrest. Evidently she was mistaken.

'Oh, there you are, Hallie.' The woman's voice echoed as she approached, smiling. 'I've been looking all over for you. Oops, sorry. I didn't mean to interrupt.' The woman glanced briefly at the man beside Hallie, then down at her watch. 'Are you ready to go?'

Hallie nodded quickly and stepped away from the armed man. The woman moved in beside her, providing a shield. 'At the stairway go right,' she commanded, 'Sam Harris is waiting for you.'

'But how did you know?' asked Hallie as she turned to look over her shoulder at the man who had accosted her. But he was gone.

The detective, an attractive blonde in her late thirties, smiled as they approached Sam. 'You may have refused protective custody,' she said, 'but that doesn't mean we haven't been watching out for you. In here,' she directed as Sam stepped out and held the door open for them.

The room was long and narrow and appeared to be a conference room. A dark wood table took up most of the space. Sturdy but scuffed chairs lined each side.

'This way, Hallie,' directed Sam. 'Obviously, we have a problem,' he began. From the far end of the room a second door opened and a woman signaled them to follow her. Hallie looked around curiously as they entered an office. Here the walls were lined with law books, and the desk and chairs, while of the same vintage as those in the outer room, had received much better treatment. To her left yet another door opened and this time they were joined by four men. One of them was Henry Sinclair, the presiding judge at the Mathews trial, two were lawyers representing each side. The fourth man was Grant Keeler.

'Let's get down to business,' directed Judge Sinclair, his tone clearly indicating that this was a serious matter. With his pen pointed at Hallie, he said, 'I understand that you are a witness for the prosecution in this trial and that just a few minutes ago you received a serious threat against your life.

'Yes, sir,' she said timidly.

'Do you understand your role in this procedure, Mrs Prescott?'

'Yes, I do.' This time she spoke with more assurance.

'And in view of this threat, are you still willing to testify?'

Hallie looked toward Grant, and she could see the conflict in his eyes. He desperately wanted to see Mathews convicted, but not by risking her life again. She thought of Billie, and the tranquil, uncomplicated life that awaited her at home in Mimosa. She could walk out right now and be free and clear of all danger and all responsibility. But now that she had come this far, she couldn't back out. 'I am,' she announced with more confidence than she felt.

'Hallie!' exclaimed Grant and Sam simultaneously.

'Your Honor!' objected the prosecuting attorney.

The judge fixed his eyes on the group that surrounded his desk, silencing them. To the attorneys

326

he said, 'It is your responsibility to proceed with this trial.'

To Grant and Sam he said, 'It is your responsibility to protect this witness during this trial.'

To Hallie, he said, 'It is your responsibility to tell the truth. After your encounter today, do you still think you can do that?'

'Yes, I can. I just want this to be over as quickly as possible.'

The judge stood, indicating that this meeting was over.

A few minutes later, Hallie had been hustled out of the courthouse and was now seated next to Grant in the back of an unmarked car. In the front seat Sam sat next to the driver.

'Are you out of your mind?' he shouted. 'You could be killed tomorrow! This is not some game these guys are playing, and believe me, Hallie, they're not just counting on you to run and hide, or to conveniently "forget" what you saw. They are going to do whatever it takes to make sure you don't testify. Damn! All you had to do was tell the judge you were scared. He would have postponed, or the prosecution could have asked for a change of venue.'

'And would either of those things have kept those men from coming after me?' asked Hallie. 'Really, Grant, you should have thought about all this before you asked me to gather evidence against Mathews. Without my testimony tomorrow he'll walk out of that courtroom a free man.'

Grant ran his hands through his dark hair in frustration.

'Well, well. What are we going to do now?' Sam asked quietly.

After spending a sleepless night in a hotel near the airport with a team of police officers that included the same blonde detective that had come to her rescue the previous day, Hallie was escorted back to the courthouse.

There she was taken in though a secured passageway that was used to bring prisoners in and out of the building, then escorted to a room where she was met by Grant.

'There will be police scattered all over the courtroom. We will do our best to protect you.'

'I know you will,' Hallie said, looking up at him.

His gray eyes searched her eyes, and she could see the fear in them. Or was that only a reflection of the fear she felt?

'You can still back out, Hallie. You don't have to go through with this.' His voice was husky. All night long he had thought about her. About her courage. About her foolishness. About how much he loved her and how he would die if anything, or anyone, harmed her. He ranted at his inability to protect her, remembering his failure to protect Libby and the terrible, tragic consequences. 'I don't want to lose you.'

'It's time,' announced the bailiff as he opened the door.

Grant nodded. He placed his hands on her shoulders and kissed her gently. Then left her in the care of the bailiff.

A few minutes later her name was called and she

walked to the witness stand. Outwardly, she looked calm. Inside she was quivering with fear. Over and over she recited the prayers of her youth, asking God to protect her.

Grant entered the courtroom and slipped into a vacant seat in the back row.

Jack Collins, the prosecuting attorney, stood before the witness stand and addressed his question to Hallie. 'Mrs Prescott, while you were in his presence did Edwin Mathews admit to having Senator Rawlins killed?'

The defense attorney, a big swarthy man who appeared to be in his early sixties, sat at the other table staring at her, waiting for her answer. He was one of a team of four lawyers who sat at Mathews's table. It was rumored that in previous cases involving the powerful man, this legal team had done whatever necessary, even bought off jurors, in order to keep Mathews out of prison. This, of course, meant that no one had ever successfully prosecuted Edwin Mathews.

Hallie's gaze traveled across the rows of spectators and locked with Grant's for a moment. Then she looked away and wished she wasn't so acutely aware of his presence. At this very moment her life depended on how she answered.

Forget and live. Or testify and die.

She opened her mouth, but no sound came out. She swallowed. *Dear God . . .*

When she failed to answer the question immediately, the prosecutor prompted, 'Mrs Prescott? We are waiting for your answer.'

Still, she was silent. Her eyes searched out Grant's

once more, and she thought about their time together. He was always so sure of who he was, and what he had to do. He represented justice. He had chosen it as his life's work, but even he had advised her not to proceed with this. The threat was real; the smell of danger was all around her. Was she strong enough to tell the truth as she had sworn to do before God and put this evil man away?

'Please answer the question, Ms Prescott,' instructed Judge Sinclair.

Hallie turned, breaking eye contact with Grant, and met the steady blue eyes of the judge.

'I'm sorry,' she said, weakly, and turned back to face Jack Collins. She was determined to keep her eyes off Grant. In a strong, clear voice she answered, 'Yes, he did.'

A collective exclamation by those sitting in the courtroom broke the silence and caused the judge to pound his gavel repeatedly, calling for order.

'And is it true that that very same day, in your presence, Edwin Mathews ordered the murder of your husband, Casey Prescott?'

'Yes,' answered Hallie firmly.

Her answer was nearly lost in the popping sounds, so sharp and quick, that followed only seconds later. Grant sprang to his feet, calling out her name as he helplessly watched the force of the bullets spin her around, knocking out of her chair and sending her crashing to the floor.

Panic ensued while the police, who had been scattered around the courtroom, searched for the person who had fired the shots. In the midst of shrieks and screams from the panicked crowd as they scrambled to exit the courtroom, he was nowhere to be found.

Grant leaped over the wooden benches and raced toward Hallie. Her face was white. Fear nearly smothered him. She had put herself at risk, and once more he had failed to protect the woman he loved.

Paramedics moved him out of the way as they carefully and quickly secured her still form on a stretcher, then wheeled her to the waiting ambulance.

Grant hesitated only a second before his years of training kicked in and he raced to join the search team. Even as he moved swiftly and efficiently through the courtroom, into the corridor then out onto the street, he swallowed his bitterness at having to do his job, especially in the face of the devastating event he had just witnessed.

Within hours the police had located the gun which had been tossed in a trash dumpster a few blocks away. There were no fingerprints, and neither Sam nor Grant held much hope that they would ever find the hit man. He was probably already on his way out of town.

All those who had been present in the courtroom had been prevented from leaving the building until they could be questioned. It was doubtful anyone would remember seeing anything either before the shooting or afterward. In cases of this kind, the hit men were skilled, moving fast, then blending in with their surroundings and doing nothing out of the ordinary to arouse suspicion. Afterward they always counted on the pandemonium that usually followed a hit to cover their exit.

But the damage to Mathews's defense was devastating. No matter what happened now, or what tactic his lawyers took in his defense, he had been positively identified as a killer.

It was hours later before Grant went in search of Hallie. The nurses' station on the third floor of the hospital repeatedly denied that they had any record of a patient named Hallie Prescott ever being admitted for treatment that afternoon. Even after Grant showed them his badge, they continued to deny it.

He raced to a pay phone in the waiting area. Of course, they had no record of it. What the devil had he been thinking of? In his panic he had failed to realize that she would have been admitted under a different name.

'I can't find her,' Grant said to Sam a few minutes later. 'Are you sure this is where the paramedics took her?'

'Positive,' replied Sam, unable to disguise his enjoyment at having the upper hand over Grant, only if momentarily. Then, feeling guilty for capitalizing on his anxiety over Hallie, Sam said, 'Relax. She's in a private room on the fifth floor. According to the records, her name is Susan Lawson and she has just given birth to her second child.'

Within minutes Grant located Hallie's room. Relief at finding her alive and unharmed caused his voice to thicken with emotion. 'You look pretty good for a woman who just had a baby,' he quipped.

'Yeah, I do, don't I?' she answered with a smile, struggling to sit up.

'Here, let me help you,' he said and easily lifted her higher on the pillows.

'When can I leave here?' she asked.

'As soon as the jury comes back with a verdict. If it doesn't drag out it could be as soon as tomorrow. Where did you get hit?' he asked with concern.

'I'm not sure,' she answered. 'I'm sore all over. The impact was enough to knock me out. I thought I was dead.'

'You would have been, Hallie, if it hadn't been for the bulletproof vest you were wearing.'

Grant sat on the side of the bed, taking her hand. 'Do you have any idea how risky that was?'

She smiled. 'I do now.'

'No one would have blamed you, you know, if you had decided not to testify.' His eyes were soft as they gently scanned her delicate face.

'I know,' she said. 'But for the rest of my life I would have felt like such a coward.'

Grant smiled at her words. 'Hallie, honey, if things had gone wrong you wouldn't have had . . . well, you know.'

He stayed until she fell asleep, then he kissed her – a soft, tender kiss that would have told her how deeply he cared for her. In the hallway, the lights were dim, and taking a deep breath he said goodnight to the officer who was guarding Hallie's room. Shoving his hands into his pockets, he walked slowly toward the elevator and wondered what he was going to do about Hallie when this was all over.

Two days later the trial ended. The jury found Edwin Mathews guilty. That same day Hallie left the hospital. Each time she heard the familiar ding of the elevator as the doors opened, her hopes had soared that it was Grant coming to see her. But after that first night he had not come back. Even though she tried to act as though she didn't care, her heart ached. For the second time Grant Keeler had walked away from her.

CHAPTER 24

Joseph Aaron had protested when Hallie had given him a month's notice that she would be leaving her job to return home to Mississippi. Her decision had been made and now it was time to move on. Secretly, she had longed to give him only the standard two weeks' notice. But her conscience would not let her shortchange her mentor and friend, the man who had given her the chance to develop her talent, and the setting in which to showcase her creations.

'This is crazy, Hallie. You have been working too hard, too many hours. And this trial, this "trouble" you neglected to tell me about – you are just burnt out. Take a week or two off and rethink this decision. Los Angeles is where you belong. Don't bury yourself in some dried-up town, just because you're homesick. Go home for a visit, say hello to your family, all your friends, then come back.'

Hallie smiled, sadly, and shook her head. 'I'm sorry, Joseph. You've been very good to me, and I love working here, but . . .'

'Then what's the problem, Hallie?'

'It's hard to explain, and even if I did, I'm not sure you would understand.'

'Try me.'

'Well,' she said, biting her lip, 'you see, there was this man . . .'

Joseph held up his hand, stopping her. 'I don't think I want to hear this after all.'

Her smile this time was broader. 'No, you don't,' she agreed. 'But there's more. You see, I need to go home, Joseph. It's very difficult to explain. The South is more than a place or a culture. It's a state of mind.'

'Go, Hallie,' he said, sighing and smoothing his thinning hair. 'Whenever you're ready. If you change your mind you can always come back, you know that, don't you?'

She nodded, not trusting herself to speak.

Joseph looked toward the window, disturbed by the thought of losing Hallie. He regarded her as more than an employee; she had become his friend. He waved his hand in the air. 'Now get back to work. You can't leave me with so much.'

'Oh, Hallie! You can't leave. Not only will I be losing a friend, but Mother's friends are all dying to know who designed the dress she wore to the party. Your "design debut" was such a success. They all want your name. I can almost guarantee that you will get some clients out of this.'

Hallie laughed. 'Your mother was the success, Dana. Selena would command attention even if she was wearing a flour sack!' If Hallie had aspired to be a movie star, she would have wanted Dana to be her

336

agent. Her enthusiasm for Hallie's talent was boundless. 'I can design clothes just as well at home as I can here,' she said.

'I know,' admitted Dana.

'You can come for a visit to Mimosa.'

'I will, I promise, but meanwhile what do you want my mother to tell all her friends?'

'Tell her to stall for at least two weeks until I get moved and settled. Then I can start taking orders. If I get overloaded, there are quite a few seamstresses in town who might be willing to help me,' replied Hallie.

'But why, after all this time . . .?' asked Dana, and they both knew she was referring to Grant.

'I should have gone home months ago, right after Grant left.' Hallie admitted. 'It was something Sam said the night of the party that triggered my decision.'

'Poor Sam,' said Dana. 'No matter how hard he tries, he seems to say things he shouldn't. I wonder what kind of a lawyer he will make?'

'An exceptionally fine one,' Hallie said. 'And if I were you I'd keep an eye on him.'

Dana smiled. 'I plan to,' she admitted.

'Are you sure you don't want me to park and wait until your plane takes off?' asked Dana. 'I hate to just drop you off outside the airport and leave.'

'No,' replied Hallie. 'This is not going to be easy. Saying goodbye never is.'

Dana nodded in understanding. 'Okay,' she said. 'Curb-side delivery is all you get from this limousine service.'

Hallie nodded, then gave her friend a quick hug.

Inside the terminal she checked her bags and with her ticket in hand she walked toward the concourse, following along with the crowd. She looked up in surprise when a strong hand reached out and fastened a hold on her wrist, sweeping her in a different direction.

'What are you . . .?' Hallie began, then she recognized Grant. If anything, he was even more handsome in the bright sunlight that filtered through the windows along the concourse. Briskly he pulled her along a short distance until they reached a vacant seating area.

His eyes, intense and nearly silver, scanned her from head to toe then rested on her face. 'Hello, Hallie,' he said softly.

Her heart was pounding so hard it was impossible for her to do more than stare at him.

'I just wanted to make sure you were okay,' he said.

'I . . . I'm fine,' she stammered.

'You're leaving?' he asked, when he saw the ticket she held.

She nodded. 'I'm going home.'

'For a visit?'

'No, this is a permanent move.'

'I see. Let's go somewhere and have a drink. *Bon voyage*?' he suggested with an assurance he was far from feeling.

'No, that's not a good idea,' stated Hallie as she began to recover from the shock of being this close to him again.

'Why not?' he asked with a smile. 'What's wrong with two old friends spending some time together?'

'Tell me something, Grant. Would you have called

338

me and asked me out for a drink or dinner tonight if you hadn't seen me here this afternoon?'

Grant hesitated. He had been back in town once before the trial and he hadn't called her. And it had been over a month since he had seen her at the hospital. Every day, every hour since that time he had wanted to call her, to see her, but it would have only added to the pain of parting. Then there would be questions. Things he couldn't answer.

'No?' she continued when no answer was forthcoming. 'I didn't think so.' Nothing between them had changed since the night she had asked him about their future. 'We may have been a lot of things to each other, but old friends isn't one of them. Goodbye, Grant,' she said softly. Her message was unmistakable. Hallie pulled her arm free of his grasp, turned and walked away.

In the midst of the busy concourse the only sound in Grant's head was the retreating echo of her heels tapping against the terrazzo floor.

When the 757 banked for its wide, silver sweep over the Mississippi River on its approach to Memphis, Hallie was once again in awe of the winding muddy giant below that seemed to wield a power of its own, eroding its banks and cutting new paths at a whim. In less than three hours she would be back in Mimosa again. Her home town. It would be a painful and emotional reunion.

There was really nothing to fear in Mimosa, she reminded herself. She had known everyone for as long as she could remember. But she had left, restless and ambitious, wanting more than the languid town could offer, while the others had stayed.

Now she wanted to go home, to hide. She was tired and battered by the ugly things that had touched her while she was away. She wanted nothing more than to run to Billie like she had as a child and hide her face in the starched white apron that smelled of sunshine and bleach, then sit at the kitchen table across from Lacy, who had been a real pain sometimes, but had always been her friend, and pour out her troubles. But Hallie was a woman now. She couldn't run to Billie or to Lacy. She had to come to grips with her problems on her own.

'I suppose nothing much has changed in Mimosa,' Hallie remarked idly, as she straightened in her seat after they had been on the road for quite a while.

'A few things have,' Billie said, keeping her eyes on the road ahead. 'You probably haven't given this any thought, honey, but for quite a while you provided all the gossips in town with something to talk about. The *US Star Gazette*, that trashy tabloid, was the best-selling newspaper for weeks. The Piggly Wiggly couldn't keep enough of them in the store. I thought you should know. People will ask questions about you and Casey and Jasmine Turner.'

'And the trial,' Hallie added with a sigh.

'That, too,' agreed Billie, 'but mostly the other stuff.'

'This has been hard on you, hasn't it?' asked Hallie, suddenly realizing that her aunt had also been tainted by all that had happened.

'It's nothing compared to what you've been through. But I should tell you that for a while some people in

340

town actually thought that you might have killed that Turner woman. The rest of them didn't believe it for a moment. It has been a while since you've lived in Mimosa, Hallie. Remember, it's a very small town. People will entertain themselves with almost anything. It's better than being bored. But having Benton around has helped me put things in perspective.

'Benton? Benton Wilder?' Hallie swiveled in her seat so she could get a better look at Billie whose cheeks were now flushed. Hallie had always though her aunt was pretty, but she noticed now, at the mention of Benton, that there was a certain sparkle in her brown eyes that she hadn't noticed earlier.

Billie nodded and continued to look straight ahead as she steered the big Cadillac down the Interstate.

'Oh,' Hallie murmured and turned to look out the window, knowing that in her own good time Billie would tell all. Benton Wilder was the editor and owner of the Mimosa newspaper. He was also a relative newcomer to town, having moved there only a few years ago after his wife died.

'Well,' said Billie after a few minutes of silence, 'there *is* a little more to tell.

'Umm,' Hallie said, pretending to be engrossed in the lush green landscape.

'We've been dating.'

'Really? Well, I think that's nice. You two are about the same age and Benton is a widower, isn't he? I would think that at your age the companionship would be a welcome change,' teased Hallie.

'Companionship?' croaked Billie, casting a quick glance in Hallie's direction.

'Isn't that what women your age want in a man?'

Billie looked over at her niece, but she couldn't see the grin that Hallie was hiding. 'Listen, my dear, what women my age want in a man is exactly what women of your age want!'

Unable to keep still any longer, Hallie burst out laughing. 'Now you have to tell me everything, Billie!'

And Billie did, unable to hide her interest in the handsome newspaper man. 'Benton has been a regular at the restaurant, and we've been friends for a while. Then one day, out of the clear blue sky, he asked me out on a date. After that we began spending more and more time together.'

'But why didn't you tell me all this was going on?' asked Hallie, bewildered. It wasn't like her aunt to hold news this important back.

'I wanted to,' replied Billie. 'It was something that seemed so natural. Our relationship just seemed to progress from one stage to another. Besides, things were not going too well for you at the time, honey. When I thought about what you had been through, I felt almost guilty about being as happy as I was.'

'Oh, Billie, you deserve all the happiness in the world. So, tell me now, do you think Benton's intentions are honorable?'

Billie shrugged, her brown eyes dancing as she appeared to weigh Hallie's question. 'Gosh, I hope not.'

This time it was Hallie's turn to blush.

In the competent hands of Billie Dean Barrett the big blue Cadillac seemed to streak down I-55 South, smoothing the miles and the tension away. After a while Hallie rolled the window down, leaned her head against the back of the seat, and breathed deeply of the humid, fragrant air, so soft and caressing. Her eyes feasted on the land, serene and abundant. Her soul, serenaded by the melodies of legions of birds and insects, was calmed. She was home.

In the weeks that followed her return, Hallie spent some of her days helping Billie at the Mimosa Café, just as she had while growing up. The little café with its dark redbrick façade and the faded green striped awnings that covered the door and windows was as much home to her as the house she and her aunt shared.

One by one, people she had known all her life stopped by the café or the house to see her. And, with few exceptions, uppermost in their minds was Casey's affair with Jasmine, followed by Jasmine's murder. As much as possible Billie and June Gilroy, a waitress at the café, tried to run interference, shielding Hallie from as many embarrassing questions as possible.

'I should just take out an ad in the newspaper,' Hallie announced one Saturday morning after breakfast. 'That way, I could tell everyone all the sordid details about Casey and Jasmine.'

'Wouldn't work, honey,' said Billie as she poured herself another cup of coffee. 'They'd still want to hear you tell about it in person.'

As Dana had predicted, Hallie began to get requests for her dress designs. At Billie's insistence she converted one of the upstairs bedrooms into her studio. Here among fabrics, laces and sketches she worked, design-

343

ing, cutting patterns and stitching, creating things she loved. And each day, the memories of her time in Los Angeles faded a little more, the images growing fuzzier, slipping further away. All except one.

Hallie had done her best to put all thoughts of Grant Keeler out of her mind, but her longing for him was just as strong as it ever was. What was it about this man that kept her from sleeping, that made her start out each morning and each night thinking about him, aching to touch him?

CHAPTER 25

During these same months Grant had concentrated on tying up all the loose ends of his life. From Sam he had learned that after his arrest Irwin Turner had made a full confession to killing his wife. He also admitted to hiring someone to rough Casey up. The man he hired was the one who was accidentally hit by the car – the same man that Hallie had mistakenly identified as Casey.

Now he was almost finished with the business that pertained to Edward Mathews; though the number of people implicated in this case had grown, Grant was finally free to go about his own affairs. While he had been in Washington and involved with the preparations for the case Grant had, for the most part, been able to push his thoughts of Hallie aside. Except for those nights when it was dark, and he was alone, and painfully aware of his solitude and his longing for her.

He should have felt relieved and satisfied that things had turned out the way they did. In some measure, those that were responsible for Libby's death would pay for their crime. He had done what he could to see that justice was done.

But the feelings of restlessness persisted, and no matter how much Grant denied them, he knew that until he brought Hallie into his life again, he would never be happy.

But the time was not right. Not yet. There was still something holding him back. Instinctively, he would know when it was time to go to her.

When it all became too much for him he left the country for a brief vacation. But while his days in Grand Cayman were spent in solitude under the Caribbean sun, the warm, humid nights brought him nothing but more restless dreams.

The island had changed since his last visit. It was still paradise – the vivid, glistening aquamarine of the Caribbean, the gentle breezes that swept the sparkling beaches – but not quite as unspoiled as it had been a few years back. There were more hotels now and more condos, which meant more tourists arriving and departing through Georgetown. Still, the island was one of unbelievable beauty.

He had been there for three days before they found him. It wasn't a complete surprise; he had expected that he would be contacted sooner or later. Anderson had another case for him. Of that, he was positive. There was always one more crime to be solved, one more file to be closed, one more assignment that only he could handle. He had been dogged by Anderson for the past three years to return to work but, up until the Mathews case, he had always been able to withstand the offers.

This time, though, it wasn't Anderson himself who came to find him. In fact, the thought of his former boss dressed in anything but a gray rumpled suit and scuffed winged-tip shoes brought a broad smile to Grant's face. No, Anderson would not venture to the island. Grant knew for a fact that his former boss would never be caught dead barefooted or in a pair of shorts. He could never remember the man ever taking a vacation.

In Anderson's place there was a sleek and beautiful woman with wondrous, smooth, bronzed skin, the result of generations of inter-marriage that was common in the islands. And Victoria Camden had obviously inherited the best characteristics of both races.

This was not the first time Grant had seen Victoria, for the island was relatively small and many of the tourists stayed away during the off-season, leaving, for the most part, only the locals. Besides, Victoria was not a woman that any red-blooded man could ignore. She had been at the same restaurant he was the evening before and the hotel bar after that.

If he hadn't been so preoccupied with his own thoughts, Grant might have recognized that she was an agent with an interest in him before now. Maybe his instincts were getting rusty. Or maybe he just didn't give a damn any more.

Now she was here in Georgetown, beside him as he browsed in one of the many duty-free shops that sold precious jewelry, china and crystal from around the world.

'Isn't it strange how we keep showing up at the same places?' he asked in a low voice.

'It is a small island,' she replied without looking up at him. 'Perhaps it is nothing more than coincidence.'

Grant smiled. 'I doubt that. Exactly what does our

mutual friend want this time?' he asked, not bothering to look her way while he quickly cut to the business at hand.

Victoria turned her head and this time her deep brown eyes met his. She masked her surprise. 'I wasn't aware that we shared a mutual acquaintance,' she protested.

'Who sent you?' asked Grant.

Smiling ruefully, she asked, 'Am I that bad, that you were able to recognize me before I even made my move?'

Grant smiled in return. 'No, actually I didn't realize who you were until today. I was preoccupied,' he confessed, then added, 'and you are a little hard to ignore, even here in the islands.'

'I shall take that as a compliment,' Victoria replied, her speech a lilting combination of melodious vowels and the precise, clipped consonants that reflected the British influence in the Caribbean. 'And in answer to your inquiry,' she continued, 'there is another assignment he would like you to consider.'

'Sorry,' replied Grant without hesitation.

'Ah. He told me you would say that. Might I suggest that we continue our discussion over a cool drink at The Plantation House?'

Once more Grant smiled. She was beautiful and charming, and while he had no intention of taking on another assignment, or even engaging in a harmless flirtation, he also had nothing better to do than to enjoy drinks and, more than likely, dinner with a beautiful agent.

The Plantation House, built in the early twenties,

had once been the home of a wealthy French business-man. After his death it had fallen into disrepair, then sustained additional damage from the many tropical storms that had battered the island through the years. In the mid-eighties, an American couple had undertaken the restoration of the home, turning it into a small hotel with a charming restaurant.

From their table on the veranda they had an unobstructed view of Lime Tree Bay. Nearby, a number of sailboats were docked, and the rhythmic clanking sounds that filled the air as the vessels rode the swells of the tide provided musical accompaniment.

Victoria raised her frothy pina colada in salute. 'I would like to have you at my side,' she said. 'This is a small project, involving the movement of illegal funds. It will require only a few days and I am already in place. Besides, your return ticket is not good until the end of the week. Think of this as a working vacation.'

Grant laughed out loud. 'Anything that has Anderson's stamp of approval is definitely not going to be a vacation, Victoria. Haven't you found that out yet?'

She nodded sheepishly and leaned forward. 'Please, Grant, let me tell you more about it,' she whispered. 'I could really use your help.'

On the surface it sounded easy enough, and Grant had to admit that it was tempting. Kind of a hit-and-run operation, which would require minimal effort on his part. In fact, it was somewhat curious that Anderson would even attempt to involve him in something this elementary, unless he simply wanted to make sure that Victoria had the benefit of his experience.

Since he had left Los Angeles Grant had eased off on his criticism of his old employer, realizing that much of what he had felt about the FBI had to do with his bitterness following Libby's death. For a moment he had even considered accepting Victoria's offer.

'Tell Anderson thanks for thinking of me, but I think not,' he said.

Victoria nodded, disappointed. Grant Keeler was a very attractive man, and she had no qualms about mixing a little pleasure with her business. 'What will happen?' she asked, drawing upon his experience.

'You will notify Anderson that I'm not a player and before the night is out a replacement will be on his way here. He will be briefed before his feet touch the ground.' Suddenly Grant leaned forward. 'How long have you been at this?' he asked.

She shrugged. 'Long enough.'

'Be careful, Victoria. It's the ones that seem so simple that can turn nasty,' he warned.

'Will I see you again?' she asked as they parted after dinner that evening.

'I'm sure our paths will cross again, Victoria.'

At midnight, two nights later, his prediction came true, and like it or not Grant became involved when Victoria appeared at the door of his hotel. She quickly pushed against the door and slipped inside. 'I need your help,' she said breathlessly as if she had been running. 'Something has gone wrong.'

'Did Anderson send you here again, Victoria?'

'No, no, Grant. You've got to help me, please! The agent they were supposed to send when you turned the assignment down never arrived. My instructions were to proceed without him. Someone would take his place. But that hasn't happened.' Victoria went on to explain that in her position at the Dominion Royal Bank, she had reason to believe that someone inside the bank, another employee, was onto her.

'On the surface, there don't seem to be any irregularities,' she admitted, 'but I am frightened, Grant.'

At first it was only a fleeting impression, intuition, a sense of something not quite right. The story she told, while plausible, didn't quite ring true.

'Of what, Victoria?' he asked cautiously.

She lowered her jet lashes and stepped towards him, running her plum-glazed nails over his bare chest. 'Let me stay with you tonight,' she said softly, with just the right amount of urgency. She pressed closer.

'Who are you afraid of?' he asked. 'Were you threatened?'

Without answering, Victoria moved closer, slithering her bronzed body against his, maneuvering him until he stood in the center of the room. Alarm bells sounded in Grant's head as he spun away from her and away from the glass doors that led to the balcony. Suddenly the room lit up like a fireworks display as the fire of an automatic weapon sprayed the walls of his room. Throwing himself across the bed and landing on the other side, Grant reached for his gun and fired, taking the shooter on the balcony out.

He snaked along the length of the room on his stomach. Where was Victoria? Cautiously, he raised himself to a crouching position. His question was answered with a single shot from the doorway that

351

caught him in the right thigh. He stumbled, and before Victoria could fire again, Grant had taken cover.

Outside, the dead man hung precariously over the balcony railing. Inside, Grant searched the room. In the confusion Victoria had disappeared. He acted quickly, tying his bleeding thigh with a T-shirt. He didn't know how badly he was hurt; right now he didn't have time to worry about the pain. In the critical minutes that followed, he knew that he, too, must disappear into the night.

With only a few police on the island, it would be a long time before the identity of the killer would be established. Grand Cayman was indeed paradise, and virtually crime-free, but he could not afford to be detained in a local investigation that was almost guaranteed to be excruciatingly precise and prolonged.

This time he had almost been killed, and he had walked right into the set-up. How could he have been so careless as to allow Victoria Camden to blindside him? He should have known that she wasn't one of them. It had been too easy. She had been a plant and by all rights Grant should have been dead by now.

Mathews might be in jail, but there were still people out there that took orders from him. His influence and his money were still powerful and far-reaching. It was obvious that this had been retaliation against Grant's testimony at the trial.

In the early hours of the morning, while it was still dark, he left the island on a small charter boat, bleeding and in dire need of medical care.

* * *

'You look like hell,' said Sam Harris.

In the bright morning light Grant opened one eye slowly, then the other. 'Yeah, nice to see you, too.'

'What happened?'

Grant reached for the controls at the side of his bed and pushed the button that would raise him to a sitting position.

'According to the doc, I failed to seek the proper medical attention,' said Grant with a wry grin.

'You going to be okay?' asked Sam with concern.

'Umph,' mumbled Grant as he tried to sit up straighter. 'I will be in another few days. What are you doing here? Isn't this a little out of your jurisdiction?' he asked Sam.

'Just a little. You disappeared for a while, and Anderson got worried and sent me to look for you.'

'You? Why not one of his men?'

Sam shrugged. 'Maybe he didn't want to call attention to the fact that he lost you. If he sent one of his guys, it would have to be official, and, well . . .'

'Yeah, I get it.' Unofficially, Sam Harris could arrange for a few days off to take a vacation and no one would give it a second thought.

Sam nodded. 'I got to Grand Cayman, the day after you departed. Too bad. Man, that is one great place.'

'How long did you get to stay?' asked Grant with a grin.

'Less than twenty-four hours. I was on the last flight in one afternoon and the first flight out the next morning for Miami. It never occurred to me to look for you here in the hospital. You know, that was one time I really didn't give a damn about finding you,

Grant. On Cayman there was this one sizzlin' babe in a string bikini . . .'

'What color?' asked Grant.

Sam looked at him strangely, then shifted his gaze toward the ceiling. 'I don't know, yellow maybe.'

'Not the bikini, the girl.'

Sam grinned. 'Oh, the girl. Well, that's the thing that made her so unusual. She was . . .'

'Bronze. With dark hair that hung to her waist,' finished Grant.

'Yes, yes, she was,' Sam agreed vaguely, as if he was far away. 'How'd you know?'

'She tried to kill me,' said Grant. 'Her name is Victoria Camden.'

'Damn,' said Sam. 'That's a real shame.'

'Yes, it is,' agreed Grant, knowing that Sam was only thinking about the beautiful Caymanian woman and not his wounds. 'You'll let Anderson know about her?'

Sam nodded, reluctant to dismiss the vision of her in his mind. 'What are your plans when you get out of here?' he asked after a moment.

'Well, first I'm going back to Virginia.

'And then?'

'Then I'm going to see Hallie.'

Immediately following his release from the hospital, Grant left Miami to spend a few quiet days at a friend's house in Virginia Beach. His friend, who was out of town, told him to stay as long as he wanted. This place had not been chosen as a getaway at random; he and Libby had come here the first year they were married.

A delayed honeymoon. This destination had been chosen for sentimental reasons.

Now he just wanted to quietly remember, to savor the sweet, brief time he and Libby had had together, to dream of what their life together might have been and what their child might have become.

The late afternoon sun had dipped behind the horizon, but he could still feel the warmth of it on his bronzed skin as he walked alone on the beach. The ever-present breeze ruffled his dark hair except for one sobering moment when there was a perfect stillness and he felt her presence. She was there with him.

Libby.

God, how he missed her.

He could smell the faint, familiar fragrance of her, and he could feel her warmth surrounding him, almost as if she had wrapped her arms around him.

I miss you so much. The words were only a thought. He never said them aloud.

Her touch, when it came, was fleeting but very real. And there was no doubt in Grant's mind that the fluttering whisper in his head was Libby's. *I'll always love you, but I can't come back to you.*

Then she was gone and he felt a loss as great as it had been the moment he had first learned of her death. Almost immediately it was replaced with a sense of peace and well-being that he hadn't had before. It settled over him. Her presence had assured him that she was safe and happy.

He breathed deeply, deliberately letting his anger and his sense of loss slip away. He had felt her gentleness and her love surround him, and he knew with

certainty that for the span of one brief heartbeat she had
come back to him.

He also knew she would never come back again.

It was time to move on.

CHAPTER 26

'That's right, Ronnie, a Buick Regal. Yep, just got an OK from the rental car company. Might be able to get this fella here fixed up and on his way by this afternoon if you can drop that part off on your afternoon run to Clarksdale.' Lifting his John Deere cap, Eldon Henderson wiped at the beads of sweat that had gathered on his forehead with the sleeve of his gray shirt then smoothed the sparse strands of hair on his nearly bald head and replaced the cap, tilting the bill low over his eyes until it was almost even with his glasses.

'Well, son,' Eldon said turning to the stranger who stood before him, 'you're welcome to wait here, but if I were you I would head on over to the Mimosa Café and get something nice and cool to drink. All I got here is that coke machine out front and half the time it just swallows up your money without spittin' anything out. I can't do much with your car until I get that part.'

Grant Keeler looked around him, noting the greasy beige naugahyde couch in the office and the stacks of newspaper that were wedged between it and the wall. The desk was just another workbench, covered with tools, rags and parts. He decided to take Eldon's advice.

'I came to Mimosa to find Hallie Prescott. Do you know her?'

Early this morning Grant had caught a flight directly from Virginia Beach to Memphis, then rented a car which broke down a mile north of here when he had stopped to ask directions to this sleepy Mississippi town.

Before he left the rental car agency at the airport, he had checked the map and decided that Mimosa was slightly over two hours south of Memphis at a point just about halfway between I-55 and the Mississippi River. But he had made a wrong turn somewhere after he had left the Interstate.

'Known Hallie all her life. What're you wantin' with her?' Eldon asked cautiously.

'We're friends,' he answered. 'I knew her when she lived in Los Angeles.'

'Is that so? Say, did you know that writer-husband of hers? Casey Prescott?' asked Eldon, suddenly interested in what Grant would tell him.

'No, I didn't meet Hallie until later, after her husband's death.'

'Oh.' Eldon digested this information for a moment before continuing, 'Well, we always wondered what he was like, but he never came to visit after they were married. Hallie always came to see her aunt alone. I saw a picture of him, though, in the newspaper. But the wife, now, she read his book. His picture was there on the back of the book, too.' Eldon tipped his hat back slightly as he considered his words. 'Don't mean to speak ill of the dead, but he looked a little slick to me. Know what I mean?'

Grant raised his brows inquiringly.

It was all the mechanic needed to continue. 'Too smooth, yes, sir, not an ounce of character in that face. Reminded me of a certain auto parts salesman that used to come in here every so often – the kind that could be anything anybody wanted him to be.

'Too bad, what happened, though, and it's sad the way things went wrong. That little Hallie mopes around more than she should. I guess she still misses that husband of hers.'

Grant raised his head at this.

Eldon hastened to explain. 'Oh, she's just as pleasant as can be over at the café. She helps out sometimes, you know – Billie Dean Barrett, she's Hallie's aunt and the closest thing to a mother that little girl has ever known, owns the Mimosa Café. It's just that sometimes Hallie will be serving me my lunch and she gets a faraway look in her eyes like she was in another world.'

'She was,' muttered Grant as he took in his surroundings.

'Beg your pardon?'

'Nothing, Mr Henderson. Just let me know when the car's ready.'

Outside the garage the blistering, late September heat rose from the pavement in visible waves, causing Grant to stagger for a moment. Squinting in the bright light, his gaze focused on the recently whitewashed concrete-block building across the street. According to the mobile sign whose lights would begin to flash at dusk, forming an arrow that pointed to the Spirit of Holiness Gospel Church, everyone was invited to attend on Sunday and receive a double portion. Of what? he wondered and made a mental note to ask Eldon about it when he returned to pick up his car.

How could anyone stand to live in this heat? Already his shirt was damp with sweat and he seriously doubted that hell could be any hotter than it was right here at this moment. Realizing he hadn't asked directions, he paused. A quick glance up and down Mimosa's main street told him he didn't need any. The town only had one café.

Inside the café the air conditioning provided a welcome relief from the stifling, humid temperatures outside. It took a minute for his eyes to adjust from the bright sunlight as he made his way to the booth next to the window. Glancing outside, Grant thought that if all the cars were taken off the street Mimosa would look much the same as it did a hundred years ago.

The three-story, red brick Gladston County Court-house occupied the center of the town square and was flanked on each side by a park. In spite of the stately old homes that surrounded the minuscule business district, the place lacked the polished, prosperous air that many small towns had been able to retain. Mimosa reminded Grant of an old pair of shoes – comfortable, but a little rundown at the heels.

'What can I get for you, sir?' asked June Gilroy with her best smile. She placed a glass of ice water in front of him.

'Iced tea, please,' he replied with an answering smile.

June hurried away to get the tea, fanning herself with one hand, the rapid movement of her chubby fingers causing the three diamond rings she wore to glitter in the light, and patting her blonde, lacquered French twist with the other hand. It wasn't very often that a man as good-looking as this one came into the café. When she returned to the table, Grant asked if Hallie was there.

'No, sir,' June replied with a smile. 'Hallie and Miss Billie are gettin' ready for the weddin'. I'm closing up in an hour, then I have to hurry home to get ready, too. Miss Billie asked me to help serve punch at the reception.'

Wedding? Grant's pulse raced, while his mind leaped to conclusions. *Hallie was getting married?* True, there had been no communication between them since they had left Los Angeles months ago, but they had both needed time to put the past aside.

'Where can I find her?' Grant inquired, taking a quick gulp of his tea, then standing to reach for his wallet.

'Hallie? Why, up at the house, I suppose.' At his puzzled look, June added, 'It's not far. Three blocks up that way from the park. The name on the gate is Barrett.'

Grant nearly ran the three blocks to the house, then wished he hadn't. Sweat trickled from his forehead and his shirt was plastered to his back. At the waist-high black iron gate he paused, taking in the slender white columns that dominated the pale pink two-story home, admiring the elegant architecture that belonged to another era, and failing to see beyond that beauty to the faded paint and the warped and sagging wood. Slowly he lifted the catch on the gate and followed the uneven brick walkway that led to the porch.

He climbed the few steps, but before he could reach for the bell the front door opened and two teenage girls slipped past him.

'Hi . . . I'm looking for Hallie Prescott,' he said.

'Inside,' said one of the girls, 'get-ting read-y. The big day is fin-a-lly here!' She sang the reply.

The second girl punched her in the arm. 'No, she's not, silly. Miss Hallie went over to the the Beauti-Bar to have her nails done.' Both girls giggled, and after a second look at Grant, flashed him big smiles and hurried off.

He looked past the open doorway and, seeing no one, paused, then stepped inside. The inside, which had a faint scent of lemon oil, gleamed from its recent cleaning. The breathtaking beauty of the wide hallway ran from the front door to the back of the house, ending with a pair of French doors. In the midst of this splendor Grant didn't notice the frayed edges of the oriental carpets that dotted the polished hardwood floors, or the once-elegant furniture with its thin and faded upholstery.

From a room that was located off the hall, a tall thin woman with black hair and dark skin darted out into the hallway, then stopped suddenly at the sight of him, studying him with sharp eyes that seemed to take in every detail of his appearance. 'Are you from the florist?' she asked.

'No . . .'

'The caterer?'

'No –' he began, intending to offer an explanation.

Before he could finish she interrupted, 'Of course not. I'll get Miss Billie. You stay right there. Sit down, please.' She indicated a small settee to her left. 'I guess I'm just a little nervous with the wedding and all,' she muttered as she disappeared into another room.

A few minutes later the voice to his right was soft; nevertheless Grant started at the sound of it.

'How do you do? I'm Billie Dean Barrett,' she said as she approached him with her hand extended and her head tilted slightly to one side in an invitation for him to speak. She appeared to be in her early fifties, with only a slight gathering of lines near her eyes marring her delicate peach complexion. Her brown eyes studied him intently, taking in every detail including his dark hair and the intense gray eyes.

Grant stood and took her hand, intending to introduce himself, but he never got that far.

'Oh, my goodness, you must be Grant Keeler,' she said graciously in a rush of recognition, as if finding strangers in her house was an everyday occurrence. 'How silly of me not to recognize you. I've heard so much about you.' He was everything Hallie had described to her, she thought, as her mouth curved in a welcoming smile.

At his puzzled look, Billie continued, 'I knew you'd show up sooner or later, when the time was right. And I'm so glad you made it here before the wedding.'

So am I, thought Grant. Out loud he said, 'I'm pleased to meet you, Ms Barrett. I'm here to see Hallie. I have to talk to her.'

'Of course you do,' Billie agreed. 'She'll be back shortly to get ready. Now if you'll excuse me I have some things to tend to. We can talk later.' She paused and looked up at him as if she were sizing him up. Evidently pleased with what she saw, Billie said, 'Well, it is just so nice to finally meet you, Grant. I do hope you'll stay for the festivities. Hallie will be most surprised.'

'I wouldn't miss it, ma'am,' he assured her, 'but as you can see I'm not really dressed for an occasion like this. My luggage is at Henderson's Garage along with my car.' In Billie's presence, Grant felt like he was ten again instead of thirty-two.

Billie dismissed his concerns with a gesture. 'I'll ask Lacy to call over to Eldon to see that your things are delivered here in time for you to change. We have plenty of time since the wedding isn't until this evening. You do plan to stay with us for a while, don't you, Grant?' she asked with a smile.

'Yes, ma'am, thank you.' *I intend to stay until Hallie comes to her senses.*

Billie Dean leaned forward and patted Grant on the arm. 'Make yourself at home. Lacy will be right back.' With a wave of her hand she disappeared up the stairs.

Left alone once more, Grant squinted at the ornate plaster molding overhead while the whirring blades of the ceiling fans on the front porch moved the fragrant air from outdoors through the hallway. It was intoxicating, and he had the strangest feeling he had stumbled right into the middle of a Tennessee Williams play, where all the characters were soft-spoken and genteel but eccentric as hell.

Tired of waiting, he glanced around and, seeing no one else, bounded up and began to walk the length of the hall, glancing into each room. He hadn't gotten past the halfway mark when the tall thin woman who had first greeted him reappeared at the bottom of the staircase. 'Mr Keeler, I'm Lacy Webster, the housekeeper. Miss Billie says for me to take you into the library and get you something cool to drink. Please follow me.'

Grant ran his hand through his dark hair in indecision. He looked toward the front door. 'I was going to look for Hallie, Ms Webster. I need to see her. I have to see her before . . .'

'Miss Billie says please to wait in the library, Mr Keeler.' The look on Lacy's face was not one that encouraged any argument. 'Miss Hallie will be back soon. I'll make sure she knows you're here.'

Reluctantly, Grant turned and retraced his steps.

In the library, he paced, too nervous to sit. This place explained so much about Hallie. Everything in Grant's life had hard edges, rigid rules, beginning with his stint in the military, and later with his career with the FBI. Things were either black or white. There were no allowances for shades of gray.

Here everything was soft and hazy, the edges blurred. Time seemed to stand still. Here, life could have many interpretations, depending on the point of view. There was room for a full palette of color and all the subtle shades that fell in between.

He didn't doubt that the harshness of the past year had taken its toll on Hallie, but beneath all her softness, she had shown a surprising inner strength. Through it all, she had endured. Now he had come to find out if she was ready to begin again. With him.

Grant leaned against the framework of the library French doors. Outside, sheltered by the overhanging trees, was a small brick patio which was nearly covered over with ivy. Behind him he heard the door open. Lacy placed a small tray of cookies with a pitcher of iced tea on the desk.

'You won't forget to tell Hallie I'm here, will you?' he asked, needing assurance.

'I'll tell her, Mr Keeler.'

Grant thanked her and turned back toward the patio, his thoughts drifting back six months earlier to that night in Los Angeles, the first time he had seen Hallie Prescott.

In the big old-fashioned kitchen, Hallie was met by Lacy as she came through the back door. 'He's here,' Lacy announced. 'Miss Billie has already met him.'

'Who?' asked Hallie as she reached inside the refrigerator and poured herself some iced tea from a glass pitcher.

'Your man, honey,' said Lacy.

Hallie spun around.

'Mr Keeler,' clarified Lacy with a smile.

Hallie's eyes grew wide. She swallowed. 'Are you sure?'

Lacy nodded. 'He's in the library, and he's handsome as the devil hisself.'

'He *is* the devil himself,' proclaimed Hallie.

'Uh huh.'

'Besides, I didn't think you would notice a thing like that, Lacy,' teased Hallie.

'Hmm. Person would have to be dead not to notice that man. Besides, I notice more around here than you think, girl.' Hallie and Lacy had been verbally sparring since she was in her teens and had decided to challenge Lacy's authority in her Aunt Billie's house.

366

Hallie sank into the nearest chair, feeling suddenly weak.

'You look a little pale, honey,' said Lacy. 'Must be cause things are heatin' up. And Lord knows it's about time, if you ask me.'

Hallie shook her head, unable to answer.

Dear God. He was here.

CHAPTER 27

Later Hallie would admit to Billie and Lacy that at the very moment she realized that Grant was actually there in their house, she had been equally tempted by the desire to run into his arms and never to let go, and the desire to run like hell as far in the opposite direction as she could. There was so much between them, so much to be reckoned with, so many memories to sweep away.

But for now she was reluctant to leave the old-fashioned kitchen of the house where she had lived most of her life, knowing that in a few minutes she would have to face the man she loved, the man who had left her without any promises, without hope, and without words of love.

'He's waitin' for you, girl.'

'Oh, Lacy, I don't think I want to see him. There's so much that you don't know.'

'But I do know, honey. I know that anytime a man who looks like that comes to a place like this, he's plenty serious. Now get on out there and talk to him.'

'I will,' said Hallie uncertainly.

'When, tomorrow?' Lacy's sarcasm was lost on Hallie.

'No . . . just not right this minute. This is such a shock to find him here . . . today.'

'Hallie, honey, you and I been pullin' and tuggin' at one another for most of your life. If I say it's rainin', you say it ain't. If I say it's hot, you say it's not. But for once in your life, child, you listen to your Lacy. That man is in a sweat to see you, girl. And the secret is knowin' just how long to let him stay that way. Now get on out of here and go see him.'

'I know, Lacy, I'm going.' Hallie stood and walked reluctantly out the door that separated the kitchen from the rest of the house.

But after a few minutes, Lacy frowned. There was no familiar squeal of the library door as it opened, no sound of footsteps or voices raised in greeting.

Where did that crazy girl sneak off to?

Grant emerged from his reverie certain that he had heard voices. It was Hallie. He was sure it was her. Turning from the French doors, he crossed the library and yanked open the door. But the hall was empty and his footsteps echoed against the polished hardwood floor as he looked toward the back of the house. From the kitchen doorway Lacy appeared.

Grant raised his brows. 'Where's Hallie?' he asked uncertainly.

'I'm not sure she's at all pleased that you're here, Mr Keeler,' Lacy announced with her arms crossed, leaning indolently against the door frame.

Grant took two steps forward. 'You promised,' he reminded her. 'You promised you would let me know when she arrived.'

'She said you was the devil hisself,' announced Lacy, ignoring his reminder.

In spite of his tenseness, Grant grinned at this and stepped closer. His probing gray eyes met Lacy's, dark and unreadable. 'But you don't believe that, do you?'

They stood face to face while Lacy silently weighed this question. Then she bestowed one of her rare smiles on him. 'Uh huh. I believe I do, Mr Keeler. Yes, sir, I believe I do.'

Grant's eyes sparkled with humor at her assessment. 'Where is she?' he asked.

Without moving from her spot against the door, Lacy unfolded her crossed arms and pointed her index finger toward the ceiling. 'Up there,' she said.

She watched as Grant turned on his heel and sprinted toward the stairway. 'You sure danced your way around this one, Lord,' she muttered with a smile, 'but I thank you for finally sending Mr Keeler here for my Hallie. This time I think we got the right man.'

At the first door at the top of the stairs he knocked, then turned the knob, but the room was empty. He had just approached the second door when it swung open and before him stood Hallie, looking younger than he remembered, with her hair slightly damp, her face scrubbed and free of makeup, and wearing a pair of faded denim shorts and a blue T-shirt. Draped carefully over her arm was a tea-length bridal gown of pale ivory.

For a moment neither of them spoke. They stood, drinking in the sight of one another. Finally, Grant broke the silence, his voice deeper than Hallie had remembered it. 'Looks like I got here just in time,' he said, indicating the dress over her arm. 'So much for the grieving-widow act.'

'What are you doing here?' Hallie demanded, bristling at his words and not bothering to explain that neither the dress nor the wedding was hers.

'Sorry to spoil your plans, Hallie.'

Grant advanced.

She retreated.

'Didn't you know I would come for you? The woman I met downstairs, your aunt, she didn't seem surprised. She even knew who I was, and she was a hell of a lot more gracious than you.'

'Billie is gracious to everyone,' Hallie replied. 'It's the way she is. I don't have to be gracious, especially to you, showing up without any warning and expecting everyone to drop whatever they're doing and be happy to see you. Well, let me tell you, Grant Keeler, your timing stinks. We all have a wedding to get ready for.'

'What's the matter, Hallie? Aren't you glad to see me?' he asked, with a slight trace of hurt in his voice.

'Well, you certainly took your sweet time getting here. Tell me, Grant, did you think I was coming home to spend my days on the veranda, reduced by this heat to a mindless, whimpering state, rocking to and fro while I died of a broken heart?' Having delivered her speech, Hallie turned away from him, intent on laying Billie's gown on the bed.

'Do you have a broken heart, Hallie?' he asked quietly, suddenly needing to hear her answer.

'No, I most certainly do not!' She spun around and found him much too close. 'Don't come near me,

371

Grant. You can't just ignore me for months, then show up at my door and expect me to fall into your arms.'

'Is that what you think I want?' he asked as he took another step toward her.

'Umm, so far all the signals point that way,' said Hallie.

'And exactly what is it that you would do if I suddenly pulled you into my arms and . . .' Moving as he spoke, Grant reached out for Hallie and easily pulled her close. With his lips against hers he whispered, 'I've missed you, babe.'

'Hallie? Do you know where –?' Billie stopped in mid-sentence at the sight of Grant kissing Hallie. 'Oh, dear. Excuse me, I didn't realize . . .'

'It's okay,' said Hallie, breathlessly, without moving from Grant's embrace. 'I'll be ready in a few minutes. Billie, this is –'

Billie looked from Grant to Hallie with a wide smile. 'I know who he is, honey. What I don't know is what took him so long to get here. Honestly, Grant, I thought it over since we met downstairs a while ago, and I just have to ask you – what did take you so long? I had almost given up on you.'

'Well, there were some things I had to take care of before I could come for Hallie.' Grant smiled down at Hallie.

'I see,' Billie said, seriously considering his reply. 'And are those, uh, matters fully resolved?'

'Oh, yes ma'am,' Grant assured her with a conspiratorial smile. 'Completely resolved.'

Hallie cleared her throat to remind her aunt and

Grant that she was still there. The look that she gave Grant said that things between them were far from being resolved. 'I don't know about you two, but I've got a wedding to get ready for,' she announced.

'By the way, who is the lucky guy?' asked Grant with a scowl.

Billie blushed. 'Benton Wilder,' she answered.

'Well, tell Benton when you see him that his luck just ran out. Hallie is not marrying anyone but me.'

'I'm not?' Hallie's eyes were wide with feigned surprise, and she was doing her best to keep from laughing out loud.

'Why, Grant Keeler,' said Billie, realizing for the first time that Grant had assumed Hallie was the bride-to-be, 'this wedding is due to take place this evening whether you approve or not. Your arrival in Mimosa is not going to change that one bit.'

'I love Hallie,' protested Grant, 'and I'm not going to lose her.'

'And you won't,' Billie assured him, scooping the wedding dress from the bed and marching toward the door. Then she added, 'If you handle things right.'

At the doorway she paused. 'Hallie, you don't have long to get ready. The photographer will want to take pictures of us before the ceremony, I'm sure. And, honey, before Grant decides to throw a punch at Benton, will you please explain things to him?'

Hallie did, and was almost late for the photographer. Each time she went to get dressed, Grant would trail kisses over her body, making it nearly impossible to put, or keep, her clothes on.

* * *

The string quartet from the junior college played the wedding march as a radiant Billie, wearing the beautiful dress her niece had designed for her, walked down the brick pathway through the well-tended garden to join Benton Wilder. Under an arbor of flowering vines he waited, handsome and tall, in front of Reverend Frazier.

Only the quivering ribbons that cascaded from the bouquet of ivory and peach roses that lay nestled in her arms betrayed Billie's nervousness. Throughout the brief ceremony, Hallie stood proudly next to her aunt, confident that with Benton Wilder at her side, Billie would be truly cherished and loved.

At the reception that followed, Hallie made sure that Grant was introduced to the other guests and made to feel comfortable. Whenever she left his side, she could feel his eyes following her, and when her eyes would meet his across the gathering of friends and family, there was no mistaking the message there.

'Will you stop that?' she hissed, finally making her way to his side.

'What?' he asked innocently.

'You know, staring at me like that. This is a small town and tomorrow the whole town will be talking about us.'

'Don't you want them to know about us?'

'Look, Grant, I have been the topic of gossip in this town since . . . well, you know. I still have to live here, and things are just now getting back to normal.'

'Is that what you want, Hallie? Normal? Somehow I can't picture you that way.'

'What's wrong with that?' she asked defensively.

'Nothing, except it's so boring.'

'I like boring,' she insisted stubbornly.

'Come on, honey,' he said, dropping his voice to a suggestive whisper. 'I know better than that and so do you.'

Hallie blushed.

'Underneath that lovely, but prim, pale blue dress you're wearing, there's a savage woman who can't wait to tear my clothes off and have her way with me.'

'Grant!' Hallie blushed again and looked around to see if anyone had heard him.

'Well, it's true, isn't it?' he asked with a grin.

Hallie smiled self-consciously at Jim Burton and his wife, giving them a little wiggle of her fingers, then she leaned close to Grant and whispered, 'That's all you can think about, isn't it?'

Across the way Lacy studied the newlyweds. It had been a wonderful day, she concluded, pleased that her dear friend Billie was now married to a wonderful man like Benton Wilder, and that the wedding and the reception she had helped to plan had come off without a hitch.

Letting her sharp eyes roam farther, she could see Grant leaning down whispering something in Hallie's ear. At his words Hallie's face turned almost as red as her hair.

Lacy raised her glass of champagne. *Hmm . . . that Mr Keeler must be talkin' some kind of trash to make my girl blush like that*. She smiled with satisfaction. Soon, she thought, she would more than likely be busy with preparations for another wedding.

* * *

It was after midnight before the last guest had departed and all the candles on the tables had been extinguished. Lacy and one of her daughters were in the kitchen cleaning up. After changing into a pair of jeans and tennis shoes, Hallie returned to the kitchen to lend a hand.

'Where's Mr Keeler?' Lacy asked as she carefully boxed up the top layer of the wedding cake.

'Oh, he's out there helping Jim put the chairs away.' Jim was Lacy's husband; on Monday, he would load the chairs and tables that had been rented for the occasion into his pickup truck and return them to the rental store in Clarksdale.

After her daughter left, Lacy declared that the rest of the work could wait until the following morning. The cake had been carefully placed in the freezer where it would remain until the bride and groom celebrated their first anniversary. Hallie slid into a chair at the kitchen table. In a few minutes she was joined by Lacy.

'Billie looked so beautiful,' announced Lacy with a sigh as she stretched her legs and flexed her narrow shoulders.

'And so happy,' added Hallie. 'She and Benton are perfect for each other.'

'So are you and Mr Keeler, honey.'

Hallie blushed and shook her head. 'I don't know about that, Lacy. Grant and I are nothing like Billie and Benton,' she protested. 'Whenever we're together sparks seem to fly. We bring out the worst in each other.'

'All the time?' Lacy asked as she straightened in her chair.

'Well, not *all* the time,' replied Hallie. Two red spots stained her cheeks.

'Uh huh.'

'You don't believe me?'

'Oh, I believe you, but that isn't what's important. What's important is that he came all this way down here because he loves you.'

'How do you know?' asked Hallie, wanting to believe what Lacy had just told her.

'I seen in his eyes, honey. He 'bout had a stroke when he thought you were the bride-to-be. Just string him along a little while longer, keep him dancing to your tune, and you'll have that man exactly where you want him,' advised Lacy.

Just then Jim came into the kitchen followed by Grant.

Lacy stood and stretched. 'Well, it's been a long day.' She turned toward her husband and looped her arm affectionately through his. 'I'll be over tomorrow to finish up, but not until late afternoon.'

'Stay home, Lacy. You deserve a few days off. Don't come back until Tuesday.'

Lacy looked from Hallie to Grant, her gaze still sharp and probing in spite of the late hour. 'How long will you be staying, Mr Keeler? Will I see you again?' asked Lacy. Hallie might be a grown woman, but she still needed looking after.

Her pointed question and her unspoken admonishment to behave himself weren't lost on Grant. 'Indeed, you will, Miss Lacy,' Grant said with a wicked smile and a nod of his dark head. 'Goodnight,' he said as he shook hands with Jim and promised to help him on Monday.

After they had left, Hallie ushered Grant out of the kitchen and turned out the lights.

'I suppose you want me to stay at the local motel?' he offered.

'No, Billie invited you to stay here, so here it shall be.'

'And what about you? Do you want me to stay here also?' he asked suggestively.

'I think the motel would suit you nicely,' she replied sarcastically as she led the way through the dark hallway toward the stairs. 'Unfortunately, we don't have a motel in Mimosa.'

'Your hospitality overwhelms me,' he muttered as he followed her up the stairway.

When they reached the door to her room, Grant peeked inside and said, 'I don't suppose this is the room you had in mind for me?'

Hallie continued down the hallway, remembering Lacy's latest words of wisdom on how to handle Grant. She stopped at the bedroom farthest from hers. 'Not likely. This will be your room for the duration of your visit.'

Grant reluctantly joined her at the door to the guest room. Leaning against the wall, he reached out and fingered the shiny strands of copper hair that had escaped her elegant French twist.

'Don't do that,' she whispered, twisting her head away from his touch.

'Why not?' asked Grant. He brought his fingers to her lips, brushing them lightly, then softly ran them down her chin and her neck. His destination became clear when his fingers continued their downward decent.

'It bothers me,' she murmured, capturing his hand with hers just as it reached her breast.

'It's supposed to,' Grant whispered as he kissed her softly.

Hallie's heartbeat escalated as she waited for the pressure of his lips to demand more, the teasing of his tongue to suggest more, the press of his aroused body to promise more. So many nights she had dreamed of this, and for months had waited for this moment.

Without warning Grant raised his head without doing any of those things, breaking the only physical contact between them.

'Goodnight, Hallie,' he said softly as he stepped around her and into the room. 'Pleasant dreams.'

Hallie spent a restless night, flip-flopping between disappointment that Grant had not pressured her to make love, and anger that he had so casually dismissed her with a goodnight kiss. What was it Lacy had said? Make him dance to your tune? She should have been the one to leave him at his door, all hot and bothered and still panting for her. Well, she had failed her first test miserably. She was the one who was left wanting more.

'What do you usually do around here on Sundays?' Grant asked as he joined her in the kitchen the next morning. He had showered and shaved and was dressed in a pair of jeans that fit like a second skin.

'Nothing,' Hallie answered as she poured him a cup of coffee. 'Billie usually goes to church and I go along, but it's too late for that today. Then we drive over to one of the neighboring towns and have brunch or an early dinner.

'Electrifying,' said Grant as he took in Hallie's tousled hair and her sleepy, sexy eyes. His jeans got a little tighter as he thought about waking up with her next to him. Last night had taken all his willpower to walk away from her, but it was clear that she hadn't yet forgiven him for leaving her in Los Angeles like he had, and he intended to keep her off-balance.

'Don't you have trouble staying awake here?'

'Some days,' she laughed. 'Those days you can lie in the hammock out back or sit in the swing and just enjoy doing nothing. Life here is slow and comfortable.'

And predictable. 'So what would you do on a really exciting day?' he asked with a grin. In the back of his mind he knew he, too, could get used to this lazy lifestyle.

'Well, we would drive to Jackson or Memphis and go shopping, have dinner and maybe see a movie.'

'Okay,' he said as he stood. 'Get ready and we'll go.'

'Where?' asked Hallie, bewildered.

'Out,' he called back to her as he left the kitchen.

'Out' turned into a lazy afternoon drive along winding back roads where the branches of massive oak trees sometimes extended overhead forming a thick, intimate canopy of greenery. At the first town they came to they stopped at a small country grocery and bought drinks and sandwiches for a picnic lunch. Then they resumed their back-road meandering.

'I love driving like this,' said Grant. 'You miss so many quaint places when you travel the Interstate.

Let's look for a place to stop. Are you getting hungry?'

'Starved,' Hallie replied with a quick smile.

After a few more miles Grant pulled off onto the side of the road and together they carried their picnic to a secluded grassy spot.

'You know, we never had a chance to spend time together like this in Los Angeles,' he observed as he spread out the blanket he had brought along.

'That seems so long ago, but it's only been a few months,' Hallie replied as she unwrapped the sandwiches they bought. 'So much has happened.'

The afternoon sun warmed their skin while they ate in silence, solemnly studying one another now that they were finally alone.

'You first,' directed Grant with a sparkle in his expressive gray eyes. Today he appeared relaxed and unguarded, and younger than she had ever remembered.

'What?' asked Hallie, pretending she didn't know what he was talking about.

'You have been dying to ask me something since yesterday. So go ahead.'

'Why did you come all this way?' she began, easing into the question she had so carefully guarded in her heart.

Grant finished his sandwich and reached for another. 'You know the answer to that – I came to see you.'

Hallie pulled her knees up to her chin and wrapped her arms around them, wondering if she was brave enough to ask what was really on her mind. But when she thought about the miserable months she had spent hoping for some word from him, she realized that she had nothing to lose, not even her pride. She took a shallow breath, and she could feel her heart clench. 'Yesterday you told Billie that I couldn't marry anyone but you.'

Grant nodded, as he watched the slight quivering of her lower lip.

'Did you mean that?' she asked quietly.

He was silent as if he was giving her question great consideration.

Her heart was pounding so hard it hurt. She couldn't breathe.

'I meant it.'

She should have been relieved, but instinctively she knew it wasn't that simple. Nothing with Grant had ever been simple. She waited for him to speak, but his silence seemed go on forever.

'After I left Los Angeles I went to the Cayman Islands,' he said finally. 'I needed to get away for a while. But the answers I was looking for weren't there. Along the way I ran into a little trouble.' Briefly he recounted his episode with Victoria Camden and his near brush with death.

'When I got out of the hospital I went to Virginia Beach. Libby and I spent our honeymoon there. For some crazy reason I felt compelled to return.'

'You still miss her,' whispered Hallie.

'No. That's the strangest part. She was there, Hallie. With me. I felt her touch me. For a few minutes she was as real as you are. She spoke to me and I heard her. I'll always love her, but she knows that. After a while she was gone. And I knew then that she was safe and happy.

But she's gone for good. She'll never come back. In those brief moments Libby gave me something very special. It's difficult to explain, but for the first time I feel free of guilt and full of hope for the future.'

Hallie digested what he had just told her, resisting the impulse to reach out and touch him. She believed him, alright, but she had no idea what his revelation meant for the two of them.

'I know you're waiting for me to say something, Grant, but honestly, I don't know what to say. I wish I could tell you that I've had a similar experience, that I felt that kind of peace, but I would be making it up. After the trial I came home to heal, to come to some understanding of the things that had happened. And to forget.'

'And have you forgotten?' He studied her face intently.

'No,' she answered solemnly, raising her eyes to meet his. 'But I have forgiven him.'

'I see,' he said quietly.

'No, you don't. Oh, Grant, I loved the image of Casey, but in reality, I don't think I ever knew who he was. He was a chameleon, adapting his personality to his surroundings, using his charm to get what he wanted, using anyone he could to achieve his dreams. Looking back, the only thing that seems genuine about him was *Journey to Fear*. Even though it was fiction, it probably revealed more about Casey than he would ever reveal of himself.'

Hallie leaned back on her elbows, then shifted on her side, aligning herself with Grant, who was now stretched out on the blanket next to her. Tentatively, she reached out to touch his face, to reassure herself that he was really here. His skin felt warm and surprisingly smooth to her touch. 'I came here to wait for you,' she whispered, 'but I thought you'd never come for me.'

Grant pulled her down next to him, wrapping both his arms about her. He buried his face in her hair, and held her like that for a long while as if he couldn't get enough of her. 'You are so beautiful. Did I ever tell you that?'

'Once,' she whispered, remembering that night at the Prescott house.

'I almost stayed away too long, didn't I?' Grant murmured against her lips. 'What if you had found someone else? What if I hadn't made it back from Grand Cayman? What if I had been lost at sea?'

Hallie smiled, 'I would have waited the rest of my life for you.'

'In your rocking chair, on your sagging, crumbling veranda, wilting in the heat?'

'Year after year.' Hallie kissed him slowly, softly, and her lips were as seductive as the warmth of the sun. Lazily, Grant allowed her access into the moist recesses of his mouth, enjoying her exploration immensely. When he could no longer stand what she was doing to him, he rolled her over on her back. But when she looked up, he saw his passion mirrored in her eyes.

Greedily his lips sought her skin, while his hands began the task of unbuttoning the dress that hid her from him, then pushed the fabric off her shoulders. His lips traveled downward to her breasts, seeking their softness before capturing one and then the other, teasing each with his tongue.

384

Hallie moaned, arching her back while Grant reached down and pushed her skirt up and explored what he uncovered. Deep down, in that secret place where passion begins, a slow heat began to radiate and a yearning, more powerful, more demanding than ever, washed over her.

Grant, having discarded his shirt and jeans, raised his hard lean body over hers and positioned himself between her slender thighs. It was then that he noticed the first drops of moisture that had gathered on her face and her breasts. He reached up, wiping the dampness from her face.

'I think we have company,' she murmured.

'Anyone we know?' Grant asked lazily as he moved against her silky skin.

'Just some clouds and a few raindrops,' she answered with a sigh.

A few minutes later the rain, warm and soft, slid over their bare skin. Drops of water danced slowly, sensually, over Hallie's breasts. With his tongue Grant traced their path as they slithered in a downward trail to her stomach.

The rain had increased now, falling in a steady rhythm against his broad bare back as Hallie readily arched to meet his first thrust. With unleashed passion, she cried out, meeting thrust after thrust as he pushed her higher and higher. The driving intensity of the rain, seemingly in concert with their escalating passion, obscured their cries when finally they took one another to a place of stunning, shining pleasure.

Later, laying still across her rain-slicked skin, Grant breathed heavily. 'I want to spend the rest of my life here. Just like this,' he whispered huskily when he could manage to speak. 'Want to stay with me?'

'Naked and wet?' she whispered.

'Yeah.'

Hallie was just about to answer when a sudden crack of lightning lit up the afternoon sky, followed by the rolling roar of thunder. It was enough to send them scrambling to gather their clothes. With the blanket wrapped unevenly around both of them they ran for the car, where they sorted though their soaked clothing and dressed as best they could in embarrassed silence.

'Did you do a rain dance or something?' Hallie asked shyly when he reached out and attempted to wipe the raindrops from her face.

'Nope.'

'Have you ever done that before?' she asked curiously.

'Made love in the rain?' he asked with a grin. 'Hmm. I'm not sure. There have been so many . . . ouch!' exclaimed Grant laughingly, when Hallie punched him in the arm. 'What was that for?'

'That's for making fun of me,' she replied primly. 'And I insist on knowing.'

'Not that I can remember,' he said after a pause. 'Which means that either I never have, or if I did, it wasn't all that memorable.'

This time, when Hallie reached out to punch him, he dodged.

It was nearly dark and still raining by the time they returned home. Hallie, still in her damp clothes, hurried through the house, turning on lamps as she went. 'I'll make us some coffee,' she said, hurrying past Grant toward the kitchen.

'Slow down, honey. We have all the time in the world for coffee. How about a nice hot shower?'

'You go ahead,' she said, turning and taking another step toward the kitchen.

'Whoa! I was talking about *us* taking a shower. Together.'

'I know,' she answered, her eyes fixed on the floor.

'Is there something wrong with that idea?'

Hallie didn't answer.

Grant reached out and tilted her head up, forcing her eyes to meet his.

She blushed at his scrutiny.

It took a moment, but suddenly he understood the reason for her shyness. 'You've never done that, have you?'

Hallie tried to turn her head away, to escape his amused inspection, but Grant held her face firmly between his hands. Then he leaned over and kissed her. In one sweeping motion he lifted her in his arms and headed for the stairs.

'Grant!' she protested weakly.

At the top of the stairs he paused and nuzzled his face against hers. 'I'll just bet there are a lot of things you haven't done yet,' he said in a husky voice.

At the door to her bathroom, he paused, letting her slide slowly down the length of his body until she stood pressed against him. 'We'll make a list, and we won't stop until we've mastered them all.'

Hallie buried her face against his chest and smiled. 'Promise?' she asked.

'Promise.'

Later that night, next to the tall, ornate, white iron bed that sat in the middle of her bedroom, Hallie stood wrapped in Grant's arms. The ceiling fan above them sent cool drafts of air downward over their heated bodies, while the soft whirring of the blades added a steady rhythm to the musical sounds of the night that drifted inside through the open double doors.

Grant breathed deeply, inhaling the sweet, intoxicating fragrance that surrounded them and knew that he had found a place where he belonged. Against her hair he whispered, 'I never suspected when I took a beautiful woman with me that night to my hotel, that she would leave the next morning with a piece of my heart.'

'And I never expected to fall in love with a complete stranger,' murmured Hallie as she turned and placed her hands on his shoulders, then began to sway against him, compelling him to sway along with her in a silent, sensual, dance.

The music was soft, the tempo slow, and the lyrics spoke to them of things to come. It was a prelude to the rest of their lives.

THE EXCITING NEW NAME IN WOMEN'S FICTION!

PLEASE HELP ME TO HELP YOU!

Dear *Scarlet* Reader,

As Editor of *Scarlet* Books I want to make sure that the books I offer you every month are up to the high standards *Scarlet* readers expect. And to do that I need to know a little more about you and your reading likes and dislikes. So please spare a few minutes to fill in the short questionnaire on the following pages and send it to me.

Looking forward to hearing from you,

Sally Cooper

Editor-in-Chief, *Scarlet*

QUESTIONNAIRE

Please tick the appropriate boxes to indicate your answers

1 **Where did you get this Scarlet title?**
Bought in supermarket ☐
Bought at my local bookstore ☐ Bought at chain bookstore ☐
Bought at book exchange or used bookstore ☐
Borrowed from a friend ☐
Other (please indicate) _____

2 **Did you enjoy reading it?**
A lot ☐   A little ☐   Not at all ☐

3 **What did you particularly like about this book?**
Believable characters ☐   Easy to read ☐
Good value for money ☐   Enjoyable locations ☐
Interesting story ☐   Modern setting ☐
Other _____

4 **What did you particularly dislike about this book?**
_____

5 **Would you buy another Scarlet book?**
Yes ☐   No ☐

6 **What other kinds of book do you enjoy reading?**
Horror ☐   Puzzle books ☐   Historical fiction ☐
General fiction ☐   Crime/Detective ☐   Cookery ☐
Other (please indicate) _____

7 **Which magazines do you enjoy reading?**
1. _____
2. _____
3. _____

And now a little about you –
8 **How old are you?**
Under 25 ☐   25–34 ☐   35–44 ☐
45–54 ☐   55–64 ☐   over 65 ☐

cont.

9 What is your marital status?

Single ☐   Married/living with partner ☐

Widowed ☐   Separated/divorced ☐

10 What is your current occupation?

Employed full-time ☐   Employed part-time ☐

Student ☐   Housewife full-time ☐

Unemployed ☐   Retired ☐

11 Do you have children? If so, how many and how old are they?

_____

_____

12 What is your annual household income?

under $15,000	☐	or	£10,000	☐
$15–25,000	☐	or	£10–20,000	☐
$25–35,000	☐	or	£20–30,000	☐
$35–50,000	☐	or	£30–40,000	☐
over $50,000	☐	or	£40,000	☐

Miss/Mrs/Ms _____

Address _____

_____

_____ Postcode:_____

Thank you for completing this questionnaire. Now tear it out – put it in an envelope and send it, before 31 July 1998, to:

Sally Cooper, Editor-in-Chief

USA/Can. address
SCARLET c/o London Bridge
85 River Rock Drive
Suite 202
Buffalo
NY 14207
USA

UK address/No stamp required
SCARLET
FREEPOST LON 3335
LONDON W8 4BR
Please use block capitals for address

SLDAN/1/98

***Scarlet* titles coming next month:**

THE MOST DANGEROUS GAME Mary Wibberley
Scarlet is delighted to announce the return to writing of
this very popular author! 'Devlin' comes into Catherine's
life when she is in need of protection and finds herself in that
most clichéd of all situations – she's fallen in love with her
bodyguard! The problem is that Devlin will leave when the
job's over . . . won't he?

DANGEROUS DECEPTION Lisa Andrews
Luis Quevedo needs a fiancée in a hurry to please his
grandfather. Emma fits the bill and desperately needs the
money. Then she makes the mistake of falling in love with
her 'fiancé' . . .

CRAVEN'S BRIDE Danielle Shaw
For ten years, Max Craven has blamed Alison for the death
of his daughter. Now he returns home and finds his feelings
for Alison have undergone a transformation. Surely he can't
be in love with her?

BLUE SILK PROMISE Julia Wild
When Nick recovers consciousness after a serious accident,
he finds himself married within days. Nick can't believe he's
forgotten the woman he loves so passionately. Then little by
little, he begins to realize that his beloved Kayanne thinks
he's his own brother!